What others are saying about **ANN SIMAS** *books ...*

"...Ann Simas seamlessly intertwines a [...] with a budding romance [and] a love th[...]
– Stacie Theis, BeachBoundBooks.c[...]

"...you won't want to put [FIRST STAF[...]
– lfb68 (Reader, Amazon Kindle)

"[FIRST STAR]...is Romantic Suspens[...]
– Linda Strong (Reader, Amazon Kin[...]

"BLESSED ARE THE EAGLES should be made into a movie, it was that good."
– Dee Matt (Reader, Amazon Kindle)

"[BLESSED ARE THE EAGLES] is a gripping story..."
– Bella's Blog (Reader, Amazon Canada)

"If I was ever to write a book involving steamy passages, LOOSE ENDS would be the template for style and dialogue. [Simas] is a breath of sultry air."
– Dolores Walker (Reader, Ottawa, Canada)

"[LOOSE ENDS] kept me reading late into the night...thank you Ann Simas for an excellent read."
– Michelle Turner (Reader, Amazon United Kingdom)

"[Ann Simas] did a great job blending the forensic and investigative elements [in DRESSED TO DIE]."
– Lt. Mike Hurley (Ret.), Director, Oregon State Crime Lab, Springfield

"Take one part mysterious death, add two parts religion, combine with a dollop of horror and a dash of romance and you have the intoxicating mixture that is...HOLY SMOKE."
– Woodeene Koenig-Bricker, Author of *365 Saints*

"HOLY SMOKE...is awesome! The depth of subject is something this author is extremely good at."
– Josephine Musumeci (Reader, Amazon Kindle)

"[HEAVEN SENT] is a truly remarkable story filled will love, faith, determination and suspense."
– Niki Driscoll (Reader, Amazon Kindle)

"[HEAVEN SENT] is a wonderful, scary, and uplifting book."
– Christine Holmes (Reader, Amazon United Kingdom)

"I give [SANTA'S HELPER] 6 Candi Kisses because 5 is not enough."
– Candace Fox, Candi's Books & Reviews

"SLICED TO DIE...has characters you like, is easy to read, and hard to put down! This book does not disappoint...[Simas's] wit, imagination and writing skills are amazing."
– Rebecca Hunter (Reader, Amazon Kindle)

"[PENITENCE]...leaves you in suspense right up until the end."
– Gary Wolfe (Reader, Amazon Kindle)

"[BLACK MOON RISING is] a heart pumping, rush of adrenaline story. You won't be disappointed...it has everything in you can imagine: romance, adventure, mystery, and mayhem all rolled into one spectacular book!"
– Jessica Mitchell (Reader, Amazon Kindle).

"Ann Simas has struck gold with [BURIED TO DIE}. It's a great read."
– Chuck Wallace, Reader (via Ann Simas Facebook page)

"[BLACK MOON RISING] was holy wow."
– Starswarlover (Reader, Amazon Kindle)

"Grab a warm cup of hot cocoa and curl up [with LET IT SNOW]."
– Jaime Kurp (Reader, Amazon Kindle)

Books by Ann Simas…

Chloe's Spirit[†]
Chloe's Spirit Afterstories
First Star[†]
First Star Afterstories
Blessed Are the Eagles[†]
Loose Ends
Heaven Sent
Black Moon Rising
Here and Gone

Grace Gabbiano Mysteries
Dressed to Die
Sliced to Die
Buried to Die
Quilted to Die
Taken to Die *(coming Summer 2019)*

Andi Comstock Supernatural Mysteries
Holy Smoke
Penitence
Angel Babies
Hellfire *(coming Spring 2019)*

Christmas Valley Romances
Santa's Helper
Candy Cane Lane
Let It Snow
Fruitycakes
Sleigh Bride
Angels on the Rooftop
Deck the Gnomes
Back-Door Santa

Short Story Collection
All's Well

[†]RWA Golden Heart Finalists

HERE & GONE

ANN SIMAS

Ann Simas

MAGIC
MOON
PRESS

HERE AND GONE

May 2018

Here and Gone is a work of fiction. Names, characters, places, and incidents are either the product of the author's imagination or are used fictitiously. Any resemblance to actual persons, living or dead, or events described herein, is entirely coincidental.

ISBN 978-0-9993858-1-4 (print book)

Magic Moon Press . POB 41634 . Eugene, OR 97404-0386

Editing by Nancy Jankow

Printed in U.S.A.
112718/11pthyph
CS 6969120

If you're going through hell, keep going.

— *Winston Churchill*

Chapter 1

Hannah Mason didn't actually move into her new home under the cover of darkness, but she might as well have, for all the subterfuge involved in her relocation.

That's what happened when you were a major front-page headline in the local papers for months on end. Hannah called it crucifixion by journalism.

In the beginning, it had been difficult to crawl out of bed and face the world. No one except her family got that she was immersed in grief. Outside, vigilantism prevailed and nothing short of burning her at the stake would have satisfied those who had assumed the role of judge, jury, and executioner.

If not for the diligence of that self-appointed lynch mob, she might have crawled under the covers and given up living altogether. Instead, being a woman of strong will and determination, she forced herself to get up, get dressed, and accomplish something every day, no matter how small the task or how difficult the effort to climb out of bed.

At first, that meant repairing the daily damage wrought by those who persisted in leaving hateful graffiti on her front door, or painted threats on her house. After almost a year, the entrance to her home had so many coats of paint, she gave up trying to conceal the messages and replaced the door. Her brother-in-law installed a glass storm door over that, which she locked every night, and cleaned with a one-sided razor blade first thing almost every morning. There wasn't a nasty negative word in the dictionary that hadn't been used against her.

Regardless of the absurd lies and conjectures the media invented, or how many times the police pounded her with the same questions they'd asked a dozen times before, or who the life insurance company sent to interrogate her, Hannah refused to cave into depression or desperation. She also worked hard not to succumb to the grief that consumed her from the inside out.

After the vile defacements had been obliterated each day, she forced herself to sit at her home-office work station. As a scientific illustrator, she'd taken on jobs from various publishers and authors and, by God, she'd complete them. She called them her rejuvenation pills. She also made time every day to work on the book she'd started for Jay. Getting lost in line drawings and colorations had turned out to be an unexpected salve against the sorrow she experienced for her lost little boy every hellacious day.

When she couldn't keep her eyes open any longer, she tumbled into bed, hoping, praying, for a dreamless slumber. If she was lucky, she only cried herself to sleep. If she wasn't, she had nightmares about how horrific it must have been for Jason and Jay, her husband and five-year-old son, out there on the vastness of the Pacific Ocean, in a sailboat, all alone, with no one to rescue them from drowning when the boat capsized.

She tried not to think about the creatures that lived and thrived beneath the water and how they'd react to the temptation of human flesh.

She tried not to think about the dying thoughts of the two people she cared about and loved more than her own life.

And most of all, she tried not to think about how she would face the rest of her life without them.

Chapter 2

Hannah thanked God for the support of her siblings and their spouses. Without them, she might have gone crazy over the past two years, or given in to the haunting desire to join her husband and son in death.

Her sister Emily, six months pregnant, and her husband Craig, along with their brother Seth, and his wife Deena, had been instrumental in keeping Hannah's move and her final destination a secret. Much as she missed her parents, who had died before her marriage to Jason, she was grateful they hadn't lived to witness the lynch-mob mentality of the people they had called friends during their lifetime. The upside of them being in Heaven meant that her sweet little Jay had someone up there who loved him.

In conjunction with the move, Hannah had taken her illustrator *nom de plume* permanently, and backed it up with a legal name change. She clung to a wild hope that it would keep the media from tracking her down. For some obscure reason that she still didn't fully comprehend, they'd been so focused on denigrating and persecuting her with their words, they'd yet to discover her occupation. Both they and the police were under the mistaken assumption that she was nothing more than a rich housewife, bored with her husband and child. Even during the whole-house search, when the cops had torn out every drawer and emptied every closet, no one had ever questioned what she did with all the art supplies in her workroom.

The police hadn't found anything in the search, and why would they? They were completely misguided about her being either rich or bored. Yes, Jason had earned a big salary, but neither their joint personal bank account, nor their joint savings account had held any funds at his death. She'd opened a savings account under her illustrator name before she and Jason had married and all her payments and royalties were direct-deposited. If he'd had access, that account probably would have been emptied, too.

Hannah found it odd that the other accounts had been cleaned out down to a dollar each, but she had attributed it to Jason's strange behavior for the last year of his life. She figured he had a gambling problem, since he'd gone frequently to Las Vegas, or maybe he'd adopted an expensive drug habit. Certainly, he was doing something he shouldn't have been during the evening hours he claimed to be at work. Otherwise, wouldn't he have answered his phone, or been at his desk when she and Jay had dropped in to bring him a surprise dinner?

Her husband had a small life insurance policy through his work and another, larger one he'd bought personally. She hadn't spent one cent of that one, but had taken five thousand from the smaller one as a cushion and put the remaining balance in the safe deposit box. With frugal budgeting, she managed to live comfortably on the money generated from the sale of her house and what she earned from her illustrations. The five-thousand-dollar cushion had yet to be touched.

In the overall scheme of life, what she needed most wasn't money, but a snuggle and a sloppy kiss from her little boy, and unfortunately, that was never going to happen again.

Hannah tried to shake off the dark cloud hovering over her. This was a new place. She had a new life. The daytime was for work. Nighttime was for climbing into her big, lonely bed, where she could spend all the time she wanted thinking about Jason and Jay, missing them so much it left her in physical pain.

She especially agonized over Jay's loss. Jay, who would never have a chance to be a teenager or a man or have a family of his own. God, she hoped Jason had wrapped his arms around his son to comfort him when they were drowning. She couldn't bear the thought of her boy thrashing about in the water, scared out of his mind, maybe even crying out for her to save him.

Little puppy claws clickety-clacked over the hardwood floors. Hannah forced the morbid thoughts from her mind and allowed herself to smile. She'd never had a dog before, and even though Bowie was still a pup, she was loving every minute of canine ownership. It would be even better when she got the golden retriever properly housebroken. He'd shown his intelligence already with his quick grasp of commands and his understanding of simple phrases, which gave her hope she wasn't simply cultivating a pipe dream about his smarts. "Ready to go outside?"

Bowie puppy-woofed.

Hannah grabbed her jacket. "Let's go."

Bowie raced to the door, but hadn't mastered the art of slowing down yet. He tried to put on his puppy brakes, but despite the belated effort, he slid the last five feet into the glass door. He yelped, as he always did, though he wasn't hurt, simply disgruntled.

Hannah laughed. These days, it was Bowie who kept her sane. What a horrible responsibility to thrust upon an innocent little puppy.

On Thanksgiving day, Hannah decorated a large Milk-Bone treat with a squirt of whipped cream from the Reddi-wip can in honor of Bowie's five-month birthday. For old-time's sake, she shot a squirt into her mouth, too. Even after all these years, her mother's warning still came through loud and clear…and it still made her smile. *Don't squirt whipped cream into your mouths from the can. We're civilized, you know!* When her mom wasn't looking, her dad would sneak into the kitchen and join her and Emily and Seth in what her brother had dubbed The Forbidden Whipped-Cream Adventure.

Hannah had carried on the tradition with her son. Her heart ached remembering how Jay had opened his little mouth in anticipation of receiving the Reddi-wip squirt. They'd giggle and giggle and Jason would scowl and tell them only pigs ate directly from the container. It was one of the many grudges her husband had come to nurture against her. For the life of her, Hannah had no idea what had caused the nice guy she'd married to morph into a mean malcontent who seemed to take pleasure from hurting her.

Bowie yipped to remind her she was still holding his treat. Every day, the yips and squeals out of his mouth were sounding more and more like real barks. Hannah glanced down and said, "Happy almost-half-year birthday, Bowie."

Bowie's butt, and consequently his tail, waggled about a hundred miles an hour in response.

"Sit."

Like the smart dog he was, Bowie sat.

Hannah leaned over and held the treat out for him to lick. That done, she handed over the Milk-Bone, which Bowie promptly took over by the patio door. He loved to lay in the winter sunlight.

She repeated the Milk-Bone treat for the next six days, until the Reddi-wip can was empty. Not bad. Four days for a human and her dog to polish off a can of whipped cream. "Don't get too used to this," she said, handing Bowie the biscuit. "Thanksgiving only comes once a year."

His tongue came out and licked his chops in anticipation.

Hannah laughed. "You don't even know what I'm saying, do you?"

In response, Bowie gave her one of his sweet smiles.

It was almost time for their morning walk around the property. The pup chewed contently on the biscuit, occasionally glancing at Hannah. Once it was devoured, he jumped up and ran over to her, then back to the door.

Hannah slipped into her snow boots, then pulled on her coat and gloves. "You're in for a new experience today, Bowie. It snowed last night."

He announced his excitement over the prospect of meeting

snow by dancing a doggie two-step.

"When we get back, I'm going to build our first fire."

He smiled up at her.

"Let's go."

Bowie ran to the family room, then back toward the door, nearly managing to stop this time before he crashed into it.

Hannah chuckled. "You've almost got it, haven't you?" She reached down and patted his head.

The dog nuzzled her gloved hand.

She opened the door and Bowie shot outside. He got as far as the edge of the patio, which was dry because it had a cover, and came to a screeching halt. He lowered his muzzle to smell the snow, then lifted a paw and tentatively tested it. In the next instant, he backed away, turning to glance at Hannah as he did so.

She pulled the patio door closed and took off running into the yard. Twenty feet out, she turned to see what was keeping her dog. His butt was firmly planted on the cold concrete patio. "Chicken," Hannah said, laughing. "Bowie, come."

He stood, but other than that, made no move to follow the command.

"Bowie, come!"

This time he stepped gingerly into the snow, decided he liked it, and went down on his belly, licking the wet stuff as he crawled toward her.

"I'll go without you," Hannah threatened.

Bowie apparently didn't care. He rolled over and wriggled around on his back. Talk about a quick attitude conversion.

"Bowie, *come!*"

With obvious reluctance, he got up on all fours again and took a tentative step forward, and then another, and the next thing she knew, he was loping through the six-inch layer of snow, puppy-yipping for all he was worth.

Hannah laughed again and continued on toward the back of the property. Familiar with the route by now, she knew she wouldn't encounter anything beneath the snow to trip her up.

Bowie frolicked alongside her as she climbed the gentle slope. At the top of the hill, he went off to take care of business under his favorite tree. Five minutes later, he came back to her, cavorting like the puppy he still was, amusing her with his antics.

Half an hour later, they were back at the house. Hannah dried him off on the patio, including his wet little paws, before she let him inside. He thanked her with a generous lick.

She removed her boots outside the door, then took those and her coat to the mudroom, where she deposited her boots in the boot tray to drip dry. Her coat went on the last hook of the rack and her hat and gloves in a basket hanging from the first hook.

Not for the first time, Hannah marveled at the differences between beach living and mountain living. She'd never seen snow in person before moving to Fossil, so she and Bowie had that first experience in common. The snowman she'd built up on the hill, with Bowie's help, was no Frosty, but she'd have plenty of time to learn the proper way to make one.

Next on the agenda, breakfast. She put together a casserole using Italian sausage she'd browned and crumbled the day before, green chiles, grated cheddar, and eggs. While it baked, she put her boots back on and went out to get firewood. Whether it was ridiculous or not, she'd been waiting for the first snow to build her first fire. She found herself almost giddy with excitement.

After that, she walked out to the mailbox. Not that there would be anything other than bills, but she didn't want the mail carrier to report to authorities that she must be dead because her mailbox was stuffed full. Company, or anyone wearing a badge, was the last thing she wanted at her door.

Back inside, she made a pot of coffee, checked the timer on the oven, and went to her office to boot up her laptop. Emily sent her an email every morning, usually with a picture of her pregnant self. Today was no exception, if the little paperclip beside Em's name was any indication.

Hannah didn't eat while she was drawing, but she usually took her breakfast to her laptop to read the few emails she got and the day's news. She deleted three junk transmissions, read one from the editor she worked with at a publishing house, replied to a query from an author who was indie-publishing a children's book, and finally, it was time to read Emily's. She resisted looking at the attachments first. How much could her sister's belly have grown in one day, anyway?

Hannah,

I tried to call you last night and this morning, but your phone goes directly to voice mail. Please, please, please, since you insist on living in the wilderness, at least keep your phone on and charged if you're not going to check your email regularly!

Craig just returned from his East Coast trip. The way airlines are these days, with all the bumping and overbooking, he got bumped and had to take a different flight home, which necessitated changing planes in Denver to catch the flight home to San Diego.

Hannah shook her head. Emily always did take the long way around a story.

You may be wondering where all this is leading and all I can say is, I wanted you to understand how Craig came to be in Denver, but didn't stop to call or see you. He only had a 30-minute layover and he missed his connecting flight because the first leg was late. He tried to get another one, but at that point, they said they had nothing else available until morning. He was pissed, but he went out to catch a courtesy bus to a nearby hotel because he didn't want to sleep in the airport. He was waiting at the curb, when he got a call from the airline that they were going to get him on an 7:20 p.m. flight out, after all.

Before you read further, open the attachments I sent, then come back and read my second email.

em

Hannah's mouth twisted in a wry smile. Her sister could be such a drama queen. She put down her breakfast and used the mouse to open the first attachment.

Shock immobilized her. Instead of Emily's pregnant belly, up popped a picture of Jason. Although he sported a short beard, there was no mistaking him. Hannah enlarged the photo, then grabbed her magnifier to examine it more closely.

It was Jason, all right, unless he had an identical twin he'd never mentioned.

Or, it could be that she was losing her mind.

She jumped up and went to grab her cell phone, which was on the kitchen counter. She turned it on, on her way back to the workroom, where she opened the second attachment. Again, she stared at the photo, stunned.

Jason, Jay, and Sabine. How could that be? Jay looked older, which didn't compute with her memory of how he'd looked nearly two years before. Besides, how could that be, unless....

Unless he was still alive. Then, of course, he would be older. Had he lived, Jay would be almost seven now. And what was Sabine doing in the picture? She'd left San Diego a couple of weeks before Jason had taken Jay out on that fateful boat ride. Hannah had missed her friend terribly during those dark days when everyone else, including her neighbors, had treated her like a pariah.

She enlarged the photo and took the magnifier to it. There was no question. It was Jason with Jay and Sabine. Her mind was intact, but the facts in front of her didn't make sense.

She'd never seen Jason with a beard and though Jay was older, she still recognized him. Was this some good-intentioned effort on Craig's part to help make her feel better?

Her breakfast forgotten, Hannah hit speed dial for Emily. Instead of a greeting, she went straight to it. "What the hell is going on?"

Chapter 3

Hannah couldn't take her eyes off the picture of Jason with Jay and Sabine, but she had to. There was one more attachment she hadn't looked at yet. A video.

"I take it you opened the emails," Emily said.

"No! I got so rattled, I forgot to open the video and I haven't read your second email yet." Hannah opened the attachment and stared at the screen. Jason was kissing Sabine, way more passionately than he'd ever kissed her. Jay, stuck between them, was wriggling against Sabine's hold on his hand. Her son never had liked Sabine and now Hannah knew why. Her little boy had been a better judge of character. "This isn't a joke, is it?"

"I knew I should've gotten on a plane and told you in person," Emily said, her tone clearly a mix of exasperation and concern. "Geez, Hannah. Keep your phone on, will you?"

Hannah took a deep breath, trying to make sense of what she was seeing on the screen. Sabine finally pulled out of Jason's embrace and bent down to shake Jay. She was so rough, his little head jiggled back and forth like it was a bobblehead. Jay started crying. Jason looked on, but didn't try to stop the bitch from hurting Jay. Is that what the two of them called discipline, and why was it even warranted?

"Hannah, I want you to stop watching now and listen to

me. Craig's here and he's going to fill in the details, okay?"

Hannah nodded, then realized they couldn't see her. "I can't believe what I'm seeing," she said, barely able to find her voice.

"Believe it," Emily said. "Here's Craig."

"Hi, Hannah. Look, let me preface this by saying I agonized over this all the way home yesterday. I wanted to use Jason for a punching bag and keep hitting him until he couldn't stand up anymore. God, I was so pissed! You're like a sister to me, Hannah. I know how much you've suffered these past two years, both because of the loss you experienced, and the way you were treated by the cops and the media."

"Please...please, tell me...."

"Em already filled you in via email how I happened to be at DIA yesterday."

"Did you take the pictures?" Hannah asked. Belatedly, she opened the second email and read quickly. "Never mind, I see you did. Was it really Jason with Jay and Sabine?"

"It was. I'm so, so sorry."

"Tell me."

"She picked him up at the curb. It was a hurry-up greeting, but they took time for a nice long welcome-back, as you could tell." He blew out a quick breath. "Let me back up a minute. I saw Jason as soon as I walked out the door. He didn't see me, and at first, I thought I was mistaken because of the beard, but I pulled out my phone anyway and took some pictures. I thought he looked right at me once, but I was bundled up, because you know I'm a warm-weather guy not a freezing-ass-cold guy, so he apparently didn't recognize me. A minute or so later, this Lexus SUV pulls up and Sabine jumps out. The back passenger door opens, too, and Jay gets out. I think the pictures tell the rest."

"I don't get it...Jason and Jay...they're alive?"

"Yes, unless we've all been transported to some alternate universe," he said with no humor.

"Where did they go from there?" she asked. "If she was picking him up, they must live in the Denver area."

"Not necessarily. Denver and the Springs have the only big

airports. People drive from all over Colorado to use them."

The enormity of what she was seeing, of what had *really* transpired over two years earlier, hit her with the force of a wrecking ball colliding with a brick wall. "Ohmygod. *Ohmygod!*" she cried. "Jason took Jay out on the boat against my specific wishes and then he *faked* the accident. He took all our money, effectively setting me up to be the fall guy for his and Jay's deaths. He stole my son away from me to be with Sabine! What kind of man *is* he?"

"Not a good one," Emily said, her tone grim.

"That's for damned sure," Craig agreed. "I would have taken more video, but as you can see from the one we sent you, the security guard told them to take off before he ticketed them."

"Jay's alive! My little boy is alive!" Hannah tried hard to hold back her tears. She could cry later. Right now, she had to think. "I don't know what to do next."

"We can hire a private investigator to find him," Emily said.

"I know it's weird, Hannah," Craig said, "but thinking back, I thought I saw Jason's head at the front of the business-class section on my flight. After the three of them took off, I went to the United counter and asked who'd been sitting in seat six-A. I told them my brother had been missing for a while and I thought that was him. The clerk wouldn't tell me, so I asked for a supervisor. I laid it on a little thick about an open police case, and I guess she didn't want to go through the hassle of checking out my story, so she pulled up the passenger manifest for my flight and told me the guy's name was Jason Hendrickson. I slipped her a twenty and my thanks, then I had to run like crazy to catch the train over to my terminal so I wouldn't miss my rebooked flight."

"Hendrickson," Hannah said, her tone dull. "He did the same thing I did. He's using his mother's maiden name."

"He's such a bastard," Emily said, her voice heated. "All those months before the boat capsized, you kept worrying that you'd done something wrong and it wasn't you at all. It was all Jason, and Sabine."

"I would have given him a divorce," Hannah said. "We

could have shared custody of Jay. Why'd he have to steal him? I don't get it."

"I think you should contact the local police," Craig said. "We can still hire a PI, but Jason crossed the line by faking his and Jay's deaths. He also cleaned out all your bank accounts, and what he did to his business...that's got to be criminal fraud."

"What about the life insurance?" Emily asked. "When the company finds out, Hannah will have to pay it back."

"I haven't spent any of the large policy and only tapped five-K of the one through his work," Hannah said, "and I haven't spent any of that yet, either. I live off the money I got for the house and whatever I make from my illustrations." She paused, thinking. "I know you're right about the police, Craig, but I'm reluctant to do so. The entire incident...all the accusations...the grillings Twombly gave me...it's left a bad taste in my mouth. If haranguing me was the best they could do, I certainly don't trust them with this new information."

"I have a sneaking suspicion that was in part because Jason's parents kept after them to make you confess," Craig said, "but I understand where you're coming from and I don't disagree."

"His folks never liked me, I know, but I never thought they'd turn on me like they did. Do you think they know Jason is still alive?"

"I have no idea, but I wouldn't be surprised if they do. Nothing their little pissant-of-a-son does could be wrong."

Hannah knew that to be true.

"Em and I have a friend who's a PI. We can trust him to be discreet and also to keep things confidential."

"Have I met him?" Hannah asked.

"I don't think so, but Seth has."

"I wondered if you contacted Seth."

"He feels responsible," Emily said.

"It's not his fault Jason took Jay out when I asked him not to."

"True, but he's the one who introduced you to Jason."

"He didn't make me fall in love with him, though, did he?"

"Hey, Hannah."

"Hi, Seth. I should have known you'd be there."

"This is a pretty big deal," her brother said.

"No kidding, but I don't want you taking any guilt trips over introducing me to Jason."

"Kinda hard *not* to."

"Please, Seth, don't. I made my own decisions and I accept full responsibility for those choices."

"Look, we want to hire the PI, okay? Jason is a prick and if I'm being completely honest here, I kind of suspected something a month or so before the accident when I saw him and Sabine out together."

"I wish you'd told me," Hannah said, disappointed but not angry with her brother.

"I wish I had, too. Em told me this morning that you thought something was up, but you never suspected cheating."

"If I'd known, I would have taken Jay and walked out the door."

"It wasn't anything I could prove, or I would've told you. They were with a group and I went over to say 'hi.' Jason said it was a business dinner and since Sabine did business with his firm, I had no reason to doubt it."

"I'm not blaming you, Seth, so don't blame yourself. Jason is the one at fault here."

"Craig's right, though, you should contact the police. Jay needs to be back with you, not getting shaken by Sabine until his teeth rattle."

Dared she hope that's the way this would end up? One thing was for certain, she wasn't going to call Dickhead Twombly, the cop who had hounded her unmercifully for nearly two years. "I need some time to think about this. Let me call you guys back later, okay?"

"Give us a time so we can all be here together," Seth said. "Deena wanted to be here, too, but she had a thing at pre-school with Haley this morning."

Hannah glanced at the clock. It was not yet 9:00 a.m., Colorado time. "I'll call you back at noon my time, so eleven o'clock your time."

"Perfect," Emily said. "Talk to you then."

Noon came and went, but Hannah couldn't make herself pick up her phone. Instead, she sat rooted in her chair, staring at the video playing over and over and over again on her laptop.

Jason taking Sabine in a passionate embrace.

Jay, squished between them, unheeded, never acknowledged until Sabine shook him like he was a dirty rug or something. Her son managed to wiggle out of her grasp, and in typical little-boy fashion, took off. That netted him a spanking, which the security guard interrupted with a warning to move on.

After four hours, Hannah pushed away from her desk and stood up.

Every muscle and bone in her body protested.

She picked up her forgotten breakfast plate and her cold, but full coffee cup and moved with wooden motions back to the kitchen.

Her cell phone rang for the sixth time.

For the sixth time, she ignored it.

All those late nights and weekends Jason was away from home. Hannah had asked him point-blank once if he had a woman on the side. He'd laughed and pinched her cheek in that pseudo-playful way he had that she loathed.

His words rang in her ears, even now. *Of course not, Hannah. You're the one and only girl for me.*

Girl. Hannah was a woman, not a girl. She'd recognized at the time that the words lacked sincerity, but fool that she was, she hadn't dwelled on it.

And then there was the day he'd walked out the front door holding Jay's little hand in his. *Taking the birthday boy out for a sail*, he'd said. *Expect us back when you see us.*

Of course, Jay had been excited and scared all at once about his first trip out on the sailboat. Hannah had run after them, begging Jason not to take him yet. It was the Pacific Ocean, for God's sake. Jay had just turned five. Sure, he'd had swimming lessons, but his little body was no match for an ocean that covered half the world.

Hannah, *Did you at least get him a life vest?*

Jason, *Don't worry. I've got everything covered.*

Jay, *'Bye, Mom. I love you! Don't worry about me.*

Dissecting Jason's words now was too little, too late.

Expect us when you see us. She should have realized how ambiguous that statement was at the time.

I've got everything covered. Translation, I'm taking Jay with me and we're meeting up with my lover, Sabine, and you're out of my life forever, Hannah. Screw you!

Hannah dropped her dishes into the sink. They shattered on impact, but she never noticed. She grasped the edge of the counter and began to sob. Her body shook so badly, her knees gave out on her. Inch by inch, she went down and crumpled into a heap on the hardwood floor.

Wracked with emotions that ranged from anger to fear to hatred to vengeful, she had only two coherent thoughts—Jay was alive and Jason was going to pay for what he'd done.

Chapter 4

Sheriff Noah Ward was having the kind of day that made him regret he hadn't re-upped and spent another ten years as a Navy SEAL. One goddamned thing after another had gone wrong, beginning at 7:00 a.m., when his hot water heater had taken a hike.

After that, he'd burned his frickin' eggs, and to add insult to injury, the toaster had somehow gotten turned up to 7, so his toast had come out blacker than midnight. By then, his only alternative was to hit the drive-thru, which also turned into a fiasco. Instead of two sausage egg McMuffins and a hashbrown, they'd given him two McGriddles, which he hated, and a yogurt parfait. Plus, his coffee had been laden with cream and sugar, when he was a staunch black-coffee drinker.

At the office, things hadn't gone any better. The county's only two jail cells were occupied by the Otto brothers. Jimbo and Bimbo, as they were known around the small town of Fossil, had been overnight guests. Neither one seemed to be able to stay away from an alcoholic beverage, but when it really got ugly was when the brothers both decided they wanted the same woman for the night over at the Flop House.

Noah didn't think the two knuckleheads were ever going to get it through their thick skulls that they needed to agree before they went out and got stinkin'-ass drunk whether they wanted Suzzie or Maryellen or Teddie. They could each have one, or they could agree to share one, or they could take on two, or all three sister-whores at once, but they could not both be alone at the same time, with the same one, ever. Fortunately, drunk-and-disorderly was a jailable offense, even if stupidity wasn't.

He peeked in through the wired windows of each cell, scowling. "Keep 'em both an extra night," he said to his deputy, Derek Parker. "I'm so sick of their juvenile bullshit, I could spit nails."

Derek's eyebrows went up in surprise. "If they stay two nights, they'll have to go up before Judge Fury."

The muni court judge lived up to his last name and didn't suffer fools lightly. "That's right. Maybe this time, when they're told to sober up, they'll take it seriously."

"I hope so. The sister-whores said they've had it with them."

Noah raised an eyebrow. "Must have gotten pretty bad."

"Only if you count black eyes," Derek said.

The sheriff blew out a disgusted breath.

Martha Nilsson, Pike County Sheriff's Office receptionist and dispatcher, handed Noah a cup of hot coffee. "Wake up late, did you?"

"No, I burned my damned breakfast."

Martha, more commonly known as Marty, folded her arms, which always made her look like a female Viking. All she needed was a battle axe and a helmet with two horns to complete the picture.

Because he never, ever asked Marty to get his coffee for him, he added, "Thanks for the cupp'a."

"You're welcome. As long as you're in a bad mood already, you might as well know that some punks hit the high school last night. Took five laptops out of the computer lab, spray painted graffiti all over the lockers in the senior hall, and whizzed on the trophy case in the main entrance."

Noah didn't need a crystal ball to tell him who the culprits were. He glanced at Derek. "You and Toad head out to the Miller farm. See which idiot you can shake loose first."

"One of these times," Deputy Toad Hoffman said, his

voice a little croaky, and hence his nickname, "I'd like to see you send Barbie and Flip out to deal with these little shits."

"If Barbie and Flip ever showed up for work on time, I would," Noah said. He looked at Marty. "What's their excuse today?"

"Same as it always is. They got busy doing something else."

Noah grunted. He should have nipped that romance in the bud, but neither Barbie nor Flipster supervised the other, so he'd let it slide. Did they think he didn't know that *busy doing something else* was an overused euphemism for *screwing*? "Switch one of them to graveyard, I don't care who, and let Kenny know he'll be on days for a while. Maybe the two of them will finally get the message." Either that, or he'd have to fire both of them and be down two deputies, which meant a probable long and excruciating hiring process to find two more.

The Otto brothers. The Miller boys. Barbie and Flip. Eggs and toast. Water heater and hot water. Every damned thing came in pairs today.

By two o'clock, Noah decided he'd had enough. He left the SO, with instructions to Marty to call him only if it was a dire emergency. He had a water heater to replace.

He stopped by the lumberyard and picked out a more efficient unit than the current piece of crap currently hooked up to his water line. With any luck, the savings on his gas bill would eventually, in about five years, help offset the cost of the new one.

Herb offered to help him load it into the back of his truck, but Noah declined. "'Preciate the offer, Herb, but I gotta get it out by myself, so I might as well load it by myself."

"See your point," Herb said, rubbing his chin. "Don't forget to save your receipt. The gas company's doing rebates on these new models. Good through the end of December."

"Good to know. Thanks."

After that, Noah took off toward home. His stomach growled before he left the city limits, so he veered into Sig's Sandwiches and got a footlong and some chips to go.

Half a mile from home, he passed the old Kirby place. He

eased his foot off the gas and slowed to a crawl. There, in the snow, were footprints. Two sets of them. One coming, one going.

Surprised, he came to a dead stand-still. He went up-and-down County Road 8, which everyone referred to as Creight, at least twice every day and he hadn't seen hide nor hair of any activity around the place for what, a year? Of course, he'd been gone for ten weeks earlier in the Fall to attend the FBI Field Police Training Program. Had someone moved in? That didn't seem likely, unless they'd done it while no one was looking, which was also entirely possible. The parcels out this way were large and easily separated by a half-mile of roadway between front doors, if not more.

He shoved the gear shift into PARK and got out of the truck to examine the prints left in the snow. One set led to the mailbox and the other pointed back toward the house. By the size of them, they belonged to a woman.

He raised his head and studied the sky. It was the middle of the day, but overhead, the gray blanket of snow clouds made it seem like twilight. He lowered his gaze and ran it over the structure. There weren't any lights on inside, which didn't mean anything. He'd been in the house years earlier, as a kid. With the main living area at the back, you wouldn't see any lights from the road.

Frowning, he debated what to do.

His stomach rumbled again.

He decided to head on home, unload the water heater, and eat his lunch. Then he'd come back and knock on the door, see who answered. God help whoever it was taking up residence if they were homesteading or squatting.

On this particular day, he was done taking shit from idiots.

Noah turned off the gas and disconnected the line, shut off the water, drained the tank, disconnected the pressure-and-temperature relief line, and unhooked the safety band before carting the water heater off to the corner of the garage.

He unwrapped the new one and realized even before he tried to place it where the old one had stood that he had a problem. The new water heaters had a larger diameter. The only way this one would fit in the space was if he took a sledgehammer to it.

Given that the day had started out shitty, he wasn't surprised.

Noah pulled out his phone and called Herb at Locke Lumber. "Got a problem," he said. "The tank's too big. It won't fit."

"I was afraid of that," Herb said. "It's all this new conservation crap. The outsides are bigger around to allow for insulation, ergo higher efficiency."

"Do you have smaller ones?"

"Not in stock, but I can order you one."

"Great. How long?"

"Probably take a week to get here."

"A week!" He added a WTF for good measure.

"Sorry, Noah. We're kind of in the middle of nowhere up here. You know that."

Noah dropped another f-bomb. "I already disconnected the other one."

"You don't want to hook it up again, anyway," Herb said, his tone a little too logical for Noah's taste, under the circumstances. "Cold showers suck."

"Tell me about it," he said, remembering how much he'd hated the one he'd had that morning. He considered his options. They had a shower at the jail. He could shower there, as long as it got a sterile cleaning first. "Call me when it comes in," he said, and gave Herb the dimensions of the old water heater.

His next call was to Marty. He explained the situation. "Call Olsson's and have them come give our facilities a good cleaning. When they're finished, don't let the Otto boys use anything but the head, got it?"

"Loud and clear," Marty said, her amusement evident. "You know, you could always come use the shower at our house."

"Marty, I appreciate that, but you have four girls. How many times have I heard you complain that you can't get into the bathroom in the mornings?"

Marty laughed. "You have a point, boss. I'll give Ole a call. I'm sure he'll appreciate the extra work, since his business is usually slack while people are busy decorating for Christmas."

"Before you hang up," Noah said, "do you know if the old Kirby place has sold or rented out?"

"No, I haven't heard anything about it. You want me to buzz the recorder's office and see if anything pops?"

"Yeah. Call me back." He disconnected as soon as he heard the *hmph* that always signaled Marty's okay and her goodbye at the same time.

Fifteen minutes later, his phone rang. Munching on the other, soggier half of his sandwich, Noah asked by way of greeting, "What did you find out?"

"Sold last summer to someone by the name of H.L. Mason. Rice Realty handled the transaction, so I called Kimmy for particulars. She says she's never met the buyer, although she initially showed the house to some guy who said he was the buyer's brother-in-law. He hung around to do some fix-it stuff, hired some subcontractors to come in and do some work, too, then left town without a word. Kimmy didn't know anyone had actually moved in, or she'd'a been out there with a welcome basket."

Kimmy Rice was famous for her welcome baskets. Whoever got one, probably wouldn't have to cook for a week afterward. "Thanks, Marty."

"You seen something going on out there?"

"No activity, just a trail of footprints to-and-from the mailbox. I'm headed over there now to take a look, make sure no one's taken up residence who shouldn't be there."

"I guess you'll call if you need backup," she said, her tone dry.

"I guess I will," he answered, his tone equally dry.

A *hmph* later and the line went dead.

He tossed the sandwich into the trash, then wondered if he should have eaten it, anyway, because he was still hungry. How many times had he told Toby *not* to put so much vinegar and oil on the bread? If he didn't get to eat it right away, it tasted like crap, plus it dripped all over him.

That reminded him to look down at his front. He dropped another f-bomb and stormed off to his bedroom to change into a clean shirt.

Ten minutes later, he pulled part-way into the driveway of the Kirby house, blocking the exit. He climbed out of the F-150 Police Responder that served as his duty vehicle and unbuttoned his jacket so he had easy access to the weapon holstered on his hip.

In the mountains, daylight faded quickly as winter neared. Noah pulled out his mini tactical flashlight, activating it. He examined the footprints again, then followed them to the back of the house. Odd that they didn't lead to the front door, which was a helluva lot closer to the mailbox.

He stopped at the edge of the patio and unsnapped his holster. The house was dark inside. He moved closer, not making a sound, keeping the light aimed at the ground.

A screeching noise threw him off for a moment. He glanced down and noticed a golden retriever puppy scratching at the patio door. It didn't bark or yip, but it was whining and wagging its little butt for all it was worth. Nice welcoming committee.

Noah knocked, the corner of his mouth quirked up in momentary amusement.

No one responded, but the dog jumped up to put his front paws on the glass again. This time, he did yip.

An uneasy feel crept up Noah's spine. Footprints out to the mailbox and back, but no vehicle had left the property via the road. He swung around and aimed his light around the yard. Footprints and paw prints, coming and going, up the slope. He turned back and aimed his light inside the darkened house. The entire place, or what he could see of it, had been renovated.

His light crept over the family room, the fireplace, the dining area, and on to the kitchen. He almost missed the bare hint of a foot sticking out between the island and the L-end of the cabinets. He jerked his hand back. Yep, definitely a foot, and by the size of it, a woman's foot.

He raised the tactical light, intent on shattering the patio door to get inside. Just before he connected heavy metal to glass, he pulled back and tried the door. Unlocked. When the hell would people learn not to leave their doors unlocked?

He slid it open, then pulled out his Glock, holding the light over the barrel as he stepped inside. His gaze and his gun arm swept the room, searching for intruders. The only commotion was from the puppy, circling his ankles. "Sit," he hissed, and was surprised when the dog did exactly that. "Good boy."

The dog yipped.

Noah couldn't contain a shadow of a smile. Someone had done a good job training the puppy.

He aimed his light at the wall, looking for the light switches. He flipped on both, which lit up the kitchen and the patio, and continued around to the island.

A woman lay on the floor, curled up into a ball. He could see no signs of a struggle, and thank God, no blood. As he studied her, he noticed she was breathing. He decided to take a chance that no intruders were lurking in the shadows or one of the other rooms. He holstered his Glock and turned off the flashlight before he shoved it into his pocket.

Kneeling down, he felt for the pulse at her neck. Steady, strong.

He gave her shoulder a slight shake.

She moaned.

He did it again.

Her eyes came open slowly. An instant later, her head jerked back and her eyes widened in fright.

And then she screamed so loud he was absolutely certain they heard it on Main Street.

Chapter 5

Quicker than the blink of an eye, Hannah was on her butt and scrambling backward toward the end wall that housed her pantry cupboard. Bowie jumped in her lap, as if he could protect her.

She didn't realize until she found herself trapped, that she'd aimed for a corner with no egress. Damn! "Who are you? What do you want?" She had knives. If she got on her feet, she could open the pantry door and grab the meanest, longest knife in the block.

"Calm down," the stranger said, standing.

She had to look up, and up, to meet his eyes.

"I am calm," she shouted. "Who the hell are you?"

"I'm Pike County Sheriff No—"

"Does that give you the right to break into my house?" she screamed.

"How do I know this is your house?" he countered, his hand on the butt of his weapon.

"Because I bought it."

"I'd like to see some ID, please."

Hannah's breaths were shallow and erratic. She ordered herself to breathe deeply, but she couldn't seem to take her breaths slowly. She began to hyperventilate.

He took three steps and there he was, kneeling down in

front of her again. "With me," he said. "In...out...in...out...
in...out...."

The sheriff, if that's what he really was, kept at it for a
least a minute by her estimation, and finally, she was breathing normally again. Bowie curled up in her lap, completely
content with the odd situation.

The stranger held out a hand to her.

She stared at it, as if his fingertips were loaded with poison
darts.

He let out a resigned sigh and said, "Okay, let's do it the
hard way."

Before she realized his intent, he picked up Bowie and set
him aside, then put one arm beneath her knees and the other
around her back and lifted her off the floor. Hannah had never been picked up before. She panicked and squealed, wrap-
ping her arms around his neck.

He let go of her legs slowly, until her feet hit the floor. "As
soon as I know you can stand unaided, I'll let go of you," he
said, "but in the meantime, please, let go of my neck. You're
choking me."

As if he'd suddenly developed a temperature of a thousand
degrees, she released him and lost her balance at the same
time.

He grabbed her with both arms. What resulted could only
be called an awkward position between two people who
didn't know each other intimately.

Neither one spoke.

Hannah was mortified. She'd gotten dressed that morning
in sweats and a long-sleeve T-shirt, sans bra. His jacket was
undone. Could he feel her through his shirt?

"You okay now?" he asked, his voice tight.

She nodded, afraid she'd squeal again if she tried to answer. Still, he held on longer than she thought politely appropriate.

"I'm going to let go. Grab the edge of the counter for support."

She nodded again, her eyes downcast because she couldn't
face him. Consequently, her gaze was aimed right at his
crotch as he backed away. What she saw answered the ques-

tion of whether or not he'd been able to feel her breasts pressed against his chest. Her face flamed with embarrassment. Her eyes darted wildly around the room, landing anywhere but on him.

"You all right?"

She managed to get out a tentative, "Yes."

He came back and grabbed her arm, steering her toward the table. He pulled out a chair and said, "Sit."

Trailing behind them, Bowie sat, as well.

He spared a wry glance at the dog. "You must be doing a good job of training him."

"I'm trying," she said. "I've never had a dog before."

"What's his name?"

"Bowie."

He squatted down and petted the puppy. "Hello, Bowie. You're a good dog, aren't you?"

Bowie woofed in response.

"I have a golden retriever, too, although Fiona's not quite as well-mannered as Bowie. Did you get him after you came to Fossil?"

She nodded. "From Arch Kimball." Good God, they were having a normal conversation, like they'd known each other forever. Is this what Alice felt like when she fell down the rabbit hole and had tea with the Mad Hatter?

"Fiona and Bowie are siblings, then."

"Maybe they can play together sometime," she said, sounding inane, even to herself.

He shook his head, as if trying to clear it. "Maybe they can."

Hannah stared at his big, strong hand petting Bowie into a frenzy and felt a tingle of something she'd never felt before. She ignored it and said, "Why did you break into my house?"

Still squatting, he said, "As soon as you show me some ID, I'd be glad to explain why I'm here. Otherwise, if you have no ID, I'll be happy to offer you alternative accommodations at the county jail tonight."

Hannah stared at him, half in shock. He couldn't be serious! "Is it okay if I get my purse?"

"Is it in this room?"

"No, it's hanging on a hook in the mudroom."

His eyes scanned the room. "Through there?"

She nodded.

"Stay put. I'll bring it to you."

Traitor that he was, Bowie abandoned her to follow the stranger.

He returned moments later, her purse dangling from his index finger by the strap.

She took it from him and dug around inside for her wallet, eternally grateful that she taken care of name changes on everything—her driver's license, her social security card, her library card, her credit cards. One by one, she pulled out every form of ID she had in her wallet and lined them up on the table.

The sheriff, if that's who he was, reached for the Colorado driver's license. "Hannah L. Mason." He looked at her again, this time with amusement. "I guess if you also go by H.L. Mason, then you're the homeowner, all right."

She felt like giving him a good swift kick where it would count the most. What right did he have to be amused by all this when she'd been scared shitless to find him looming over her?

Without a word, she picked up every credit card and piece of identification and put them back into her wallet.

He said, "You shouldn't carry your social security card in your wallet. If it gets stolen, you'll be in a world of hurt."

Hannah had never carried her card with her before, but she'd gotten it before she left San Diego, and truthfully, she'd forgotten it was even there. "Thank you for the reminder," she said and removed it from the slot.

"No problem." He leaned back against the island and crossed one foot over the other and then his arms over his chest. "How long have you been living here?"

"Since October fifteenth."

He grunted. "Guess that's why I didn't know you'd moved in. As soon as I got back from training I took at the FBI, I went elk hunting."

She eyed him with suspicion. "Elk hunting?"

"Yes, you know what an elk is, don't you?"

Hannah thought about telling him to go do something ana-tomically impossible because of his slightly snarky tone, but decided not to stir the waters. In her current state, she might have imagined the snarkiness, anyway. "Actually, I illustrated a book of antler animals. I thought the elk were quite magnif-icent. I've never met anyone who hunted them before."

"My family and I eat the meat," he said a bit defensively, and then his eyes widened. "H.L. Mason. Of course! I gave that book to my dad last year for Christmas. He spends hours looking at the drawings." He shook his head. "Small world."

"Not small enough," she muttered, "but I'm glad he likes it. I worked on that book for over a year."

"You're talented."

"It's God-given."

"Still...."

Bowie ran toward the patio door, managing to stop his slide a foot from the glass.

"He wants to go out."

"I'll take him."

"You don't have to do that."

"I know I don't have to, but nonetheless, I'm offering."

"Thank you." She closed her purse and stood. "Would you, uh, like some coffee?"

"Coffee sounds great. Thanks." He went to the patio door and opened it.

Bowie shot through like he was running a puppy marathon.

"There's a particular tree at the top of the incline where he likes to complete his business."

The sheriff, if he was indeed the sheriff, said, "I'll let him lead me."

"You can stay on the patio. I have him trained to come back after five minutes."

"A dog who tells time. Amazing." His lips quirked and his dark eyes lit up. "Maybe I should let you have a go at my golden. She likes life best when she ignores my commands."

"Bring her over any time," Hannah said. "Bowie would like a playmate, I'm sure, and I'm always up for a challenge." The moment the words were out, she wanted them back. What on earth was she thinking, making future plans with a stranger and his dog?

Noah stepped outside and pulled the door closed behind him, slightly bemused. He went over to the edge of the patio, watching Bowie cavort through the snow before he tore up the hillside. His thoughts were on the woman inside. Had she really been sending him a message? Did she consider him a challenge, too, or just his dog?

H.L. Mason was not at all what he expected. From the top of her head, with its floppy knot of hair, to the pink polish on her toenails, *Hannah* Mason was all woman. Not even the T-shirt or the sweats could hide her curves. Had that been her intent? He hadn't had an instant reaction to a female like the one he'd experienced mere minutes ago since…hell! Since he was knee-high to losing his virginity with Maryalice Farraday when he was fifteen and she was eighteen. She'd long ago left town, but it was an experience he'd never forget.

Bowie raced back down, circled his ankles, then tore out over the snow-covered yard again, yipping his version of a puppy bark. When the dog showed no signs of wanting to come back, Noah likened him to a little kid, testing his limits. "Bowie, come!" he called out.

Bowie came to a dead standstill and lifted his head.

"Come!" Noah said again.

The dog wagged his tail and leaped through the snow, then ran directly to the patio door and sat, staring through the glass. Noah glanced inside, wondering what he was looking at. Hannah Mason stood there, holding a towel. The little rascal knew he had to be dried off before being allowed back inside on what was obviously recently installed hard-wood flooring.

She opened the door and handed the towel out. "If you wouldn't mind taking off your boots this time?"

"Yes, ma'am," he said, noticing she'd already cleaned up his earlier mess.

There had been a time in Hannah's life when she'd allowed

people to fluster her. After the reported deaths of her husband and son, being hounded by both cops and the media, she'd somehow managed to quell that reaction. Being pissed was a heckuva motivator, even if it was on the opposite side of friendliness.

Stay angry, she always told herself, and nothing will get to you. No one will be able to mess with your psyche or intimidate you or rock you in any way.

She met the stranger's gaze without flinching.

He didn't bat an eyelash, either.

The battle of wills was on.

Finally, he gave her what she thought was a knowing smirk and bent to towel Bowie dry. Moments later, she opened the door and the puppy jetted inside, only to plop his doggie butt down right next to her while he watched the alleged sheriff bend over to take off his shit-kickers. Emily had warned her she'd better start calling boots by another name, but so far, Hannah hadn't been given a good reason why she should.

He straightened before removing the boots. "I need to go move my truck into the driveway. Be right back." As quick as that, he disappeared around the side of the house.

Hannah hurried to the living room to look out the front window. Though the day had grown dark between twilight and the snow clouds, she could make out the large pickup truck blocking the entrance to her fenced property. She almost couldn't fathom that he'd expected her to try and make a getaway. The absurdity of it made her chuckle, something she rarely did these days if it didn't pertain to Bowie.

He fired up the engine, backed up to straighten the vehicle, then drove straight in and parked up close to the garage door. She went back to the patio door, hoping he hadn't seen her watching him.

He reappeared less than a minute later, removed his boots, and stood on the cold patio in his stockinged feet.

She slid the door open.

He looked her in the eye and said, "May I?"

"What's your name?"

"Noah Ward."

She stepped back to allow him room to pass by without

touching her.

He went straight to the mudroom and deposited his boots in the boot tray.

Hannah slid the patio door closed and locked it, giving herself a silent lecture about locking it at all times, to prevent future intrusions by the likes of people such as Noah Ward, who might or might not be the sheriff.

The man himself returned to the kitchen and bent down to play with Bowie.

"How do you take your coffee?"

He glanced up and smiled. "Black."

That smile did something to her insides she didn't like. She tamped down the curl of desire and went to pour French roast into two mugs. She took both to the table, but didn't sit down. "I'd like to see your identification now."

"Shit!" he muttered, then said, "Excuse me," and pulled out his phone and dialed. "Marty, it's me. Everything clear at thirteen-three-sixty-five Creight."

Startled to hear the numbers of her address come out of his mouth, Hannah stiffened.

"Yeah, H.L. Mason is here, alive and well," he said, his tone wry. "No, no problems. See you in the morning." He disconnected in a hurry, as if he didn't want to talk about his stop at what he called *crate*.

"Why did you say crate after my street numbers?"

"It's c-r-e-i-g-h-t," he said, spelling out the word. "Short for County Road Eight."

"I see," she said, though she really didn't, but who was she to argue over the local jargon of Pike County. "About *your* identification."

He slid his phone back into his pocket and withdrew a black wallet and flipped it open. It held a miniature gold shield with a five-point star centered on it. SHERIFF was emblazoned across the arching top, and PIKE COUNTY circled the county emblem in the center. His print identification was on the opposite flap.

Hannah reached for the wallet so she could read the ID card. Noah Ward, Sheriff, Pike County, Badge 125, and a photo, which, as far as she could tell, didn't do him justice.

She handed back the wallet and her eyes went to the black ball cap on his head. Embroidered with two-inch white letters, PCSO, it should have given her a clue regarding his identity. In the old days, it might have. These days, she didn't trust anyone. Not even him, even after she noticed when he'd taken his boots to the mudroom that the back of his hat had been embroidered with the word SHERIFF.

She said, "I'm sorry if I gave you a hard time, Sheriff, but you really gave me a start."

"I understand, and I'm sorry, too. I live up the road, and when I passed by, I noticed imprints in the snow. I didn't know the old Kirby place had sold, so I assumed someone was squatting. Being sheriff, I felt obliged to stop and check things out."

"I appreciate your concern." She waved a hand toward the table. "Let's sit, shall we?" She headed to the chair she normally sat in, but he beat her to it and held it out for her. "Thank you."

He said, "You're welcome," and headed for the opposite side of the table. "What brought you to Fossil?"

Hannah had prepared herself for this exact question, though she'd been such a hermit since moving in, she hadn't given anyone a chance to ask it. "Dinosaurs." While it wasn't the exact truth of how she'd chosen Fossil, it sufficed for an answer, especially since Jay had loved the now-extinct creatures.

He nodded, as if he understood her explanation, but said, "And yet, you're an artist, not an paleontologist."

"Regardless, I'm working on a dinosaur book and when I read that new bones had been discovered in Fossil, I said to myself, Why not?"

He stared at her for a moment, then picked up his mug and took a sip, his eyes still on her.

Hannah met his gaze without blinking. Two could play the stare-down game, as she'd learned well over the past two years.

"You planning on staying?" he asked.

"Yes."

Finally, he glanced around the kitchen–dining area, and the

family room it fed into. "You've done an amazing job refurbishing the place.

"Thank you," she said, inexplicably warmed by the compliment. "My brother-in-law sent me photos and I worked from those. He's a contractor in California, so he offered to oversee the renovations for me."

"I wouldn't have thought a long-distance reno could be successful, but I guess anything's possible," he said, studying her intently again.

"Where there's a will, there's a way," she said, citing an old proverb she'd found to be true in her recent past.

He nodded, a slight smile turning up one corner of his mouth.

Hannah felt like she'd lost all ability for small talk, but she had a million questions for Sheriff Ward, one being, "Is there something else I can do for you?"

If she hadn't had her gaze locked on to his, she never would have seen the flicker of…not surprise, but something in his eyes. Had he found her comment rude, or was he taken aback by her bluntness?

"No, ma'am." He made a move to stand.

She stayed him with her hand. "Please, finish your coffee."

His eyebrows dipped in obvious confusion, and no wonder. She'd just been thinking she wanted him gone five minutes ago, and suddenly, she encouraged him to stay longer. He no doubt thought her a flake.

While she considered that contradiction, her phone rang. She got up to grab it off the counter, intending to turn it off. When she saw it was Emily, she finally caved in and took the call. "Hi, Em."

"Hannah, are you okay? You said noon, dammit! Craig and I are going crazy worrying about you!"

"I'm fine," Hannah said, her eyes locked with the sheriff's. "In fact, I've just had a visit from the county sheriff."

"OMG, you did it!"

"No, I'd left a trail in the snow out to the mailbox and he thought squatters had settled into the house. I guess you could say he's doing a wellness check." She omitted the parts between her crying jag and falling asleep where she'd collapsed on the floor, and the sheriff entering her house because he thought she must be injured or dead. No sense fueling the flames of her sister's worry, or her imagination.

"Have you told him about Jason and Jay?"

"No."

"Are you going to?"

"I don't know. We'll see how it goes."

"What the devil does that mean? Hannah, this is serious. Jason broke some laws here and he's obviously living in Colorado now. Maybe the sheriff can help you."

"Maybe, but I haven't gotten the lay of the land yet, if you get my drift."

"We're coming out there."

"You are not! You're six months pregnant."

"So? I have no travel restrictions."

"Emily, stop! I'll take care of it."

"Call me back after he leaves. It's apparent this conversation is stifled because he's still there."

"That's astute of you to notice," Hannah said. "Talk to you later." She disconnected and turned off her phone. "My sister," she offered by way of explanation, retaking her seat.

"I have a sister," he said, his tone wry, "so I can relate. I also have two brothers."

"I have a brother, too. Emily and Seth are both married. Seth has a four-year-old daughter and Emily is expecting her first child in March."

"My parents crave grandchildren, and none of us are married, but they keep ragging on us to 'get with the program,' as my mom likes to say."

"My folks were like that, too, so even if your folks rag on you, consider yourself lucky."

"I do." He stared at her with narrowed eyes. "What really brought you to the smallest county in Colorado, to a town hardly anyone's heard of?"

"I needed a change of pace," she said.

And that, at least, was the God's honest truth.

Chapter 6

Noah finished his coffee and rose from the table, intending to take his cup to the sink.

Hannah popped up out of her chair and hustled after him. "Excuse me," she said, leaning over the sink. She removed the broken dishes he'd noticed earlier, tossing the shards into the plastic wastebasket she kept beneath the sink. The food went down the garbage disposal.

"Accident?" he asked.

"Sort of," she said, but didn't elaborate.

Man, she was going to be one tough nut to crack. "Thanks for the coffee."

"You're welcome."

"Anything I can do for you?" He was eager to hear her response. From the side of the conversation he'd overheard with her sister, it sounded like she might be in need of some assistance, law enforcement-wise.

"No, I'm good. Thank you."

She was good, but that was beside the point. He pulled a business card from his pocket and a pen. He jotted down both his cell number and his landline at home and handed it to her. "Call me if you need anything."

She stared at the card for at least fifteen seconds before she took it.

He couldn't decide whether or not to press the issue or let it go. He got it, she was skittish, but she was also wound tighter than line on a fishing reel. "If you can't reach me, call the sheriff's office directly and someone will respond within ten minutes."

"Okay."

That's it? Okay? "Look, I don't know your situation—"

"I don't have a situation!" she cut in way too quickly and a lot too emphatically. Her gaze skittered away, which he took to be a tell that she had something to hide.

"Let me rephrase. Everyone has crap going on. If your crap requires assistance, I'm here for you, and so are my officers."

When she didn't respond, Noah sighed. He was not a guy who liked beating his head against a brick wall. He headed for the mudroom to retrieve his coat and boots. Hannah followed, as if he needed watching. He slipped into his lined jacket and waited for her to move so he could head back to the patio and pull his boots on.

"You might as well go out the garage door," she said, after working her lower lip over for a bit. "No sense going all the way around the house when your truck is parked in the driveway."

Noah looked around, trying to get his bearings. The mudroom had one door that led outside, so by default, the other most likely led into the garage.

She slipped past him, so obvious about not brushing against him he almost laughed. He might have, if her expression hadn't been so serious. She flipped on the light switch and opened the door, then reached around the jamb to activate the garage door opener.

"Um, I appreciate that you were only trying to help when you thought I was in trouble," she said, not meeting his gaze.

"It's my job, remember?"

She jammed his card into the pocket of her sweats. "I'm not likely to forget it."

He eased past her and skirted her truck on his way outside. "Goodnight, Miss Mason."

"Goodnight, Sheriff Ward."

The garage door came down before Noah had his F-150

unlocked. He climbed inside and started the engine, gripping the steering wheel as he stared at the dark house in front of him. "That went really well," he said, his tone facetious. "I can hardly wait until Act Two starts up."

Hannah called her sister as soon as she heard the sheriff's truck pull away.

"What are we going to do with you?" Emily demanded. "You can't keep us in suspense like this!"

"Sorry, but it just didn't feel right blurting out my life story when I'd just met the guy."

"Why was he there, anyway?"

"I told you before, he thought squatters had settled in."

"God, spare me from small-town America. So, you really didn't tell him?"

"I just said I didn't."

"Don't get snarky with me, little sister."

"Sorry. It's been a rough day."

"I know. I'm sorry, too. This deal with Jason is the last news we ever thought we'd be giving you."

"It's really left me flummoxed. I don't quite know what to do."

"Seems like a no-brainer to me—we've got to hire the private investigator."

"I appreciate the suggestion, Em, but I want to think about this a little more."

"I don't know what there is to think about," Emily said. "Isn't it pretty straightforward?"

"Not from where I'm standing. Look, let me sleep on it and start with a clear head tomorrow. I'll call you as soon I decide what I want to do."

"What if that's three weeks from now? Do you really think that's fair to us?"

"It's not going to be three weeks. Primarily, I want to think through the ramifications of involving the sheriff. After that bastard in San Diego got through with me, I'm afraid I have real trust issues concerning cops."

"I understand, but can you at least commit to checking

back with me in twenty-four hours?"

Hannah considered the request. It wasn't her intention to cause her pregnant sister any undue stress. "I'll call you no later than nine o'clock tomorrow night. That'll be eight your time. Does that work for you?"

"It's not like I have a choice, is it?"

"I love you, Em."

"I love you, too, Hannah. Craig and I and Seth and Deena are ready to kick some ass for you."

"I know you are, and I appreciate it. Talk to you tomorrow."

"Wait!"

"What?"

"Tell me about the sheriff."

Hannah could have summed it up in four words—tall, dark, and handsome—but decided not to. "He's mid-thirties, stern, but pleasant, and obviously dedicated to his job."

"Hunh."

"What's that supposed to mean?"

"You might as well have been describing the Twinkie food tester."

The description she'd given was pretty generic. She tried again. "He seems intelligent, and he has a sense of humor." She thought another moment and added, "He also has kind eyes and he likes my dog."

"Next time he's there, take a picture with your phone and send it to me. I'm a pretty good judge of character, based strictly on seeing but not talking to a person."

Hannah laughed. "Says you."

"And Craig," her sister said her own defense. "He uses me to weed out bad construction workers, you know."

Hannah knew that to be a fact, though she still wasn't certain how Emily managed it. "If I can accomplish it without him knowing I'm doing it, I might—and I stress *might*—try. Better yet, why don't you go to Pike County Sheriff's Office on the Internet and see if he has a photo and a bio. You can use mental telepathy on him."

"Did I ever tell you that you have a smart mouth?" Emily said, amused.

"Plenty of times. You set a good example for me, didn't you?"

"Tomorrow night, nine o'clock. Don't forget."

"I won't. G'night."

Hannah's phone rang ten minutes later. Emily again. She ignored it, but moments after that, her phone signaled a text message. Waiting at the door for Bowie to finish with his nighttime business, she reached for her phone on the counter.

> OMG, he's hot! No wonder you didn't give me a proper description—you didn't want me to know you're attracted to him. His bio says he's a former Navy SEAL. He'll be able to beat the crap out of Jason when he finds him.

Hannah's first inclination was to deny Emily's assertion, but after a second thought, decided not to feed her sister's over-active imagination. Instead, she let Bowie in, dried him on the mat by the door, then locked up and turned off all the lights.

Bowie followed her into her workroom, where she booted up her laptop and accessed the Pike County Sheriff's Office website. Like the photo in the Sheriff's ID wallet, this one didn't do Noah Ward justice, which in no way took away from his good looks.

She read his bio with interest. He was a home-town boy who'd gone off to college at Colorado State University, graduated in three years with a degree in International Studies, specifically, Middle East and North African Studies, then entered the Navy, where he became a SEAL and spent ten years in service. Upon his return to Colorado, he completed police academy training and was subsequently elected sheriff of Pike County. Twenty-two months into his four-year term, he was quoted as saying he considered it an honor to have been accepted for the FBI training he'd attended in the Fall.

Three hours later, Hannah paced her house in darkness eased only by nightlights. She stopped occasionally to reread the sheriff's bio. There was a reason why the constituency had elected him to what some might consider the most important position in Pike County. Granted, some voters probably just checked the box next to his name without knowing anything about him, but for those who were informed, they must have trusted him, right? A decorated Navy SEAL, son of a retired FBI agent and a retired community college instructor. The bio had even included information about his siblings. One brother was an architect in Denver, the other was a former U.S. Marshal who now worked for Colorado Bureau of Investigation, and his sister owned her own business, a Christmas shop, in Estes Park. In addition to his job as sheriff, Noah Ward leased out his land to a local farmer and an adjacent horse rancher.

Hannah had driven further up the road the day she'd moved in, wondering about her neighbors. She'd seen a sign stretching over one set of gateposts that day, BELLA VISTA RANCH. If that was the Sheriff's place, the name indicated he had a place with a view.

She went back to pacing until two a.m., still in the dark in case a passing sheriff stopped to ask why she was up at such odd hours.

She suspected he was already suspicious as hell about her behavior.

At seven-fifteen the next morning, with four hours sleep behind her, Hannah walked the hillock with Bowie. Big, fat snowflakes tumbled down from the dark clouds, obscuring her view to the top of the slope. It reminded her that she'd never got her fire built the day before.

All the way up, and all the way back, she discussed aloud with Bowie the pros and cons of involving Sheriff Ward in her quest to track down Jason. She found it uncanny the way Bowie barked once or twice in response, like he knew that once meant *yes* and twice meant *no*.

Silly or ludicrous as it might seem, she trusted her canine's opinion. Hadn't she read that dogs were the best judge of character? Bowie had hit it off with Sheriff Ward. That had to mean something.

With the decision made to seek his assistance, she headed back to the house. Bowie frolicked in the snow beside her. The snowfall had gotten so serious in such a short amount of time, it surprised her. A sunny-SoCal girl, she had a lot to learn about the Colorado mountains.

Outside the mudroom door, she and Bowie went through their usual drying routine that they normally completed on the patio. Irrational as it might be, she couldn't face going in and out of a door she couldn't lock behind her.

Having the sheriff enter her home through the patio door had rattled her, despite the fact that he'd done so for purely benevolent reasons. The next person who tried it might not be so helpful. Small town or not, from now on, she planned to take Bowie out for walks via the mudroom door, which she *could* lock behind her. What was a few extra steps to ensure their safety?

Inside, she put on a water–milk mixture to boil for oatmeal before she filled Bowie's food and water dishes. She left a Milk-Bone on top of his kibble.

Pleased that she'd adopted the habit of brewing a pot of coffee before heading outside every morning, she was grateful for a hot cup of java to warm her. With her first sip, her mental to-do list grew to include purchasing a warmer coat, warmer gloves, a scarf, and a knit cap for her head. Colorado at nearly nine thousand feet was freaking cold in winter.

She added oats to the boiling water and set the timer for five minutes. When it was ready, she took both cereal and coffee to her workroom, where she reread the sheriff's bio one last time, then closed the page.

On a lark, she plugged his name into the search engine and spent the next hour reading newspaper articles about various crimes he'd dealt with throughout the county, which ranged from drug-related activity to car crashes to missing persons. Locals and the weekly newspaper lauded him for an excellent rate of apprehension and crimes solved. Chalk one up for Sheriff Ward.

At nine, she loaded her dirty dishes into the dishwasher, poured another cup of coffee and returned to her workroom. Still chilled from her morning hike up the hill with Bowie, she detoured to her bedroom for a sweater, then went back to work on her latest freelance project, which involved illustrating insects for a children's book. Today, she'd tackle the Elvis Presley Shield Bug, so named, she presumed, because its black tail-end resembled Elvis' hair

With several projects going at once, she had the ability to rotate projects when she felt like it. The new system allowed her to keep each job fresh and exciting.

By noon, she still hadn't picked up the phone to call the sheriff, though she'd thought about it several times. She ventured to the kitchen for another cup of coffee and made herself a ham-and-cheese sandwich. She ate it in front of the kitchen window, watching the heavy snowfall pile up outside. At least another six inches had fallen since her early-morning walk with Bowie. It blew her away that it could snow that much in a few hours.

Minutes later, the front doorbell sounded. Even though she had easy-listening music playing at a low volume on the whole-house sound system, the musical chime startled her. Aside from the Sheriff, she hadn't had one visitor since she'd moved in. Who could possibly be venturing out on a day like this? She peered out the front window, surprised to see a pickup truck with a snow plow attached to the front of it parked in the driveway.

The configuration of her recessed entry way didn't allow her to see who had rung the doorbell, but the door had a peephole. If she stood on tiptoe, she could see who was there. The boy on the other side looked serious, but not dangerous. Hannah opened the door.

"Hi," the young man said, "I'm Sonny Meacham. Sheriff Ward asked me to drop by and plow your driveway, in case you want to go out."

Stunned, Hannah stared at the boy, who looked to be around eighteen.

He went on. "If you'll raise the garage door, I can set the plow down at the opening without damaging the door. I'll get that area scraped quick, so you can put the door right back down." He looked at her expectantly.

"I hadn't planned on going out," she said for lack of any other coherent response.

"We could get another twelve inches," Sonny said. "It'll be easier to clear it now, and then I'll come back when the storm's over and do it again."

"If you say so," Hannah said. Who was she to disagree with someone who plowed snow for a living?

He smiled at her then, softening his serious countenance. The kid must be breaking a lot of hearts at the local high school.

"Will you have time to come in for a hot chocolate when you're done?"

"No, ma'am, but thank you. I've got a number of other plow jobs this afternoon."

Bowie chose that moment to come charging to the door to see who'd come to visit. At five months, he already had his priorities straight—dog biscuit first, company second.

Sonny laughed and knelt down to pet him. "Hey, boy, what's your name?"

"He's Bowie."

"Bowie, huh? You're full of piss-and-vinegar, huh?"

Hannah laughed. "I guess he is, at that. How much for the plowing, and will you take a check?"

Sonny gave Bowie one last scrub between his ears, then straightened. "Oh, there's no charge, ma'am. Sheriff Ward is taking care of it."

"Please, call me Hannah." She sucked in her lips, debating how best to straighten out the situation the sheriff had created. "Look, I appreciate the sheriff offering to pay for the plowing, but I'd rather assume that responsibility myself. In fact, if you're up for an additional customer, I'd like you to add me to your regular plowing list." She tacked snow shovel on to her mental list of things to buy. She could at least do her own sidewalks and the patio, if the wind came up and blew snow over it.

Sonny frowned, considering her proposal. "The sheriff told me you would probably argue with me, and he said to tell you that this one's on him because he scared the crap out of you yesterday." He tilted his head at her. "What did he do to you, anyway?"

Since the sheriff hadn't blabbed about how he'd found her, Hannah certainly wasn't going to explain it, either. "He did a wellness check and I wasn't expecting anyone, so it...startled me."

"He does like to make sure folks are okay," Sonny said, his eyes back on Bowie. "The sheriff has a golden."

"So he told me."

"Her name is Fiona. Bet she'd like playing with Bowie."

"They're brother and sister," she said. "I got him from the same breeder."

"Wow." He shuffled his boots against the concrete porch. "So, are we okay about the first-time payment?"

Hannah smiled at him, hoping to relieve his obvious anxiety. No need to embroil a kid in this when she could take it up directly with the sheriff, when and if she ever decided to make contact with him again. God, when had she become so indecisive? "Yeah, we're good, but can you hold up a minute?"

He nodded.

Hannah ran off to get her purse. She pulled a ten from her wallet and went back to the door. "This is a little something extra from me to you, thanking you for your courtesy."

His eyes widened when he noted the denomination. "Thank you, ma'am, I mean, Hannah. That sure is generous of you."

"Maybe some other time, you can plan to stay for hot chocolate when you're done."

"I'd like that," he said. He tilted his head at her. "The sheriff was right about you."

"Oh?"

The boy's cheeks flushed. "He said you were nice…and pretty, and you sure are."

Hannah's face blossomed with color and she lost her ability to speak.

Sonny flashed her another smile, this one shy, and said goodbye.

Hannah responded with a wave of her hand and closed the door.

The sheriff thought she was pretty?

Chapter 7

At three o'clock, Hannah took a break and wandered out through the garage to look at her driveway. A light dusting of snow had covered it since Sonny plowed, but the day was young yet, and still dark with heavy snow clouds. She didn't doubt for a minute that more was on the way.

With no coat on and only loafers on her feet, she walked down the drive to the mailbox. The local paper was the only thing inside. Not for the first time, Hannah wondered why Thursday was publication day and why it was cheaper to mail it out than to deliver it to driveways. Not a question of world importance, certainly, but she was curious, nonetheless.

On the way back up the driveway, she slipped on the icy concrete and went down hard on her bottom. By the time she righted herself, and took extra care where and how she stepped, she was freezing. No more going out in these temperatures without a coat on. Inside, she lowered the door, then stopped at the sink in the mudroom to run her hands under warm water, shivering all the while.

Back in the kitchen, she put on the tea kettle, then headed to the thermostat, raising the temperature a degree. She also went in search of her bedroom slippers, since she'd left her loafers in the mudroom. Ten minutes later, not even a cup of hot chocolate had warmed her. She went back to the thermostat and raised it another two degrees.

At five, she stood and did some bends and leg lifts. Bowie, curled up beside the desk in one of his beds, raised a head to watch her, his tail wagging.

"You probably wonder why humans do such weird stuff, huh?"

One woof came in response.

"It's because I get stiff sitting at my drawing board all day. I'm also freezing to death."

He smiled up at her, then put his head back down and promptly went back to sleep.

"You lazy bum," she teased with affection.

At six, she decided to heat up the previous day's breakfast casserole for dinner. Just as she slid it into the oven, the doorbell sounded.

Startled, even though she'd heard the sound one other time that day, Hannah made her way to the front window and peeked out.

The big red truck parked in her driveway could only belong to one person, especially since it had the sheriff's office seal on the door.

Hannah flipped on the porch light and pulled the door open.

"Hi," Noah Ward said.

"Hello. What brings you by?"

"Just checking on you," he said. "Everything okay today?"

"Yes. Thanks for sending Sonny over to plow my drive-way. I appreciate the gesture, but I'd like to reimburse you for it."

"No need. Consider it a welcome-to-the-neighborhood pre-sent."

Sheriff Ward looked nothing like what Hannah imagined a representative from the Welcome Wagon might look like, but she decided to let the matter drop. "Thank you."

"You're welcome."

And just like that, she decided to invite him to stay to din-ner. How better to interrogate him than over a home-cooked meal, even if it was reheated leftovers?

Noah accepted Hannah's invitation to stay to dinner without hesitation. He told himself it was because he wanted to find out why she'd *really* settled in Pike County, and Fossil, in particular. After all, he rationalized, the sheriff should be up-to-date on all new residents.

He offered to help prepare the meal, but she declined his assistance.

"It's nothing fancy, just a chile relleno casserole I made for breakfast yesterday morning. It's reheating now."

He recalled the broken dishes and discarded food in the sink the day before. It definitely had green chiles in the mix. "Sounds good."

She narrowed her eyes on him, as if trying to decide if he meant what he said.

"I rarely have a home-cooked meal, unless the folks invite me over."

"Does that mean you eat out a lot?"

"Not really, but I do eat a lot of peanut butter and jelly sandwiches."

"Nothing wrong with that. I have one for lunch lots of times."

"I guess we have something in common, then"

She narrowed her eyes on him again. "I wouldn't bank on it."

He winced. She really knew how to inflict a barb. "You always so prickly?"

She hesitated, as if she'd never considered it before. "I didn't used to be."

If he read her expression and her tone correctly, something negative had occurred in her life and she'd just realized it had changed her. "What happened?"

Hannah bit her lower lip and looked away, her eyes filled with unshed tears. She looked so vulnerable and sad in that moment, he thought about crossing the room and offering her solace in his arms. Not in a lover's kind of way, but in a caring person's kind of way.

When she looked back at him, she had her emotions under

control. "My husband and son drowned almost two years ago. Their deaths...were hard on me."

Noah felt like shit. Losing the two people in the world you loved most *would* change you. He hadn't meant to dredge up her grief, for God's sake. "I'm sorry, Hannah. My condolences on your loss. It must have been horrible for you."

"It was...it is...I...."

He joined her at the counter, since she showed no indication of approaching him. She gripped the edge of the granite so tightly, her knuckles were white. The pain in her eyes undid him. "You don't have to tell me."

"There isn't much to tell. Jason took Jay out against my wishes. The next thing I knew, Harbor Patrol was at my door telling me the sailboat had capsized." She sucked in a shuddery breath. "No bodies were ever recovered."

"How old was your boy?"

"He'd just turned five. He was too young to be out in a sailboat on the Pacific Ocean."

Noah could understand that. A lake, maybe, but not the freaking ocean.

The timer sounded on the oven. Hannah swiped at a stray tear before she pulled open a drawer and withdrew a potholder. The casserole was bubbling and one whiff of it made Noah realize how much he missed out on by not learning how to cook.

She set the hot dish on a trivet and turned off the oven. "If you'd like to wash up, you know where the mudroom is. I'll get the table set."

He hesitated a moment, but recognizing that she needed a moment to get her emotions under control, he headed off to the mudroom sink. When he came back, the table was set.

Hannah placed the casserole in the center, then added a plate of fresh-cut fruit. "Would you like Tapatio or salsa?"

"Sure."

She added both to the table, along with salt and pepper. "Would you like a beer?"

He glanced at his watch. Technically, he was off duty. "Please."

She brought two bottles to the table, then pulled out her

chair before he could do it for her. He waited for her to sit before he took his own seat.

"Would you like a glass for your beer?"

"No, the bottle's fine, thanks. Everything looks delicious, and it smells great."

"Help yourself."

"You first."

She shook her head. "Guests first."

Noah believed in ladies first, but she had her chin jutted up in a way that told him she was ready to have a go at him if he disagreed. No sense causing a stir over it. He served himself, but didn't start until she'd done the same. He tasted before he added anything. "Wow, this is amazing. It doesn't need any additional seasoning. What's in it?"

"Italian sausage, green chiles, cheddar cheese, eggs, and a little flour-and-milk mixture."

He cleared his plate too quickly, which is what happened when a big guy like him had to miss lunch. He eyed the casserole, wondering if it was okay to take seconds.

"Please, have some more," she said, as if reading his mind.

"I missed lunch."

"Does that happen often?"

"No, but when you have a four-car collision on Main Street because of icy roads, and people who are in a big hurry to get wherever they were going, you do what you have to do."

"I read about you on the Internet. How did you happen to decide you wanted to be sheriff?"

At that point, Noah understood she didn't intend to talk further about herself. For the moment, he decided to let her get away with it.

Hannah could have listened to Sheriff Ward talk all night. He had a deep, soothing voice that somehow lulled her into a comfort zone she hadn't expected.

By the time they'd finished the casserole, she knew all about him and his family. He'd even shared a few tidbits about his time in the military, which she knew from talking to her brother's best friend, didn't come easily to anyone who had served.

She concluded from the revelation that he either really trusted her, or more likely, he was in law enforcement mode, specifically, playing good cop as a means to draw her out about Jason and Jay.

Not going to happen, at least not today. Hannah was stubborn that way. Yes, she'd made up her mind for a second time to enlist his help, but first, she had to get all her ducks in a row. That meant printing out copies of the JPGs Craig had sent to her, digging out all the police reports, unpacking the family photo album, and most importantly, getting her thoughts in order. She'd need at least another day before she told him anything else.

"Are you still with me, or have I bored you to death talking about myself?" he asked, his tone wry.

"Still here, and you're far from boring."

He smirked. "From my perspective, talking about myself is a complete and utter bore. I'd rather hear more about you."

Unexpectedly, Hannah yawned. "Sorry. I didn't get much sleep last night."

He considered her with a serious expression. "Did that have anything to do with why I found you on the floor, out cold?"

To his credit, he was determined. "I wasn't out cold. I'd been crying and I fell asleep."

He nodded, as if that explained something he'd been wondering about.

"Sometimes, I get restless. That's what happens to us creative minds," she improvised. "We get ideas when we're trying to sleep, so we have to get up and deal with them."

"If you say so."

"I do." She softened her response with a smile.

He blinked in response.

"Tell you what, can you come for dinner tomorrow night? I'll do a tell-all."

He shook his head, as if he were in on her little joke.

"I'm serious."

"What's wrong with right now?"

She glanced at the clock. "I know eight-thirty seems early

to most people, but when you're going on four hours of sleep, it's bedtime."

"Four hours? Must have been quite some idea you were dealing with."

If only you knew. "It was."

He rose from the table. "I'll help you clean up."

Hannah didn't feel like arguing, so she said, "You can clear the table and I'll rinse and load the dishwasher."

He nodded. "Want me to take Bowie out?"

"No, but you can dry him off when you let him out the patio door and he comes back."

He gave her a lopsided grin. "I think I can handle that." He looked down at his boots. "I apologize for not removing my boots."

"It's not a problem. You cleaned them off sufficiently on the rug in the entryway."

Fifteen minutes later, he let Bowie back in and dried him. Hannah gave the pup a dog biscuit, which he took to the family room to eat in front of the fireplace, even though it still had no fire going.

"It's cold in here," Noah said, a little surprised that he'd just noticed. That's what a hot woman did to him, apparently.

"I've got the heat cranked up to seventy-two, which is way higher than I usually keep it."

Noah went over to the thermostat. "It says the temperature is sixty degrees in here."

"You're kidding!"

"Where's the furnace?"

"In the garage." She turned toward the mudroom and he followed.

Noah gave the unit a once-over. "The pilot light is out. Do you have any matches?"

"No, but I have one of those long lighter thingies."

"That'll do."

Hannah went back inside to the kitchen and returned moments later with the lighter.

Noah took care of relighting the furnace. "I wonder why it went out. That's not normal."

"I raised the door earlier so Sonny could plow without hitting it. I remember thinking it was breezy when I opened it."

"You should call someone to come take a look at it. The pilot light isn't supposed to go out when the door goes up." He handed her the lighter. "I'd recommend Charlie Crispin. He's good with all HVAC systems."

"Does he have a website, so I can look up his number?"

"Pretty sure he does, but I have it in my phone."

They went back inside and Hannah grabbed a pad and pen. She glanced up at him. "Seems like you keep rescuing me." She added wryly, "I never considered myself a damsel in distress before."

His eyes blazed. "Just a public servant doing his job."

Yeah, and the moon was made of green cheese, too.

Chapter 8

Hannah spent the next morning on her drawing of the Elvis bug. Her afternoon, on the other hand, was spent pulling together everything she wanted to present to the sheriff when he came back for dinner that evening.

She considered that it wasn't really fair to hit him with her thoughts and problems when he'd probably rather be home watching TV and relaxing on Friday night, but selfishly, she couldn't hold off talking to him one more day.

There was also the fact that Emily had told her in no uncertain terms the night before, "If you don't get the sheriff involved by this time tomorrow night, Craig and I will be on the first plane out Saturday morning and we'll talk to him ourselves."

Emily was two years older and bossier, but beyond that, Hannah knew her sister had a point and it was a good one. Jason couldn't be allowed to get away with what he'd done.

By the time Hannah finished her preparations concerning what she planned to discuss with Sheriff Ward, she was a basketcase. She'd alternately cried and ranted the entire afternoon. In between those times, she lectured herself to grow a pair. She wanted her son back! She didn't have time for theatrics or tears or anger. She needed to focus, to stay calm, to pray. The latter, she hadn't been much good at over the past two years, but as of three days earlier, she'd begun to pray earnestly to God, asking him to help her find the sonofabitch who taken Jay from her.

With or without his help, she didn't know of any other way than to start the ball rolling with the sheriff of Pike County, or perhaps that *was* God's answer and she simply didn't recognize it.

Noah arrived early, which she suspected he did on purpose, to throw her off. Dinner wasn't ready yet. In fact, he was so early, she hadn't started preparing it yet.

She greeted him at the door with an apology. "Dinner isn't even in the oven yet."

He slipped out of his coat, seemingly unconcerned. "I'm a little early, so no need to apologize."

She took his coat and hung it in the guest closet. "You're more than a little early."

"I thought maybe you could give me a few cooking pointers."

She turned back and noticed he wasn't wearing his uniform shirt. He'd swapped it out for a cranberry-colored shawl-collar sweater worn over a red-and-black plaid shirt, but he still had on jeans. Hannah gave him an A+ for knowing how to dress. "I'm no Barefoot Contessa, but if you're game, I'll try."

He shot her a crooked grin. "Be forewarned. My mom says I'm hopeless in the kitchen."

Suspicious that he was trying to butter her up by playing the cooking and mom cards, Hannah shrugged without saying anything and led him to the kitchen.

"It's much warmer in here tonight."

"Mr. Crispin came right out today and looked at my furnace. He said it was probably just a fluke that it went out."

"I hope he's right."

"Me, too, since he said he only installed it two years ago."

Hannah worked efficiently, filleting two chicken breasts before pounding them with a wooden kitchen mallet. After that, she layered them with slices of swiss cheese and black forest ham, then rolled them up and coated them with fine bread crumbs that she'd seasoned with salt, pepper, and garlic powder.

The pan went into the pre-heated oven, where she set the top timer for forty-five minutes and the bottom timer for thirty minutes.

"What are we having?" he asked.

She started and he wondered if she'd forgotten about him. "Didn't I say?"

"No." While she'd broken the silence to list her ingredients and explain what she was doing, it had been otherwise quiet in the kitchen for fifteen minutes while she worked. The silence had been comfortable, which surprised him.

"Chicken cordon bleu, modified."

"Hunh. Never had it before. Sounds too fancy for a spur-of-the-moment dinner."

"It's not really spur-of-the-moment, since I invited you last night. Besides, I was planning on fixing it tonight and freezing one serving for later. I do that a lot, so I don't have to cook so much."

He nodded. "Sounds efficient."

She wiped down the counter and inside the sink with Clorox wipes. "That's me, Miss Efficiency."

He hadn't said it in a negative or condescending tone, but he realized she'd taken it that way. "I meant it as a compliment."

Her arm froze, then she finished up what she was doing and tossed the used wipes into the wastebasket. "Sorry," she said, facing him. "I'm afraid I used to know someone who ridiculed me with that moniker."

Someone who was a dipshit, he thought. "Let me try again—that sounds smart. I never considered preparing multiple quantities and freezing some." He shrugged. "I suppose that's why I rarely cook for myself, unless it's a single steak and a baked potato."

"I suspected you were a meat-and-potatoes man."

"Is that bad?"

"No, I love a good steak and a baked potato myself."

She glanced at the stove, then back at him. "We have time

before I have to get everything else together. Would you like a drink? My brother-in-law left a bottle of Maker's Mark behind, or there's wine, or beer."

"A beer is good, thanks."

She retrieved a bottle from the fridge, then poured herself a glass of red wine from a bottle she'd already uncorked. "Are you sure I can't get you a glass?"

"No, thanks. The bottle's fine." Noah accepted the beer from her, noting that she was so fidgety, she was practically vibrating. "What's going on, Hannah?"

She took a long sip from her wine glass before she met his gaze. "I'd rather not discuss it until after dinner."

That might have been good enough for her, but it wasn't good enough for Noah. He wanted to ask more questions, and he needed more answers, but before he could open his mouth, she slammed her glass down on the counter and ran from the room.

Noah debated following her, or letting her be. The cop in him won the argument. He tracked her down the long hall to the bedroom at the end where the only light in the room came from within and to the left. He gave the room a cursory glance, then strode across the wood floor and to the bathroom, where she was heaving her guts out in the toilet.

"Leave me alone!" she cried. "For God's sake, let me puke in peace."

Noah turned on his heel and retraced his steps. He stood in the kitchen alone for so long, the first timer sounded. He turned it off and wondered why she'd set two timers, then he got it. Time to get the rice going. A box of Uncle Ben's Long Grain and Wild Rice sat on the counter. What the hell did he know about cooking rice? He read the directions, then followed them to the letter. Once he'd added the rice, he gave it a stir, put the lid on the pan, and lowered the temperature. He reset the bottom timer for twenty-five minutes and went back to her bedroom.

She was bent over the sink in the bathroom, brushing her teeth. He knew that she knew he was there, watching her. "The rice is on."

"Thank you," she muttered through toothpaste lips, then

cupped some water in her left hand and rinsed three times before she put her toothbrush away and splashed water on her face. She towel-dried her hands and face, and with her gaze cast downward said, "I'm sorry you had to see that."

"I've seen worse."

"I bet you have, but I've never...well, you know, hurled in public before."

"You're not exactly in public."

"But I'm in front of you and...."

"And what?"

Her head came up and she glared at him. "I'm embarrassed, okay? I feel like shit, both because I puked and because you saw me do it."

"As I said, I've seen worse. Are you sick?"

"No, and I'm not like one of the scumbags you arrest and throw in jail, either."

Her belligerent reply made him smile. "Let's finish this discussion in the kitchen, shall we? You said something about making a sauce for the chicken?"

Her mouth formed an O and in the next instant, she turned off the light and bolted past him.

Noah hesitated before he followed her, wondering what kind of surreal path she'd take him down next.

Hannah was already pulling things from the cupboards by the time Noah reached the kitchen.

"What took you so long?" she asked.

"I was snooping around your bedroom."

She stiffened for a moment, but didn't turn around. "Nothing much to find."

"Your son was a fine-looking boy."

"Thank you."

Her body stiffened to the consistency of a two-by-twelve. Noah imagined it was rare these days that anyone mentioned her son to her. She hung her head for a moment, gripping the edge of the counter with white-knuckled fists, probably trying to corral her emotions before she spoke.

"Life's a bitch, ain't it? One minute, Jay is here, happy and sweet, and the next, he's gone, and I'm supposed to get over it just like that." She released her death grip on the counter and snapped her fingers.

"I'm sorry for what happened, Hannah."

She shook her head, but didn't speak before pulling a small whip from a crock next to the stove. A moment later, she began to have her way with a flour-and-water mixture, which she then dumped into a pan of chicken broth. She added salt and pepper and once it had boiled and thickened, she pulled the chicken dish from the oven and poured the sauce over it. "Can you peel a carrot?" she asked.

"Probably." His response, laconic even to his own ears, caused her to turn and face him with a smirk.

"Grab the bag out of the vegetable drawer." She pointed to in the general vicinity to the left of where he stood. "I'll show you how it's done."

Noah did as she instructed, but didn't bother to wait for a peeling how-to. Potatoes were the one chore his mother left to him at holiday dinners. How difficult could a carrot be?

Hannah stopped to observe his technique, then moved on to set the table. "And you said you couldn't cook," she said, her tone facetious. "What would you like to drink with your meal? Another beer or wine, or if you prefer, milk or soda, or water?"

"Another beer is fine, unless it's too gauche to have a brewsky with a gourmet meal." He wanted to be clear-headed for whatever was coming next from this paradoxical woman, but one more beer wasn't going to dull his senses or his brain. "Otherwise, I'll take water."

"This is a modified version of the French recipe, so nothing gourmet about it." She looked at him from the far side of the table. "And FYI, there's nothing gauche about a beer with any meal I cook in this house."

"Just so you know, I have no idea what modified means in this instance."

"I don't do the fancy French mustard or spices."

"See, I have no idea if that makes a difference to the taste or not." He considered not uttering his next words, but then decided, the hell with it. "And if you're inviting me to future meals, I accept."

Hannah blinked at him, as if she didn't know what to make of his comment, then went to the fridge and pulled out another Fat Tire.

He turned back to his carrot-peeling.

"I like your style."

He glanced over his shoulder at her and discovered she was actually smiling. He sucked in a breath, taken aback by her beauty.

"If you wouldn't mind cutting the carrots into pieces about three-quarters of an inch long?" she said, holding up her fingers spaced apart so he could have a visual gauge.

Did she think he was some kind of idiot?

Never mind. In this case, he already knew the answer to that question.

Hannah had fixed a beautiful dinner. Whether in the Julia Child culinary way, or her way, she knew the chicken cordon bleu would be tasty, and Noah proved it by cleaning his plate. Her dinner, on the other hand, had barely been touched.

God, what a mess. She'd worked herself into a dither, getting ready to tell him her life story, or at least the last two years of it. Puking? She couldn't even remember the last time she'd up-chucked, and to do it in front of the sheriff. The hunky sheriff. She glanced over at him, wondering what he *really* thought of the episode and found him staring at her with concern.

"Are you sure you're okay? You've hardly touched your dinner."

"I kind of worked myself into a state because…."

"Because what?"

She fiddled with her water glass for several moments, then said, "I kind of invited you to dinner tonight with an ulterior motive."

He grinned, and said in a teasing tone, "If you're planning on jumping my bones, be gentle."

The thought of jumping his bones hadn't crossed Hannah's mind, but to be honest, she had to admit, she was attracted to him. Who wouldn't be?

When she didn't respond, he said, "Hey, I was just kidding."

"I know," she said, her voice barely audible. "It...I...that is, I need to talk to you about Jay's...death."

He frowned, not with anger, but with concern.

Hannah knew she'd worked herself up into quite a state, to warrant the kind of reaction she had earlier. His compassion had undone her.

"I can't begin to imagine how difficult the last couple of years have been for you."

"They have been, but I lived through them. I made life changes. I moved here...." She shrugged, overwhelmed with a sense of helplessness that left her feeling lost and weary.

"I don't know quite how to take you, Hannah."

"I don't know quite how to take myself sometimes," she said with a sigh, "so don't feel like the Lone Ranger."

The corner of his mouth quirked up.

"If you're still hungry, you can have mine."

He patted his belly. "That was the best meal I've had in ages, including anything I've eaten at my parents' place." He grimaced. "Please, don't tell my mother I said that."

"You presume I'll meet your mom sometime."

"Oh, I'm sure you will, as soon as she finds out about you. She fancies herself a committee-of-one greeter."

"From what you've already told me about her, I'm sure I'd like her."

"She's going to like you, too."

A little sad because she no longer had a mom of her own, Hannah picked up her wine glass and took the last sip it had to offer.

One thing Noah knew how to do in a kitchen was rinse dishes. That was always his chore after family dinners. His mother even trusted him to rinse her good china.

"You're good at this," Hannah said, accepting the last pan to put in the dishwasher.

"I've got plenty of experience cleaning up after myself."

"How are you at building a fire?"

He spared a glance for the fireplace on the end wall of the family room. "Don't tell me you didn't get a gas insert when you renovated."

"I didn't get a gas insert when I renovated."

"Why not?"

"I thought I'd like to have a real fire for a change. Not one that came on with the flick of a switch."

"Did you have the flue cleaned?"

"Yes, but I was never a Girl Scout, and I've never been camping, so I don't know how to build a fire." She frowned. "I suppose I could look it up on the Internet. There's a video for everything these days."

"God save us from the 'Net."

"Amen," Hannah agreed with mock seriousness.

"Are you a wiseacre, Hannah Mason?"

"Somewhat," she admitted.

He grinned at her. "You did, after all, give me a cooking lesson, so I guess it's only fair that I return the favor by showing you how to build a fire."

She giggled, enchanting him all over again.

He rinsed out the sink and wiped down the countertops, then hung up the dish towel and glanced over at her. She worried her bottom lip so hard, he thought she might draw blood. "Are you afraid to be here alone?"

"What? On, no, it's just that…." She heaved a giant sigh and uttered a non sequitor. "You seem like a nice man and a competent cop."

"Thanks, I think," he said, his tone droll. When she didn't go on, he prompted with, "Isn't it about time to cut the bullshit, Hannah? What's going on?"

Hannah forgot about learning how to build a fire. She sucked in a deep breath, hoping the extra oxygen would give her some added courage. Aside from her sister and brother, and their spouses, she hadn't had any deep discussions about Jason and Jay and what had happened that day, excluding all the interrogations she'd undergone, of course.

Leaning against the island, she took another breath and said a silent prayer that she wouldn't come off sounding like a crazed maniac. "Jason never understood that I don't like the ocean, but because I loved him, I went out once. I was practically catatonic the entire time. All the slimy, crawly things under the water with big teeth and claws and tentacles creep me out." An involuntary shudder wracked her body thinking about the creatures that dwelled under the surface. "When our son was born, Jason must have said a hundred times that he couldn't wait until Jay was old enough to go out on the water with him. When Jay turned three, we fought for a solid week about it. As he approached four, we started arguing three weeks in advance of his birthday. A week before his fifth birthday, the argument stopped, and I thought I'd won."

She swiped at a stray tear and went on. "They were supposed to go to the zoo that day, but the bastard told me on his way out the door he was taking Jay on the sailboat. The neighbors must have thought I was insane, running after them, screaming. When they didn't come home on time, I knew something had happened. That evening, someone from San Diego Harbor Police Department came to my door to tell me Jason's boat had capsized and he was presumed drowned." Her voice caught. "I asked them about Jay, but they had no idea Jay was with him."

She pulled a glass from the cupboard and filled it with water, drinking half of it before she continued. "If Jason had survived, I think I might have killed him myself for what he did to our son."

The sheriff stiffened. "Are you inferring someone killed your husband?"

"No, everyone loved Jason. Even though Jason was a self-centered user, he had a way of schmoozing people so they didn't really notice that about him." She grimaced. "I didn't even notice it about him until we'd been married for a year. Even so, murder never crossed my mind until the homicide detective from San Diego PD came around and started asking me questions about my relationship with Jason. He hounded me relentlessly for almost two years, certain I'd somehow gotten Jason and Jay on that boat, then managed to capsize it and left them to drown. He accused me of swimming a mile back to shore and going home like nothing had happened."

By then, tears streamed down her face. "Another boat found the sailboat and made every effort to retrieve the detritus floating around it, so it wouldn't be lost."

"What kind of detritus?" Sheriff Ward asked.

"Two adult life vests and one that was child-sized. A lifebuoy and an empty cooler. Well, not exactly empty. It had three soda cans in it that were empty." She swiped at her tears. "The fact that there were three life vests and three empty soda cans was apparently enough to convict me in the eyes of the world. At the news conference, the detective told the press that I was a person of interest, and these days, as you probably already know, when that happens, you're guilty, no matter what."

She ripped the damp dish towel off its hook and wiped her face. "I'm scared of the ocean, dammit. Everyone who knows me knows that, but everyone I knew started treating me like I was some kind of murdering pariah." She choked on a sob. "Like I'd kill my baby!"

Chapter 9

Noah watched her carefully. If Hannah Mason was acting, get ready to move over Ingrid Bergman, because someone is about to take triple Oscars this year and put you in third place. He chose his words carefully, but he knew they'd still rile her. "The police always look at those closest to the victims when a crime's been committed."

"I understand that, but that doesn't mean I have to like it. I also didn't have to like being harassed by Detective Twombly week after week, month after month, for almost two years. I can't count on two hands how many times he told the media I was still a person of interest, even though he had absolutely no proof in that direction."

Noah hardened his heart against her anguish. "Did your husband have life insurance?"

"Of course! It's not cheap living in San Diego. Everything Jason did or had was the best. He bragged to everyone that he had a five-hundred-K life insurance policy. Our so-called friends were happy to report that to both the police and the media."

"Did the life insurance company investigate, too, or did they just pay out?"

"Oh, they investigated me all right, both of them. One was a policy through Jason's work and the other, he'd taken out himself. The check for twenty-five thousand came in the mail, but the other one for five hundred thousand was hand-delivered. When the guy came to my door, he told me to be prepared to pay back every last cent when San Diego PD finally arrested me."

"Did you cash the checks?"

"Yes."

"Is the money spent?"

"I held back five thousand from the smaller policy to supplement my income if I needed it, but I haven't spent a single dime of the large one."

Well, that was something, at least. "What did you do with it?"

"I converted it to gold coins and put it in a safety deposit box, along with the remaining twenty thousand from the other policy."

"What about the house you lived in?"

"I sold it. That was mine, anyway. My parents lived there and it was paid off when they died. My siblings—"

His warning radar went off like wildfire. "Your parents died, too?"

She straightened and glared at him. "You needn't make it sound like I'm some kind of serial killer!"

He might have said, *I didn't mean it like that*, but the fact was, he did. "How did they die, and when?"

She practically gaped at him. "Ohmygod, I can't believe I misread you so badly. I *knew* I shouldn't trust you. You're just like Twombly!"

Noah stood his ground. He'd been a Navy SEAL, for God's sake, and now he was a county sheriff. People lied to him every day in Pike County, just like locals had lied to him every day in Afghanistan or Iraq or whatever hellhole he happened to be in for the ten years he'd served. "How did they die?" he asked again.

Hannah took a fortifying breath. "Dad soloed and got his pilot's license. He bought a little Tri-Pacer and he and Mom decided to fly to Mexico for a short vacation. They encountered weather on the way back and the plane went down. They were both killed." She couldn't resist one final snide comment. "Satisfied?"

"You're the one who initiated this conversation. I can't imagine you didn't expect questions."

"Questions, okay. Interrogation, no way! I've had it up to here with being interrogated!" She swiped her hand across her throat.

His internal radar alert went off again. "Why did you bring all this up, anyway?"

"Because," she screamed at him, her eyes wild and streaming fresh tears, "my brother-in-law saw my dead husband and my dead son at the Denver airport two days ago, along with my so-called friend, Sabine, and they were all as alive as you and I are right now." She lunged at him and pounded her fist against his chest. "Feel better now that you wormed a confession out of me?"

Noah was usually pretty quick on his feet, and his mind was agile and able to leap tall conclusions in a single bound, but for some reason, all he could think of when Hannah socked him, then collapsed against his chest, sobbing her heart out, was that he wanted to kiss her senseless, and after that, he'd like to haul her off to her bedroom and make passionate love to her all night long.

That's what the sexual-animal part of him wanted to do.

The rational-man part of him that was a law enforcement official grabbed her upper arms and set her away from his body. "I could arrest you right now for assaulting a police officer."

Her head reared up.

He couldn't remember when he'd last witnessed someone with so many emotions reflected in an expression—pain, anger, sadness, hope, frustration…and back in a nanosecond to being thoroughly pissed off.

"Go ahead!" she shouted. "Then take me down to the town square and string me up with a rope. Put me out of my misery and save the taxpayers some money, because if you don't, when I find Jason, I'm going to kill the sonofabitch for stealing my son from me!"

A glare-match ensued. Hannah made no effort to wipe her eyes or her nose.

Noah-the-man ached for her anguish and inner turmoil. What kind of asshole stole a child from the woman who'd created that child with him and carried it within her body for nine months?

A monster, for sure, and possibly a sociopath. Hadn't she said he was self-centered user? That fit, too.

Even as he had the thought, another idea wiggled into his law-enforcement brain. What if she was making all this up to cover for a crime she'd committed? Shit, either he believed her or he didn't. He couldn't keep jigsawing back-and-forth like this.

She lowered her gaze, then leveled agonized eyes on him. "I need to find Jay, which means I have to locate Jason, and I don't know how to go about doing that. Colorado isn't a big state, but there are plenty of places he could be hiding, especially with all these mountains. Or, maybe he isn't hiding at all, but has a new life in plain sight. The only thing I'm sure of is that he won't have the same last name."

"Jason Mason," Noah said. The name felt bitter on his tongue and that's when he realized he believed her. "I suppose I could run him in our system, see what pops.

"His surname wasn't Mason."

He shrugged, knowing some women kept their maiden names. "What was it?"

"Clarke, with an E at the end. Mason was my mom's maiden name. I use it as a pseudonym for my art projects and books, so when I decided to leave San Diego, I had my name legally changed from Hannah Clarke to Hannah L. Mason, or H.L. Mason, as it appears on books. I don't actually have a middle name, but I got the idea for adding an initial from one of my uncles, who also didn't have a middle name."

"A name change seems pretty drastic."

"If you knew how badly I was hounded by the media, you'd think it wasn't drastic enough."

He frowned. "I've had my fair share of run-ins with the media, so I can pretty much guess how severe it got."

"There were times when I thought it might be easier to...."

She didn't finish, but he didn't need to hear the rest of her thought to know what she'd been thinking. Hadn't he experienced a similar thought once in Afghanistan, when he was the only one of six out on a reconnaissance patrol to make it back alive? Lying in a hospital bed for three weeks had given him plenty of time to think about how it might be in the afterlife.

She gave her head a quick shake, as if trying to ward off evil thoughts. "I consider myself fortunate that neither the cops nor the media vultures ever discovered my *nom de plume* or the fact that I actually had a career."

"More important than hiding your name is keeping your location secret."

"In addition to my name change, I got all new credit cards, too. The only bills I get now are related to my life here in Fossil, and all my contract payments and royalty checks are automatically deposited in my bank account."

"All that subterfuge that sounds like a pain in the ass."

"Making all the changes were, but right now everything works."

"Dish towels?" he asked. He'd made his decision, with what had to be self-imposed stipulations.

She pointed toward a drawer to the left of the sink.

He grabbed one and handed it to her. "Dry your face."

She opened a drawer behind her and pulled two tissues out of a box. After she blew her nose, she wiped her face with the dry towel.

"I'll tackle the fire now."

"Thanks."

She went back to biting her lower lip and he couldn't help thinking he might enjoy nibbling on it, too. What the hell was wrong with him?

"Do you think…that is, if I get my laptop, would you mind taking a look at the video my brother-in-law sent me?"

Now what? "Not at all."

"I also have a lot of other stuff accumulated."

"Might as well look at everything."

"Thank you." She hustled off and returned quickly, watching while he laid the fire with kindling, then logs, and crumpled up newsprint to fill the empty spaces.

"Will you get the igniter?"

She went to a drawer in the kitchen and pulled out the device. She handed it over to him, then went back to the kitchen and poured two coffees and put some homemade cookies on a plate. She brought everything to the family room on a tray and set it beside her laptop on the big leather ottoman. She opened the laptop and hit a button to wake it up.

"How's that?" he asked, staring down at the flames.

"It's the most beautiful fire I've ever seen."

He glanced at her, thinking she had put on her wise-ass hat again, but her expression was sincere, and she seemed to actually be in awe of the flames. He went to the kitchen to return the lighter to the drawer and give his hands a quick wash. Back in the family room, he sat beside her on the sofa.

She had the first JPG pulled up and enlarged. "Here's a paper copy, too. This is Jason. He's grown a beard." She scowled at the photo. "Some disguise. I'd recognize the bastard anywhere."

She pulled up the next photo and enlarged it, as well. "Jay's grown so much."

She ran the tip of her index finger over the image of the boy's face. Noah studied her, wondering what she was thinking, knowing it must be difficult to learn your spouse had betrayed you in such a horrific way.

"His baby fat is all gone," she said, her voice sad. "I've missed almost two years of his life, and for what? So Jason could run off with Sabine and leave me in hell, thinking there must have been something I could have done to stop him from going out on that damned sailboat? Was there some clue I should have picked up on ahead of time?" She looked at him, her expression tortured. "What kind of man does something like this?"

"A piece of shit," Noah said, his tone grim, "but then, I think you already know that now."

"I do, and even calling him that doesn't seem harsh enough," she said, almost whispering. "Why didn't he just ask me for a divorce?"

"When we find him, you'll have to ask him." Noah started, surprised by his own words. He hadn't realized until that moment that he was fully behind Hannah one hundred percent on the search for Jason-whoever-the-hell-he-was-now.

No stipulations required.

Hannah had lost all desire to be demonstrative with her emotions or her affection—Jason had done that to her, long before the day he'd played out his and Jay's fake drowning—but she experienced a sudden, wild urge to throw her arms around Noah Ward's neck and kiss his face all over in thanks for believing in her.

Instead, she grasped his big hand and squeezed it. "Thank you, Sheriff."

He looked down at their joined hands, then up at her. "I haven't done anything yet."

"It doesn't matter." She gave his hand one last squeeze, then released it. "If only you knew how it feels to be accused of killing two people you love…it's just such a relief to know I have someone in my corner for a change."

"It sounds like your family has stood with you."

"They have, but family is expected to do that, regardless, right? You're a total stranger, and yet you're willing to help me."

"I still have reservations," he warned her.

Hannah's heart lurched in her chest. Was he backing away already? "What kind of reservations?"

"The usual cop questions."

Her hopes sank all the way. Cop questions. Where were you? What was your relationship with your husband? Were you having an extramarital affair? Did you take to motherhood? Did you ever hit your child? How often did you and your husband fight? When did you first start thinking about how best to kill them both? How long did it take you to swim back to shore? How far could you swim when you were on the swim team in high school?

Questions, questions, questions. Some dredged up from her past, others from supposed information Detective Twombly had gleaned from hers and Jason's mutual friends, or Jason's parents, or the life insurance company.

Twombly and his team of police officers had torn the house apart the day he'd shown up with a search warrant. Of course, he'd found nothing incriminating, but the search had not only left her home in shambles, it had generated more questions. Why did Jay's room have scary monsters on the walls? Why did she have a cupboard full of booze? Why weren't her art tools up higher, where a little boy couldn't reach them? The monsters were dinosaurs, the booze was Jason's, and the art tools were kept on a shelf, in containers. Jay might have been inquisitive, but he'd never been in danger because of those tools.

"Ask your questions now and get it over with," she said, suddenly exhausted beyond belief.

"Who's the woman?"

"Sabine Borreau. She immigrated from France with her parents when she was a child. Her mother planted the idea in her head that she'd make it big in Hollywood. By the time she was a teenager, she managed a few bit parts, but it was obvious she couldn't act, and looks and a fabulous body can only take you so far in Tinsel Town."

"How did you meet her?"

"She and her husband moved into our neighborhood right after we did. We could tell right away that their marriage was rocky, and it wasn't long before Henri left. She told me she got everything in the divorce, which I found surprising. I ran into Henri once, about a year after that. In the vein of too much information, he said sex with Sabine was incredible, but he couldn't live with her cheating, knowing other men were getting the same 'fuck job'" —she air-quoted those two words— "he was, and he particularly couldn't turn a blind eye when she started screwing his boss."

She stared at the third picture of Jason and Sabine locked in a passionate kiss, with Jay squished between them. "In retrospect, Henri must have been giving me a heads-up, only I was too stupid to realize it."

"Hindsight has a way of tormenting all of us."

Startled by his observation, her gaze flew to meet his. Like her, he must have his regrets, but now was not the time to probe for them. In fact, there might never be a right time. She said, "Sabine left town without a word about a month before the sailboat capsized. I was worried about her, because despite her infidelities, I liked her. I went to visit Emily one weekend, and when I came back, Sabine was gone and her house was completely empty. I contacted the real estate agent who listed the property, but got nowhere. Jason urged me to forget about her and Jay told me he was glad she was gone because she was always mean to him."

Hannah glanced at the sheriff. "This is another retrospective moment...Jason's behavior had changed the last year we were together. I knew he was working toward a partnership in the firm, but even so, I see now that him being gone all those nights and weekends was excessive, even for a forensic accountant."

"They say the wife is always the last to know."

She made a face, dissecting his expression and his tone for sarcasm. She found none. "But she shouldn't be, if she really knows her husband."

"That may be, but having had a similar experience during my one year of marriage, I can attest that a spouse may think their other half is acting strange, but once you exchange those wedding vows, you don't really expect to be cheated on, do you?"

"I'm sorry you went through it, too," Hannah said.

He shrugged as if it were no big deal, but she knew it was, otherwise he wouldn't have brought it up.

"It was twelve years ago. I was young and newly enlisted, she was young and lonely and apparently didn't fully comprehend the concept of fidelity."

"Did you ever forgive her?"

"Not really, but as I said, it was a long time ago. Time eases stuff like that."

"So maybe in twelve years, I'll be over Jason's deception?"

"That old saying, forgive and forget? It ain't necessarily cast in stone, you know."

She nodded because what he said made perfect sense. Why should you have to forgive someone who had done to her what Jason had? "The strange thing is, Sabine doesn't like kids. When she came over, she avoided Jay like he was some kind of germ-infested mongrel. I can see her being involved with a friend's husband, but to plan a fake drowning and run off with that man and his five-year-old child when she hates kids...I don't get it."

"You might as well give up trying to figure it out. I know psychiatrists who can't fathom human behavior."

"Please, don't mention the word psychiatrist to me. Detective Twombly insisted I be interviewed by the department shrink. I thought I felt horrible before that, but I was thoroughly humiliated and denigrated by the time that guy got through with me."

"That's odd."

"What, you think I should have been able to take it?" she demanded.

"No, it's odd that he had a department shrink interview you. Are you sure it was? I mean, did you see an ID?"

Stunned, Hannah shook her head. "No, I...I just believed him. Are you saying police departments don't have their counseling personnel talk to suspects?"

"That's exactly what I'm saying. They're in place to deal with department personnel issues."

She gritted her teeth. "Twombly is another one I'd like to remove from the face of the planet."

"Please, don't do anything you or I will regret. You're kind of growing on me."

Despite the fact that his admission sent a little thrill of something through her, Hannah kept on track. "I've been mulling this new development over for two days. I think Jason took Jay because Sabine *doesn't* like kids. Even though he was in love with her, he knew she'd never consent to giving him a child."

"Doesn't sound much like love to me, at least on her part," he said.

"Given what I learned from Henri, maybe it was sex more than love."

"Some guys do only think with their second head."

His observation didn't make her feel any better.

"I wonder who watches Jay while Jason goes off to work."

"That's what scares me. Unless Jason works from home now, Sabine would be Jay's primary caregiver after school, and for holiday breaks, and during summer vacation. What kind of mental damage is she inflicting on my little boy?"

"Hannah, try not to dwell on that aspect of this. Your son is alive, and if the photo is anything to go by, he looks healthy and he's well-fed."

She glanced at her laptop again and wondered if that was true. Did children really go from baby fat to angular in two years? "Anyone can feed a child, but kids need love and affection as much as they need nourishment. Jason isn't big in the emotions department, despite the fact that he took a lover."

Noah's expression conveyed his compassion for her.

Hannah struggled not to lose it again, but her voice caught and new tears burned her eyes as memories surged through her. "I was the one Jay always came to for hugs and kisses and snuggles."

"We'll get him back," Noah said.

"Promise?"

"Promise."

Chapter 10

Half a cup of coffee later, Noah squinted at the laptop screen. "Do you have a magnifying glass?"

"Yes, in my workroom."

"Will you get it? I'd like a better look at these photos and the video. Maybe something will jump out at me."

Hannah popped up and went to her workroom. She was back with the magnifier in less than a minute. She also had a small, battery-powered gooseneck lamp, which she turned on and aimed at the screen.

"Thanks," the sheriff said and leaned forward, examining every square inch of the first photo. He did the same with the second one, and the third. For the video, he enlarged it to fit the screen, then continually hit pause while he ran the magnifying glass over the screen. At one point, he pulled a pen from his pocket and jotted down something on a napkin.

"What did you find?"

"A license plate partial." He glanced at her. "Would you mind giving your brother-in-law a call to see if he has more video or photos he didn't send?"

"Sure." She jumped up to retrieve her phone from the kitchen counter and called Emily. "It's me. Can I talk to Craig? ... Thanks. ... Hey, Craig. The sheriff and I are looking at the photos and video you sent and he'd like to know if there are more. ... Really? Thanks, that would be great."

Hannah sat back down next to Sheriff Ward and reduced the JPGs and video so she could access her email. The laptop pinged, and then it pinged again, four more times. "Got 'em," she said, opening the first JPG. It was a shot of the vehicle driving away, but the characters on the license plate were fuzzy. "What do you think?" she asked Noah.

"I think we have a crummy lab at the station, but since my dad is retired FBI, he still has friends who might help get this cleared up enough to read."

"Did you hear that?" Hannah asked Craig.

"Sure did. Put us on speaker."

Hannah activated the speaker and said, "It's on."

"Sheriff, Emily and I can't thank you enough for helping Hannah out with this."

"It's all part of the job," Noah said. "Hannah's told me what happened. Do either of you have anything to add that might be pertinent?"

"I do," Emily said. "I've spent my day scouring the Internet for every news item even remotely related to Jason or Sabine. I found an obituary for Sabine's husband, so I kept looking for the news story, because the obit said he'd been murdered." She took a breath. "Sabine and an unknown accomplice are wanted for questioning in connection with his death."

"Henri is dead?" Hannah asked, shocked. "Why would she want him dead? She got everything he had in the divorce."

"That's the thing," Emily said. "The article says they were never divorced. Henri left her, but he was fighting a huge court battle over the house, the possessions, and his finances."

"But...he never said anything about it when I ran into him."

"Male pride."

"I don't know about that. Remember, he did tell me she screwed around on him."

"True enough, but Sabine manufactured a story about the divorce, didn't she?" Emily said. "That bitch is a liar if ever there was one."

Hannah said, "Send me the links you found. I want to read the articles."

"Maybe you shouldn't," Emily warned.

"Why not?"

With seeming reluctance, Emily said, "They have an eye-witness who describes Jason to a T."

Hannah closed her eyes for a moment, trying to regain her composure. *Please, God, do not let my son be living with murderers.*

Noah gave Hannah his work email address so she could forward the JPGs and videos to him. He planned to have Shari Deitermann, his crime scene technician, give them a go first, before he involved his dad.

He ate two cookies and finished his coffee. The clock on the fireplace mantel struck ten. "I need to get going. Fiona probably thinks I left the country." He stood and his body creaked from sitting too long staring at the laptop. "Thanks again for a great dinner. I haven't had anything that delicious for a long time."

She stood, as well. "You're welcome. I...enjoyed the company."

He stared down at her, but she avoided his gaze. "Me, too."

That brought her head up from whatever had her interest on the floor. "I hope it's not too much of an imposition that I asked for help in finding Jason."

"It's not an imposition at all. I'm the sheriff, remember? I can take any case I damned well please."

"I...it's just that I feel like I've taken advantage of the situation."

He made a grunting noise. "You citizen, me sheriff."

That made her grin. "You sure you're not a caveman?"

He shrugged. "I've been called worse."

"Just so you know, I'm not angry about you coming in un-invited the other day."

"I didn't think you were, but just so *you* know, when I see someone lying on the floor, whether I'm invited in or not, I will find out if that person is dead or alive."

She did that slow-blink thing and visibly swallowed. "I'm afraid I haven't been at my best since I found out about Jason and Jay."

"Could've fooled me. From where I'm standing, you look pretty good." Good God, what the hell was he thinking, admitting that? She'd been victimized, he was the law in these parts. Unlike her POS husband, he couldn't afford to think with the wrong head.

"I let my emotions get the best of me when I saw the pictures," she said, her gaze elsewhere again. "I haven't had a meltdown like that since the day Harbor Police came to my door."

"Everyone deserves to have a meltdown once in a while, and in this instance, I'd say it was warranted."

Her chin went up and she turned her head to face him eye-to-eye. "I don't have time to be a pussy. I need to stay strong. I have a feeling that whatever lies ahead, the going is about to become rough."

"You've handled worse."

"Not really."

"Hannah."

"What?"

He tilted that chin up a little further, and she trained her eyes downward again. "Look at me."

With obvious reluctance, she raised her gaze to meet his.

"After all you've been through, thinking your husband and son were both dead, what could possibly come at you that would be worse? You've managed to live beyond that, haven't you?"

She was silent for so long, he thought she wasn't going to answer. Finally, she said, "I hadn't thought of it like that."

He gave her a quick nod and pulled his hand back. "Want me to take Bowie out before I go?"

"Thanks, but I could use a bit of fresh air. Maybe it'll clear my brain."

The dog in question raised his head and yawned. When he realized Noah and Hannah were both standing, he bounded to his feet and wagged his way over to them. Cute as Bowie was, Noah preferred to keep his eyes on Hannah, as she squatted down and rubbed the fur between the pup's ears.

As a boy, he'd never done any serious thinking about girls. He liked them, they liked him. End of story. Today, though, he was a man. One who wore a star, and who'd served for ten years performing covert operations that required critical thinking. Right now, he was wondering if Hannah needed her brain cleared because of the issue with her son, or because— and maybe this was nothing more than wishful thinking on his part—of him. In his mind, he envisioned a giant red neon sign flashing DANGER.

Maybe she did, too.

Sheriff Noah Ward, who'd managed to avoid romantic en- tanglements since his divorce, was in danger of taking a ro- mantic plunge over what seemed to be a really high cliff.

Maybe she did, too.

Watching her pet Bowie, all Noah could think about was what it might feel like if she ran her fingers through *his* hair like that.

Maybe she was thinking about that, too.

Hannah walked Noah to the front door, where she retrieved his coat from the guest closet.

"I put your chicken cordon bleu and some rice in a micro- wavable container," she said. "You do have a microwave, don't you?"

He gave her a look. "Doesn't everyone?"

She couldn't help giving him back half a smile. "I'd rec- ommend cutting the chicken in half before you heat it. That will cut down on warming time."

"How long?" he asked, accepting the plastic container.

"Four minutes ought to do it. I usually leave the lid on, but rotate it so that the corners are open a tiny bit."

He glanced down at the container and frowned. "I have a better idea. You keep it and I'll come back tomorrow night to give you an update. We can eat leftovers together."

An unexpected tingle of excitement shot through her. "That would be fine, but I don't want you to make a special trip be- cause of me."

He planted his hands on his hips. "I live *up* the road, so I pass by here at least twice every day, and besides, I'll need to return all this paperwork after I have Marty make copies." He glanced at the container again. "I'll bring dessert."

"I thought you didn't cook."

"I don't, but we have a great bakery in town."

He flashed her a wry smile that endeared him to her even more. "I'll look forward to it. What time shall I expect you?"

"Six? That is, unless I'm being too forward by inviting myself to dinner."

"You're not and six is fine." She held out her right hand. "Thanks again for all your help, Sheriff."

He took it and gave her a firm handshake. "I think we know each other well enough by now that you can call me Noah."

"All right. Thanks for helping me, Noah."

He smiled at her then. "Happy to oblige, Hannah."

Her traitorous toes curled in her socks.

What the hell?

Soon after Noah drove away, Hannah and Bowie went outside through the patio door. It was literally freezing-cold, so she waited on the concrete, shivering in her coat. Her brain seemed okay now. She didn't know whether to attribute that to the frigid air or the fact that Noah was no longer within inches of her body.

Bowie came barreling back after less than two minutes. Apparently, freezing temperatures and eight more inches of snow put a damper on his nighttime routine, poor little guy.

Hannah opened the door and stepped back inside. Bowie hesitated. Because she had an aversion to freezing, she said, "For tonight, I'm drying you off inside." Still, the pup didn't move. "Bowie, come."

The dog planted his bottom on the cold concrete.

"Bowie, come."

His head dropped down to study the open doorway.

"It's okay, buddy." She squatted and patted the throw rug.

Finally, Bowie understood. Like the well-trained dog he

was becoming, he rose and stepped over the threshold, stopping once he had four paws on the throw rug. She closed and locked the door and picked up the towel.

As soon as he was dry, Bowie darted over to his food dish, then drank a bit of water, and after that, he raced back to the fireplace, where he promptly curled himself into a ball and fell asleep.

Hannah shut off all the lights and checked that the other doors were locked, then headed to her bedroom to get into her flannel pajamas. She'd bought them on a whim, and a cold night like this made her glad she had. She slipped her feet into a pair of warm, Sherpa-lined slippers and pulled on a robe. On her way to her workroom, she detoured to the family room to get her laptop.

She had some reading to do. Once she'd finished, she sat back and ruminated on the unimaginable situation she now faced. Sabine had made a play for Jason the day after she and Henri had moved into the neighborhood. Hannah distinctly remembered her flirting with Jason when they'd taken over a welcome-to-the-block bottle of Cabernet Sauvignon. At the time, she'd chalked it up to too much wine for both of them.

A year after that, Henri had taken off and Sabine had bragged that she got everything in the divorce, only Hannah now knew that to be a lie.

Shortly thereafter, Jason had begun to change. He'd become secretive, while at the same time, working longer hours and often on weekends. He's also lost all interest in making love. Hannah had to admit feeling relief over that, even though she really wanted another child. The problem was, she and Jason had never really clicked in that department. She'd been rather naïve prior to the wedding, thinking that once they were married, all restraints would be off and passion would reign. If only it had worked like that, maybe Jason wouldn't have strayed.

There were other tells during that year leading up to what she'd believed were the deaths of her husband and child. If only she'd known what Jay had been babbling about when he told her, *Sabine sweeped at our house*. Hannah had taken the comment literally, because Sabine had offered to look in on

Jason and Jay while she was away for a few days, presenting an illustration workshop in Carmel. Why hadn't she realized her boy, who sometimes had problems pronouncing the letter L, had meant "sleeping" when he said "sweeping"?

A shiver of disgust wracked Hannah's body. Sabine sleeping with Jason in the bed he shared with his wife. Could the two of them have gone any lower?

Belatedly, it struck her that they *had* gone lower, so low, in fact, that they could be considered residents of Hell.

Soon after that, Sabine had taken off without a word. Her traitorous friend had waited until Hannah had taken Jay to her brother's for a weekend visit. No doubt Jason had lied about having to work so that he could help Sabine move. Rat bastard!

And now, almost two years later, either by fluke or by divine intervention, her brother-in-law had encountered Jason. Jason, who had done something wrong, something illegal, and something immoral. He may have even compounded his heinous action by helping Sabine kill Henri. That kind of evil behavior might well be punishable under the laws of the land, but it was also subject to celestial oversight, as in karma-is-a-bitch, baby.

Jason had deplaned at DIA. Sabine and Jay had picked him up at the curb…to take him home.

Now all she had to do was figure out where that was.

Hannah plugged *jason clarke accountant* into the search engine to see what would come up. With over three hundred thousand results, the most pertinent to the Jason she knew were on the first three pages. She located one additional article that Emily hadn't sent to her and read it with mounting horror.

If she'd had any doubts that Detective Twombly had gone overboard to implicate her in Jason and Jay's deaths, they were forevermore erased. There, in living color, from Jason's hometown newspaper, was a photograph of Jason, Sabine, and Twombly, and three other people Hannah didn't recognize, at the twentieth class reunion of Santa Monica High School.

The date coincided with a weekend Jason had said he was

making a quick trip home to visit his folks before they left on a three-month trip to Europe. Did Merle and Susan Clarke know that their only child, the spoiled, self-centered, evil-minded Jason, was not only a user, but a child-stealing sonofabitch who wasn't really dead?

God, all those accusations they'd hurled at her, all the taunts, all the promises of retribution—had they actually known he was still alive, or had they truly been grieving and meant every word of what they said? Granted, they had never liked or approved of her, but how could they believe she'd kill her own child?

Hannah had half a mind to call the Clarkes and fill them in on what a bastard their son was.

After a moment of rational thought, she decided not to. No sense giving them a heads-up, if they didn't already know what their perfect rat-bastard offspring had done. Once she found Jason, once she had Jay safe and sound in her arms again, *then* she'd contact them.

She dropped her head into her hands, overwhelmed. So much for clearing her brain.

Lies. Everything her husband had ever said to her became suspect. And now he had their son. Had he been indoctrinating Jay to the ways of lying and cheating while on the lam?

A bullet was flat out too good for him. When she found Jason, Hannah decided the first thing she'd do was cut off his balls, and after that, she'd force him to jump off a really high bridge, maybe the Royal Gorge. As the world's highest suspension bridge, it would give him time to repent all the shit he'd been responsible for during his sorry lifetime.

Who was she kidding? Jason obviously didn't have a penitent bone in his body.

Chapter 11

Despite her emotional rollercoaster-of-a-day, Hannah dozed off immediately.

Her dreams started out rocky, literally, primarily because her last thoughts before turning in centered around all the horrible ways she could torture Jason for his ill deeds. Even in dreamland, she was pretty certain he'd look a lot worse if he really fell more than a thousand feet to his death, landing on jagged canyon rocks.

Somewhere in the middle of the night, those dreams morphed from payback time to erotic time, starring Sheriff Noah Ward.

Hannah awoke all hot and bothered. She didn't know how to deal with the sexual longings swamping her, or the all-consuming desire. She'd never experienced either, not even after almost seven years of marriage.

To add to the confusion, she didn't understand how a man she'd known only a few days could play so prominently in her nocturnal wanderings. And the things they'd done....

God help her, she was afraid she really *would* jump the poor guy's bones as soon as he walked through her door again, and that was *so* not her.

Somehow, she managed to push thoughts of Jason's possible demise by torture, and Sheriff Ward's possible sexual prowess, to the back of her mind.

Throughout the day, she answered her phone four times. One call was from Craig, asking if she'd heard anything from the sheriff yet. Two were from Emily, wondering what the sheriff was like, because not only did he look *hot* in his PCSO photo, but he had a *hot* voice. The fourth call was from her brother, Seth, asking what was being done about *that fucking bastard, Jason*, because he wasn't sure he had the complete story from Emily and Craig. Even though she was certain he *did* know everything, Hannah repeated it all, assuring him that when she knew more, he'd know more.

She switched to the dinosaur book, extra motivated because the little boy she'd planned to dedicate it to was actually alive, rather than drowned, as his father had left her to believe.

Dirty. Rotten. Stinkin'. Bastard.

Hannah had never hated anything or anyone in her life. She'd read once that you have to love in order to hate, so perhaps that's why the hate festering inside her for Jason threatened to detonate into a full-blown nuclear explosion.

She glanced at the clock. Four-thirty-four. Nearly an hour-and-a-half before Noah arrived.

Restless, she decided that eight hours of drawing was enough for the day. She straightened her art supplies before she called out to Bowie. Time to clear the cobwebs from her brain again with some fresh mountain air.

The puppy careened around the corner, sliding three feet wide of his intended destination, which was where she sat at her desk.

"Outside?" she asked him, standing.

Bowie yip-woofed.

Hannah used the bathroom, then pulled on her snow boots, wool coat, and her hat and gloves. Bowie raced her to the patio door and plopped his puppy butt down to wait for her.

It was going to take a few days to retrain him, but she was certain he was smart enough to understand that sometimes, their routine would vary.

She grabbed her keys and said to the dog, "From now on, when we both leave the house, it'll be by the mudroom door.

No more unlocked doors for us, remember? You never know who might walk in uninvited."

Bowie, still sitting, wiggled his butt on the floor, sweeping the hardwood with his tail.

"Good, then we're in agreement. Come."

Bowie tilted his head at her, as if in question.

"Bowie, come!"

In an instant, he was up on all fours and trotted over to her, circling her feet.

She took a step forward. He ceased his circular movement and raced ahead to the mudroom.

"You're one smart puppy, you know that?"

Bowie yipped. When she arrived in the mudroom, he flashed her one of his fabulous puppy smiles.

They trekked all the way to the top of the hillock. Looking down, Hannah wished she had a sled, or maybe one of those saucer things she'd seen in pictures. She added two more items to her mental list of what to buy next time she went into town. No one ever said you had to stop having fun just because you were thirty.

At the bottom of the hill, she examined the white expanse from an artist's perspective. It definitely needed a snow angel, but how did a person go about *making* one? By the looks of the landscape, another six inches had fallen overnight, give or take an inch. If Sonny was correct, that made nearly two feet of snow total. That should be a sufficient depth to cushion her fall. She held her arms at her sides and fell backward, surprised and relieved when she realized she'd guessed right.

She lay there for a moment, deciding what to do next. Bowie barked and took off in a frenzy, probably after another squirrel.

Hannah closed her eyes, trying to envision what a snow angel looked like.

"You're off to a good start," came an unexpected though welcome voice.

Hannah's eyes flew open.

Noah towered over her, grinning.

Good thing she was down here and he was up there, although the view from this angle was pretty darned good

"Bring your arms up from your sides, to shoulder height, then back down to your sides again, and do that several times. Once you get the wings done, you're ready for the skirt. You do that by opening your legs as far as you can and closing them, several times."

She was fine until he got to the *open your legs* part, at which point, she became totally self-conscious about her childlike antics, not to mention that her thoughts also went to what could happen between a man and a woman who opened her legs.

For God's sake, Hannah! Sex, out. Snow angel, in.

She moved her legs as instructed. Good grief, he must think her a silly idiot for even lying in the snow.

Only, apparently, he didn't. He said, "I haven't made a snow angel since I was a kid. Mind if I join you?" He didn't wait for an answer, but fell down backward about six feet away from her. He immediately began to move his arms and legs.

"You're a lot bigger than I am," she said. "I hope it didn't hurt when you landed."

"It was harder than I thought," he admitted with a laugh, "but I'll live." He lolled his head to the side and looked at her. "How's yours going?"

"I guess I'll know when I get up."

"I guess you will." In one quick movement, he was on his feet and stepping outside the compacted area where he'd made his angel. He leaned over and offered Hannah a hand up. As soon as he had a good grasp on her hand, he gave her a yank. Her feet left the ground and the next thing she knew, she was in his arms. Not even a piece of paper would have fit between them.

She threw back her head and looked up at him.

He peered down at her from beneath the brim of his PCSO ball cap. "Hello, Hannah."

"Hi, Noah."

"Did you have a good day?"

She nodded, wishing he would...*stop!* "It was productive. How about you?"

"Same." He continued to stare into her eyes, then his gaze

dropped to her lips.

Hannah had a burning desire to stand on her tiptoes and offer her mouth to him. But that was crazy, especially since her feet weren't touching the ground.

He blinked and just like that, the connection was broken. He eased his hold on her and let her slide down his body until her feet were again planted on good ole terra firma. "Want to see what your angel looks like?"

She nodded, but couldn't seem to find her voice.

He took one step back, then turned her around so she could admire the fruits of her labor.

"Wow," she said, too aware that her backside was pressed against the front of him, "it really does look like an angel."

He chuckled. "Why are you so surprised?"

"Did I forget to mention that I'd never seen snow in person before I moved here?"

"As a matter of fact, you did." He wrapped his arms around her middle. "What else have you experienced for the first time since you came here?"

"You," she blurted out before she thought.

"Funny, I've been thinking the same thing all day."

"You have?"

"Yes, and for the life of me, I don't know what the hell that means."

"Me, either," she admitted. "It's frightening, but it's also …exhilarating."

He let out a little sigh. "I guess that's as good a way as any to describe it."

Bowie nipped at the hem of Hannah's jeans, then tried to run with the fabric still clutched between his sharp puppy teeth. His misguided efforts brought her back to reality.

She stepped out of Noah's arms, disappointed when he made no attempt maintain his hold on her. "I thought you weren't coming until six."

He shrugged and looked up the hillside. "This was one of those days where I happened to catch a break, schedule-wise, so I decided to cut out early."

"I'm glad you did."

That brought his eyes back to hers. "Are you?" He grunted. "Of course, you are. You're dying to know what I found out, right?"

"It's not just that," she said, "though, of course, I am anxious to hear what you learned."

"Then what?"

"I…I was looking forward to seeing you again."

"I was looking forward to seeing you, too."

They stared at each other in silence for at least another minute.

Finally, Hannah said. "I'm going to get a sled or a saucer or both, so I can ride down the hill."

His gaze went to the top of the incline. "I used to sled down this hill with Ned Kirby."

"Kirby…they used to own this place, didn't they?"

"Yeah. After Ned died, his folks both kind of lost the will to live. Jeannie passed in March and Kent in June."

"How'd Ned die?"

"He was killed in Afghanistan, when his Humvee was hit by mortar fire."

"That's so sad. Was he their only child?"

"They had a daughter, Evelyn, but she died of leukemia when she was just a little kid."

"How awful for them!" Even though she'd never met the Kirbys, she did live in their house, and it was a place she'd come to love. She felt their grief as if it were her own.

"You're an interesting woman, Hannah."

"Why do you say that? I'm nothing extraordinary."

"I disagree."

Her face grew warm in the frigid air.

"You've heard the expression, 'beauty is in the eye of the beholder'? Well, extraordinary works the same way, and since I'm doing the evaluating in this instance, it's my opinion that counts."

"What, like I'm a vacuum cleaner or something?" she challenged, a little incensed by the word *evaluate*.

His eyes lit with amusement. "I was thinking more like a sparkly diamond, with all these hidden facets you can't see unless you look deep."

"Diamonds are hard and sharp," she countered.

"But under the right light, they can also be warm and soft."

Hannah gulped. She'd like to be warm and soft right now and doing some of the stuff she'd spent her night dreaming about, with hot and hard on top of her. "We should go in. It's getting cold out here."

He acknowledged that with a quick nod. "It's snowing again, but if you'd like to stay out a little longer, I could warm you up."

Hannah almost took him up on it, but common sense prevailed.

He was the sheriff. She was the victim of a vicious scam.

Scam. That seemed too tame to describe what Jason had done to her, but regardless, the twain between her and the sheriff wasn't supposed to meet, except to find her dickhead, snake-in-the-grass husband.

Therein lay the problem with making her nighttime dreams a daytime reality. She was no longer a widow, therefore, she was not free to engage in a physical relationship with a man who was not her husband.

She took a step backward and tripped over Bowie.

Noah reached for her and managed to grab her hand. He over-corrected and they both went reeling the other way.

Fortunately for Hannah, she landed on Noah, rather than the other way around.

Unfortunately for Hannah, she landed full-length on top of him.

Her breaths came faster.

Noah's eyes burned with obvious desire. "I'm going to kiss you."

She scootched up a little, to let him know her lips were available. It was just a kiss, after all. A simple kiss. Not sex.

He lifted his head and tilted it so the brim of his cap didn't hit her forehead.

Hannah's lips parted the tiniest little bit.

Their mouths connected.

The kiss went on forever.

Hannah didn't even realize she was clutching his shoulders

with her gloved hands. If only they weren't wearing heavy coats. Or gloves. Or clothes. That final thought poked a hole in the haze of desire that had her in its grip.

"This is wrong." She uttered the words, staring at his lips, but once they were out, she let her gaze wander up to meet his.

"How could anything that feels that good be wrong?" He pulled her head back down and took her mouth again, this time, pressing his tongue against her lips, urging her to open them.

Hannah could have no more denied him entrance than she could have boarded a rocket ship headed for Mars.

When they came up for air, he said, "You're shivering."

"It's cold out here, but my insides are all hot and bothered."

His eyes flared. "We should go in."

"We should."

"Hold on." He had such strength in him, he somehow managed to get to his feet while holding her in his arms.

Beside them, Bowie chased snowflakes, happy as a little clam and totally unaware of what he'd started.

By the time she unlocked the mudroom door, Hannah had gone from having second thoughts to having third and fourth thoughts about what she'd decided out in the snow.

It was too soon. She didn't know him well enough. He was too much man for her. She didn't know what she was doing. Life was short, eat dessert first. Conflicting thoughts, all designed to turn her into a sinner.

"Bowie, stay," she said to the puppy who had tripped her up but good.

He plopped his puppy butt down on the mat.

Noah helped her out of her coat, then her boots, before he shucked his own boots and hung his coat beside hers on the rack. "I'll dry off Cupid, if you want to put on the tea kettle."

Hannah nodded like one of those dogs whose head goes up-and-down on the dashboard, but said, "You give Bowie too much credit. I haven't yet reached the matchmaking section of his training manual."

Noah stared at her for a moment, then began to laugh.

Hannah hustled into the kitchen and filled the kettle with hot water and placed it on the burner. "Hot chocolate or tea?" she asked.

"Hot chocolate. I hear it's a great aphrodisiac."

"Like you need any help in that department," she shot back with a smirk.

He laughed again and for the second time, the sound of his amusement made her insides tingle.

He removed his ball cap and hung it beside his jacket. His dark hair hadn't seen a barber's shears for quite some time. She imagined running her fingers through it, and rubbing her cheek against the beard stubble on his face. Overall, he had the appearance of a dashing rogue, which seemed to be having a wildly carnal effect on her feminine side.

"I need to use the bathroom," he said.

Hannah swallowed hard, hoping to tamp down her lusty thoughts. "Down the hall, first door on the left."

"I remember." Again, he stared at her for several moments.

Had she been a romantic, she would've had flowery thoughts...like his dark, sexy eyes were devouring her, turning her insides to mush.

While the kettle came to a boil, she got down two mugs and spooned powdered hot chocolate into them. Her insides really were jittery with longing. Funny word, longing. It implied that you were never going to get what it was you were pining over, and in this case, nothing could be truer.

Why had she let him kiss her? As a mature, adult woman, she'd known what it would start, and where it would lead.

What if Noah didn't understand why she couldn't go down that path with him? Would he storm off in anger? Would that be the last she saw of him? Worse yet, how would she handle being around him if they couldn't kiss again?

Was she over-thinking all of it, when it really was a simple problem with a simple solution? Regardless of how hot they both got, there was no sexual relationship in their future. Period.

"Hannah?"

She glanced up to find him watching her intently from the doorway. "Yes?"

"Would you like a fire?"

"That sounds great."

He looked as if he wanted to say something else, but instead, he went to the fireplace and did his fire-building thing.

"Do you like marshmallows on your hot chocolate?"

"Only if you do."

Did that mean what she thought it meant? Marshmallow lips kissing marshmallow lips? Or, did it simply mean, don't bother if you're not having any?

She went with marshmallow lips, even though, regrettably, there wouldn't be anymore kissing.

As soon as Noah got the fire going and settled the screen back in place, Bowie curled up in front of the flames and went to sleep.

"Dogs have it so easy," Hannah said.

Noah grinned. "They do."

She turned off the stove and poured boiling water into both mugs, stirred, then sprinkled mini-marshmallows on top. She carried them into the family room, where Noah had already made himself comfortable on the sofa. Hannah set the mugs on coasters and went back to turn off the kitchen light.

While she hadn't deliberately planned it, only firelight lit the room, giving it an ambiance that could only be described as romantic.

Her logical brain considered how to rectify the unplanned ambiance, but her recalcitrant heart had other ideas and refused to cooperate in the discussion.

Chapter 12

Hannah intended to sit next to Noah, but he had other ideas. He took her hand and pulled her down, settling her on his lap.

She thought he would kiss her again, but instead, he put his arms around her so she could nestle against his nice, wide chest. It took her a minute to relax, but as soon as she did, Hannah realized she'd never felt as comfortable or as secure than she did at that moment. "Whatever this is between us, it seems like it's moving too quick."

"I thought so, too, but then I thought, what the hell? If I kiss her and she kisses me back, how slow does it have to go after that?"

"Is that Kissing one-oh-one at the police academy?"

He grinned. "No, I must have missed that class, but it *is* the way my mind works."

"I like your honesty."

"I like yours, too."

At least they understood each other. Even so, she felt compelled to clarify. "We're not going to end up in bed."

"Why not?"

She tilted her head back so she could meet his gaze. "It's not that I don't want to."

"Then what's the hold up?"

"I've only ever been with one other man in my life and

look where that got me."

"Please, don't compare me to that POS you were married to. I'm nothing like him."

"I know." She bit her bottom lip. "This has turned into a heckuva conundrum."

"Maybe if you tell me what you're thinking?"

"I wasn't offering my inexperience as a reason. I was trying to get to my reasoning behind my refusal to let this... whatever *this* is...go any further."

He nodded, his expression resigned.

"If Jason is still alive, then that means I'm still a married woman, and I feel strongly about marriage vows. Regardless of what he's done to me, I don't intend to break mine."

Noah blew out a breath of frustration. "Somehow, I knew you were going to say that."

"I'm sorry I had to."

"I'm not. You wouldn't be the woman you are if you were like Sabine." He cupped the side of her face with his big hand and rubbed her cheek with the pad of his thumb. "In some ways, it's like I've known you forever. I don't know if that's because I finally found the woman I want to spend the rest of my life with, or because my brain and my heart are messing with my dick and I'm horny as hell for you."

Hannah laughed softly, a little scandalized by his frank admission. "Maybe it's both."

With a rueful smirk, he said, "Maybe it is."

"If it makes you feel any better, I'm horny as hell for you, too, and as far as I know, I don't have a dick for my brain and my heart to mess with."

For a startled moment, he stared at her, then laughed.

"I've never experienced anything like this before, either," she admitted with all seriousness.

"Not even with Jason?"

"Not even, and that's really sad, isn't it? I had high hopes and good intentions, but in retrospect, I think I married him for all the wrong reasons."

He tilted her head up by lifting her chin with his finger. "What're we going to do about this, Hannah? It seems like we're at an impasse, because I don't fool around with married women, either."

"My brother Seth is a lawyer. Let's call him and see what his take is on where I stand legally regarding my marriage."

"I have a pretty good idea of what he'll say."

"I do, too, but maybe he'll surprise us."

Noah dropped his head and took her mouth.

Hannah turned in his embrace, pressing her breasts against his chest.

With a growl of satisfaction, he lifted his groin against her bottom, leaving her no doubts of exactly how horny he was.

When they broke apart a good five minutes later, he said, "This is going to be hell if I don't find that SOB pretty damned quick so you can divorce him."

"I know," Hannah whispered, "but in good conscience, even the kissing has got to stop…until we find him."

"In law enforcement, there isn't a *we* when it comes to civilians and cops, love."

Love. Jason had never used endearments. It warmed her and frightened her at the same time. "We'll see," Hannah said. She cupped his face. "Just one more."

Even though she knew it wasn't right, she needed one last kiss to sustain her. They'd have to be satisfied with mating tongues, even though it was a reminder of the ultimate mating ritual, just out of reach to them.

Noah obliged and somehow managed to make it last longer than any kiss Hannah had ever experienced.

After dinner, Hannah suggested they work at the desk in her workroom.

Noah agreed.

They both knew what could happen if they got cozy in front of the fire again.

Noah reread in silence the latest article she'd found. When he finished, he leaned back in the chair and said, "Twombly is the cop who tried to pressure you into confessing you'd killed Jason?"

She nodded.

"I wonder what the hell he was getting out of the deal?

Friends help friends out all the time, but this crosses the line."
He linked his fingers behind his head. "Did you speak to the
partners at Jason's accounting firm?"

"They came to the funeral, so we exchanged a few words
then, but not since. Why?"

"Money is usually a key ingredient in crap like this. I wonder if Jason embezzled funds from the firm or any of its clients? Being a forensic accountant, he'd sure as hell know
how to do it without getting caught."

"Ohmygod! My brother mentioned something about what
Jason had done to the firm, but I was sidetracked by everything else, and I didn't remember the comment until just this
second! Don't you think the partners would have asked me
about it?"

"Not necessarily. Depending on how much he took, and
how many people he fleeced, they might have wanted to keep
it hush-hush, so it didn't kill the business altogether."

Hannah considered that. "So, you think because they believed as I did that he died in the ocean, they decided to let
sleeping dogs lie?"

"Essentially." He straightened in the chair. "How comfortable do you feel contacting one of the partners and asking
him straight out?"

"It probably won't be the easiest conversation I've ever
had, but I'm willing to give it a go. I always got along great
with Gary Simpson and his wife, and I used to watch their
twins occasionally so they could get away for a weekend."
She collapsed against the back of her chair. "I just realized! If
Jason took money from his firm or clients, then he's a thief
on top of everything else! My God, what kind of man is he?"
She straightened and pulled out a drawer, withdrawing a
small address book. "I'll call now, while Gary's not in the office. He may feel freer to speak when he's at home."

"Good idea."

Hannah flipped to the S section and ran her finger down
the entries. *Simpson, Gary and Alison.* Before she dialed, she
said, "Alison, his wife, was one of the few people who tried
to keep in contact with me...after. I'm afraid I never recipro-
cated. I hope that doesn't mean Gary won't talk to me."

"I'm sure they understood you were in a bad place," Noah said.

With that assurance ringing in her ears, Hannah pushed the sequence of eleven numbers and put her phone on speaker.

After two rings, Alison Simpson answered.

"Hi, Ali, it's Hannah."

"Ohmygod, I've been wondering what happened to you!" Alison said. "How are you, Hannah? Is everything okay?"

"I'm fine. I just…well, I had to get away from all the memories, and the media was still hounding me…."

"Vultures!" Alison said with disdain. "You don't have to tell me where you are, but is it better for you there? I've felt so bad, because it seemed like I couldn't do anything to help you through your grief."

"I'm in a good place and I suppose you could say that grief is like a bad injury. You eventually learn to live with the scar."

"That's an apt analogy, I'm sure, but still…."

"How are the twins?"

"Loving second grade. They ask about you. They loved playing with Jay and…oh, dear! Me and my big mouth."

"It's okay, Ali. Jay liked playing with them, too. Every time we got home, he'd say, 'Mom, when you gonna get me a bruddah?'" The memory caused Hannah to choke up.

"It's okay, Hannah. Cry if you want to, sweetie."

"No time for tears now," Hannah said, forcing her emotions back. "Are the kids already in bed?"

"Yes, thank God. Gary and I were just getting ready to have some chill time before we watch TV for a while."

"I need to talk to him," Hannah said. "It's about Jason. You may want to put me on speaker, or not. You two decide."

A murmur of voices carried over the line and Gary came on. "We're on speaker, Hannah. It's damned good to hear from you. How are you, really?"

"For the first time in a long time, I can actually say I'm coping well."

"Glad to hear it. Ali and I have been worried about you, taking off like you did."

"I appreciate all the support you offered me and I'm sorry I left without saying goodbye."

"Past history," Gary assured her. "Now what's this about Jason? Don't take this the wrong way, Hannah, but I honestly never wanted to hear that bastard's name again."

Hannah sighed. "I was hoping it wasn't true, but from that, I'm guessing Jason absconded with funds from the firm."

"Not just the firm, but from three of our biggest clients. It nearly broke us to replenish funds to their accounts so they wouldn't know what Jason had done."

So, Noah's theory was spot on. "Why didn't you tell me?"

"No need to bring you down further than you already were," Gary said. "We only lost money. You lost your husband and your son."

"It was as rough time," Hannah admitted, "but...." She faltered, unsure how to phrase what she had to say. She decided on straight out. "Did you consider, with Jason dead, that I might have the money?"

After a slight hesitation, Gary said, "We did, but after the funeral, when you told us Jason had cleaned out your bank accounts, we realized you were as in-the-dark about his activities as we were. Bringing it up would have only added salt to your already wounded soul, and we couldn't do that."

His admission made her feel worse than ever about not bothering to say goodbye, or even keep in touch with them. "I'm on speaker at this end, too. The sheriff of the county where I live now is here with me."

"First of all," Gary said, "let me say how relieved Ali and I both are to have you confirm you knew nothing about what Jason did, but I don't see how law enforcement in whatever county you're in now can help resolve this issue."

"My involvement comes from a different angle," Noah said.

"How so?" Gary asked.

"I'll let Hannah explain."

Hannah took a deep breath and described recent events.

"What a depraved, horrible sonofabitch!" Ali cried.

"Are you sure it was Jason?" Gary asked.

"Positive. Seeing Jay in the photos, and Sabine Borreau, pretty much clinched it."

"The siren keeps on singing her song, huh?" Ali asked, her tone sardonic.

"I suppose that means she put the make on Gary."

"Boy, did she. I thought Gary was going to have to visit me at the state pen after we left your house for the Fourth of July barbeque."

"I remember that. She also hit on my brother-in-law, and Emily was pissed beyond belief." Hannah uttered a self-deprecating laugh. "You'd think, knowing how Sabine was constantly on the prowl, I would have suspected she'd try for Jason, too. I guess I thought she was...I don't know, innocently flirting." Hannah held back the information she'd found about Jason and Sabine knowing each other from high school.

"I don't think Sabine Borreau has an innocent bone in her body," Ali said, her tone grim.

"Simmer down, honey," Gary said, his tone gentle and loving. "I didn't take her bait, did I?"

"No," Ali said, placated. Hannah could hear the smile in her voice.

"Before this conversation goes any further," Noah said, "I'd like to ask that you keep our discussion confidential until such time as Jason has been arrested. If he gets wind that we know he's alive and kicking, I'm afraid you can kiss any restitution goodbye."

The cold tickle of dread slithered down Hannah's spine. Noah's warning made her realize she hadn't considered what might happened to Jay if Jason discovered he'd been outted before she managed to get their son out of his grasp.

"Our lips are sealed," Gary assured Noah. "The partners and I paid back the embezzled funds to the tune of four-point-six-three million, so I think I speak for all of us when I say I wouldn't want to jeopardize recouping some of it."

"I'm so sorry, Gary."

"It's not for you to apologize, Hannah. Jason is the one who stole the money and he's the one who should offer an apology...and pay us back."

"Is there anything we can do from this end?" Ali asked.

"We don't know yet," Noah said. "We needed confirmation of the theft, and now that we have it, we'll keep it in mind as we make further inquiries. Obviously, we'll have to involve your local law enforcement at some point."

"As long as we don't have to deal with that jerk who hassled Hannah," Gary said. "Listen, Hannah, if you need financial assistance tracking Jason down, I'm sure the partners would be amenable to ponying up some funds. We're all still pretty pissed about what he did."

"I appreciate the offer," Hannah said. "Thank you."

"I'll keep you in my prayers," Ali said, "and I'll pray for Jay's safe return." She sniffled and added with emotion, "I can't believe Jason did such a horrible thing to you."

Almost overcome with emotion herself, Hannah said, "Thank you, Ali."

"You doing okay financially, Hannah?" Gary asked.

"I'm fine. I'm free and clear on the house, so I only have monthly expenses, plus taxes. My work keeps me busy and brings in a steady income."

"Promise you'll let me know if you need any financial assistance," Gary said.

"I promise," Hannah said, but she knew she'd never do it. That just wasn't her way, and besides, he and Ali had already taken a big hit because of Jason.

"Thank you for your candor, sir," Noah said. "We'll be in touch."

"You sound like former military," Gary said. "You don't have to 'sir' me, but I'd like to thank you for your service. What branch?"

"Navy."

"A SEAL, by chance?"

"Yes."

"My cousin was a SEAL. He died when his 'copter went down in Afghanistan. Damned shame, too. Newly married and a baby on the way. Life ain't fair, is it?"

"No," Noah agreed, his voice somber, "it isn't. My condolences on your loss."

"Thank you. Good luck, both of you."

"Thanks," Hannah said. "I have a feeling we're going to need it."

Chapter 13

Hannah disconnected and looked at Noah, who was still staring at the phone. "That wasn't as hard as I thought it would be." When he still didn't say anything, she asked, "Is something wrong?"

He shook his head, as if to clear it. "Sometimes, I have a tough time remembering that there are good people in the world. Gary and Alison sound like they're part of that circle."

"I've always thought so, but then I loved my husband and I liked Sabine. That pretty much puts the skids on my ability to judge character, wouldn't you say?"

He offered her a wan smile. "Not necessarily. Ted Bundy had everyone around him fooled into thinking he was a nice guy, and look how that turned out."

"I take your point, but unfortunately, it doesn't make me feel any better." She shook her head. "Four-point-six-three million. That's a lot of money. Can three people live off of that comfortably for the duration of their lives?"

"I suppose if they don't buy yachts and the Hope diamond. Why are you asking?"

"Did I mention that Jason was ten years my senior?"

"No. What does that have to do with anything?"

"He never talked much about his life before we got together. I mean, I met his parents, and I knew he was a spoiled rich kid, and his folks didn't much care for me—I guess that was because I'd never been a debutante, or even a prom queen— but I didn't have to worry too much about it, because they lived up near San Francisco, and we saw them only infrequently."

"Where's this going?"

"Jay was new to San Diego when I met him. What if he's a serial embezzler?"

Noah's eyes widened slightly. "You've got a quick mind, you know that?"

"Do I? Lot of good it's done me so far."

"Don't sell yourself short, Hannah. You've got a good brain in your head."

"Jason used to tell me I didn't have a brain the size of a flea's."

"When I meet this prick, I'm going to punch him in the nose."

"I reserve the right to give him a good, swift kick in the balls first."

Noah laughed. "I'd pay to see that."

Hannah grinned in response. "We can sell tickets."

Growing serious again, he asked, "Why didn't you just leave him?"

"When Jay turned four, I started thinking about it. I took my wedding vows seriously, so it wasn't an easy decision, but the day Jason disregarded my concerns and took Jay out on the sailboat, he decided it for me. Unfortunately, it was too late by then."

Noah reached for her hand and gave it a compassionate squeeze.

Hannah accepted his consolation for the space of a heartbeat. "I may have an idea about where Jason worked before he signed on at Simpson Tunney and Hargreaves."

Though his expression said he was disappointed that she'd reclaimed her hand, he followed her lead and got back to business. "Do tell."

"I went through every box and every piece of paper in the house before I moved here. I wanted to get rid of as much as I could…you know, out with the old, in with the new."

He nodded. "You wanted a fresh start."

"I found a box at the back of Jason's closet, up on the highest shelf. I guess he must have forgotten about it."

"Do you still have it?"

"I do. Follow me."

Noah trailed her to one of the two spare bedrooms. She stepped inside and turned on the light and opened the closet, pointing upward. "There."

"It's heavy. How the hell did you get it up there?"

"Sheer force of will."

"I need to check out your arm muscles," he said. "I might need to get a suit of armor if you ever decide to tangle with me."

"Relax, I'm kidding," she said, but her mind got a little stuck on tangling with Noah and all that would entail. "I had the mover hoist it up there for me. No way could I have done it myself. That box weighs a ton."

"What's in it?"

"I have no idea. I opened it once and when I realized it was Jason's stuff, I closed it again, thinking I'd look at it when I got here. Once I did, I realized, I didn't have any burning desire to know." She shrugged. "Now I do. I have a feeling there's important stuff in there and one of these days, Jason's going to be sorry he didn't take this box with him, or destroy it before he left."

"I hope you're right, because frankly, we don't have much to go on right now." He placed the box on the bed.

"Does that mean you didn't have any luck unfuzzying the license plate number?"

"Shari's working on it now, but she warned me, our software is lacking in some regards. I gave her until tomorrow afternoon to see what she can do."

"I'll keep my fingers crossed."

"Where do you want to open the box?"

"How about the kitchen table? We can pull open the hidden leaf to expand it."

"That'll work."

Hannah waited until he'd left the room before she shut off the light and followed him to the kitchen. "Coffee?"

"I'd rather have a beer, but I suppose I should keep a clear head while I'm looking this stuff over."

"Do you get your drunk on after one beer?"

He glanced at her in surprise. "You serious, or are you having fun at my expense?"

"Yes," she said, deadpan.

He gave her a wry smile. "I'm starting to get that you have wicked sense of humor, H.L. Mason."

"While my unscrupulous reptile-of-a-husband used to tell me I wouldn't know humor if it bit me in the ass, my sister and brother would counterbalance that assertion, since they have encouraged my wicked tongue for over thirty years."

"Forewarned is forearmed," he said, his tone amused.

"Now back to the original question, coffee, or beer?"

"I'll take the beer. I think I'm gonna need it."

Hannah chuckled on her way to the fridge. She chose a diet cola for herself and a Fat Tire for him.

An hour later, with stacks all over the kitchen table, Hannah said, "I had no idea Jason kept a journal."

"Anything interesting?" Noah asked without looking up.

"I suppose all of it would be interesting if you didn't know him and wanted to live vicariously through his many lowlife adventures. However, from a wife's point-of-view, I'm appalled by his behavior and his rationalizations for resorting to criminal behavior and infidelity."

He did look up at that. "Break those down for me. Is that a recent journal?"

"It's dated the first year we were married. There are three more in this pouch. This is the oldest."

"Okay, I'm sure you don't want to dwell on the infidelities, so let's focus on the criminal behavior."

"He worked for a company called Squires Essentials when I met him. I thought he left there rather suddenly, but what did I know? He went to work shortly thereafter at Simpson et al., so I suppose I took it for granted that it was a step up on his ladder to success."

"What happened at Squires?"

"He notes with some jubilance that he managed to make off with two hundred and eight-K and according to him, 'the dipshits never noticed it was gone.'" She moved forward several pages. "Here's where he starts noting how much he's taking from Simpson et al. Ten-K on the first go-round." She leaned back in her chair. "Numbers have never been my strong suit, but I can't begin to fathom how someone can steal money from a company and not have anyone notice."

"It happens all the time. Usually, though, embezzlement is a woman's crime because it's nice and clean."

"Really?"

"Really."

She moved ahead, page-by-page, reading off amounts, which she jotted down on a piece of paper. She jumped up once to retrieve her calculator and ran a total. "At the end of year one, he'd taken two hundred and twelve thousand from the firm and sixty-five thousand from one of the clients."

"He's a smooth operator, I'll give him that, but like all criminals, he got too cocky for his own good."

"How do you figure that?"

"He left the box behind, and now we have proof, written in his own hand, of his criminal activity."

"Do you think he killed Henri?"

Noah's expression hardened. "Any man who would do what he did to you is capable of anything."

"That was my first inclination, too, but I was hoping I was wrong."

"One thing I learned on the battlefield, which has also stood me in good stead in law enforcement, is to trust my instincts. You need to do the same, Hannah, even if you doubt those instincts. They're ninety-nine-point-nine percent right."

"What about the one time they're not?"

"I don't know. I've never been wrong when I went with my gut."

After Noah left, Hannah went through her usual nighttime routine—let Bowie out, dry him off, get into her PJs, brush her teeth, go to bed.

It was all pretty humdrum, and after two years of it, except for adding Bowie to the mix, she still hadn't adjusted to it. Alone and lonely. That was her.

She wondered what Noah did when he got home. She was certain he let Fiona out, but did he dry off his dog? Did he use a regular toothbrush or an electric one? Did he wear pajamas to bed, or just his underwear, or better yet, nothing at all? What did he have for breakfast? Did he eat lunch at his desk? Did he have a girlfriend? OMG! Was he married? No, of course not. He didn't mess around with other men's wives, so he wouldn't mess around on his own, either.

She tried not to think about him after she crawled into bed, still alone and lonely, but her mind refused to cooperate with her heart. She may have made a grave error with Jason, thinking the sex would get better after marriage, but with Noah, there were different, scintillating signals. She knew without a doubt that sex would be good between the two of them, but it wasn't the carnal possibilities that drew her to him.

He was a good-looking guy, in a well-honed body, but she'd be willing to bet he didn't spend hours on gym equipment building muscle strength. Thirty minutes, maybe, but not hours. He also didn't strike her as the type of man to down protein drinks like water, or blended vegetable juices, or caffeine enhancements. But his appeal went beyond that.

It was the guy *inside* the man who appealed to her. He'd stopped to check the house because he was concerned someone had taken up residence inside who shouldn't have, and when he'd noticed her on the floor, he hadn't hesitated to come inside to render aid. Yeah, that could have been in part because of his law enforcement training, but she had a feeling he'd acted more out of concern than duty.

He actually listened to her when she talked, too, and he not only kept up with her in a conversation, but he could give her back as good as she gave. God knows, the creative side of her took twists and turns that left a lot of people in the dust when conversing with her, but not Noah.

He was courteous and considerate, and honest. How many men would have understood why she chose to honor her wedding vows, despite what Jason had done to her? How many men actually believed you shouldn't partake of another man's wife and stood by that conviction? God knows, her own husband hadn't, and if statistics were anything to go by, forty percent of marriages involved infidelity. Hannah found that figure not only astounding, but sad. If a person wanted to cheat, get a divorce and save your spouse the heartache of suffering through your infidelity.

She drifted off to sleep wondering if kissing really crossed the line.

Her last thought was, of course, it does.

No more kissing Noah Ward.

Fortunately, she had that one long, hot last kiss to keep her going. But for how long?

Noah tossed and turned for hours. He couldn't quell the memory of Hannah in his arms, or how her lips tasted, or what it felt like to duel tongue-to-tongue with her. His imagination ran rampant, envisioning what it would be like to make love with her all night long.

God, he must be a masochist! He knew damned good and well, by law, she was still married. Jason Clarke was a no-good piece of shit, who'd trapped Hannah in a legal and moral agreement that he, himself, had no problem violating.

At two a.m., Noah threw back the covers and left his bed. He went to the kitchen and pulled a bottle of whiskey down from the cupboard. His intention wasn't to get drunk as the proverbial skunk, but to fog his brain enough to bury all thoughts of Hannah Mason.

What if he'd met her a month ago and they'd let their attraction take it's natural course? Everything about their relationship would be good and effed up right now, because he didn't doubt for a minute that they'd be having sex every damned day.

He downed the liquid in his glass, ignoring the burn as it passed through his throat, and poured another.

No more kissing. In his book, the kisses they'd exchanged were cheating, no matter how he tried to spin it, but he'd had to give in that one last time. No more sitting in his lap, either.

No more thinking about sex. Okay, he could think about it, but he wouldn't discuss it with her.

Jesus, did he have no willpower at all where she was concerned?

The thought scared him so badly, he poured a third drink. His mind grew hazy, but still thoughts of her lingered, doing weird things to his mind and a certain part of his body.

Furious because he'd never been a man who wasn't in control of either his mind or his dick, he slammed the glass down on the countertop and stormed to the bathroom, where he turned on the shower.

A moment later, he'd stripped out of his boxers and T-shirt and stepped under the icy cold spray.

He gritted his teeth against the chill and slapped his hands against the tile wall. It took everything he had not to grab his junk and finish what thoughts of Hannah Mason had started.

Chapter 14

After two days of not hearing a word from Noah, Hannah decided to pay him an official visit, in person, at Pike County Sheriff's Office. An audience of deputies, and the woman he'd called Marty, would help keep the discussion on a professional level. In other words, no miscellaneous thoughts about kissing or what it felt like to have his hands on her.

Sonny had been back twice to clear her driveway. She'd never driven on snowy roads before, but the snowplow had gone by on Creight the day before, so she assumed that meant the road was clear enough to drive. No guts, no glory.

She'd also never left Bowie in the house alone before. Each time she'd gone out, she'd allowed him to ride in the back seat, in his crate, but he was getting so darned big, that didn't seem to work well anymore. For sure, she wasn't letting him ride in the bed of the truck.

She studied her pet as he slept in front of the fireplace, even though there was no fire burning. Fortunately, he wasn't a dog who liked to chew on everything in sight. He was also fairly well behaved, except when they went out into the snow. There, he liked to cavort, no-holds-barred. He loped as if he were a gazelle and rolled like a panda and burrowed like a mole. She'd captured some of his antics on video with the camera on her phone and sent it to Emily and Seth, since they'd never seen her dog and still couldn't imagine that she actually owned one.

She pondered what to do with him, then decided it was time for him to learn how to travel in the truck without his crate. She went to the hall closet and rummaged through her linens looking for a thermal blanket she could live without. The selection was made easily, thanks to the loosened binding on the top edge on one of them.

She took the blanket out to her truck and folded it so that it would fit across the bench seat. Back inside, she filled a baggie with dog biscuits, then woke Bowie. "Out you go for a quick run, and do your business while you're out there."

He followed her to the patio door, eager to get outside. Five minutes later, she called him back in. For the first time, he resisted minding her, more intent on playing in the snow. "Bowie, come!" She said it three more times before he finally listened.

She dried him off, giving him a lecture about minding her, then told him to sit. At least he did that promptly.

"We're going to *go* in the truck."

His tail began to wag against the wood floor.

"I know you like to *go*, but if you don't mind me, you're going to be grounded."

Woof-woof.

"Yes, and I mean it. You better be a good dog, or else."

He smiled up at her.

"So, do we have an understanding?"

Woof.

"Good. Let's go."

He rushed off toward the door leading out to the garage, doing a doggie four-step while he waited for her to put on her coat, hat, and gloves.

Hannah grabbed her purse, turned out the light, and stepped into the garage. Once at the truck, she had to help Bowie up into the backseat. "Stay on the blanket," she instructed him. "Understand?"

Woof.

She stared at him for several seconds.

Bowie stared back, smiling.

"I'm trusting you." She shook a finger at him. "You'd better not make me sorry I did."

His tail began to move at warp speed. He yipped, then gave her face a swipe with his tongue.

"Thanks a lot," she said, using her glove to wipe away the puppy slobber. "I love you, too." She closed the door, second-guessing her decision to take Bowie with her. He sat immediately and looked out the window, ready for his big adventure.

Resigned to sticking with her decision, she climbed into the cab, raised the overhead door, and started the truck. It wasn't far into town. If need be, she could pull over or even turn around and come back home if he acted up, but he had to learn sometime, right?

She drove slowly, grateful the road had been plowed. Being a newcomer to snowy roadways, she'd read up on how to handle a skid, how to brake, and how to keep out of a ditch, but reading wasn't the same as experiencing. Not that she wanted a real-life experience, but she hoped she could remember what to do if she found herself in a pickle.

Fortunately, there wasn't a lot of traffic on the road. Two trucks behind her gave her a honk and a friendly wave when they passed her, but other than that, she didn't encounter anyone until she hit the city limits. Having preprogrammed the sheriff's office into her GPS, she took the opportunity to activate the navigation system,

It wasn't until she was parked in front of PCSO that she realized she hadn't thought the visit through, as it pertained to Bowie. Did she dare leave him alone in the vehicle? Would he get too cold? Would he take the opportunity to start a chewing campaign?

She removed one of the dog biscuits from the baggie. "I need to go inside, Bowie. You have to stay in the truck. Will you be a good dog while I'm gone?"

His eyes on the Milk-Bone treat, he came up on all fours and wagged his doggie butt for all it was worth.

Hannah rolled her eyes. How far she had digressed, to have a conversation with a dog about her plans. She handed over the biscuit and he settled right back down on the blanket.

Though it was frigid outside, she cracked the driver's side window half an inch before she climbed out. She didn't want anyone stealing Bowie, so she locked the door with the key fob.

"Be good," she said again, looking at him through the back window. He chewed contently on the doggie treat, sparing her only a quick glance.

With a sigh that was part resignation, part what-have-I-done-now, she climbed the steps and entered the sheriff's office.

"'Morning," said the woman behind the front counter.

"Good morning. Is Sheriff Ward in?"

"Nope. He'll be back tomorrow."

"Is he off today?" Hannah asked, thinking she could drive to his house instead.

"No, ma'am. He's out of town."

Well, that explained why she hadn't seen him for two days.

"Is there something I can do for you?" the woman asked.

"Are you Marty?"

She nodded, but her courteous countenance became a little stilted. "Do I know you?"

"No. I'm sorry. I'm Hannah Mason. Sheriff Ward mentioned your name when he called you from my place the other day."

If a light bulb had gone off over Marty's head, the transformation from curious to friendly couldn't have been any more obvious. "So, you're H.L. Mason."

Hannah didn't quite know what to make of that. "Yes."

The woman extended her hand across the counter. "Martha Nilsson. Everyone calls me Marty, except the sheriff when he's irritated. Then he calls me Martha, like that will make me behave better." She finished on a laugh. "Good luck with that."

"Nice to meet you, Marty."

"Got time for a coffee and some conversation?"

Hannah remembered her passenger and said with genuine regret, "Maybe another time. I have my dog in the truck, and he's never been left alone before."

"Bring him in! We get dogs in here all the time."

"You do?"

"Sure. Just know that you're responsible if he triple-*P*s."

"What's that?" Hannah asked, stymied.

"Pees, poops, or pukes," Marty said, grinning.

"He's housebroken, and I've never seen him puke, but I promise to clean up after him if he does any of those."

"Noah said your dog is better behaved than Fiona, so I'm not worried about it."

"He did?"

"Yep. Go get your pooch. I'll put on a fresh pot of coffee."

By the time Hannah returned with Bowie, who was on a leash for the first time, two others had joined Marty behind the counter. Another stood over near the radio, talking into a microphone tethered to it. "Yeah, she's here now," he said, and quickly disconnected.

"Bowie, sit," she said to the dog.

Little showoff that he was, Bowie minded.

"This is part of our crew," Marty said. "Derek Parker and Kenny Tigard are deputies and Shari Deitermann is our crime-scene gal."

They all stepped forward to shake her hand and to a person said, "Nice to meet you, Hannah."

A little surprised that they were treating her like she was some sort of celebrity, Hannah said, "It's good to meet all of you, too."

"Sorry I couldn't do better on that license plate," Shari said. "Noah's dad is former FBI, so we're hoping he can capitalize on that."

That answered one of Hannah's questions. Noah obviously had discussed her case with his staff. "Thanks for your effort, Shari. I hope they can clean it up."

"Me, too. We're lucky the sheriff has friends in high places." She grinned, revealing a dimple in each cheek.

Before Hannah could say anything more, the front door opened. Two more deputies walked in.

"Toad Hoffman, ma'am," said the first man. His voice was so deep he practically rumbled. He offered her his hand.

"Flip Valdez," said the second, also with his hand extended.

"We're only missing Barbie Fleming," Marty said, casting a wry glance at Flip. "She's on graveyard shift right now." She herded everyone into the conference room, some with coffee in their cups, and two with hot chocolate.

Hannah pulled out another dog biscuit for Bowie. She'd let go of his leash and he was making the rounds sniffing everyone and letting them pet him.

"He really *is* better-behaved than Fiona," Shari said. "I thought the sheriff was kidding."

Marty plopped down in the chair next to Hannah. "You got some new information on your case for Noah?"

Hannah pulled off her gloves and hat and slipped out of her coat. "No, I was hoping he'd have some news for me."

"These past couple of years must have been horrible for you," Shari said.

"They haven't been any picnic, that's for sure."

"I don't know what kind of asswipe does something like this," Kenny said.

"You just answered yourself," Derek said with a frown. "Asswipe covers it."

Hannah couldn't disagree.

"The sheriff's got all of us working on this," Toady said.

Flip nodded. "We're taking turns going out on patrol, but we each got an assignment."

"Like what?" Hannah asked. Her only cop experience had been with Twombly, and he was pretty much an asswipe himself.

Shari said, "I requested the accident report and any accompanying photos."

Hannah let out a startled a breath.

"Don't worry. I went straight to the Harbor Patrol supervisor and spoke to him in confidence. I specifically asked him not to bring Twombly in on it." She sucked in her cheeks and glanced at her co-workers. "Actually, I guess it's okay for me to tell you that Detective Twombly is no longer with SDPD."

"He isn't? But...he seemed too young to retire."

"He didn't. From what I gather, he walked in one day and quit. No one's seen or heard from him since."

The first thought that went through Hannah's head was, *I*

hope he's not dead, too. Then the term "thick as thieves" popped into her head, and her mind went a different route. Once she'd disappeared, maybe he'd sensed something was up. Had he subsequently contacted Jason and Sabine to warn them he didn't have an eye on her any longer?

Good grief! Now she sounded like some master plotter for a BBC mystery series!

"My assignment is to locate Twombly," Kenny said.

"And I'm looking for your husband's parents," Toad said.

"They're missing, too?"

"Not missing as in dead, missing," he said for clarification. "According to a neighbor, they were planning a short trip to Connecticut, so we're trying to confirm that."

"I think Merle, Jason's dad, has a brother there."

Toad nodded. "That's what we understand."

Hannah had no idea how you went about checking someone's whereabouts without them knowing that you were checking, but she decided to trust PCSO's methodology.

Flip said, "I'm going through Colorado law enforcement databases to look at anyone with the first name of Jason."

"I'm doing the same thing, only for Sabine," Derek said.

"And I," Marty said, "am working with the state's records division to see if there's been a marriage license issued, or legal name changes."

"Wow," Hannah said. "Is Noah, that is, the sheriff, out of town because of this case?"

"Sort of. We had prisoner in the jail who was extradited to Wyoming. Noah and his dad drove him up to Cheyenne, then they were going to hit the FBI office in Denver on the way back."

Hannah sank back in her chair, stunned. She'd asked Noah for help, but she honestly hadn't expected him to put his entire department to work on it. "This is...amazing. Thank you all for what you're doing."

Toad's chair squeaked when he leaned back and crossed his arms over his massive chest. "We don't like dirty cops and we can't stomach people who do to others what your husband did to you. That's why we signed up to be police officers."

Hannah didn't think she had any tears left to cry, but several fell nonetheless. Aside from her family, she simply wasn't used to others helping…or caring.

Bowie came running back to her. He jumped up and put his paws on her knees, whimpering.

Noah stood in the doorway, surveying the scene in silence.

Kenny, who like everyone else in the room, had his eyes on Hannah, must have sensed an undercurrent in the air. He jerked his head toward the door and said, "Hey, boss."

In unison, the rest of his staff also greeted him.

"Glad to see there's no crime in Pike County today," Noah said, his tone wry.

"We're just taking a quick coffee break," Flip said, rising.

"So I see." He scanned the group, his gaze coming to rest last on Hannah. She swiped at her eyes and stood.

Bowie took that as a sign it was okay to welcome his new friend, the sheriff. He took the shortest route to Noah, jetting beneath the conference table to reach the doorway.

Noah squatted down to give him a few pats and scratches between his ears.

Bowie responded by squirming in ecstasy.

Noah straightened. "Miss Mason, if you wouldn't mind, I need a moment with my deputies."

"I should take off anyway." Her gaze bounced from one person to the next. "It's been really nice meeting all of you. Thank you for what you're doing."

When she reached the doorway, Noah said, "Please, wait in the lobby. I need to speak to you, too."

Hannah looked up into his dark eyes, fearful she'd find anger. Instead, she read no emotion whatsoever. Neither his inscrutable expression nor his tone gave away his thoughts. She nodded, then bent to grab Bowie's leash and stepped through to the outer office. At the last moment, she turned to at least say hello to him, but he closed the door in her face.

For a stunned moment, she considered barging back into

the conference room. Bowie whined, as if he might be in agreement. She reached for the doorknob, but a voice behind her put the skids to her plan.

"I wouldn't do that, if I were you."

She whirled around to see who had spoken.

An older man with silver hair and Noah's eyes stood at the counter. "He's going to give them a lecture on procedure."

"How do you know that?"

"Lucky guess?" The man grinned and came toward her, his hand extended. "Hannah Mason, I presume?"

She accepted his handshake. "Yes. How did you know?"

"Beautiful woman, friendly golden retriever puppy."

That's how Noah had described her? Beautiful? "I take it you're Noah's dad. He takes after you."

"Pete Ward." He cast a wry glance at the closed door and said, "He takes after me more than he should, probably." With that curious comment, he squatted, just as his son had done, to show Bowie some attention. "Fine looking pup."

"Thank you. I've never had a dog before, but I'm really loving this one."

"Noah says you're doing a fine job training him."

"I did a lot of reading about how to do it, and I watched a couple of videos."

He straightened. "What say we go down to the diner and grab a cup of joe while we're waiting?"

Hannah bit her lip in indecision. "He told me to wait out here."

"I'll leave him a note."

"What about Bowie? He's not a service dog."

"You can leave him outside. No one will take him."

"Are you sure?"

"This isn't Southern California, Hannah. He'll be perfectly safe. Darius, who owns the diner, has a place set up for dogs. C'mon. You'll see." He reached over the counter and grabbed a pad and pen and scribbled out a note.

Hannah had her doubts about taking Bowie into a diner, but for some inexplicable reason, she trusted Pete Ward. Whether that was because he was retired FBI or because he was Noah's father, she had no clue.

Chapter 15

"Wow," Hannah said when they reached the diner.

"Thought you might like it," Pete said.

The owner had provided a doggie area alongside the eating establishment. Two other dogs were already inside, playing with tennis balls. "How is there green grass, when everything else is covered with snow?"

"Heated artificial turf," Pete explained.

"Wow." For a moment, she watched the two full-grown dogs, one a black Lab, the other a German shepherd. "Bowie's never played with other dogs before."

"About time he did, then, wouldn't you say?"

Hannah wasn't certain. Bowie was friendly, but she'd been around dogs that weren't.

"If you worried about the other dogs, don't be. I recognize them and they'll take to Bowie like he's always been here."

She walked her pup over to the gate and opened it. She bent to unleash him and much to her astonishment, didn't have to encourage him to go inside the enclosure. Within seconds, he forgot all about her. "Will he get too cold?"

"Nah. We won't be here long enough for him to even feel the cold, the way he's playing."

She closed the gate and watched for another couple of moments.

"We'll get a table by the window, so you can keep an eye on him."

That was a plan she could live with. "Okay."

He gave her a quick nod and grasped her elbow in a gentlemanly way to escort her inside the diner. The place was nearly deserted.

"Too late for breakfast, too early for lunch," Pete said, as if he could read her mind.

"Not for me," Hannah said. "I'm starved."

Noah's dad grinned, as if he approved of her response. "Bring us a menu, will you, Darry?"

"Sure thing, hon. Brought me a new one, did ya?"

"Pretty new. She's been here for a couple of months, but settling in, she hasn't gotten around much."

Hannah appreciated the way Noah's father had explained away her lack of involvement in the community.

"This is Darius Smith, owner and chef of Darry's Diner," Pete said. "Darry, this is Hannah Mason. Her pup outside is Bowie."

Hannah stood and offered the older woman her hand. "It's nice to meet you."

Darius sized Hannah up with one swift up-and-down glance. "Nice to meet you, too, young lady. Where do you hail from?"

Hannah thought about lying, but did it really matter? "San Diego."

"No snow out that way," the diner owner noted.

"Not a single flake," Hannah agreed as she retook her seat. "I have to say, I'm really impressed with the doggie playground."

Darius grinned. "Had to do something for my dog-owning customers who thought they could just bring their pooches inside and to hell with the health department."

"I'm sure this keeps everyone happy."

"It sure does. If you're still hungry for breakfast, you might want to try the hot ham-and-cheese roll. Hunh. Come to think of it, it's good for lunch, too."

"Sounds perfect. Thank you." Hannah slipped out of her coat and folded it over the back of her chair. She cast a glance outside. Bowie was still a happy camper.

"Coffee?"

They both nodded and Hannah said, "I take mine black."

Darius scooted off toward the counter.

Hannah's gaze wandered around the diner. "This is a cute little place."

"Best hot food in town. Sig's has sandwiches, but on a cold day, there's nothing like a hot meal."

Darius returned with two coffees. "You want a ham-and-cheese, too, Pete?"

"Sure, why not? It's been a long time since we had breakfast at six."

Hannah considered him curiously. "The people over at the sheriff's office didn't expect Noah back until tomorrow."

Pete grinned wryly. "So I gathered, or they wouldn't have all been sitting around in the conference room having tea and crumpets with you."

"I didn't mean to get anyone in trouble."

"Don't worry, you didn't. The deputies all know their assignments, but they should've known better than to all come in off the streets at once."

"I went in to see Noah."

"About your problem."

"Problem. That's a good descriptive of it, even though it really doesn't describe what's going on at all."

"Noah has some news for you."

Hannah froze with her coffee mug halfway to her mouth. She placed it back on the table, gripping it like a lifeline. "Did he find Jason?"

"No."

Her heart and her hopes both sank.

"Don't be disheartened." He rubbed his moustache. "I'd tell you, except this is Noah's gig, not mine. I'm just along for the ride."

Before she could question him further, Darius delivered their order and the front door of the diner opened, admitting Noah.

Hannah's gaze latched onto his. She tracked him all the way to the table, where he turned to Darius and said, "Coffee and whatever they're having, please."

"You got it, Sheriff."

He pulled out the chair next to his father and sat down. "Hello, Hannah."

"Hi, Noah." Did she apologize for the apparent disruption of his office? Better, in this case, to err on the side of contrition. "I'm sorry I caused a stir."

"You didn't cause it, although you were the cause of it."

That's all he had, riddles?

"Don't worry about it. I've spoken to them and I can't say as I blame them for wanting to get to meet you in person."

"Why would they? I mean, based on the assignments you passed out, I'm just another citizen who needs help."

Pete made a noise that sounded like stifled laughter, which had the effect of unsettling her.

"I'd rather not go into the particulars," Noah said, giving his father a stern look.

"Your dad says you have news."

Darius came back to the table with another coffee and a steaming ham-and-cheese roll.

"Thanks, Darry."

"No problem, Noah." She eyed Hannah one last time, smiled, and went back into the kitchen.

"Well?"

"They found Twombly."

That was the last thing Hannah expected from him. "Did he own up to being part of whatever it is that Jason and Sabine are up to?"

"No."

"Can't they put the screws to him, or something?"

"No. Hannah—"

"Why not? If anyone deserves it, he does, especially after the hell he put me through."

"Hannah—"

"I'm serious!"

"I know you are, but he's dead, Hannah."

Shocked washed over. "What?"

"He's dead. They found his car in a ravine up the Big Thompson Canyon. Forensics said the brake line had been tampered with."

"So…not an accident. Someone deliberately killed him?"

"It would appear so."

She stared down at the cheesy roll on her plate. Minutes ago, it had looked appetizing. Now it simply looked congealed. Her mind churned furiously, processing his words, trying to sort out what it all meant. "Big Thompson Canyon?"

He nodded. "Are you familiar with Loveland and Estes Park?"

"Sort of. I remember where they are on the map."

"Big Thompson runs between the two."

She gaped at him with wide eyes. "He was found dead in Colorado?"

Noah nodded.

"He came here because Jason and Sabine are here."

"That's what we think."

"Is it possible they live Estes Park?"

"We're looking into it."

She sank back in her chair. "Do you think they killed him?"

"When we find them, we'll ask."

"This is unbelievable. I didn't like him, but I certainly never wanted to see him dead."

To Noah's credit, he didn't remind her that she'd made at least one comment to the contrary. "Too bad whoever killed him didn't feel the same way," he said instead. "We might have gotten some answers out of him."

"Tell her about the license plate," Pete said.

"The FBI are your people," Noah said to his father. "You tell it."

"You sure I won't be stepping on your toes?" his father asked in a teasing tone.

"You're a little different than the people who work for me, Dad."

Pete grinned with a shrug. "Just checking."

Hannah couldn't say she wasn't enjoying their banter, but she had a burning need to know more about the license plate. "Was someone able to clean up the image to read it?"

Pete turned to her. "They could make out all but two characters. They're either a B, a three, an eight, or an S. Right about now, I'm sure someone at PCSO is checking all possibilities in the Colorado DMV records."

"Isn't there some kind of software that can do that?" she asked Noah.

"There probably is, but PCSO doesn't own it," Noah said. "We pick and choose our requests to the Feds, and since this is something we can do ourselves, we'll reserve our next assistance request for if and when we find your husband, or for something we can't accomplish, manually or otherwise."

"I have faith that it's going to be *when* we find him," she said, hating the *husband* reference, "but in the meantime, what can I do? I feel like a lump, not being involved."

"Right now, eat your breakfast."

She glanced down at the roll, then back at him.

"I'm serious. This is going to be grueling on you. You need to keep up your strength."

"If you two will excuse me, I need to use the john," Pete said.

As soon as he was out of earshot, Noah said, "You're going to have to trust me on this, Hannah."

"I do," she said, and meant it, "but I still want to help. There must be something I can do."

He frowned. "Let me think about it. If I can come up with something that won't throw you into the thick of it, I'll let you know."

She leaned forward and placed her elbows on the table. "I've been in the thick of it for the past two years, Noah, and lived to talk about it. I doubt there's anything more coming that I can't handle."

"If I hadn't been in the service for ten years and witnessed other similar proclamations shot to hell, I'd agree with you, but unfortunately, that's not the way of the world."

"How far is Estes Park from here?"

His frown morphed into a scowl. "Forget it. You're not taking off by yourself to go off searching every single mountain town in Colorado for Jason."

"You can't tell me what to do."

He leaned across the table, not quite nose-to-nose with her.

"One thing I can damned well do is put you in protective custody, and if I have to do that, I'll be pissed beyond belief because my budget really can't tolerate hiring an extra person right now just to babysit you."

"Babysit?" she practically hissed.

"That's what it would amount to. Look, just let me do my job, all right? Once we get into this a little further, I promise I'll let you help if it's not something that's going to get you killed, too." He sat back and delivered his final bombshell. "It wouldn't be so great if I found your little boy, but he no longer had a mom to come home to, now would it?"

That effectively silenced Hannah, at least verbally.

Determination-wise, her brain and her heart were just getting started on their shouting match.

While she was in town, Hannah made a stop at Mountain Meadow Mercantile to buy all the items on her mental shopping list. There, she met Evangeline Hardy, proprietress.

"Haven't seen you in before," the owner said. "Just visiting?"

"No, I moved here in the fall," Hannah said, browsing through the ladies' coats. "I bought the old Kirby place."

"Lord'a mercy! Glad someone finally did. That was a house of sadness for too long."

"So I understand." Hannah slipped out of her coat and tried on the insulated, flannel-lined barn coat. "Ooh, this feels toasty warm."

"It will be, especially compared to the one you're wearing now. If you spend any extended periods of time outdoors, you'll love it."

"I take Bowie out for walks."

"Who's Bowie?"

"My golden retriever puppy."

"Where is he now?" Evangeline asked, looked around, as if Bowie might be hiding in the clothing racks.

"I left him in the truck." She cast a worried glance toward the door. "I've never left him in the truck alone before."

"You could'a brought him in. I don't serve food here, so

the health department can't rag on me about it."

"I left him with two doggie treats, plus I think he might've gotten tuckered out playing with the other dogs at the diner."

Evangeline grinned. "Darius really struck gold with that doggie play area."

Hannah removed the coat. "I'll take it. I need to get a few other things, too."

"Sure. Can I help you find what you're looking for?"

Hannah mentally ticked off her list. "Snow saucer, a sled, a knit cap, or maybe two, and two pairs of gloves, one of them leather. Oh, yeah, and some socks, and maybe snow boots. Seems like I might need two pair."

Evangeline nodded in approval. "Sounds like you've been in snow country before."

"Actually, I haven't, but I'm a quick study."

The owner laughed. "Don't take but a mite of cold to convince you to dress warmer and smarter, does it?"

"Not a mite," Hannah agreed.

The snow picked up again as Hannah drove home. She was starting to wonder if she'd chosen the right place to begin her new life.

Then she remembered every cloud had a silver lining. In this case, the silver lining stood a couple of inches over six feet and had dark, sexy eyes, and a well-built body that had felt pretty darned good every time she encountered it.

The silver lining had also taken a prominent place in her dreams the past couple of nights. She felt a mixture of both shame and regret because she'd never once had a sex dream about her husband.

She pulled into the driveway and stopped to check her mailbox. It was empty save for one envelope that had no return address, no stamp, and no postmark.

Curious, but not concerned, she raised the garage door and eased the truck inside.

Recognizing that they were home, Bowie let out a woof of excitement.

Hannah laughed. "I'm glad to be home, too." She lowered

the door before she helped Bowie out of the truck and let him into the house. After that, it took three trips to bring all her parcels inside.

She no sooner had the patio door open to let Bowie out than the doorbell sounded. Still in her coat, she made her way to the front window to see who was there. Noah.

Her heart did a little somersault.

"Stop it!" she muttered. "Still a married woman, remember?"

She opened the front door, unbuttoning her coat as she did.

Noah's gaze raked her. "Coming or going?"

"Just got home. I had some shopping to do after I left the diner." She stood back. "Come in."

He stepped over the threshold and shut the door behind him. "I was wondering if you'd like to join me for dinner with the folks tonight."

Chapter 16

Whoa! Dinner with Noah's parents? Her heart urged her to say yes, but her brain warned her to decline politely. Her heart won the argument. "That sounds nice."

Nice? Who was she kidding? An evening with Noah, even if his parents were there, sounded like heaven.

"Dad didn't know how to get hold of you," Noah said, "so he asked me to extend the invitation."

Hannah hadn't met Jason's parents until the wedding, and it hadn't gone well. They'd eyed her like she was some gold-digger or maybe even a street floozy. Did Noah's parents have some ulterior motive for inviting her over, or were the Wards simply being neighborly? "I…." She shoved her hands into her pockets and encountered the envelope. She pulled it out, momentarily distracted from his invitation. "I got mail today, but it has no postmark or stamp."

Noah glanced down at it and frowned.

Hannah opened the flap and pulled out a single piece of paper. She made a strangled sound in her throat as she read it.

"What is it?"

She handed the paper to him.

Noah read the message aloud. "'I'm here.'" He met her gaze. "Who do you think left it?"

"Several hours ago, I would've said Twombly, but you've

since told me he's dead." She blew out a wobbly breath. "Do you think he found me and told Jason before he died?"

"Anything's possible."

A shiver wracked her body. Was it possible Jason knew where she was, or had someone made a mistake and put the note in the wrong mailbox?

"Get me a baggie. There might be prints on it."

Hannah hurried to the kitchen and retrieved a Ziplock bag from the drawer. She returned to find Noah scowling at the short missive.

"Open it, please."

She did as he asked.

"Good thing we both still had our gloves on."

Startled, Hannah looked down at her hands, surprised that she was, indeed, still wearing her gloves.

He dropped the envelope in, as well, and sealed the bag before he shoved it in his pocket. "If you've already got other plans for tonight...."

Way to take her mind off the note. "No, it's not that." Think fast! Aside from wondering about his parents' motivation, she'd had another thought...oh, yeah, her dog. "I'm wondering how Bowie will handle being alone for the evening."

Noah smirked. "Forgot to say. The invite includes your dog."

"Surely not!"

"Surely, yes. Dad was impressed with how mannerly Bowie is." He made a face. "He suggested that I should let you have a go at Fiona."

"I can't believe she's as bad as everyone says. Goldens are supposed to be gentle and well-mannered."

"Who's everyone?"

"You want me to list them?"

"Damned straight. I want to know who's talking about my dog behind my back."

Hannah took a mental step back before she realized he was amused. The twinkle in his eyes gave him away. "I'm sure they've all said to your face what they said to me."

"Name them and I'll let you know."

With his amusement even more evident in his tone, she played a long. "Sonny, the people at your office, your dad, Darius."

He laughed. "You're right. The truth of it is, the list is a lot longer than that."

She pursed her lips. "I should amend my comment to say that no one claims Fiona's not gentle, just that she doesn't mind."

He tilted his head at her. "You wouldn't be interested in working with her, would you?"

Hannah hedged her response. "I'm hardly qualified as a dog trainer."

"And yet, there's Bowie, whose behavior clearly says otherwise."

She couldn't argue with his logic. "I'd have to meet her first. She might not like me."

"Let's go."

"What, right now? I should at least change my clothes, if we're having dinner with your folks."

"Why? Dinner at the Ward house is casual. You don't want to make my mom feel bad because she didn't dress up, do you?"

"No, of course not, but I'd still like to change."

His gaze roamed her from head to foot and back up again. "I don't see anything wrong with what you're wearing."

"Humor me." She braced herself for the big explosion like she usually got when she dared challenge Jason.

Noah shrugged with a smile. "Not a problem. I have to change out of my uniform, anyway, and I also need to feed Fiona. What if I come back in thirty minutes to pick you up? Will that give you enough time?"

"You're not upset with me?"

"No. Why would I be?"

"I defied you."

He stared at her for a moment with another one of his enigmatic expressions. "I'd hardly call wanting to change into something else defiance." And then, as if he wanted to lighten the conversation, he added, "Unless, of course, you show up at the door wearing your pajamas."

Relief washed over her in a giant wave. She cracked a smile. "Don't worry, I won't, and I promise not to change into a ballgown and four-inch heels, either."

He jammed his hands into the pockets of his jacket and studied her with a new gleam in his eye. "You wear four-inch heels?"

"No, but apparently you might like it if I did." Good grief! Who knew she could be the queen of suggestive repartee?

He laughed again. "The thought does conjure up some possibilities."

How had she gone from worrying about a strange note to a vision of herself dressed only in black lingerie, thigh-high black stockings, and four-inch stilettos flashing through her mind? Flustered by where the conversation seemed to be headed, she went to the door and opened it. "We both have to change and I need to get Bowie back inside. He's probably wondering why I'm not at the patio door." As if on cue, her dog let loose with a series of impatient woofs.

Noah's eyes skimmed her one last time, and she wondered what *he* was thinking. Maybe it was better not to know, especially since she sure as hell knew what *she* was thinking.

Finally, he pulled his hands out of his pockets. In two long strides, he was out the door. "Thirty minutes," he called over his shoulder.

Hannah locked the door and collapsed against it.

She blew out a huge breath. It was not one of relief, but of anxiety. Never, ever, had she played sexual word games with a man. Unsure of her own feelings about it, she was pretty certain Noah had enjoyed it.

She pushed away from the door and headed for the kitchen so she could let Bowie in.

If she wasn't careful, she'd be an adulteress before she knew it.

Noah arrived early. Two minutes, to be exact. He didn't honk, or sit waiting for her to come out, like Jason had been prone to do. Instead, he walked up to the front door, rang the bell, and stepped inside when she opened the door.

Bowie circled his ankles, begging for attention.

She opened the closet and reached inside for her coat. "Better give him some love."

"He can wait," Noah said. He took her long wool coat in his big hands and held it open.

Hannah pulled on her scarf and presented her back to him. "Thank you."

"My pleasure."

While she buttoned up and tugged on her gloves, he squatted down to give Bowie that attention he was so anxious for.

"Ready," Hannah said, enjoying the simple pleasure of watching Noah pet her dog. He had such strong hands. Long fingers. Capable fingers. Sensuous fingers. She couldn't help but imagine them skimming across her skin, teasing the tips of her breasts, visiting her secret places.

A shiver of desire coursed through her.

"Hannah?"

"Yes?"

"You look quite lovely in your non-ballgown."

She grinned. "Thank you." Her non-ballgown consisted of black slacks, a vibrant teal-colored sweater, and her brand new black leather snow boots. She'd also taken her hair down out of its usual topsy-turvy knot and let it hang loose.

He pushed up and said, "Can I help get your hair out of the coat?"

"Sure."

She turned again so her back faced him.

His fingers brushed against her neck, sending yet another shiver through her. He managed to release her hair from the confines of the wool coat, then fingered it for several moments. "You have beautiful hair. It's so soft and silky."

She turned slowly to face him. "You could do a commercial for my shampoo and conditioner," she teased.

"Only if it could be filmed in the shower, while I'm washing it for you. Although, on second thought, no cameras allowed. Just you and me and that's it."

For a stunned moment, she was speechless. "You're not playing fair."

"All is fair in love and war. We may have put the skids to

physical contact, but we didn't make any rules about what comes out of our mouths, as you proved earlier."

True enough. "Still." Her gaze dropped from his eyes to his mouth. If only he'd slobbered or something, but no, he had to be the world's best kisser. Life wasn't fair! "We should go."

"We should."

She knew what he was thinking. One little kiss wouldn't hurt. The problem was, one little kiss would lead to more and longer kisses, and that would lead to a place they had both committed to avoid. "Noah, I can't be the only one who has to resist temptation. We have to do it together."

He let out a long sigh. "I didn't know it would be this difficult."

"Me, either, but this is the way it has to be."

"I know." He brought his hand up and caressed the side of her face. "You really are beautiful."

She captured his hand with hers. "Only in your eyes."

"Why do you do that?"

"Do what?"

"Disparage yourself."

"I don't—"

"You do. What did that prick of a husband do to you that you have to counter every compliment?"

"Do you mind if we don't discuss this right now? Can't we just enjoy our evening?"

His jaw worked furiously, though he obviously wasn't angry. "Someday, I hope you'll trust me enough to be completely honest with me about all of this."

"I trust you enough now," she admitted, "but talking about Jason and how he treated me will put a pall on the evening. For a change, I'd simply like to enjoy myself and the company I'm keeping."

"Fair enough." He dropped his hand and said to Bowie, "Come."

Bowie, who'd apparently grown bored of their human interaction, had curled up in a ball and observed them from beneath dancing eyebrows. He leaped to his paws, his tail wagging.

Noah scooped him up. "You get to hitch a ride to the SUV,

buddy. Fiona's waiting for you."

"Oh, good, you brought her."

"I wasn't going to, but decided, why not? You wait here and I'll come back and walk you out. I'm surprised Sonny didn't get your front walk. It's icy."

"That's my fault. I told him I planned to buy a snow shovel, but I didn't get it until today."

"Nonetheless, I did hire him to clear *every*thing."

Hannah didn't want to cause trouble for the boy, but she also didn't want to argue with Noah. "Don't scold him for it, okay? It's my fault the walk's icy."

He looked as if he had a ready rebuttal, but instead, he said, "You have a soft heart, Hannah. I like that about you." He turned and left the house with Bowie in his arms.

The unexpected remark warmed her. She did have a soft heart. It was one of the things about her that always drove Jason crazy. Many an argument had ensued between them over things like leaving Jay to lie crying in his crib when all he wanted was to be held by his mama. She'd never understood that, especially since Jason rarely ever held Jay himself.

He was back in a minute. "Fiona and Bowie hit it off immediately."

"So, no growl-fest on the way to your parents' house?"

He grinned. "No, and they'd better keep it that way." He helped her into the passenger side of his Toyota 4Runner.

"I never would have figured you for an SUV guy."

"The truck is department-owned. Even though I'm on-call twenty-four/seven, I try to drive my personal vehicle when I'm on my own time. This one has four-wheel drive, so it's good in the snow."

"I relied on the salesman at the dealership to point me toward a reliable truck for snow driving," she said, admiring the interior of the 4Runner SUV. "He said either a Tacoma or a Tundra would do. I thought the Tundra was a little big for me and I wasn't sure it would fit in my garage."

"The Tacoma has four-wheel drive, but if you're ever worried about how the light back-end will handle, you can stop in at Locke Lumber and have Herb throw some sandbags into the bed. The extra weight will help keep the vehicle situated on the road."

"Thanks for the tip. I think I'll do that tomorrow. I had a couple of harrowing experiences on the way home today."

He shot her a quick glance, then put his eyes back on the road. "Better to be safe than sorry."

She glanced back at the two dogs. Both had settled in for the drive and curled up on the rear seat. She looked back at Noah. "Is it written in blood that your vehicles have to be red?"

He was silent for a moment, then chuckled. "Very punny."

"Thank you."

"Actually, being in snow country, I decided red was a good color, in case I ever went over an embankment. Whoever came looking for me would be able to spot the vehicle right off the bat."

"I never thought of that. I guess I'm glad I chose the Inferno color, in that case."

"Something tells me there's a story behind that choice."

She shrugged. "Only that it spoke to me because my life's felt like an inferno for the past two years. It seemed appropriate."

He nodded.

"Will your siblings be there, as well?"

"They'll all be here for Christmas, but not tonight."

"Who's the oldest?"

"Brant, then me, then Simon. Jules is the baby of the family."

"You and Simon are following in your dad's footsteps."

"I guess you could say that." He glanced at her. "I take it you've been on the department website."

"I have. I thought it was nice that they mentioned both Pete and your mom, too. Is Liza short for Elizabeth?"

"Nope, my grandmother was just in love with the name Liza."

"Your dad apparently still dabbles in law enforcement."

"Occasionally," he replied with humor.

"And your mom, what does she do since she retired from the community college?"

"She quilts and does needlework and putters around in the

yard when the weather's good, but mostly, she harangues me and my brothers and my sister because we haven't given her any grandchildren."

Hannah smiled. "You mentioned that before."

"With any luck, you won't be a target."

"Why is that?"

He shot her a look that answered her nonverbally. "Just so you know, I made it clear to Dad today that you're still a married woman and I called Mom and told her not to get her hopes up."

"That's telling it like it is."

"Right now, there's no other way to tell it."

Fiona chose that moment to sit up and bark.

"She knows we're here."

Hannah searched the darkness, wondering how a dog could be so in tune with her surroundings. A moment later, they rounded a curve and a lighted driveway came into view. Clear out here, in the middle of nowhere, Christmas lights everywhere.

"I take it your parents are into Christmas," she said, her tone dry.

"Let's just say Mom is and Dad loves her like crazy, so he'll put up every light and deco she orders or brings home from the mercantile."

"No wonder she wants grandkids," Hannah said, her heart suddenly aching with memories of how much Jay had loved Christmas. Truth be told, she hadn't celebrated Christmas since he'd died.

Only he hadn't died, but even so, she had no idea if she'd ever see her little boy again.

"Oh, God, Hannah, I didn't think. I'm sorry, I should have warned you."

"It's okay," she said. "Jay loved everything about Christmas. It won't kill me to pretend I still love it, too."

Chapter 17

Pete opened the door with a big smile on his face. "Glad you could make it, Hannah."

"Thank you for inviting me," she said, accepting his hug.

Noah helped her slip out of her coat, then removed his own and hung them both in the guest closet.

"Liza's in the kitchen. Let's go join her, shall we?"

"Absolutely. Whatever she's cooking smells delicious."

"She usually fixes pot roast," Noah said, "but tonight I can tell that's definitely not on the menu."

Pete grinned. "Mom got a wild hair to try something different. You know how she loves the Barefoot Contessa, so she went with filet mignon with mustard and mushrooms."

"She's a great cook, so no matter what she fixes, I'm a fan," Noah said. "Hi, Mom."

His mother looked up from stove, where she'd been adjusting the flame beneath the pot, and smiled. "Hi, honey." Her gaze swung to Hannah. "And you must be Hannah. I'm so glad you could make it." She came around the end of the counter, her hand extended.

"Thank you for inviting me," Hannah said, extending her own hand. "I love Ina Garten, too, so I'm excited to try this dish."

"I hate to experiment on company," Liza admitted, "but I

usually hit a home run with her recipes, so I think we'll all be fine."

It took Hannah a moment to realize Liza had a wicked, if understated, sense of humor. "You're right about that. She has the best recipe for prime rib I've ever made."

"Ooh, I'll have to try it," Liza said. "How about something to drink before dinner? Wine? A cocktail? Beer?"

"Nothing for me, thanks, but I might have a glass of wine with dinner," Hannah said.

Noah strode over to the fridge and opened it. "You want a beer, Dad?"

Pete glanced at his wife. "Do we have time before dinner to nurse one?"

Liza looked at the stove timer. "Twenty minutes, so I guess so."

"What can I do to help?" Hannah asked.

Liza linked arms with her and steered her toward the family room. "When Pete told me your story, I sat down and cried, it was so horrific. I'm glad he and Noah are helping you, but now I want you to tell me what *I* can do to help." She pulled Hannah down beside her on the sofa.

"I…"

"Mom, I thought this was a social affair," Noah said without censure.

"It is, but you can't expect me to sit idle while you and Dad and Hannah plug away over this mess, now can you?"

Noah glanced at Hannah with an expression that could have been read as a mix of apologetic and resigned.

"It's okay," she said to him, then focused again on his mother. "This all came about so suddenly, I haven't really got my head wrapped around it yet, but let me give it some thought."

Liza smiled and patted her knee. "Good. Now tell me about your little boy. Your heart must have broken when he was reported as drowned."

Hannah spent the remaining time before Liza went back into the kitchen talking about Jay. For the first time in two years, it didn't hurt to remember his sense of humor or his intelligence or his artistic talent.

Over dinner, a discussion of the past and current events, and what could be done to find her husband and son, dominated the conversation. By the time dessert was served, Hannah's brain was fried. "I hope it's okay if we change topics. You've all given me a lot to process later, but for now, I'd like to know more about you and your family."

Hannah wasn't just casting out a red herring. She genuinely wanted to know more about the Wards, who apparently had taken her under their wing, as if she were some little lost soul.

To a person, they must be mindreaders, because that was exactly how she'd felt over the past two years.

"I think I owe you an apology," Noah said on the drive back to Hannah's.

"Why?"

"I had no idea this was going to be the Hannah Inquisition at dinner tonight."

"It didn't feel like an inquisition."

"It didn't?" He grunted. "From where I sat, it seemed like you were in the interrogation room down at PCSO."

Hannah turned slightly in her seat. "From where I sat, it seemed like I was with three people who actually cared about what happened in the past and what could be done to rectify it now."

He eased up to a stop sign and faced her without saying anything.

"What's wrong?"

"I thought you'd be ticked." He shook his head. "Maybe even blame me for setting you up."

"You still don't get it, do you?"

"Get what?"

"I got the shaft from nearly everyone I know for almost two years. People left hate mail in my mailbox and gruesome graffiti on my house and dolls soaked in red paint with their heads torn off on my front porch. Friends deserted me. Neighbors shunned me. Jason's family threatened me. The cops lied about me. Except for my siblings and their spouses, not a single person stood in my corner."

"You didn't mention all of that when you explained the situation tonight."

"I thought it was too much to heap on your folks."

"Eventually, Mom will get it all out of you."

"Eventually, I might tell her, anyway. She's a caring, kind-hearted woman."

"She is."

"I like your dad, too. He's certainly not what I envisioned an FBI agent to be like."

"That's what TV does for the profession."

She gave up the ghost of a smile. "I suppose so, even though I don't watch much TV anymore." Her heart clenched with memories. She looked away from him so he couldn't read the agony she knew would show up in her eyes. "You wouldn't believe the vitriol I used to hear about myself on local news. They talk about fake news today and I can relate so well, it's scary."

"I'm so sorry for what you've endured, Hannah."

"Thank you." She bit her lip, considering how to convey her thoughts. "As I look back on it, being treated like that toughened me up. I used to let Jason get away with belittling me and ragging on me about the dumbest things. Having to put up with all the shit being dished out about me…well, I either had to grow a spine or wither away into nothingness, as if I no longer existed."

"It's hard for me to imagine that you tolerated that kind of behavior from your husband."

With a wry twist to her lips she said, "I guess I've succeeded in transforming myself, then haven't I?"

"It's not a bad thing."

"No, I guess it's not. Quite honestly, I don't even know how I subsisted as that other Hannah. I can't believe I let Jason walk all over me like he did. I don't even think I stayed with him because of Jay, because frankly, he wasn't much of a dad. He was more in love with the idea of having a son than he was with actually having a little boy he could play with and read to and explore the world with." She sighed. "In those days, I took everything Jason dished out and stayed around for more. How pathetic is that?"

"Every cloud has a silver lining."

Like minds. Nevertheless, a tear streaked down her cheek. "Losing a child is a helluva way to become a woman of character."

With his foot still on the brake, Noah reached over and wiped the tear from her cheek. "You're still the same person, Hannah, whether you realize it or not. You've just readjusted your attitude in a positive way."

That brought a sad smile to her lips. "I think I like you, Noah Ward."

"I know I like you, Hannah Mason."

Behind them, a horn honked.

Startled, they broke eye contact.

In the back seat, both dogs barked.

Hannah had a hard time getting to sleep. After an hour, she gave up, and climbed out of bed. She slipped into her heavy chenille robe and Sherpa-lined slippers and began to prowl the house.

Bowie trailed her for a few minutes, but when he discovered she wasn't doing anything interesting or productive, he moseyed back to his doggie bed and dozed off.

In the kitchen, she made herself a cup of tea, using the hot water dispenser, though she much preferred boiling water from the teapot. Tonight, it just seemed like too much effort, and then there was the fact that she wanted to remain in the dark.

Darkness was much better for thinking and planning.

Darkness helped you keep your secrets to yourself.

Darkness could be your friend.

Technically, it wasn't completely dark. As with any house these days, there was a clock on the stove and the microwave and the red light on the landline charging station, and a green light on the smoke detectors, and a kind of a chartreuse green light on the readout of the security system pad. In addition to all that, the snow had stopped and the sky had cleared. The moon was almost full and illuminated all the windows, even though the window coverings were drawn.

Hannah took her tea to her favorite chair in the family room and set it on a coaster on the side table before she grabbed a throw and settled in with her feet on the ottoman. During the day, she sometimes sat and stared out the window, which gave her a nice view of the hillside she and Bowie walked every morning. But now it was nighttime and the blinds were closed. There was no view to enjoy.

Her first indication that someone was outside the house came when she heard the crunch of footsteps against the frozen snow. As if to confirm she wasn't imagining things, a shadow crept by the window on which her gaze was focused. As with any shadow, the human form it projected was slightly distorted and larger than the actual person it projected.

She placed her tea cup back on the coaster, surprised when it rattled against the Thirsty Stone. She hadn't even noticed she was shaking.

The shadow stopped in the middle of the window, apparently trying to peer past the two-inch blinds, then moved on and disappeared. Moments later, she heard a sound, as if someone were trying to open the patio door.

If her heart had picked up speed earlier, now it was pounding almost out of her chest. She watched, frozen, as the shadow proceeded further east, stopping in front of the kitchen window. At that point, she got up from the chair as quietly as possible and moved into the kitchen. It took a second for her to realize no little green or red lights illuminated the darkness. Her power had gone out.

Even though she would be barefoot, she stepped out of her slippers and made her way carefully through the darkness to the mudroom. It had a deadbolt, so if it wasn't locked, it might make a rasping sound that the prowler would hear, which wouldn't be a bad thing, if it made him run away.

Why was she second-guessing herself? The simple answer was, because. Slightly unnerved by the threatening missive in her mailbox, she'd checked all the doors and windows before bed.

Holding her breath, she reached out and felt for the bolt. Thank God, it was horizontal. Locked.

While she stood there, deafened by the sound of her own

heartbeat pulsing in her ears, the shadow appeared on the blind. Hannah, still holding her breath, didn't dare move.

The doorknob rattled. The prowler dropped the f-bomb loud enough for her to hear through the door.

At that point, she knew whoever was there, he was intent on getting in. Did he plan to burglarize the house, or did he have a more sinister plan in mind that centered on Hannah herself?

Quaking, she was uncertain what to do next. Once the shadow moved on with crunching footsteps, she moved toward the first guest bedroom. With the moon on the opposite side of the house, there was no shadow, of course, but she could still hear the intruder crunching his way through the snow. On he went to the second guest bedroom, then past the living room, and on to the front door, where he again, rattled the door handle. Next, he went past her workroom. She distinctly heard him grunt as he tried to raise a window.

Hannah raced to her bedroom for her cell phone, almost tripping over Bowie, who'd appeared out of nowhere. How did he know to be so quiet? And better yet, why had she hesitated to call Noah?

She'd never thought to train Bowie to be guard dog, but maybe she should. He liked having company. His tail was going a mile a minute in anticipation of someone visiting.

The phone light came on as soon as she picked it up. She clasped it to her middle, thinking. She wanted the prowler caught, but she didn't want him to know she was on to him. Where could she go to use the phone so he wouldn't see the light it projected?

The only room in the house without a window was her walk-in closet. She padded over and stepped in. Bowie followed her. She closed the pocket door and sank to the floor beside her pet.

Noah had given her his cell and landline numbers. She pulled up his number in the contact list, praying he'd hear his phone ring and that he was the right person to call, since he lived closest. If he called in support from his patrol staff, so be it. The more to this party, the merrier, as long as they were on the side of law enforcement.

"Ward," he answered, his voice rough with sleep, even though he sounded alert.

God help her, but she found the sound of his voice incredibly sexy. "Noah, it's Hannah. I have a prowler. I think he's trying to get in. I hear him rattling doorknobs and trying to open windows."

"Where are you?"

"In my walk-in closet."

"I don't suppose you have a weapon."

Hannah had completely forgotten about the gun. "I do."

After a moment of silence, he said. "I hope you know how to use it."

"I do, but I was hoping I'd never have to."

"I'd rather not break down your door when I get there, but I don't want you coming out of that closet. Do you have a key hidden outside?"

"There's a slide-out on the mailbox, on the bottom. Push up, pull out."

He gave a grunt that sounded more like disgust than thank goodness. "Be right there."

The line went dead, but she'd heard him making getting-dressed noises as he spoke.

How long would it take him to get from his place to hers?

She pulled a sweater off the shelf and worked it across the bottom of the door, then activated the flashlight on her phone. The gun safe was on the shelf next to her folded jeans. She input the code and the door popped open.

She withdrew the Glock G30S. Although it was the only gun she'd ever owned, and the one she'd trained with at the gun range, it still felt foreign in her hand. Still, if it came to her or the intruder, she had to win the discussion.

Bowie whined.

"I know," she whispered. "I don't like it, either, but you're not exactly a pit bull, are you?"

He whined again, then curled up on her feet, as if that was all the protection she needed.

"Good dog," she said, and switched off the flashlight.

The next ten minutes were the longest of her life, speaking in terms of current events.

Chapter 18

The next ten minutes were even longer. Hannah's hand began to cramp, but she didn't dare let go of the Glock.

She thanked God that she'd learned the proper procedure for holding a weapon so that she didn't shoot herself or her dog. It all centered around keeping her finger off the trigger, but after twenty minutes of clutching the cold metal for all it was worth, her hand was starting to protest vehemently.

At thirty minutes, certain that Noah was outside somewhere, she shook her phone so the light came on, then set the gun back in the gun safe, but didn't close the door. Surely, the sheriff didn't expect her to wait in the closet all night long.

She bent to retrieve the sweater from the floor, but didn't bother refolding it before she tossed it toward the shelf.

Bowie, wide awake, stood nosing the closet door.

"What do you think?" she whispered. "Should we see what's going on, or stay here?"

The dog looked up at her and gave a little yip.

"That's what I think, too," Hannah said, and began to work the door open. Assailed by a brief moment of indecision, she wondered if she should take the gun with her.

Bowie tore out of the closet, then the bedroom, and ran directly to the front door, his tail wagging like crazy.

Hannah went to the front window and slanted the blinds a

bit, hoping to have a view of what was transpiring outside.

There in her driveway were Noah's truck, a patrol car, and a vehicle she'd never seen before.

A figure dressed all in black stood near the patrol vehicle, his hands apparently cuffed behind him. Noah was at the open door of his truck, talking on the radio. His female deputy kept an eye on the prowler. Noah said something to her, and she opened the back door of her Interceptor SUV, then grabbed the prowler by the arm, probably intending to get him inside the vehicle.

Instead, the guy shoved against the deputy and sent her flying across the driveway. He took off running toward the road, like he really had a chance to outrun the law.

Noah and the deputy took off in pursuit. Noah tackled him long before he reached the end of the driveway. It took both of them to get the guy, kicking and screaming, into the SUV, and even then, he landed his feet directly in the deputy's chest and sent her flying again. When she came up the second time, she had a weapon in her hand. Noah stood back and the next thing Hannah knew, the deputy fired and the prowler was consumed with spasms that left him flagging in moments. A Taser, no doubt.

Noah slammed the back door of the SUV closed and spoke with his deputy for a moment before making his way to Hannah's front door. Halfway there, he turned back and headed toward the mailbox.

Hannah ran to disarm the security system, then opened the front door. She stepped out on the stoop and said, "I'm here," like he hadn't heard her fling the door open.

He swung around and headed back. "It thought I told you to stay in the closet."

"I did, for thirty minutes."

"Good God, Hannah, what if we hadn't been able to get things under control out here?"

"I would have gone back to the closet." She curled her cold, bare toes and shoved her hands under the armpits of her robe, hoping to keep them warm.

"Get inside," he said, his tone none too gentle.

"But—"

"It's frigging cold out here. Get inside where it's warm."

She hadn't realized that she'd come out without her slippers. At the moment, she couldn't even remember where she'd taken them off. Once again inside, she turned to face him. "Do you know who he is?"

"No, and he's not talking, but we'll figure it out." He stared at her. "You okay here by yourself?"

"Of course."

"I'll come back after we get him processed."

"Really, I'm okay, Noah. It was just a little unsettling to hear him walk around the house and try to get in."

His expression didn't change. "What were you doing up at two a.m., anyway?"

"Couldn't sleep, so I got up and made myself a cup of tea. I was sitting in the dark with Bowie, drinking it, when I heard something and the next thing I knew, there was a shadow on the family room blinds."

"You didn't call it in immediately?"

"No, I waited to see what he was going to do."

"Jesus-H, Hannah, he could've broken in and raped you or killed you or—"

"But he didn't!"

Obviously angry, he shook his head in disgust. "We'll pick this discussion up when I get back." He walked out the door, then swung around. "Did you at least have your damned alarm set?"

"Of course."

He turned away again without another word.

"Wait!"

He ground to a halt. "What?"

"Just wait a minute, okay?" She ran off to the mudroom, where she'd hung a key collector, and grabbed a spare house key. When she got back to the entry, Noah stood glaring at her from just outside the door. "Take a key, in case I'm sleeping when you come back."

"You expect me to just walk in?"

She nodded. "Better that you do that than break down my door."

He glanced down at the key she extended to him.

"It'll save you having to get the spare key from the mail-box."

Still, he didn't take it.

"The code to the alarm is 20206. You'll have three minutes to disarm the system."

His gaze rose to meet hers. "Why can't I just ring the damned doorbell?"

"I told you, I might be sleeping."

"What am I supposed to do if you are, climb into bed with you?"

Hannah might have considered that a fine idea the night before, but since Noah had morphed into Mr. Growly-Face, the idea had lost some of its luster. "Actually, I thought you might put on a pot of coffee, then wake me, so I can take Bowie out while it's brewing."

He snatched the key from her fingers. "I'll take the dog out if you're asleep, and I'll put your coffee on, but I'll be damned if I'll walk into your bedroom to wake you."

With that, he spun on his booted heel one last time and let his angry strides take him to his truck.

Hannah reset the alarm and headed back to bed after letting Bowie out to relieve himself. He didn't like the freezing cold at all, so the foray outside lasted less than a minute.

She expected to toss and turn, like she had earlier, but instead, she fell asleep immediately, only to be plunged into a quagmire of nightmares involving Jason, the prowler, and Sabine. She awoke, terrified. Her breath came in shallow, rapid pants, and her heart beat so furiously, she thought it might explode in her chest.

The room was still dark. In fact, it was too dark. She glanced toward the clock radio, dismayed when the numerals weren't illuminated. She noticed at the same time that her bedroom was ice cold, and then she remembered. The power was out.

She tossed back the covers and immediately shivered. She reached for her robe, which she'd tossed across the bottom of the bed, and slid her feet into the slippers she'd finally located where the kitchen met the mudroom.

Hoping her cell phone was still in the pocket of her robe, she reached in for it. "Ah-ha!" she whispered, and activated the flashlight before she made her way to the thermostat in the hallway. Ever the optimist, she tried light switches as she went. Of course, the vague green illumination usually visible from the thermostat was gone, and the gas furnace had an electric igniter, so no heat.

At least she had a good supply of candles in the mudroom, but a battery-operated lantern would have probably been a better option. And a camp stove, so she could heat a pot of water for tea, or drip coffee. Two more items to add to her new mental shopping list.

For some reason, she'd been completely oblivious to the fact that she might experience a loss of power. Well, not completely. She and her brother-in-law Craig had discussed it briefly. He'd mentioned that both the gas stovetop and furnace had electric ignition and wouldn't work if she lost electrical.

Yikes, the water heater was gas, too. Had the water already grown too cold for a shower?

God, she had a lot of adjusting to do, living in the mountains.

With candles lit on saucers in the kitchen and family room, Hannah trudged off for the shower. It was another new experience for her...shower by cell phone flashlight. She took time to wash her hair, then regretted it when the water ran to lukewarm and then cold by the time she was ready to rinse out the conditioner.

She did the fastest towel dry in history, then climbed into her sweats and a sweatshirt and two pairs of socks.

Back in the kitchen, she decided if she really wanted coffee, she could heat a pan of water on the barbecue. That, at least, had its own internal igniter. She didn't want to ruin her teapot, so she scavenged amongst her baking pans for a pie tin. The teapot fit nicely inside the nine-incher.

She slipped into her snow boots and opened the patio door.

Even though it was still dark out, Bowie whizzed past her and leaped into the snow. "Glad someone has enthusiasm this morning," she muttered. She set the pie pan and teapot down on the patio table and got the barbie going, hoping fervently that she wasn't undertaking an experiment she'd live to regret.

The cold seeped into her while she waited for the water to boil. Hannah took a quick peek at the thermometer she'd mounted on the house. Five degrees Fahrenheit? That couldn't be right. Could it?

"Bowie, come!"

For a change, she didn't have to call him twice. She opened the patio door and the pup jetted in ahead of her, though to give him credit he did stop on the rug. Freezing, she shut the door, then went to get the puppy-drying towel. As soon as that was done, she headed for the fireplace, wondering why she hadn't thought of it right off the bat.

She laid a fire and got it going, then went back outside to check the teapot. No boil yet. Did that have something to do with the cold? Or was it more of an altitude thing? Which reminded her to grab more firewood while she was there. Inside, Bowie had already curled up in front of the fireplace. Smart dog. As soon as she had her tea made, she planned to do the same thing, only with a blanket over her.

Fifteen minutes later, she sniffed the air from the chair she'd pulled over in front of the fire. Vanilla-scented candles and burning oak. Life didn't get any better when you'd lost your electricity. Well except for maybe not having anything to munch on besides Triscuits. She really should have gone to the grocery store while she was out the day before.

Bowie twitched and she wondered what he was dreaming, if dogs even dreamed.

The crackle of the flames eating at the logs was soothing. Hannah sipped her tea and let her mind wander back over the events of the early morning hours.

Who was the prowler?

Why had he picked her house?

Had he intended to do her harm, or was he intent strictly on burglary?

When would Noah be back?

She pulled her phone out again to check the time. 7:00 a.m. Processing a criminal must take a lot of time, and speaking of time, she said to Bowie, "Do you mind missing our walk up the hill? I really don't feel up to it this morning?"

Bowie craned his neck and smiled at her.

"I'll take that as agreement," she said, relieved she didn't have to go back out into the frozen tundra.

Noah's finger hovered over the doorbell. Against his better judgment, he pulled his hand back and jammed it into his pocket to retrieve the key Hannah had given him.

Behind him, Arnie's Towing Service was hooking up the prowler's vehicle to tow down to the impound yard. What kind of dipshit prowler parked his car in plain sight, anyway?

He inserted the key into the lock, wondering if Hannah had fallen asleep, or simply wasn't in the mood to greet him at the door. Her dog wasn't in hiding, that's for sure. No sooner did he open the door than Bowie jumped up, putting his paws against Noah's knees. He squatted to pet the pup. "You haven't done that before," he said, scratching between Bowie's ears. "I don't think your mistress would like knowing you did it, either, but I won't tell, if you don't."

Bowie wriggled, as if with delight, then spun around and tore off back toward the family room.

Noah straightened and shut the door. He'd momentarily forgotten he needed to shut off the alarm. Fortunately, he had a three-minute window.

It took a moment to realize the house was quiet. And cold.

He reached for the light switch and flipped it on. Nothing. Hannah was without power. Hoping not to wake her, he made his way to the kitchen, surprised to find the fire waning and Hannah sound asleep, curled up under a blanket, in the chair.

Noah pulled out his phone and searched his contacts for Pike Power and Utility. He identified himself, then asked, "Have you got reported outages in the area?"

"No, sir."

"Well, I have one for you. Thirteen-three-sixty-five

Creight. How soon can you check it out?"

"I'll put in a work order immediately. Are other residences affected, as well?"

"I have no idea."

"All right. Thank you for letting us know."

Noah signed off, wondering if his place was affected, too. Since Hannah was asleep, he decided to go find out. He was back twenty minutes later with Fiona, a battery-powered lantern, and his camp stove. Hannah was still asleep.

While he built the fire back up as quietly as he could, he heard the rumble of a large truck outside. He pulled on his boots and coat and left the house. Two PPU employees climbed down out of the utility vehicle.

"My place is just up the road, but I have power," he told them.

"No one else has reported anything," one of the men said. "We'll take a look and see what's going on."

Noah nodded and headed back inside. An hour later, he heard a knock at the door.

While he was talking to the PPU workers, Hannah came up behind him with her trusty sidekick, who, as usual, was wagging his tail as if the movement would heat up the place.

Noah moved aside to make room for her in the doorway. "Your incoming power line has been cut."

"What?" Her eyes widened as she connected the dots. "But...I had power last night."

"The place was dark when we took the prowler in," Noah said.

"Ohmygod, you're right. I noticed all the indicator lights were out, but I didn't connect it to the prowler."

"We repaired it, ma'am." The utility worker looked at Noah. "Would you mind trying a light switch, Sheriff?"

Noah reached over and flipped on the entryway light. It lit the gloom nicely. "Thanks for coming out so quickly."

"Yes, thank you," Hannah said, looking a little dazed.

"That's what we're here for. Give us a call if you have any further problems."

She nodded.

Noah closed the door, wondering what the hell was going

on. A burglar cutting the power? That didn't compute at all, unless he wasn't really a burglar.

Chapter 19

Hannah huddled beneath the blanket, chilled to the bone, not only from the cold, but from the evil she perceived to be surrounding the home she'd come to regard as her safe haven.

"Take a good look at this guy's picture."

Noah held the photo so close, she was almost cross-eyed trying to see it. The man he'd arrested looked vaguely familiar, but with his scraggly beard, and the bandage across his forehead and his hair askew, not to mention the oxygen mask over his nose and mouth, how was she supposed to identify him? She looked up at the sheriff. "There's something familiar about him, but it's hard to say definitively when his face is mostly obscured. Did you ask why he was prowling around outside my house?"

Noah flexed his jaw.

"Well, did you?"

"I couldn't."

"Why not?"

"He's in the hospital, unconscious in the ICU. We think he may have had some kind of drug or poison stashed on him."

"Is he going to make it?"

"They don't know. They're processing a blood sample now, hoping they can figure out what he took."

"I don't understand. He went around the entire house, trying doors and windows. He wanted to get in, which meant he wanted to do me harm."

"Maybe."

"Why else would he want in?"

"To steal from you?"

"I've got nothing worth stealing!"

"He wouldn't know that."

"You may be right, but I've given this a lot of thought and it feels really personal."

He folded the photo and shoved it back into his pocket. "I don't want to scare you—"

"Too late, I'm already scared!"

He acknowledged her comment with a wry twist of his lips. "I don't believe in coincidence. First Twombly shows up dead in Estes Park, and now you're targeted in Fossil."

"Those exact thoughts are the same ones I keep having."

"I need to talk to your brother-in-law again."

"All right, but why?" His indecision concerning an explanation was clear in his expression. Gone was the man who was attracted to her. The by-the-book sheriff had taken his place. Hannah waited for one of him to make a decision about how it was going to be.

Finally, he did, and she found herself slightly disappointed that the sheriff part of him had won the inner battle.

"I want to know if there's any possibility your husband saw him at the airport."

"Craig would have said, if that was the case."

"You may be right, but I still need to speak with him."

Hannah unfurled herself from the cocoon of her blanket and went to the kitchen to grab the landline, since her smart phone was on the charger. She dialed Craig, then put the call on speaker and handed the phone over to Noah.

"Craig Fender," her brother-in-law said when he picked up the call. Hannah knew he must be working, or he would have read the screen and known it was her.

"Sheriff Ward," Noah said, keeping it professional.

"Is something wrong?" Craig asked. "Is Hannah okay?"

Noah gave him a quick rundown on the prowler. "Hannah is fine, but a bit shaken."

"What the hell! Is this related to Jason?"

"That's what I'm trying to determine. Do you think he saw you at the airport?"

"No, I stayed back and he was completely involved with Sabine."

"You're certain?"

"Yes. Absolutely," he said, but his tone had changed, reflecting something less than certainty.

"What is it?"

"I'm thinking back and there may have been something…I didn't remember it until right this minute."

"What was it?"

"Jay…he looked right at me and waved. Nothing blatant, just that quick little thing he used to do when he got ready to leave our place."

Hannah gasped. She knew exactly what Craig was talking about. It was a palm-out, quick little one-swipe wave.

"That's the connection I was looking for," Noah said.

"I don't get it," Craig said, "How would Jay noticing me relate to a prowler at Hannah's?"

"The boy could have said something to his father."

Hannah stepped forward. "Twombly was found dead not far from here, Craig. He went over an embankment. Someone had tampered with his brakes."

"Jesus! Couple that with Henri being killed and…you know I have to tell Emily and Seth about this, Hannah."

"I know, but try to downplay it with Emily. She's such a worrywart, I don't want this to affect her or the baby."

Craig was silent for several moments. "She has a checkup tomorrow. I'll give the doctor a heads-up and tell her about it while we're there, just in case."

"Good idea, although maybe you shouldn't tell her at all."

"I love my wife, Hannah. I'd really like to stay married to her."

"I get your drift." She sighed. "Of course, you have to tell her."

"Call me if anything shakes loose between now and then that might soften the delivery of what's happened."

"I will."

"Sheriff?"

"Yes?"

"Why didn't you ask the prowler directly if Jason sent him?"

"I would've, but it looks like he tried to kill himself during transport and he's currently in the ICU, in a coma. His prognosis is unknown."

"Shit."

"That's one way to describe the situation," Noah said. "Thanks for your help."

"No problem." And with that, her brother-in-law disconnected.

Noah stared at Hannah, his expression grim. "I don't like the trail of dead bodies in Jason and Sabine's wake."

A dark, ominous cloud of despair settled over her. "I have to get Jay away from them."

"There's something else you should know."

Hannah didn't know how much more she could take.

Her expression, on the other hand, must have said *go ahead*, because Noah nodded and said, "Twombly had your name and address in the NOTES section of his cell phone."

She mulled that over. "You're thinking he passed the information along to Jason and then Jason killed him."

"It's the only thing that makes sense."

"But how would Twombly even know I'd moved to Colorado? Only my immediate family was privy to that information."

"Did you ever consider the detective might follow you to Colorado?"

She shook her head.

"Or that he may have bugged your house?"

Stunned, Hannah had to grasp the edge of the counter to keep her balance. "No."

"Or followed your siblings or bugged their houses?"

"But…isn't bugging illegal?"

"What he did for Jason and Sabine was illegal, and for all we know, he got rid of Henri, too."

"Since he ended up dead himself, I guess karma really is a bitch."

"I guess it is."

"What's next?"

"The towing company just hauled the prowler's vehicle over to the impound yard. I'm going to meet Shari there and we're going to tear that car apart. There's got to be something there to tell us who this guy is and what he was after."

"Would it be okay if I went to the hospital and looked at him in person?"

"You think that will make a difference?"

"Probably not," she said, suddenly deflated, "but remember, I did say he seemed familiar Besides, what else am I supposed to do? Sit around and twiddle my thumbs?"

That seemed to amuse him. "As long as you stay out of trouble, I don't care what you do."

He didn't say it with any heat so she tried not to take umbrage, but really? Why didn't he just tell her to take a flying leap off a tall building?

"I need to go. Can you get your brother-in-law's contact info up on the phone again? I'll enter it into my phone."

Without a word, Hannah did as he asked.

Once he'd finished, he said, "I have a block on visitors to the prowler's room, but I'll call over and let them know it's okay for you to drop in."

Drop in. Like she was out for a neighborly visit. Suddenly so exhausted she could hardly move, she said, "I think I'll take nap first. I'm running on fumes right now." Then she remembered, she'd woken him up, so he couldn't be faring much better. "How about you? Will you be able to catch a catnap today?"

"I'll sleep when I get home tonight."

"Did they make you a tough guy in the military, or were you born that way?"

"A little bit of both, I suppose. I can go for forty-eight hours before I crash and burn."

"Will you let me know if you find anything?"

"Sure." He pulled on his coat and grabbed his boots, which he'd worn into the kitchen and taken off on the mat.

She didn't have the heart or the energy to chew him out for walking in wet footwear across her new wood floors. In the overall scheme of things, did it really matter, anyway?

"Come lock up behind me."

Several snide retorts circled her brain, but discretion being the better part of valor, she managed half a smile instead. "Thanks for coming out in the middle of the night to help me."

"That's my job, you know."

"Nevertheless, I still appreciate it."

A few minutes later, Hannah climbed into her bed, sweats and all. With the heat back on, it was toasty warm under the covers and she fell asleep immediately.

A couple of hours later, she drove over the icy, snow-plowed road to town, rattled by her daytime nightmare. She tuned Sirius XM to the Holly station and turned up the volume, hoping to wipe the remnants of the nightmare out of her mind with Christmas songs. "Grandma Got Run Over by a Reindeer" didn't quite cut it, but at least it was entertaining.

It was bad enough that her sleeping mind had seen fit to replay the horrible events of the past two years. Did it have to further torture her by creating dream images of what the future might hold?

There was a time when Hannah hadn't put much stock in dreams. Jason taking Jay off to the sailboat, knowing she vehemently opposed it, had changed her thinking. Two nights before, she'd dreamed Jason had taken Jay out on the water and a wave had caught the sailboat unexpectedly, overturning it, leaving her husband and son to drown. There hadn't been an alternative ending where Jason had stolen Jay and absconded with him and Sabine to parts unknown.

What did this new dream of Twombly trying to kill her mean, when Twombly was dead? If the nightmare of Jason and Jay dying had been only partially accurate, how was she supposed to be able to judge what was and wasn't correct about the nightmare she'd experienced just a short time ago?

At the hospital, she pulled into a twenty-minute visitor spot and went inside. Fossil was a small town and Pike was the smallest county in the state. The size of the facility matched the dimensions of the community it served. The ICU was on the first floor, adjacent to the urgent care. Hannah followed the signs, identified herself at the reception desk, and was admitted to the patient-care area.

"Is he still in a coma?" she asked the nurse.

"Yes."

"Is he showing any improvement?"

The nurse sent her an anxious look. "I'm not supposed to discuss patients with non-family members."

"I understand," Hannah said. "I just really hope he comes out of it so we'll know why he was prowling around my house, trying to get in."

The anxious expression turned to one of concern. The nurse glanced around, then whispered, "He'll be transported to Colorado Springs if we can't figure out what he took." She motioned toward the hallway. "Second room on the right."

Hannah hesitated in the doorway. In some ways, it seemed odd to enter a hospital room to stare at a comatose patient. On the other hand, he wouldn't be in the ICU if he hadn't been doing what he'd been doing in the first place.

"It's a little dark in here," said a second nurse. "I'll turn on a light, so you can have a better look at him."

"Thanks." As soon as the nurse hit the light switch, Hannah sucked in a deep breath, as if that would give her courage, and made her way to the side of the bed.

The man was attached to at least three different machines. Instead of an oxygen mask, he now had nasal prongs attached to his nose. A blood pressure cuff was wrapped around his arm, and a pulse oximeter clip was attached to his right index finger. The gauze bandage on his forehead covered one eyebrow.

His skin tone was pale and someone with a heart had brushed his hair. His breathing didn't seem labored, but it was obvious his body was in distress, or maybe it was Hannah in distress, and her breathing that was labored.

"Do you recognize him?"

"Yes."

"Do you know his name?"

"Yes." And here she'd thought her nightmare was nothing more than a ridiculous take on an impossibility. A really bad dream meant to torment her. One that had less than a snowball's chance in hell of happening.

Dear God, someone upstairs had a macabre sense of humor.

Whoever had died in the car crash in the Big Thompson Canyon, it wasn't Detective Richard Twombly, purveyor of emotional anguish to women who had lost their spouse and their child.

Twombly was safe, if not sound, in a hospital bed in Holy Cross Hospital's small intensive care unit.

He was not dead, even though Hannah now almost wished he was.

Almost, because as long as he was alive, there was a chance he could be saved, and if he was saved, he could tell her where Jason was, and if she knew where Jason was, she could go and get Jay and bring him home, where he belonged.

She swayed and grabbed the side rail of the bed for support.

"Are you okay?" the nurse asked.

Hannah lied and said, "Yes."

"I need to run out for a minute. Will you be all right?"

"Yes," she said, lying again. She stared down at the man who had helped Jason and Sabine pull off an egregious crime. He must have a cruel streak a mile wide to have enjoyed the mind-bending games he'd engaged in with her for all those months. How could he, a cop, even live with himself? He was sworn to protect and save, not torture and destroy and spread lies to the media about her involvement in her loved ones' deaths.

It was several moments before she realized that the eyes in Twombly's bruised face were open and staring back at her. She hardened her heart against his pain and discomfort. He'd brought this—*all* of this—on himself.

"You," he got out on a raspy whisper.

"Sorry you didn't get to complete your mission," she said, her voice remarkably calm.

"I will," he promised, which made her wonder why he'd tried to kill himself, if he was still intent on seeing her dead.

Hannah backed away, ending up at the door to call the nurse back. When the nurse reappeared, Hannah said, "He needs to be restrained. He's dangerous."

"We don't put restraints—"

Before she could finish, Twombly reared up in the bed, growling. He ripped out the nasal prongs and tore off the BP cuff, then yanked the IV from his arm. Machines beeped and screeched in unison. Somehow, he managed to lower the bed rail and lever himself out of the bed. Visibly annoyed that he'd missed removing the clip on his finger, he flipped his hand to dislodge it.

Still in the hall, the nurse screamed, "Get security! Call the sheriff's office!"

Hannah would have shoved past her and run, but as soon as Twombly stood on his own two feet, he staggered and dropped like a stone to the floor. She pulled the Glock from her purse and aimed it at him, though he wasn't moving. Had he hit his head, or was he simply trying to get his bearings?

It didn't matter. If he lunged at her, she'd shoot him. He easily outweighed her by at least eighty pounds. There was every possibility he could take her down and kill her before security showed up.

In what seemed like an hour later, footsteps pounded down the hall. A man in uniform stormed the room, his eyes wide at the sight of Hannah holding a gun on a patient.

"Ma'am," he said, "please, lower your weapon."

"Restrain him and I will."

He exchanged a look with the nurse, who shrugged.

"He's a patient, ma'am. He's not going to hurt you."

"He tried to kill me last night, so I damned well think he *will* try to hurt me as soon as he gets the chance." She sucked in a shaky breath. "I'm telling you, he needs to be restrained."

The guard and nurse stared at her, clearly undecided.

From the doorway, the nurse she'd first encountered, who was apparently not indecisive, said, "There's a pack of those plastic thingies used for bundling computer cords on the counter. Would that work?"

The security guard nodded. "Yes, get them."

Twombly managed to push up to his knees. With a feral look in his eyes, he trained his gaze on Hannah.

"Stay down," the guard said.

"Fuck you," Twombly snarled, never taking his eyes off Hannah.

The nurse returned with the pack of zip ties.

Twombly grabbed the lowered rail to help get him back on his feet. At several inches over six feet, he practically dwarfed the security guard, but that didn't stop the man in uniform from advancing on him. Before Twombly was completely on his feet, the guard flung his body at him and forced him back to the floor. The former detective began to buck and cuss, both with equal fervor and anger.

A sheriff's deputy appeared in the doorway. Hannah recognized him as Toad Hoffman. He entered the fray and made himself useful by putting a knee against Twombly's back, which effectively pinned him to the floor.

"Find a doctor to administer a sedative," the security guard instructed the nurse. "Once he's out, we can get him back into the bed and secure him to the rail."

Seconds later, the nurse rushed back into the room with a doctor right behind her.

Hannah deemed the threat to her to be minimal at that point. She placed her Glock back into her purse and edged into the corner, out of the way.

A moment later, Sheriff Ward loomed in the doorway. "What's going on?"

"The patient made an attempt to attack Ms. Mason," the nurse said. "One minute, he was in a coma, and the next, he ripped out everything and lunged for her."

Noah glanced at Hannah, then back at the scene unfolding in front of him. "If you can't get him sedated, use the damned taser, Toad."

"Don't have one on my belt," his deputy said.

Noah swore under his breath.

"We'll manage," the doctor said. "Just hold him still so I can get the needle in."

"Will that work instantly?" Noah asked.

"Damned straight," the doctor said. He jabbed the needle into the patient's upper arm and depressed the plunger.

Twombly went limp almost immediately.

Chapter 20

Hannah inched her way over to the door.

Noah stepped aside so she could exit the room, then turned to follow her.

"What happened?" he asked.

"I'm still trying to figure that out," she said, working hard not to scream at him, or to scream, period.

"Explain."

She scowled up at him, no longer sure that she could trust him. In retrospect, cops telling lies was nothing new to her, based on her experience over the past two years. Still, it was no longer something she intended to tolerate or be ignorant of, now or in the future. "It's Detective Twombly."

"What?"

Frustrated, she felt like smacking him. "You heard me! You told me he was dead."

Noah swung around to stare at the man being lifted back into the bed. It was all the security guard, Toad, the doctor, and two nurses could do to get his now-inert form back up on the mattress.

Hannah studied him while he watched them. She could almost hear the wheels turning and clacking in his head.

Finally, he faced her. "Back up a minute. Are you saying *that's* Twombly?"

"Did I stutter?" she shot back, angry, frustrated, and admit it, afraid.

"Are you sure?"

"Positive."

"What the hell is going on?"

"You're the big, bad cop in the room," Hannah said, unable to keep the accusation from her tone. "You tell me."

"If you're right, this changes everything."

"No shit, Sherlock." When it hit her what else he'd said, she added, "And, of course, I'm right. I'd know that jackass anywhere."

It was Noah's turn to scowl.

Uncowed, she went on. "This is why I have no faith in law enforcement. You can't even identify a dead body properly."

"It wasn't Pike County that made the identification."

"But it was Pike County that relayed the information to me."

"Give me a break, Hannah. You can't blame PCSO for relying on information from Larimer County."

She remained stubbornly silent.

"We'd be in a world of hurt if we couldn't depend on other agencies for information."

"It doesn't matter. That's Detective Twombly in there and that means someone else was in the vehicle that crashed."

"Are you absolutely certain it's him, Hannah? You're not transferring your dislike of Twombly to this prowler, out of some misguided sense of justice, are you?"

"Oh, for God's sake, Noah! Do I look like some loony who might do that?"

This time, he remained silent, which infuriated her.

"Look, I'm not, all right? Forget you even had the thought and chew on this one. Did the three of them kill another innocent person?"

Noah's jaw began to flex and he stormed back into the room. "How long before he's awake again?"

"Three, maybe four hours," the doctor said. "Would you mind explaining what's going on here?"

Hannah stood in the doorway, anxious to hear the sheriff's reply.

Noah had no intention of telling the doctor everything, and especially, he didn't want the entire hospital staff knowing they most likely had a murderer for a patient. "This man was prowling around a house last night and tried to make entry. The resident called to report it, we apprehended him, and on the way to lockup, he ingested something, which we presumed was meant to end his life." Noah glanced at the lump in the bed. "Either, it didn't work, or we were mistaken."

The doctor frowned. "He wasn't trying to commit suicide."

"How can you be sure?"

"The lab work came back. This patient took Dramamine and Benadryl. Separately, and in the proper dosage, they're harmless, but taken together and in larger-than-prescribed dosages, they can cause drowsiness. The end result would be like mixing alcohol with narcotics, which could present as a poisoning."

"Does that explain him slipping in to a coma?"

"It could. Though it seems counterintuitive, sleepiness can lead to over-sleeping, which can, in turn, lead to coma. My professional opinion is that he took the Dramamine because he has a motion-sickness problem, which is not surprising on the serpentine mountain roads we have around here. He may have taken the Benadryl at some point because of an allergic reaction he was experiencing. Most people don't read the contraindications on over-the-counter medications. It's probable he didn't know that those two particular OTC drugs can react in a negative way when taken together." The doctor glanced at the patient. "When he wakes up, we'll ask him."

That clarification put a different spin on things. Noah gave him a curt nod and said, "Thanks for the explanation."

"Not a problem. Do we need to keep security on this man?"

"I'm going to have my deputy here, so probably not. How soon before you deem this patient will be ready to leave the hospital?"

"I'd like to at least keep him overnight."

"Can we have him first thing in the morning?"

"I come in at eight, but he's not the only patient in the ICU.

Give me until at least nine. I should have my examination of him complete by then."

Noah didn't like it, but what choice did he have? "All right." He turned to his deputy. "Toad, if you have to leave to use the head, call security to come up and spell you."

"Will do, boss."

"I'll have someone bring you meals and Barbie will relieve you at eleven. Think you can make it until then?"

"Hell, yeah, Noah."

"Good." His gaze went back to Twombly, sleeping like a goddamned baby in the hospital bed. On Hannah's behalf, he had the urge to pummel him. On the public's behalf, he'd better damned well find out who, exactly, had died in the car Twombly had rented.

What an effing fiasco.

Noah turned away, expecting to find Hannah hovering in the doorway. She wasn't. He stepped into the hall. No sign of her there, either. He asked the nurse at the counter, "Did Ms. Mason say where she was going?"

"No. In fact, I didn't even notice her leave."

Great, like he had time to track her down. "Thanks." He stuck his head back in the hospital room. "Toad?"

His deputy lumbered out of the room.

"I know it's going to be boring as hell sitting in the hallway, but this guy is the one who gave Hannah such a hard time after her husband and son supposedly died."

"That detective prick from San Diego?"

Noah nodded.

"I thought he got killed in a car crash up near Estes."

"We all thought that. Look, if Hannah comes back, call me ASAP and keep her here, even if you have to sit on her."

Toad gave him a look that could only be called incredulous, and went back to the original topic. "Who reported the dead guy was Twombly, Larimer County or CSP?"

"Larimer County conducted the crash investigation, but CSP also responded. I'll contact LCSO first. Maybe we'll get lucky and someone will actually know something."

"Can your brother help out?"

"I don't know, but I plan to ask him."

Five minutes later, he was in his truck and headed back to PCSO. He wasn't exactly thrilled to find his father waiting there for him, but on the other hand, two heads were better than one and he could use a clear thinker chiming in. "'Morning, Dad."

"'Morning, Noah. Got time for me?"

"Sure." He glanced at Marty. "Hold any calls unrelated to last night's event." He looked back at his father. "Want a cup of coffee?"

"Sure."

Marty said, "I'll bring in two."

Noah could tell she was brimming with questions. Too bad. Even though she was volunteering to be the coffee girl, which was a first for her, he wasn't in the mood to give her any particulars. He had a bad taste in his mouth about how the case was going, and talking it over with his dad was about all he could stomach at the moment.

Within minutes, both of them were in Noah's office, with the door closed, enjoying coffee so good, it shouldn't have been allowed in a police station.

"Did we scare Hannah off last night?" Pete asked.

"No, in fact, she was concerned she might have scared you and Mom off."

Pete snorted. "Not likely."

"She isn't much into trust right now. She only gave you part of her story."

"I figured as much, and Mom thought…well, never mind what Mom thought. How's Hannah doing today, or have your spoken with her yet?"

Noah took the opportunity to give his dad the lowdown on the prowler who should have been a dead guy.

"He took a page from her husband's playbook." Pete leaned forward with his elbows on his knees. "We should call Simon and see if he can get to the bottom of who was actually in that vehicle."

"That's what I'm thinking. Technically, this is a kidnapping case, and the CBI should probably be involved, anyway." Noah hit speaker on his landline phone and speed-dialed his brother at Colorado Bureau of Investigation. He recapped Hannah's story, the reappearance of her husband and son, and the incident with the prowler.

"Geez, Noah, why'd you wait so long to contact me?" Simon asked.

Before he could answer, his dad intervened. "Noah and I have been checking out a few things first."

"Hi, Dad," Simon said. "I should've known you'd be knee deep in alligators on this."

Pete grinned. "Gotta keep my brain active somehow."

Noah could picture his brother shaking his head, torn between amusement and dismay.

"You should try online Scrabble," Simon responded, his tone a bit sardonic. "How do you spell Twombly's name?"

Noah gave it to him, letter-by-letter. "His first name is Richard and he went by Rick, but by all accounts, he should have gone by Dick."

"Good one, bro" Simon said with a chuckle. "And the woman, Hannah? Her full name and any AKAs."

Noah looked down at his notes. "Pre-marriage surname, Hamilton. Married name, Clarke, with an *e* at the end. Name now, Mason. She took her mother's maiden name in a legal name change. She also illustrates books and does that as H.L. Mason. The *L* doesn't stand for anything."

"H.L. Mason?" Pete asked. "Is that the same artist who did the antler-animal book you gave me?"

Noah nodded. "One and the same."

"Good God, the woman's got talent aplenty."

"The husband's name?" Simon asked, staying on task.

"Jason James and the boy's name is Jason James, Junior, but they call him Jay. We believe he's abandoned the last name of Clarke and taken his mother's maiden name, which is Hendrickson." He spelled that out for his brother, as well.

"Both spouses assumed their mother's maiden name?" Simon asked.

"That's not as unusual as it seems," Pete chimed in. "We saw it a lot at the FBI."

"If you say so," Simon said with obvious skepticism. "Give me thirty minutes to pull what I can on this and I'll get back to you."

"We'll go grab some lunch and be back here at one…that is, unless you're taking a lunch break, too."

"Are you kidding? I've been on the job for two weeks doing nothing but wishing I had a Fidget Spinner to occupy my time. This is an honest-to-God case with some meat to it. I'm a fly and this is going to be my red meat."

Noah and his dad, both of whom who knew what it was like when the law enforcement bug bit you, exchanged a knowing glance.

"Take an hour," Simon said. "I'm going to contact San Diego PD, too, and see what's shaking at that end."

After Noah disconnected, Pete asked, "How's Hannah doing after the episode at the hospital this morning?"

"She gave me what-for before she took off. I haven't talked to her since."

"Maybe you should."

"I will, later. I want to see what Simon digs up first."

"Maybe I should call Mom and have her make a welcome-to-the-neighborhood visit."

"Hannah will see right through that."

"Maybe so, but she needs all the friends and support she can get right now, don't you think?"

Noah considered that while his dad pulled out his phone. Of course, his father was right. Hannah had absolutely no one in Fossil she could turn to, including him. Being law enforcement, his badge came first.

Once his father hung up, he asked, "Well?"

"Mom's going to call her right now and see if she'd like some company. If Hannah says yes, she'll go get Fiona, too."

"Hannah probably doesn't want that much company."

"I think you're underestimating her, son. Hannah's a strong woman. She'd have to be to survive what she's endured for the past two years."

"I hope you're right, because the past few days would be enough to make most people run screaming into the street."

"Did you forget she has a little boy she wants back more than anything else in the world?"

That put the skids to Noah's train of thought about screamers and streets. "For a minute, I did. I guess this dead-not-dead Twombly thing pushed it out of my mind temporarily."

"Just a word of advice, Noah. Keep Jay in the forefront of your thoughts. Having him there will help you make good, sound decisions about what comes next."

"I hope so," Noah said fervently. "I've never dealt with a missing kid before."

Pete stood and pulled on his jacket. "I daresay, you've never fallen for a victim before, either."

"Shit! Is it that obvious?"

"Only to me, because, as you know, I did the same damned thing."

"You and Mom turned out okay."

"Yeah, and I'm not saying that whatever's between you and Hannah won't, but a favorable resolution could help ensure it."

"I don't want her to want me because she's grateful."

"Trust me, son. I saw the way she looked at you last night. She may still be a married woman in the eyes of the law, but in her heart, she knows which way this cookie is going to crumble."

"I hope to God you're right."

Hannah arrived home, determined not to answer either the phone or her doorbell. She had some thinking to do, and she wanted to do it alone.

Twombly. In the hospital. How could that be, when he'd been declared dead?

No matter how many times she asked herself that question, she came up with no answer and instead, circled back to the question she'd asked the sheriff. Who was in the crashed car in the Big Thompson Canyon, and had Twombly put him there?

The only plausible answer seemed to be that Twombly *had* put someone else in his vehicle in hopes of perpetrating a disappearing act, just as Jason had done. Had the detective killed the poor man before he put him in the vehicle, or had the guy died in the crash? What difference did it make? Either way, murder was murder.

Apparently, what it all boiled down to was that Jason, Sabine, and Twombly were killing machines.

Twombly knew she was in Colorado. He had her address in his phone to prove it. Had he already told Jason where she was? Or had he kept it to himself while he did a favor for his old friend, saving the juicy details of her demise for after he'd killed her?

Impatient with the progress Noah Ward and his deputies were making, Hannah stormed around and around the island in her kitchen, wondering what she personally could do to expedite things.

The only idea she could come up with was to take a drive to Estes Park and have a talk with local law enforcement there. Maybe even visit the county medical examiner. How had they determined the deceased's identity? Had they taken fingerprints? DNA? Used a photo ID? What?

Would law enforcement in that jurisdiction even talk to her, a civilian whose only tie to the death of the misidentified Twombly being that he had tried to kill her and promised he'd still get the job done?

She picked up the phone and dialed Noah. Marty answered and informed her he'd gone to lunch with his dad. Did she want to leave a message? "No, thanks, I'll call back."

Frustrated, she disconnected and kicked the island. Fortunately, she had on her snow boots, minimizing the resulting pain.

She hadn't even realized until then that she'd neglected to take off her boots when she came in the house.

Not only was stress an ugly companion, but she suddenly realized she couldn't face living the rest of her life in snowy Colorado worrying about the stupid wood floors.

Noah and his dad took fifty-five minutes for lunch, then walked back to the sheriff's office.

Marty handed him a short stack of three messages.

"Anything urgent?" he asked, hoping not to have to return any calls.

"Depends on how you define urgent."

Noah gave her a look, which she apparently didn't need defined verbally.

"Toad called from the hospital. Despite the doctor saying that the prowler would be out for several hours, he came out of the sedative after ninety minutes and smacked a nurse with his free hand while she was recording his vitals. Toad called Flip to bring over another pair of handcuffs to restrain his other arm and the nurse had to have stitches in her left eyebrow." She tilted her head at the sheriff. "It makes it hard for me to run this office when I get the goings-on second-hand."

"Who else called?" Noah asked, ignoring the mini-lecture, which he recognized as nothing but a disguised inquiry for information.

"Herb over at Locke Lumber says your water heater came in early."

"Thank God," he muttered.

"I'll help you install it," Pete said. "We'll get 'er done in a jiffy."

"Thanks, Dad. Anyone else?"

"Hannah Mason."

"Her message?" Noah asked, impatient.

"She didn't leave one. Said she'd call back."

What the hell? "I'm going to be on a call with CBI. No interruptions, unless someone is in danger."

"Got it." Marty went back to her keyboard. She made a big production of typing out the word DANGER and muttering the word repeatedly until he was out of earshot.

Not for the first time, Noah considered firing her for insubordination, but she did such a damned fine job of keeping PCSO running, how could he?

"I wonder what Hannah wanted," Pete said once they were back in Noah's office with the door closed.

"God only knows, but I'm sure I won't like whatever it is."

The phone on his desk rang and Simon's number popped up on the readout. Noah hit the speaker button. "What did you find?"

"Get ready for a rollercoaster ride," Simon said, unable to contain his excitement.

Chapter 21

Hannah's phone rang. After the fourth burble, she decided to answer it, even though she didn't recognize the number. "Hello?"

"Hi, Hannah, it's Liza."

"Oh, hi. I meant to call and thank you again for a lovely dinner last night."

"We were pleased to have you. I hope we didn't intimidate you with our interest in your case."

"Not at all."

"I was wondering, if you're not busy…could I come over for a chat?"

"I…."

"Look, I'll be honest with you. Pete called a while ago and told me about the prowler and what happened at the hospital. I just thought you might like a sounding board."

"It would be nice to have a regular person to vent to."

Liza laughed. "I know, right? These law enforcement types get all excited about solving the crime and forget the victims are human beings."

"I don't actually feel forgotten, but I do have a lot of questions and no damned answers, and I think Bowie is starting to question my sanity for discussing it with him."

Liza chuckled. "I know it's past noon, but have you had

lunch yet? I made a pot of chicken tortilla soup for me and Pete, but he's eating with Noah, so I'd love to have someone to share it with."

"That sounds lovely, Liza, but I don't feel like going out right now." Realizing that might have sounded rude, she added, "Sorry to be such a poop."

"You're not. I should have said up front that I'd like to come to your place. I thought I'd pick up Fiona so she and Bowie can romp in the snow together."

Hannah had no desire to force herself to be creative at her drawing board, and she did feel lonely and a little isolated. "I'd love to have you both. Thank you for offering."

"Sweetie, it's my pleasure. See you in about fifteen minutes, okay?"

"That's sounds fine." She disconnected and said to Bowie, "Your sister is coming for a play date. What do you think about that?"

Bowie danced in a circle, his excitement obvious. How on earth could he understand everything she said to him?

The pup trailed her around the kitchen as she gathered bowls and silverware to set the table. "You're going to trip me," she said. "Go to the fireplace."

He plopped down on his doggie butt and smiled up at her.

"Fireplace."

He nuzzled her calf, then took off for the family room.

Hannah laid placemats on the table and grabbed two napkins. With the table set, she put on a fresh pot of coffee, as well as the tea kettle. She'd been in the mood for cornbread muffins that morning, laden with corn, and drenched in oodles of butter while they were still warm, but hadn't done anything about it. She quickly mixed up a batch and slid them into the oven.

Five minutes later, the doorbell rang. Bowie beat her there, but of course he did. His playmate had arrived.

Hannah put her hand on the doorknob. "Bowie, sit." She had to tell him twice before he complied. She pulled the door open and greeted Liza.

"I'm going to stand right here so the two of them can say hello without tripping me," Noah's mother said.

"Smart move," Hannah acknowledged with a wry grin. She gave the canines a few moments, then said, "Bowie, sit." This time, he minded immediately. "Trying to show off for your sister, huh?"

He grinned up at her.

"This dog is a genius," she said to Liza.

"I hope his manners rub off on Fiona. I'm afraid she's a wild child."

"Maybe I can give her a lesson today."

"I wish you would. Noah is hopeless with training." She stepped inside and Hannah closed the door.

"God, that soup smells heavenly. I'll keep them both here if you want to go on to the kitchen. It's straight ahead."

"Good idea, but I should take off my boots first."

Hannah reached for the pot so Liza could do that. "You can use the towel there on the floor for Fiona's paws." As soon as the words were out, Hannah remembered she had decided to ease up on her wet-floor rules. Instead, she made a mental note to pick Liza's brain about the care and feeding of wood floors in snowy climates, and said, "You know what? Don't worry about your boots or Fiona's paws."

"Are you sure? I don't mind."

"I'm positive." Hannah handed the pot back to Liza, who headed for the kitchen. "Bowie, sit."

He looked up at her, his eyebrows dancing.

"Fiona, sit."

His sister resisted by prancing.

"Fiona, sit." Hannah pressed gently against the retriever's back end, forcing her to sit. It was just as simple as that. Fiona had the same doggie DNA as Bowie. She had to be smart like he was, right? "Good girl," she said, petting the dog's head, then scratching between her ears.

"Ohmygod, you've done it already," Liza said, coming back from the kitchen.

Fiona and Bowie sat side-by-side, both smiling.

"I had to help her along a little. Does she know any commands at all?"

"I know Noah has endeavored to teach her sit, stay, come, and fetch. She's heard them all, she just doesn't obey when he gives the commands."

Hannah looked down at the dogs. "Bowie, stay. Fiona, stay." She backed away, then turned and moved toward the kitchen. At the doorway, she said, "Bowie, come. Fiona, come."

Both dogs reared up and ran toward her, bypassed her, and went directly to Bowie's favorite place in front of the fire. There, they began to play tug-of-war with an old sock Hannah had knotted.

"Will wonders never cease?" Liza asked. "You may actually be a dog whisperer."

"I doubt it. I think they're both just super smart."

"Don't sell yourself short, Hannah. You've obviously got a gift." Liza sniffed the air. "What's baking?"

"I was hungry for cornbread muffins, so I thought I'd go ahead and make them to go with the soup."

"You're a girl after my own heart. I love cornbread muffins!"

"Should we put the heat on under the pot while we wait?"

"Sure."

Ten minutes later, they sat down to lunch.

"So, do you feel like talking about what happened last night and this morning, or will it give you indigestion?" Liza asked.

"I'm beyond indigestion on this," Hannah said. She described her inability to sleep and how she'd happened to notice someone creeping around outside. "I hurried around to make sure I hadn't left any doors unlocked, and I knew the windows were okay, but I couldn't fathom why anyone would want to break in."

"I'm glad you reported it and that Noah was able to apprehend the prowler. What prompted you to go to the hospital this morning?"

"Noah had taken a picture of the guy with his phone, and he looked vaguely familiar, but I couldn't place him, so I asked if could take a peek at him, since he was in a coma." Hannah couldn't control the shudder that wracked her body. "I was shocked when I realized who it was, and then he just happened to come out of his coma at that exact moment and when he realized who I was...."

"Pete said he tried to attack you."

"It took a security guard and Toad to take him down so the doctor could sedate him."

"Why didn't Toad just Taser him?"

"He didn't have it with him."

"Oh, my. Noah couldn't have been happy about that. He worked hard to get those Tasers approved for use at PCSO."

"He seemed a little upset about it, but not angry. I think he was flummoxed when I told him the man in the bed was Detective Twombly, so that might have made him forget about Toad not having his Taser on his belt."

"Who wouldn't be? I mean, really, he'd already been declared dead in the car crash, so who would expect him to show up here?"

Hannah reiterated the questions that had been burning holes in her brain, finishing up with two critical issues. "If Jason knows where I am, will he come after me next? Or will he abscond again with Jay for parts unknown?"

"No wonder you're in a tizzy."

"My mind won't shut down."

"It's all right, Hannah. You wouldn't be normal if you took all this in stride."

"I think I need to go to Estes Park and talk to the crash-scene investigator."

Liza frowned. "Don't you think you should leave that to Noah?"

"Noah is the one who told me Twombly is dead."

Seemingly unfazed by the accusatory tone of Hannah's voice, Noah's mother said, "He was only repeating what he'd been told by the investigating agency. You can't hold him responsible for Twombly being alive."

Hannah sighed and dipped her spoon into her soup. "Rationally, I know that. Irrationally, I'm angry at everyone in law enforcement for the treatment I got from Twombly, especially since he knew damned good and well that Jason and Jay were still alive."

"This is a tough situation, sweetie, but I know my son, and he'll do everything humanly possible to make sure you get

Jay back."

Hannah stared into her soup, tears burning her eyes. When she finally looked up, she said, "It's hard to trust when you've been screwed over like I was."

"I can only imagine," Liza said, her tone compassionate. "No mother should ever have to endure what you've gone through. For that matter, no wife should ever have to deal with a husband like Jason, either."

"Even though I think I know why Jason took Jay, it still baffles me. It wasn't like he ever spent any time with him, or read him a bedtime story, or played Legos with him. Jason was always all about Jason. He like *saying* he had a son."

"Why do you think he took him then? He could still say he had a son, if he wanted to brag about it."

"Saying it and actually having physical custody are two different things. Sabine hates kids. Jason knew she'd never give him a child."

"Good lord."

"I know. Sickening, right? You should want a child because you love him, not because you want to say you have one." She stared into her soup bowl. "We should eat before the food gets entirely cold."

Her tone sympathetic, Liza said, "Definitely."

"The soup is delicious."

"As are the muffins. I love them with corn added like this and lots of butter."

"Me, too."

"Back to the issue at hand for just a moment."

Hannah met Liza's gaze without flinching. Intuitively, she knew what was coming.

"Promise me you won't go tearing off to Estes by yourself."

"I can't, Liza."

"That's what I was afraid of." She dunked her spoon into her bowl and came out with a nice chunk of chicken. "What about me going along for the ride?"

Shocked, Hannah stared at her with wide eyes. "Noah and Pete probably wouldn't like that."

"I have the perfect cover story."

Suspicion warred with hope. "What might that be?"

"My daughter, Juliette, owns a little Christmas shop in Estes."

"I read about that on the PCSO website, on the page about Noah."

Liza smiled. "We could take a day trip and say we're going shopping at the best Christmas store in Colorado."

"I don't want you to get into trouble over my problems."

"Hannah, sweetie, I'm a big girl. I'm not worried about getting into trouble over this."

"When can we go?"

"Tomorrow, if you like."

"Can we make it the day after? I want to observe Noah interrogating that piece of crap Twombly when the doctor releases him in the morning."

"Noah's allowing that?"

"I haven't asked him yet."

Liza shook her head. "You are either a glutton for punishment, or one of the bravest women I've ever met."

"There's a third possibility," Hannah said. "I could also be the dumbest person you've ever met."

"Not likely, but how do you plan to handle approaching him?"

"I decided to show up unannounced and hope he'll agree."

"I have a feeling he will." Liza grinned. "For a girl, you've got balls, Hannah."

Hannah grinned back. "Fingers crossed."

"I'm with you, one hundred percent."

"Thank you, Liza. That means a lot to me."

After they cleaned up the lunch dishes, Hannah decided to let the dogs out into the back yard. "Here's hoping they don't run away."

"I don't think they will," Liza said, though she had a slight frown on her face. "We can watch from here and call them back if they do."

"True." Hannah pulled over two barstools to the patio door. "Might as well be comfortable while the kids are playing."

Liza laughed. "Jay must have had an amazing time with you."

"I hope so. I know I had an amazing time with him."

"Tell me," Liza said.

And so Hannah did. She talked about their favorite park and the zoo and the neighborhood wading pool. She went further down memory lane and talked about Jay's passion for frozen yogurt and Dairy Queen ice cream cones with the "curly" on top. She talked about how he didn't want to eat anything but noodles, the crazier the pasta shape, the better. And his love of story books, and how he could spell and write his name at age four, and how he'd sit with her at her worktable and draw while she created her illustrations. "I started a dinosaur book that I planned to dedicate to him. He loved dinosaurs."

"He *loves* dinosaurs. Now you can give him his own personal copy and still dedicate it to him," Liza said. "He sounds like an amazing child."

"He was." Emotion choked Hannah. "I hope he still is. I can't bear to think about what they've done to him and how he might have changed as a result." She pulled her gaze from the two dogs charging up the hillside and looked at Liza. "The only thing that gives me hope is the wave."

"What wave?"

"My brother-in-law said Jay saw him and gave his little half-wave." She illustrated by raising her hand. "That must mean he still remembers his old life, right?"

"I'd say so." Liza reached over and grasped her hand. "Keep the faith, sweetie. That's all you can do."

"I'm trying, but I'm so damned scared. From all indications, my son is living with murderers. What kind of loving environment can they possibly be providing for my little boy?"

"Do you pray, Hannah?"

"I lost my way for a while, but when I learned Jay was still alive" —she shrugged— "now I pray all the time."

"Do you believe everyone has a guardian angel?"

Hannah thought about that for a moment. "I don't know. Jason wasn't big on church and gave me such a hard time when I went to mass, I finally gave it up."

"He couldn't stop you from praying, though, could he?"

"No."

"Here's what I want you to do. Pray to Jay's guardian angel to protect him and to help him get through all this, and then pray to your own guardian angel to help you find your answers. If the need should arise, you can even utter a simple request, 'Guardian angel, please, help me.'"

Hannah stared at her. "You really think that will do any good?"

"I do, and besides, what could it hurt?"

"When you put it that way, nothing." One tear and then another slid down Hannah's cheeks.

"Oh, sweetie," Liza said, climbing off her barstool. She slipped her arms around Hannah and hugged her tight. "You're made of stern stuff, Hannah. I know you are, otherwise you wouldn't be here today, plotting about how to get your son back."

Hannah hugged her back. It felt so darned good to have some human contact from someone who genuinely cared about her. "I hope you're right."

"There's one other thing you should know."

"What's that?"

"Aside from Pete giving Noah some help on this, my son Simon is also pitching in now."

"He's the one who recently went to work for the Colorado Bureau of Investigation?"

"Yes. I guess Noah told you about him."

"We were talking about siblings."

"You have a sister."

"And a brother. They've both been supportive, but all this has been hard on them, too."

"I can only imagine." She scooted back up on the barstool, biting her lip. "I don't know if it will make you feel any better, Hannah, but with three Ward men on this case, it's bound to have a good outcome."

"I'll try to keep that in mind," Hannah said, her tone somewhat wry, but secretly, she despaired of trusting anyone connected to law enforcement, or of ever having any resolution at all.

Chapter 22

Noah stopped by his folks' place on the way home. He wanted a first-hand account of his mother's afternoon with Hannah.

"She's hurting," his mother said.

"Obviously. Is that all you got from her?"

"No, we talked about what happened last night and this morning. She's scared, too."

"I won't let anything happen to her."

"How's she supposed to know that?" his mother shot back. "She got screwed over by this Twombly jerk and she's gun-shy of cops now. Who could blame her?"

"What do you suggest I say to her that will change her mind?"

"It's not what you can say, honey, it's your actions that will speak louder than any words you might have."

Noah blew out an frustrated breath. "You got any beer?"

"Sure," Pete said. "I think I'll join you." He looked at his wife. "Want one?"

"No, but I'll have a red wine."

In the kitchen, Noah grabbed two Sierra Nevadas while his dad poured a Chianti for his mom.

At the table, Liza said, "Tell me what happened after Simon got back to you."

"Larimer County Sheriff's Office and Colorado State Patrol got their knickers in a knot when Simon told them they had the wrong ID on their dead guy," Pete said.

Noah added, "All it took was a look in the file and they discovered that the fingerprints didn't belong to Twombly."

"Whose are they, then?"

"A businessman out of Denver by the name of Bert Hague. He'd been reported missing several days earlier by his wife."

Liza uttered a sound of distress. "The three of them needed a patsy and just selected some poor guy off the street?"

"Apparently so."

"What happens now?" she asked.

"It's gone from a single-car crash incident to a murder investigation. No one had bothered to read the medical examiner's report yet, either. Hague had a bullet in his head, execution style, but no one took notice of that except the ME because the poor guy's head was completely bashed in."

"That will answer one of Hannah's questions."

Noah gave his mother a sharp look. "What other questions does she have?"

"Why don't you talk to her and find out?"

"Mom."

"Noah."

He picked up his bottle and took a long swallow, wondering why he was so resistant all of a sudden to going nose-to-nose with the woman he wanted to spend the rest of his life with.

"What else did Simon have to say?" she asked.

"Twombly was under investigation by Internal Affairs. Seems that he was spending a lot of time haranguing Hannah, but no time putting corresponding notes in the case file. She may not know this, but the call she made to the captain who was his supervisor bore fruit. They were ready to terminate him. He may have gotten wind of it and that's why he up and quit with same-day notice."

Pete added, "Simon's requested the autopsy report on Sabine's husband. He should have that tomorrow."

"I understand Twombly is being released from the hospital tomorrow," Lisa said.

"He is, and as soon as I have him in custody, I'm going to

interrogate the shit out of him."

"I hope he'll talk," Pete said. "I don't like the way things seem to be escalating all of a sudden."

"I'm with you on that," Noah said.

"Are you going by Hannah's this evening?" his mother asked.

"I thought about it, but she was so pissed earlier, I decided to let the waters settle before I talk to her again."

"I'm not sure that's the right approach," Liza said.

Pete nodded. "I agree with Mom on that, son."

"Right or wrong, my decision is made."

His parents exchanged a worried glance.

"What?" Noah demanded.

"You should never let the sun set on your differences," his father said.

"Exactly," his mother agreed.

"That's okay for the two of you," Noah said, "but in case you hadn't noticed, Hannah and I aren't married. In fact, we aren't even a couple." He blew out a frustrated breath. "We're not even *close* to being a couple."

"Noah—," his mother began, but he cut her off.

"Forget it, Mom. I know what I'm doing."

"I hope so, but just in case, maybe you'd better pray to your guardian angel for guidance."

"Please, don't tell me you and Hannah talked about angels."

"Why not? She's Catholic. It's not like she's never heard of angels before."

Noah rolled his eyes. "Don't get your hopes up because she also happens to be Catholic," he said, knowing it was already too late for that particular warning.

His mom glanced once more at his dad, then back at him. "It's your funeral," she said, her tone as droll as he'd ever heard it.

"I'd better get home and get the damned water heater installed."

"You sure you don't want my help?" Pete asked.

Noah had been tempted to accept his dad's offer earlier, but now, he didn't want any more lectures about what he should or shouldn't do concerning Hannah. "Thanks, Dad. I can manage it."

"Call if you get in a bind."

"I will." He polished off his beer and pushed away from the table. Any other questions he had about how his mom had spent her afternoon with Hannah went on the back burner. The two of them had engaged in girl talk and girl talk didn't get repeated. He wasn't dense. He got it.

That said, he didn't have to like it.

At eight forty-five a.m., Hannah left her house. Her nerves were shot and she'd barely slept a wink, worrying about whether or not Noah would let her observe the interrogation, and beyond that, if Twombly would give up anything of value regarding Jason's whereabouts.

The other thing she worried about was Bowie. She'd never left him alone in the house for any length of time. He wasn't a chewer and he'd never destroyed anything, but today would be the test. He was either a good dog, or a bad dog disguised as a good dog.

She'd filled his food and water dishes and left several dog-gie treats at his favorite lolling places.

One thing she knew for sure, as soon as the snow melted, she was having an Invisible Fence installed. Bowie needed to be able to go outside and romp and relieve himself without her having to watch him. He couldn't be trapped indoors all day, either, which was why she was also considering a heated dog house, for times when the weather was bad and she was gone.

Liza had offered Pete as a dog-sitter when they went off to Estes Park, and with no other options, Hannah planned to accept the offer, but that couldn't be the fall-back plan any time she needed to be away from home for the day.

Because her truck was probably the only Inferno-colored Tacoma in town, she didn't bother to park somewhere that Noah wouldn't notice. He was the sheriff, for crying out loud. He noticed everything.

At nine o'clock, she entered PCSO. Marty sat behind the

counter, talking on the phone. Flip and Derek were chatting with Shari over near the photocopier. Marty smiled and gave her a wave.

Behind her, the door opened. She knew without looking that Noah had come in with his prisoner. She didn't look around and thanked her lucky stars that she was bundled up. She moved quickly, diverting her attention to the bulletin board to study the wanted posters and community notices.

Neither Noah nor Twombly appeared to notice her.

"Get him into the lockup," Noah said to Toad. "I'll be there in a minute."

Twombly snarled. "You're about done for, girlie."

So much for not being noticed.

"Shut up!" Toad said.

Twombly made a move and the deputy tripped him, sending him crashing to the floor. Derek and Flip were at his side in an instant, helping restrain the prisoner.

"In my office," Noah said to Hannah.

She held her head high and stood her ground.

"Now," he barked, but didn't wait for her to follow.

Since she didn't want to beg in front of his staff, she went through the gate and into his office, where he slammed the door behind her as soon as she entered.

"What the hell are you doing here?"

"I'd like your permission to observe the interrogation."

"No way."

"Not in the room with him. Don't you have a one-way glass, like they do—"

"If you say 'in the movies,' I'm going to toss you out on the street."

"I was going to say, like they do at San Diego PD."

His expression altered subtly. "Why do you want to observe?"

"That man was in my face almost every day for two years. I think I know him better than anyone here. I might be able to help you catch him in a lie."

Noah worked his jaw while he thought.

"It's not against procedure, is it?"

"Not that I know of, but I've never allowed it before."

"He won't know I'm there."

"He already knows you're here."

"I meant, he won't know I'm watching."

"No, but I will."

"Will that constrain you?"

"Hell no."

"Are you worried I'll hear something I can't handle?"

"Yes…no…maybe. Shit, I don't know!"

"I think you have to admit I've already handled the worst of the worst."

"I'll grant you that."

"Please, Noah."

He really seemed to be agonizing over her request, and that puzzled her. If she hadn't needed to be in that observation room so badly, she would have taken pity on him, given up, and walked away.

"All right, but I swear to God, if I hear you scream or wail or otherwise create a disturbance, I'll make you sorry."

"I'm sure you will." He stormed over and opened the door. "Follow me."

Hannah thought he was taking her to the observation room, but instead, he went straight to Marty. He turned to Hannah. "Go grab a cup of coffee. Come back in exactly thirty minutes. That will give us time to get him booked."

She had no idea what was involved in booking a prisoner, but she didn't argue.

He turned to Marty. "When Ms. Mason returns, escort her to the obs room and nowhere else, understood?"

"Got it, boss."

He skewered Hannah with another scowl and pointed a finger at her. "Remember, no funny business."

Hannah couldn't resist. She clicked her heels together and saluted him. "Aye, aye, Sheriff."

Behind him, Marty clasped a hand over her mouth to keep from laughing.

Noah narrowed his eyes on her. "I mean it, Hannah. This isn't some kind of game for your amusement."

"Believe me, Sheriff, I've never been less amused in my life."

Instead of going for coffee, which would make her even more jittery, Hannah walked up one side of the street and down the other, ostensibly window shopping. In reality, she would've been hard pressed to name a single item she'd seen in any window.

At one minute short of half an hour, she stood outside the sheriff's office, counting down the last sixty seconds.

Marty pulled the door open from the other side. "For heaven's sake, come on in. It's freezing out there."

Hannah glanced at her watch. Twenty seconds to go.

"It's okay. He's in his office with the door closed and the prisoner is sweating it out in the interrogation room. Neither one of them will see you when you go into the obs room."

That decided Hannah. She really was practically frozen. As soon as she left PCSO, she was going out to buy something warmer to wear *under* her new heavy coat, warmer gloves, and a hat that actually kept her head warm. She might even buy some long johns.

"Can I get you a coffee?" Marty asked. "I noticed you didn't go over to the diner."

"You wouldn't happen to have any orange spice tea, would you?"

"As a matter of fact, I do. Sugar?"

"Yes, please. One teaspoon."

"C'mon." Marty led her to a room with no window in the door.

Through the one-way mirror, Hannah had a perfect view of Twombly, who practically had steam pouring from his nose, which she imagined should have looked like a pig snout to fit his vile character.

"Be right back." Marty left and closed the door behind her.

Hannah hung her coat over the back of the single stool in the room and peeled off her gloves and knit cap, shoving them into her purse, which she dropped in the corner.

A moment later, the door opened again. The deputy who had identified himself as Kenny Tigard stepped in. "Good to see you again, Hannah."

"You, too. Are you the assigned babysitter?"

He laughed. "No, ma'am. We always have someone in the obs room when an interrogation is underway."

In the other room, the door opened and Sheriff Ward and Derek Parker entered. Deputy Tigard leaned forward and flipped the switch on the wall.

Horrible guttural sounds played through the sound system. Twombly was on a roll.

The obs room door opened again and Marty handed over a paper cup with a lid. "Give a holler if you want a refill."

Hannah smiled. "Thank you."

"You want a stool, Kenny?"

"That would be great, Marty. Thanks."

A few moments later, Marty returned with the stool, then left, closing the door quietly behind her.

Noah activated the tape recorder. "Sheriff Noah Ward," he said into the microphone. "November twenty-ninth, nine-forty a.m. Also in attendance, Deputy Derek Parker." He aimed his dark gaze on Twombly. "For the record, please, state your full name and date of birth."

"Fuck you! I ain't saying nothin'!" Twombly spluttered. His spittle flew across the table toward Noah and his deputy.

Unfazed, Noah said, "Have it your way. For the record, the prisoner refuses to give his name and birth date." He opened the file in front of him and shuffled through the papers. "We may have to wait for fingerprint ID to come back from the FBI."

Twombly snarled at him.

"Fine by me," Noah said, as if he'd interpreted the sound into words. "I'll talk, you listen."

Hannah spared a quick glance at the sheriff, then her eyes shot back to Twombly. Noah had obviously thrown him a curve ball, which had silenced him for a moment.

"Two nights ago, you were found prowling a property at thirteen-three-sixty-five County Road Eight. The resident was able to track your progress around the dwelling. The resident also reported that you attempted to enter the dwelling on several occasions, specifically you tried doors and windows to see if they were unlocked." Noah tapped his pen against the file folder in front of him. "How am I doing so far?"

"You can suck my dick, motherfucker!"

Noah looked at Derek and managed a smile. "Got everything right so far, I guess."

"Guess so," Derek agreed.

"The resident—"

"The bitch has a name!" Twombly screamed.

"True, but that's not relevant here, is it?"

"That's what you think!"

"Moving on."

"You don't wanna know why I wanna see that bitch pay?"

The venom in his voice was so palpable, Hannah almost fell off her stool.

"Not really."

"What kinda cop are you? Every cop wants to know why." He sneered at Noah. "It's called *motive*, you dumb shit."

"All I care about is the fact that you were there, trying to gain entry with the intent of doing bodily harm to the resident. Let's move on."

"Let's not!" Twombly roared. "I'm on a mission. I gotta fulfill it."

"Like a religious mission?" Noah asked, affecting an astonished tone.

Hannah gave him a A+ for his acting ability.

"No, not like a religiousfuckingmission, you dipshit mountain cop."

"Then it's not important."

"The hell it ain't."

"You're welcome to explain why it is, then."

"I got my marching orders. I have to get the job done."

"I see. So, you're working for someone."

"Not *for*," he jeered, "*with*."

Hannah shared a startled look with Kenny.

"You want to name that person so we can bring him in and talk to him?"

"No, I fucking do not."

"Then there's no point in you trying to shift blame away from yourself, is there?"

"I ain't shifting blame."

Noah glanced at Derek again. "What do you think?"

"I think he's trying to make us think he's part of a team, but he's just a big dumb ass out for a joy ride...all by himself."

"That ain't true. I got two friends I work *with*. We been together for years and years."

"I find it hard to believe you have friends."

Twombly's expression clearly reflected his affront. "We been friends since high school, you prick. We're like The Three Mouseketeers, so to speak."

It was obvious he meant Musketeers, not Mouseketeers, but then he wasn't exactly the sharpest crayon in the box. Hannah said to Kenny, "Do you think the drugs he took affected him?"

"It's possible. The doc warned Noah that Twombly's brain might be a little scrambled. I think the sheriff is playing up that angle by goading him a little, too."

Hannah looked back through the glass. "No duh."

Deputy Tigard chuckled.

At that moment, the door to the interrogation room opened and Marty said from the doorway, "Sorry to interrupt, Sheriff, but I have an urgent call on the line for you from Colorado Bureau of Investigation."

Chapter 23

Noah stood, then said for the recorder, "Interview to resume momentarily. Time ten-oh-one a.m." He jabbed at the recorder, but Hannah noticed he didn't actually turn it off.

Once Noah was out of the room, Twombly said to Deputy Parker, "You fuckers think you're so smart here in Hicksville."

Derek stared at him without responding.

"You going to defend yourself, pretty boy?"

Still, Derek didn't respond.

Twombly, handcuffed to the heavy metal loop on the table, reared up out of his chair and tried to upend the table. The resistance put him back on his ass with a thud. He began to spew every vituperative word imaginable.

Derek remained silent through it all.

"The table legs are bolted to the floor," Hannah said. "You'd think Twombly would have noticed."

"I really don't think he's all there, or he would have," Kenny said, then explained, "The sheriff before Noah had a problem one day with a prisoner who did the same thing and damned near killed both the sheriff and one of his deputies with the table. It's been bolted down ever since." He smirked. "Not even a grizzly could budge it now."

"I'm gonna get her, you know," Twombly said, his tone

boastful. "I make a plan, it always succeeds."

Kenny glanced at her. "He's hell-bent on getting you."

"He ever comes after me again and I'll use my gun on him." Even though she was the one uttering the words, they chilled her. "Is leaving the room part of a ploy the sheriff is using?"

"I think so. I've never seen him leave an interrogation before, but I can't think of any other reason he would." He studied the prisoner. "If he's trying to rattle Twombly, it looks like he's succeeding."

At that moment, the interrogation room door opened and Noah returned carrying a single piece of paper. He closed the door and sat back down at the table. He stabbed the recorder button, as if he'd activated it again.

"Sheriff Ward, resuming interview at ten-ten a.m. I have just received additional information provided by Colorado Bureau of Investigation concerning the prisoner. For the record, his name is Richard Allen Twombly, age forty, born August eighteen, nineteen seventy-eight. Twombly is a former violent crimes detective with San Diego Police Department. He quit the department on September fifth, this year." Noah looked up and skewered Twombly with a dark stare.

Twombly stared back with belligerence, but didn't question where Noah or the CBI had gleaned the information.

"What the hell is a former detective doing, prowling around houses in Fossil, Colorado?"

"Not houses," Twombly growled. "House. That bitch killed her husband and child and I'm going to prove it, even if I have to torture her to get the confession."

Hannah wrapped her arms around her middle. She'd long thought Twombly wanted to hurt her. The events of the past forty-eight hours, and this blatant admission, cemented that suspicion.

"What do you mean, she killed her husband and child?" Noah asked, his expression icy. For all intents and purposes, he came across as being on Twombly's side all of a sudden.

"She lured them out to her husband's sailboat, then talked him into going further out to sea than was safe, considering the size of the boat. She must have had help at some point, or else she brought along a gun or a hammer to do the job, then tossed them overboard. Another boat came along and found flotsam in the water and the capsized boat and notified Harbor Patrol."

"If they were that far out, why didn't they notify the Coast Guard?"

That seemed to stump Twombly for a second or two. "Guess, since they were from San Diego, they only thought of the Harbor Patrol."

"Tell me about the flotsam."

He shrugged, rattling the chain connected to his handcuffs. "Three life vests, a lifebuoy, and a cooler with three empty soda cans. And the boat." He snarled again. "Guess she let 'em have something to drink before she killed them. Nice, huh?"

Noah ignored the snide comment and asked another question. "Was a search done for the bodies?"

"Hell, yeah."

"What about the woman…how do you think she got away?"

"Probably got a boyfriend on the side who helped her. We think she did it for the insurance money."

"What kind of alibi did she have?"

"She claimed she was home all day. Worst alibi ever, right?"

"Could anyone corroborate?"

"Her lying-sack-of-shit sister said she had lunch with her." He made an ugly face. "I'm taking her down for perjury after I finish with Hannah Clarke."

"Did she take a lie detector test?"

"Hell, yeah, but the bitch managed to cheat it."

"Did she get the life insurance money?"

"According to the two insurance companies, yes."

"You really think she was capable of killing her son, regardless of how she felt about her husband?"

"Hell, yeah."

"He's got his canned responses down," Kenny said.

"He's never displayed much in the way of conversational traits," Hannah acknowledged, her tone grim.

In the other room, Noah asked, "Why do you think so?"

"Because, the bitch hated being a mother. She didn't keep the kid fed properly, and he was dressed practically in rags. She used to hit him, too."

"How do you know that?"

"Uh…the neighbors reported her."

"To the police or child protective services?"

"Uh…CPS."

"God, he must really hate me to fabricate all these lies," Hannah said.

Kenny glanced at her, but said nothing.

"The neighbors said that sometimes the kid would be outside without supervision all day long until his Dad came home. Jason would gather the kid up in his arms and the kid would cry and be so happy to see him."

"Lies, all lies," Hannah said on a whisper. "Jason never came home until after Jay was in bed."

"This puts a different light on things," Noah said.

"Damned straight it does," Twombly said, his tone triumphant. "Now get me outta these fucking cuffs and let me go after that bitch."

"It's not that simple," Noah said.

"Why the fuck not?"

"There's another little matter that needs to be cleared up."

"Like what?"

"The report of you being killed in a car crash a couple weeks ago."

That shut Twombly up like nothing else could have.

Noah waited, and waited. Twombly didn't know him, or the dumb shit would have realized he could wait him out all night. That's what Navy SEAL training did for you. Taught you that patience was a virtue. And a life-saver.

After nearly twenty minutes of glaring, with only an occasional blink, Twombly faltered.

Big tough POS that he was, he couldn't withstand an unspoken challenge. Noah could hardly wait to hear the explanation that came out of his mouth.

"I don't know nothing about a car crash." His tone was still belligerent, but he avoided eye contact. "I rented a car in Denver and took it sight-seeing. While I was in Estes Park, someone stole it."

"That's original," Noah said, his tone as dry as the Gobi.

"And clever," Derek added. "Sight-seeing, my ass."

Twombly's face exploded with angry color. "You calling me a liar?"

"That would be a yes," Noah said. He leaned back in his chair and folded his arms over his chest. "I'd think, with all the stories you've heard chasing violent crimes, you'd come up with something a little more original."

"Truth is stranger than fiction," Twombly said with a sneer. "I ain't lying."

Noah slid the single sheet of paper into the file folder and closed it. "Interview terminated at ten-fifty-three." Again, he stabbed at a button on the recorder, but didn't turn it off.

"Whad'dya mean, interview terminated? I got my rights."

Noah stood. "When you're ready to start giving us some truth instead of fiction, holler and we'll come back."

"I want something to eat. And drink!"

"People in hell want ice water," Noah said. "You remember how that goes, don't you?"

Derek stood, as well, and followed Noah out the door. Noah closed it without a backward glance and they moved far enough away that Twombly couldn't hear them.

"What do you think?" Derek asked.

"He's a lying sack who can't remember what he's said to cover his ass and he can't think fast enough on his feet to come up with a plausible lie."

"You think Hannah's husband knows she's in Colorado?"

"I'd bank on it."

"Do we need to offer her protection?"

Noah glanced at the obs room door. "Maybe, but I doubt she'd take it." He had a sneaking suspicion that Hannah Mason was the type of woman whose next step would be to go on the offensive, knowing what she knew now. "But there are ways around the obvious refusals."

Derek breathed a sigh of relief. "Good to know. I was

afraid we were going to have the first murder in over a century in our quiet little county."

Noah didn't bother to elaborate on his thought. It was just damned unfortunate that the only other plan he'd come up with had to do with him sleeping at Hannah's house.

He didn't like where that asinine plan had led the part of his mind that couldn't stop thinking about Hannah.

"How long before he calls us back in there?"

"He's not that quick on the uptake. I give him an hour to come up with the another story."

"I can't believe she had to put up with him hounding her for two years."

"I can't believe his supervisors didn't get what he was doing long before they did." Noah flexed his jaw. "That was unconscionable."

"You really think we're going to be able to find her husband and the kid, boss?"

"Yes." Noah couldn't let himself believe anything else. Not if he wanted to be able to live with himself for whatever was left of the rest of his life.

An hour later, Marty ran over to the diner to get a ham-and-cheese sandwich for the prisoner. Ten minutes after that, Twombly began to bellow from the interrogation room.

Derek beelined to Noah's office. "You were pretty darned close."

"Stick your head in and ask if he's ready to talk."

Derek did as instructed, then came back and said, "He says he'll talk if you bring him something to eat."

"Yeah, right, he's going to starting singing like a damned canary now," Noah said, his tone wry. "Grab a bottle of water and the sandwich and let's go back in."

"It's more than he deserves," Marty said, frowning as she handed over the sandwich.

"You keeping an eye on Hannah?" Noah asked her.

"Yeah. She's had enough tea to float a boat, but she doesn't want to come out. She's afraid she'll miss something."

Noah nodded, unsurprised. "I'll take a fresh tape, too. Pretty sure the one that's in the machine is close to the end."

Marty went to the supply cabinet and grabbed another tape. "You want me to start transcription on the other one?"

"Yeah, I'll hand it out to you. Anyone checked the video recorder to make sure everything's copacetic with it?"

"Kenny came out and gave it a look-see," Marty said. She frowned again. "He says Hannah's holding up okay, but he can tell this is really hard on her."

"I hope the prick breaks with something this next go-round," Derek said. "It's hell trying to resist the urge to pound him into mush."

"I'm going to try to get him to talk about the two friends he mentioned," Noah said. "Maybe he'll slip and mention Jason or Sabine's names."

"Good luck," Marty said. "I have a feeling you're gonna need it."

Back inside the interrogation room, Twombly devoured the ham-and-cheese sandwich like an animal dying of hunger. After that, he drained the water bottle without once taking it from his mouth. And then he let loose a disgusting belch that made Noah glad they hadn't fed him salami.

Derek cleared away the paper plate, napkin, and water bottle.

Noah switched out the tape and by means of a nod, Derek took it and passed it to Marty. "Interview tape two with Richard Twombly commencing at twelve-fifteen. Sheriff Ward and Deputy Parker in attendance. Tell me about the two friends who you went to high school with," Noah said.

"What friends? I ain't got no friends."

"So you lied earlier, when you said you're working with two friends that you've known since high school."

"I never said that."

"Would you like me to bring the first tape back and replay it?"

Twombly stared at him with hostility. "Go ahead."

With a sigh, Noah got up and opened the door. "Marty, go to the tape about fifteen minutes in and find the mention of two friends from high school. When you find it, bring it and the small recorder so I can play it for our prisoner."

"I ain't no prisoner," Twombly shouted.

Noah returned to the table and sat. "Actually, you are. You were booked when we brought you in this morning, remember?"

Twombly blustered, but other than turning a brilliant red, he said nothing.

Several minutes later, a knock sounded on the door. Derek got up to take the recorder from Marty and pressed PLAY.

...he's just a big dumb ass out for a joy ride...all by himself.

That ain't true. I got two friends I work with. We been together for years and years.

I find it hard to believe you have friends.

We been friends since high school. We're like The Three Mouseketeers, so to speak..

Noah watched Twombly for his reaction.

"That ain't my voice," he spat. "What kinda police station you running here, anyway? Trying to frame an innocent guy!"

"Frame you for what?" Noah asked. "I only asked you to tell us about your two friends. It was a simple, straightforward question."

Twombly blustered a little more, then yelled, "Okay, but they ain't got nothing to do with this."

"This being what?"

"Whatever the fuck *this* is, that's what!"

"Let's get back to you telling me about your friends since high school. What are their names?"

From all outward appearances and contorted facial expressions, Twombly chewed that around in his brain.

Noah figured he was trying to find a way to name names without actually giving anyone's name up.

"J.J. and Sabby."

Bingo! The guy was a regular brain trust.

Inside the obs room, Hannah gasped. The former San Diego PD detective had finally tripped himself up!

"Those sound like nicknames," Noah said.

"Lots'a people got nicknames," Twombly said. "I got one myself."

"Dick?" Derek asked with apparent innocence.

"*Rick*," Twombly shot back, his eyes practically bulging out of his head.

"So, what do J.J. and Sabby stand for?" Noah asked.

After several minutes of what seemed to be confusion for him, Twombly said, "Jason James and Sabine." He got a glint in his evil eyes and added, "We do everything together, if you get my meaning."

"I don't," Noah said. "Please, elaborate."

Twombly leaned over the table. A dribble of saliva ran down the side of his mouth. "Sex, lies, drugs…you name it, we do it."

A shudder of disgust rippled through Hannah. How could any woman let a man as repugnant as Twombly lay a hand on her?

"You ever get arrested as a juvenile?" Noah asked.

"Nope."

"Where did you go to high school?"

"Corona del Mar. A Catholic high school. We were careful not to get caught doing anything we shouldn'a been doing."

Corona del Mar? That was a lie. Jason and his so-called friends had graduated from Santa Monica High School, and it wasn't a Catholic high school. It was just a regular high school. Hannah was certain of that, having read the article and seen the photos from his twentieth reunion.

"Where are your friends now?"

"Somewhere."

"You still in contact with them?"

"I said I was, didn't I?"

"Then you must know where they are."

Again, Twombly played dumb.

"Still in California?"

"No."

"Here in Colorado."

Twombly set his chin in what could only be termed defiance.

"We'll go with an affirmative on that," Noah said. "What kinds of lies did the three of you tell?"

"What, you don't wanna know about the sex? That was the best part. Hell, it still is!"

Hannah went cold all over. Jason and Sabine and Twombly in a threesome. It was...grotesque. It also raised more questions. How long had the three of them been without each other? When did they pick up again? Had they ever *not* been together?

Noah said, "I don't care about your sex life, Twombly, unless it somehow relates to the lies spewing out of your mouth."

"Lies? I ain't lying about nothing."

"See, that's the problem," Noah said. "All you have to do is open your mouth and a lie pops out."

Chapter 24

Hannah stepped out of the obs room under the guise of using the restroom. Inside the ladies' room, she locked the door and pulled out her phone. She dialed Liza. "Are we still on for tomorrow?"

"Yes. Are you still sure you want to go?"

"More than ever," Hannah said.

"Can I assume Noah let you observe the interrogation?"

"He did and, quite honestly, it's hard to take, listening to this jerk lie his way through everything. He did mention my husband and Sabine, though, so I guess that's a step in the right direction."

"What does Noah have to say about it?"

"I haven't discussed it with him. He's playing Twombly with a finesse I have to admire, and so far, Twombly is giving up tidbits I don't even think he realizes he's giving up. Noah hasn't accused him of anything, but he's doing a good job of goading him. I don't know if Twombly's mind was affected by his cross-contamination of drugs, or if something else is going on, but he doesn't seem quite cognizant."

"Noah learned his interrogation skills in the Navy, and Pete says he's a natural at it. I doubt he'll ever lose the ability."

"What time do you want to leave tomorrow?"

"Around eight, if that's not too early for you."

"No, that's fine. Will you drive? I don't really feel comfortable on snowy roads yet, especially not for a long drive."

"Not a problem. I was going to offer, anyway, and by the way, Pete reiterated that he's happy to puppy-sit while we're gone."

"Thank you, and him! I'll be sure and give Bowie a good talking-to about sleepover etiquette."

Liza laughed. "Did you tell Noah we're going?"

"No, but if I get an opportunity to speak to him, I will, although, it's really none of his business what I do with my time."

Liza *tsk-tsked*. "You're going to be contacting law enforcement up in Estes, Hannah," she said, her tone somehow chiding in it's gentle delivery, "so I'd say that pretty much makes it his business."

"You're right," Hannah admitted. "I guess I'm just resistant to answering to a man these days."

"Some men are worth answering to."

"That may be true, but I'm not ready to take that particular leap yet. I need to get back in the obs room. See you in the morning."

"Take care, Hannah."

Another double entendre, but she didn't begrudge the advice from Noah's mother, who had a few years on her, and therefore, a lot more wisdom. "Don't worry, I will."

Seated beside Kenny again, Hannah resigned herself to more of Twombly's claptrap. She'd grown weary of listening to the bullshit rolling off his tongue, but given the circumstances, there was no way she'd leave.

"Noah just asked him if he likes kids," Kenny said.

That made Hannah sit up a little straighter. "What else did I miss?"

"Nothing yet. He went all disingenuous again and asked if Noah was talking about baby goats."

Hannah leaned forward, intent on where this line of questioning would go.

"You know damned good and well we're not here about goats," Noah said. "Tell me how you feel about children."

"They should be seen and not heard."

"You ever hit a kid?"

After a brief but telling pause, Twombly said, "Yeah, a coupl'a times. He needed it, though."

He. Hannah put her hands to her mouth, horrified.

"Either of your friends have kids?"

"One of them does."

"Is that the kid you hit?"

"Yeah, but I told you, the little shit deserved it."

"How old is he?"

Twombly shrugged, as though it were of no consequence. "Six, I think."

"You asshole," Noah ground out. "What do you weigh, two-twenty, and you're pounding on a little kid?"

"He was tormenting me," Twombly practically whined. "He needed a good smack."

"Did you hurt him?"

"He cried and went flying, so I might've, but what difference does it make? His dad gave him a good whipping after that for bothering me."

Hannah didn't know if she could take anymore of Twombly being honest about his brutality. And Jason...had he really *whipped* his son? What kind of monster was he?

"His dad is J.J.?"

"Yeah. Say, I'm hungry. Can you get me something more substantial than a damned sandwich?"

"It's not dinnertime yet, but when it is, I'll see what I can do," Noah said. He looked at Derek, who nodded. "End of interview, four-fourteen." This time he clicked off the recorder for real.

"I ain't going back to no stinking lockup," Twombly said, his tone menacing.

"You'll go of your own accord, or we'll use the Taser on you and drag you back to your cell by the feet," Derek said, his hand already on the Taser clipped to his belt. "Your choice."

Noah went to the door and opened it. "Get Toad and Kenny in here," he said to Marty.

Three guys, all over six foot. That ought to do it, Hannah thought grimly, although she wouldn't mind watching

Twombly squirm in agony again from being Tasered.

"You wait here until we get him back in lockup," Kenny said.

Hannah nodded. What else could she do?

Twombly fought the trio of deputies every step of the way. Hannah only knew that because of all the shouting and screaming going on outside the obs room. When Twombly squealed like a pig, she knew they'd finally given up a peaceful transfer and resorted to the Taser again.

Ten minutes later, Noah opened the obs room door and said, "In my office." He didn't wait for a reply.

She thought about ignoring his mandate and going directly home to hide out until the next morning, when Liza picked her up, but then she remembered that she'd stupidly given him a key to her house. He could walk in any damned time he wanted to and he had the alarm code, so the monitoring company would never know the difference.

She took her time gathering her belongings, then went to Marty's desk to thank her for keeping her hydrated.

"You're very welcome, Hannah." She tilted her head. "You doing okay?"

"No, but I'll live."

"Figured as much. Strong women like you recover quickly."

Strong women. Hannah had never in her life considered herself a strong woman, but upon a moment's reflection, she supposed she had to be strong to have survived the past two years. She offered Marty a smile of gratitude for the encouraging words. "The master calls," she said, and swung around toward Noah's office.

"Hang tough, kiddo."

Hannah raised her arm to give Marty a thumbs-up. In the doorway to Noah's office, she said, "Sheriff."

He shook his head with a slight look of disgust. "We're beyond titles, aren't we?"

"Not today."

He blew out a long sigh and she wondered if he'd resigned himself to dealing with her stubborn side. "Have a seat. Would you like something to drink?"

She remained standing. "No, thanks. I'm good."

"Hannah, have a seat."

She thought about declining again, but decided that sitting or not sitting wasn't a battle she needed to win.

"Get any pearls from the interrogation?"

"Not really." She bit her lip, trying to decide if she should admit her failing. "I guess I overestimated how helpful I could be observing the interrogation, but I was impressed with how well you handled it."

He didn't thank her for the accolade. "You may think of something later."

"Really?"

"It's not uncommon to mull over responses, then wham, you make a connection later."

Hannah wasn't so sure, but there was something she *was* sure of. "I'd love to take a baseball bat to him for hitting Jay."

"I almost went at him across the table at him over that myself. What an asshole, hitting on a little kid and from his tone, apparently enjoying it." He studied her for a moment. "Backing up. You said 'not really.' Does that mean there was something?"

Hannah took the chair. She couldn't very well tell him that Twombly's comment about sightseeing in Estes Park had stoked her theory about the town being Jason and Sabine's hideaway. Besides, it was likely he'd already figured that for himself, and if he hadn't, maybe she'd have something to tell him when she and his mother returned from their overnight trip. "No, but I do have questions about the interrogation. How much longer will you go at him?"

"Another day, maybe longer."

"So, tomorrow?"

"Maybe. I'd like to let him stew in his own fabrications, so maybe day after tomorrow. At some point, I'm going to have him transferred to the El Paso County Jail. We're not set up to have a long-term incarceration here."

"That doesn't sound convenient."

"It won't be, but the fact is, we have a small staff. I can't have someone on him twenty-four/seven and still serve and protect the people of Pike County."

Hannah considered alternatives. "What if I paid for private security to watch him?"

"Out of the question."

"Why?"

"Liability issues." He must have considered that his response answered the proposal from every angle, since he offered nothing more.

"I'm going up to Estes Park tomorrow with your mom. We're going to your sister's Christmas shop."

"Okay."

"You already knew."

"I might have a heard a rumor."

"You're not going to try and stop me, are you?"

"No."

Hannah squirmed in her chair.

"Something else you want to tell me?"

"No."

"Well, I have something else to say to you, Hannah."

She girded herself for another lecture.

"My brother Simon will be in Estes tomorrow. He'll meet you at eleven at the sheriff's office. He's agreed to let you tag along with him when he interviews the deputies and CSP officers who responded to the crash. He's also going to go over the autopsy report with you and the medical examiner who performed the post mortem. After that, you'll visit the site of the crash scene with him."

Stunned, Hannah could only stare at him wide-eyed. Definitely not the lecture she'd been expecting.

"Am I missing anything?"

She shook her head. "Thank you."

He pointed a finger at her. "Do what Simon says or you'll answer to me."

"All right."

He narrowed his gaze on her, obviously suspicious of her easy capitulation. "Are you messing with me?"

"No. I'm sincerely grateful that you and your brother are willing to help me."

"We're not helping *you*, Hannah. We're investigating a child abduction and we're allowing you to observe, not be an active participant in the investigation."

She didn't like the sound of that, but again, she didn't have a ready argument. Instead, she said, "You may not think you're helping me, Sheriff, but if you find my son, you'll be doing a lot more than that."

He tapped his pen against a file folder on his desk. "I have work to do."

So do I, she thought, but said, "I'll leave you to it."

"If you think of anything later that jumps out at you, call me."

"I will." She pushed up out of her chair and pulled on her coat. "Giving up Jason and Sabine was progress, wasn't it?"

"From my perspective, yes, but then there was the denial that they were involved."

"You can break him, Noah. You're good at what you do."

"I hope so." He stared at her for several long moments, obviously conflicted about something. "One more thing, Hannah."

She tugged on her knit cap, and then her gloves before she said, "Yeah?"

"Be careful."

"I will."

Later, she wondered why he'd issued the warning. Did he know something he hadn't shared with her, or was it his standard farewell to all moms of missing children?

Pete pulled into Hannah's driveway next to Liza. Bowie, looking out the front window, went crazy with his tail-wagging when he saw them.

Hannah greeted Noah's parents at the door and invited them in. Bowie ran circles in the entryway in a frenzy of excitement.

"I'm meeting Noah for breakfast at the diner," Pete said. "Thought Bowie might like to play with the other dogs while we eat."

"I'm sure he'll love it," Hannah said, "but will he be warm enough? It's a little frigid this morning."

"Ta-da," Liza said, withdrawing a cute little sweater from

the bag she carried. "For Bowie, to keep him warm."

Hannah studied it dubiously. "How will we get him into it."

"No sweat," Liza said. "It has Velcro closures."

"Clever." She glanced down at her prancing pup. "Bowie, stay." First try and he minded. "Good boy." She watched while Liza fitted the garment around her dog. "That is so darned cute. Did you make it?"

"Yep, for Fiona, but obviously, she's outgrown it, so now it's her brother's turn."

Hannah pulled out her phone and aimed it at Bowie, who managed a cute doggie pose. She sent the photo to her sister and brother, then knelt down and said to her canine, "Remember our talk. You be good today and mind Pete, okay? If you don't, no more outings for you, buddy."

Bowie yipped and licked her hand.

"I'll take that as agreement." She stood and said to Pete, "I hope you're not going to be sorry you agreed to take him until we get back."

"Don't worry, I won't. We're going to get Fiona after breakfast, so he'll have a playmate. He'll be so exhausted tonight, he'll sleep like a log." He glanced around. "Did you say you have a bed and some toys and food for him?"

"Everything's stacked in the garage. I thought that would be easier than carting it through the house."

Pete nodded with a grin. "You're a logical thinker, just like Liza."

They got Bowie settled in Pete's SUV, then he said goodbye to his wife in the way of newlyweds. Hannah had never been kissed like that by her husband, and it left her a little melancholy. She gave a brief thought to how Noah would say goodbye to his wife, then obliterated the notion with a zap from the thought police.

She went inside to grab her things and lock up, and met Liza at her Honda Pilot.

"You ready for this?"

"I am, and I got my marching orders from your son."

Liza smirked. "I might have got a heads-up on that myself this morning." She belted in and turned the key in the ignition. "It's just as well Simon is going to look after you. You never know what kind of trouble you might encounter up there."

Hannah didn't want to admit it, but she was hoping she *would* encounter trouble, or at least that she might encounter some merchants or townspeople who had met Jason or Sabine or Jay. She was armed with photographs, just in case.

After a few minutes, Liza said, "You're awfully quiet."

"Just thinking. Yesterday gave me a lot to process."

"Anything relevant?"

"I told you that Twombly gave up Jason and Sabine."

"You did."

"He also admitted to hitting Jay. I almost came unglued over that."

"Good lord, I would've, too. How did Noah handle it?"

"He managed not to beat him to a pulp when he said it."

"That's my boy. He loves kids. He once told me that the hardest part of being a SEAL was having to witness the living conditions of the children everywhere he went." She signaled and entered the highway onramp. "I'm not certain, but I think he and his buddies may have taken some action against militants who armed kids with suicide vests."

"Oh, God, how horrible."

"Everything about war is horrible," Liza said. "I know it's a necessary evil, but that doesn't mean I have to like it."

Hannah reached over and gave her arm a comforting squeeze. "It must have been hard, having your son over there."

"It was, but it wasn't just Noah. Brant and Simon were enlisted, too."

"Wow," Hannah said.

"The good news is, they all came home alive and God willing, they'll stay that way until they're very old men."

"Amen," Hannah said, hoping the same for her own son.

Chapter 25

The drive to Estes Park was scenic and sunny. Even though the landscape was blanketed with snow, the roads were plowed and dry.

"We couldn't have come on a more beautiful day."

"I didn't know how much I'd love living in the mountains," Hannah admitted with a smile. "All this snow is beautiful."

"And bad for your eyes, too." Liza chuckled.

"Thanks for suggesting I bring my sunglasses."

"That's Doctor Mom talking."

"Regardless, I appreciate that you cared enough to warn me that the reflection off the snow is blinding when it's sunny."

"Years ago, the kids' pediatrician told me it was important to protect even children's eyes from the sun's UV rays. They used to look so cute in their sunglasses."

"I wonder if Jason cares about Jay's eyes," Hannah said, her voice sad. "He probably doesn't even get Jay's teeth cleaned or keep up his immunizations."

"It probably won't make you feel any better, Hannah, but there's a special place in hell for people like Jason and Sabine, and this Twombly character."

"The only thing that will make me feel better is getting Jay back."

"I know, sweetie." She cast Hannah a sideways glance. "Along that line, I've been thinking...."

"About what?"

"While you're doing your law enforcement thing with Simon, I'd like to get a head start on taking your photos around to the shops, to see if anyone recognizes them. You never know if they dropped a tidbit here or there that might help us find them."

"Are you sure, Liza? I mean, people might not be nice to you."

Liza snorted. "I could give a rat's behind, as long as they tell me something."

"Well...if you're sure, I'd certainly appreciate the help."

"I'm sure."

"I forgot to ask how long the drive is to Estes."

"I know it seems like a crawl when we're going through the Denver metro area, but that's only because there's so much traffic. We'll cut over at Highway thirty-six and take the road up through Lyons." Liza shook her head. "Which didn't answer your question at all, did it? The drive takes about two-and-a-half hours. We're about halfway now, so we should be there in about an hour and twenty minutes." She glanced at Hannah. "If you like, when we come back, we can take the back road. It's about a half-hour longer, but gorgeous."

"Let's see how our visit goes. We might both be anxious to get home again."

Liza smiled. "Maybe."

Antsy, Hannah decided to settle in and enjoy the ride. Denver had an interesting skyline. The Broncos stadium, which Liza maintained was still referred to as Mile High by Coloradans, was huge. She imagined taking Jay to a game there one day. Maybe with Noah.

Further north, the best thing to look at was the mountains to the west. Peak after snow-covered peak sprang like sentinels from the earth. She and Jay could take up skiing, too. Maybe with Noah.

When she realized how many plans she was concocting, Hannah put the skids on her thoughts. No one knew better than she did how fast you could plummet back to reality when you allowed yourself to have hopes and dreams, and to make matters worse, she'd envisioned Noah in every single one of those plans.

Estes Park sat at the entrance to Rocky Mountain National Park.

"I'm going to take a quick detour," Liza said, turning onto Steamer Drive, then Steamer Parkway. "That's the Stanley Hotel," she said with a nod toward a sprawling white structure. "Did you ever read *The Shining*? This is the place that influenced how King wrote about the Overlook Hotel in the book."

"I did. Is the Stanley really haunted?"

Liza grinned. "Some say so."

They returned to Highway 34 and continued on to the downtown area, where the roadway was called Elkhorn Avenue. In the business area, the street was lined on both sides with shops geared toward tourists—art galleries, gifts, candy, restaurants, bars, novelties.

"Juliette's shop is a bit further up, closer to the park entrance. She calls it Santa's Workshop and it encompasses the entire bottom floor of an old house she bought. She lives upstairs."

"Sounds like an ideal work environment," Hannah said. "I know it works for me."

Several minutes later, Liza eased her SUV into a driveway on the west side of the house. A young woman who looked very much like her mother, ran outside to greet them. Behind her, a man who had to be Noah's brother followed at a slower pace.

"You're late," Simon Ward said to his mother.

"Five minutes!" she said, laughing and hugging him at the same time. "I wanted to show Hannah the Stanley."

Juliette and Simon studied Hannah with curious expressions. "It's a beautiful place," she said. "I think I saw several ghosts dancing around on the front balcony, though."

For a moment, brother and sister looked startled, then both

broke out laughing.

"Good to meet you, Hannah," Juliette said, offering her hand.

"You, too, Juliette."

"Mom's the only one in the family who calls me Juliette. You can call me Jules."

Hannah smiled. "Okay, Jules."

Simon also extended his hand. "Glad to see you have a sense of humor, Hannah."

"I try," Hannah said.

"You can call me Simon," he said, deadpan, which made Hannah laugh.

"Simon, be a sweetie and grab our overnight bags, would you?" Liza asked. "Let's get inside. It's chilly out here."

They headed directly upstairs, where Simon deposited their bags in a large room furnished with twin beds.

"I hope you don't mind sharing a room with Mom," Juliette said. Usually, she and Dad get the room with the queen bed, but since I didn't think you'd want to share with Simon, I let him have it this time."

"It's great," Hannah said, pausing to look out the window, which offered beautiful views of the mountainous terrain. "Thank you for having me."

"Let's go sit and have some coffee and fresh-baked zucchini bread," Juliette said. "You and Simon can plan out your day, and Mom, you can tell me how you plan to spend yours."

Hannah and Liza hung up their coats on the hall tree in the alcove at the top of the stairs and followed Juliette to the kitchen, where she and her brother had apparently already been drinking coffee.

"Shop not open yet?" her mother asked.

"It is, but since there's a bell on the door, if anyone comes in, I'll know it." She pulled down two more mugs and filled them. "Help yourself to bread. How do you take your coffee, Hannah?"

"Black, thanks." Her stomach rumbled, reminding her that she hadn't eaten anything before the road trip. She reached for a slice of bread and took a big bite. "Wow, this is the best zucchini bread I've ever had."

"Secret recipe," Juliette said, *sotto voce* and with a grin.

Simon reached for a slice. "So secret, she won't even give *me* the recipe," he said, mock scowling at his sister. "Fortunately, she baked two loaves and I get to take one home."

"Unless we eat it today," Juliette said, plopping down in a chair and grabbing a slice for herself. "Aren't you having any, Mom?"

Liza smirked. "Just waiting until I could be sure I wouldn't lose my hand trying to get a piece."

Her children howled with laughter.

"I have a feeling there's a funny story behind that," Hannah said, enjoying the easy camaraderie among the Wards. It reminded her of being with her own siblings.

"Tell it and you're both disinherited," Liza warned.

The siblings exchanged a look, and apparently decided not to test the threat.

Hannah, Liza, and Juliette listened quietly while Simon proceeded to outline his schedule.

"Does that work for you?" he asked Hannah.

She couldn't think of anything he'd omitted that she wanted to accomplish. "Yes."

Juliette asked, "What are you going to do, Mom?"

"One of the things on Hannah's agenda is to take some photos around of Jason and Sabine and Jay. She's hoping to find merchants who might recognize them. I thought I could get started on the queries."

Juliette shot a worried look at her brother. "Should she be doing that?"

"It's safe enough," Simon said. "It's unlikely any of the locals are in cahoots with them. What kind of story are you going to give?"

Liza put down her mug. "I thought I'd say I was the grandma of the little boy and that my ex-son-in-law had taken him against court order."

Simon nodded. "That will work. Might garner a little more sympathy and cooperation, too."

"Can I see the photos?" Juliette asked.

Hannah dug into her purse and pulled out a small brown

envelope, which she handed over.

Juliette withdrew the pictures and went through them, one-by-one, then went back to one, in particular, of Jay. She looked up with a stunned expression on her face. "I'm pretty sure these people were in my shop just before Thanksgiving."

"Are you certain?" Simon asked.

His sister nodded. "The little boy has aged since this photo, obviously, and his hair is a little darker now, but he had that same little mole just to the left of his mouth."

Hannah nearly fell out of her chair. "Did they happen to mention where they lived?" she asked, wondering if it could all be this easy. Jason, holed away with his paramour and his son in a small mountain town in the Rockies, shopping like they were regular people.

"Not in Estes," Juliette said, dashing her hopes. "The little boy liked that he was in a Christmas shop, but he wanted to see Santa Claus. When he reminded them they had promised to take him to see Santa at the North Pole, the three adults with him didn't take it well."

"Three?" Simon said, straightening in his chair. He dug into his pocket and pulled out a sheet of paper he'd folded in quarters. "Was this one of them?"

Juliette studied the picture. "Yes. He was good-looking as all get-out, but clumsy as hell, kind of what you'd describe as the stereotypical bull in a china closet."

Hannah realized she must be talking about Twombly. She'd thought him good-looking, too, the first time she met him, but after that, she only saw the ugliness inside him. She held out her hand. "May I?"

Juliette handed the paper over.

"That's the detective who harangued me so mercilessly. Noah's got him locked up in his jail right now."

"What?" Juliette asked.

Hannah relayed the story of her prowler, the events at the hospital, and the first day of Twombly's interrogation.

"Wow, who knew things could be that exciting in Fossil," Juliette said, her eyes wide.

"Makes you want to move back, doesn't it?" Simon teased.

"Maybe next year," his sister tossed back.

"Juliette!" Liza said.

"We'll talk about it later, Mom." She turned back to Hannah. "Right now, there's a little boy missing."

Hannah asked, "Are you certain they didn't live in Estes Park?"

"Positive."

Hannah's hopes took a major nosedive.

"But that doesn't mean I don't know where they do live," Juliette went on.

"C'mon, Jules! This isn't the time to play games," her brother said, somewhat impatiently.

"I'm not. Apparently, they had promised to take Jay to the North Pole, but instead, they came up here. Kids don't like broken promises. I could hardly blame him for being miffed."

"North Pole?" Hannah asked, wondering why Juliette kept mentioning it. "There's no such thing as the North Pole, in reality."

"Oh, but there is," Liza said, her eyes alight with excitement.

Simon pulled out a slim notebook. "Where was home?" he demanded with some impatience.

"Woodland Park," Juliette said.

"The North Pole is only about fifteen minutes from Woodland Park," Liza said.

Juliette went on. "I think the only thing that kept the little boy from melting down over it was that his dad promised they'd stop on the way back home the next day." Juliette frowned. "He didn't seem very sincere about it, but then, I don't know him, so maybe he's like that all the time. They did mention that they were staying at the Stanley that night, and planned to head back to Woodland the next morning."

Simon glanced at Hannah. "Do you still want to talk to the local law enforcement folks and visit the crash site...and go over the autopsy?"

Hannah had never really *wanted* to do any of that, but forewarned was forearmed, although in this case, informed was forearmed, so whether she still wanted to or not was a moot point. She had to do it. "Yes." She looked at Liza. "If we leave early enough tomorrow, would we have time to go to Woodland Park on the way back to Fossil?"

"You bet. We can go on up through Divide and catch the back road home from there."

"I'll be finished here, too, and three can accomplish more than one of us alone," Simon said.

"Thank you all so much," Hannah said. Her gaze landed last on Juliette, who had a concerned frown on her face. "Are you worried about your mom and brother being involved in this?"

Juliette shook her head, but didn't speak.

"What's wrong, honey?" Liza asked.

"There's more to what happened when they came in the store, but I don't know if I should tell it."

"Please," Hannah begged, "don't hold back. I can take it."

Juliette drew in a shuddery breath, then said, "The little boy, Jay, saw a snowman ornament he wanted. He asked his dad if he'd buy it for him. Before his dad could speak, the woman, who I thought was his mother at the time, grabbed his little arm and shook him. She told him he was nothing but a whiny little brat and they weren't buying him anything. She also told him if he spoke again, the North Pole was cancelled." Juliette's voice caught. "I've seen people be mean to other people, but I've never witnessed a parent being so cruel to a child. I wanted to say something, but I was afraid to because...." She glanced at her brother, as if he could give her some courage to continue.

"What happened?" he asked.

"The big guy, the one in the picture...I guess he saw me open my mouth to ream her a new one and he took a step closer to me and said, 'Think carefully before you speak.' I've never been threatened before, but I recognize one when I hear it."

"You should've called the police."

"And say what? There's a mean mom being nasty to her son in my store?"

Horrified, Hannah closed her eyes, trying not to cry. Her beautiful, sweet boy, talked to in such a malicious way, treated like he was dirt on Sabine's Jimmy Choo's. How on earth could Jason put up with allowing her to treat Jay like that?

Please, God, help me find my child before they completely destroy him.

Overcome with emotion, Hannah excused herself and fled to the bathroom.

"I should've left well enough alone," Juliette said, her eyes filled with tears.

"Hannah's stronger than you think," her mother said. "Look at what she's had to endure for the past two years."

"I just hope she lets us do our job," Simon said.

"She needs to be involved," Liza said. "I think both you and Noah are smart enough to figure out how to do that without her getting in your way…or putting her in harm's way."

"She has no police training."

"She's Jay's mother."

Simon frowned. "I can see this is a go-nowhere disagreement."

"I knew you'd see reason," his mother said, "but I'm dead serious about her not coming to any harm."

"Since Twombly's in custody, it's highly likely that her husband and his girlfriend and the kid are long gone by now, probably out of the state."

"For Hannah's sake, I hope not," Juliette said.

A few moments later, Hannah returned. Her eyes were red and puffy, but she had a determined look on her face. She asked Juliette, "Did they buy anything at all?"

"Oh, my gosh, they did, or at least the bitch from hell did."

"Did she pay with a card, or by cash?" Hannah asked.

Juliette thought a moment. "By card, I think. Wait! I remember now, she wanted this god-awful pink sea shell Christmas wreath that was sent by mistake with my order. I was so happy to get rid of it, I almost offered her a discount, but then I remembered how mean she was to the little boy, and I decided not to."

"She does love her pink and her bling," Hannah said.

"Funny you should mention bling. That stupid wreath was covered with fake jewels."

Hannah gripped the back of the chair she'd sat in before.

"Do you happen to still have the snowman ornament that Jay wanted?"

"Pretty sure I do. Would you like to see it?"

"No," Hannah said. "I want to buy it."

Downstairs in Santa's Workshop, Juliette went directly to a tree in the front window and pulled off a snowman ornament. She handed it to Hannah.

Hannah cradled it in her hands. "There's a little cardinal on his shoulder."

"That's exactly what Jay said when he looked at it. He also said he's never seen a real cardinal."

Hannah blinked, hoping to hold back more tears. "We used to talk about why there weren't any cardinals where we lived. I promised him that someday, I take him where they lived."

Juliette put an arm over her shoulders. "And someday, you will."

"I hope so. God, I hope so."

"C'mon, I'll wrap the ornament up for you, so it doesn't get broken on the way home."

"Thanks. I didn't look at the tag. How much do I owe you?"

"Nothing."

"But—"

Juliette stayed Hannah's hand on her wallet. "No *buts*, okay? This is my gift to you…and Jay."

"Thank you, Jules. I appreciate your kindness."

"It's the least I can do, since I didn't haul off and punch that stupid Sabine right in her nasty mouth."

Hannah couldn't hold back a little smile. "Maybe someday, I'll meet her face-to-face and pop her one myself. I'll be sure and tell her it's from you."

Juliette grinned. "Man, what I wouldn't give to see that."

"If it ever happens, I'll try to get a photo with my phone afterward and send it to you."

As an afterthought, remembering what Liza had told her, Hannah said another little prayer, this time to her guardian angel. *Guardian angel, please, help me find them.*

Chapter 26

Hannah and Simon met with the Larimer County Sheriff's Office first, then headed over to the Estes Park Police Department, where a patrol officer from Colorado State Patrol joined them. After that, they pored over the autopsy results and spoke via phone with the deputy medical examiner, who reiterated what he'd written in the post mortem report. Bert Hague's death had resulted from a gunshot wound to the back of his head, prior to the car crash.

Hannah was amazed at his certainty. "Prior to the crash. Does that mean someone shot him as he was driving and his car went off the road?"

"Not at all. Once the body dies, the heart stops pumping blood, and after that, anything that happens to the body that would ordinarily cause it to bleed, no longer results in bleeding. This guy was dead for an hour or more before he ever went over that embankment."

"And you know this because there was no blood."

"Minute amounts, but not enough to account for the massive head trauma he experienced."

Hannah, who had been hired to illustrate one medical book in her career, found that fascinating. "Has his wife been notified yet?"

"Yes, as a matter of fact, she came up yesterday to make an

official identification."

"Was she okay?"

"Not really. Her parents brought her. They'd only been married a couple years. She's pregnant with their first child."

Though it was not her fault, and she was related only remotely to the crime, a wave of guilt swept through Hannah. Her heart ached for the widow, and the child who would never know his father. "I should do something for the wife," Hannah said to Simon when they'd hung up.

"There's nothing you can do."

"I feel like it's kind of my fault that he's dead."

"Look, Hannah, let's get something straight, okay? The only person responsible for Bert Hague's death is Twombly, although he may have had help from Jason and Sabine. They screwed you over, and apparently, they don't care who else dies while they go after what they want."

Though Simon's reassurance made sense, the former detective's motivation for killing Hague puzzled her. "Why do you think Twombly wanted the world to think he was dead?"

"Good question. I think the answer is that he wanted to disappear like Jason and Sabine did."

"Couldn't he have accomplished that with a simple name change?"

"From what you've told me, and what his supervising lieutenant said, I'm not sure he was bright enough to understand that."

"I don't get it. Aren't people who advance to the rank of detective supposed to be smarter than the average bear?"

"Theoretically."

"That sends a chill down my spine."

"Mine, too, but that's the way things happen, and there's one other thing."

"What's that?"

"Twombly's LT thinks he was using drugs. He's not sure what, but he said it would explain his mood swings and lack of ability to concentrate on his cases."

"I think that happened because he was focused solely on destroying me."

"Maybe so." He gave the autopsy report one last cursory

look. "I think we've accomplished as much as we can here. Are you ready to head back to Jules's place?"

"Actually, I could use a cup of coffee. Do you mind if we stop at the Starbucks?"

"Fine by me. I just realized, we didn't take time for lunch."

"I'm not sure I can eat anything after reading that autopsy report."

"Still, if you're going to play super sleuth, you need to keep your strength up."

He grinned at her and she found herself thinking of his brother, who had pretty much the same grin. Nice as Simon was, she experienced a longing to have this conversation with Noah instead of his brother.

They drove to Starbucks and went inside. Over coffee and lemon bread, Simon said, "Noah tells me you have a golden retriever puppy."

"I do. His name is Bowie and he's a brother to Fiona." She clarified. "By a different litter, of course."

"I have one of Fiona's brothers, from the same litter. His name is Felix, and he's much better behaved than Fiona."

"Poor Fiona. I think she gets a bad rap."

"Trust me, she doesn't."

"Noah invited me to retrain her."

Simon laughed. "I'm sure he did. Having any luck so far?"

"Actually, yes. I gave her some commands and she obeyed perfectly."

Simon grunted. "Maybe she just doesn't like taking orders from a man."

This time, Hannah grinned. "Who would?"

"Point taken," Simon acknowledged, "but sometimes, a man's gotta do what a man's gotta do."

Thinking of Jason by then, Hannah said, "That doesn't make it right."

"No," Simon said, "in some cases, it certainly doesn't."

They arrived back at Santa's Workshop just after five. Liza reported that she'd talked to three different businesses that had confirmed seeing Jason et al. in their stores—a restaurant, a toy store, and a candy emporium.

"I don't know if I should tell you this, Hannah, but if I

were you, I'd want to know," Liza said.

Hannah listened, silent, as Liza related stories from each location, similar to what Juliette had said. She could only hope that when she got Jay back, he didn't rebuff her, thinking she'd rejected him and that she was just like Jason and Sabine and Twombly. "It's hard to hear how badly my son is being treated, but if anything, it makes me more determined than ever to find Jason and Sabine and make sure they're prosecuted for what they did, and what they're doing."

The worried glance Liza shared with Simon didn't go unnoticed by Hannah. "I'll be okay," she assured them. "Much as I'd like to push each one of them out of a airplane, without a parachute, I'm not looking for vengeance. I just want Jay back."

"Glad we have that settled," Simon said, "especially since Mom's taking us all out to dinner." He tweaked his mother's cheek.

"I am?" Liza asked, as if surprised.

Hannah almost said dinner would be her treat, but she knew Liza would debate the point, so she left it and resolved to let their server know to give the check to her. It was the least she could do for all the help they'd given her. "I think I'm going to lie down for a while. What time are we going out?"

"Six?" Juliette suggested. "I need to do a little bookwork. I had a super busy day, thank goodness. At this rate, I'll need to bring in someone part-time to help out."

"That's a good thing, right?" her mother asked.

"The best possible thing," her daughter assured her. "I'm sorry you don't live closer. I'd put you to work."

"Once I finish getting my decorations up inside, maybe Dad and I can come over for a few days and help out."

"No way," Juliette said. "You've got baking to do, remember? If you're here working in the store, who's going to do that?"

Liza laughed. "Isn't it about time you learned to make some of my recipes?"

"Uh, no."

Their easy camaraderie left Hannah feeling a little blue.

She missed her parents so much, and picking up the phone to talk to her sister and brother didn't quite cut it as far as personal interaction, when smiles and hugs went so much further. Still, she'd left San Diego for a reason, and that part of her life was something she'd never long for again.

Hannah and Liza were on the road again by eight a.m. Simon had left an hour earlier, so he could check in with his office before he met them in Woodland Park.

"I wonder where we should start?" Hannah said.

"I'd suggest the post office, then the local market, and after that, maybe the Starbucks."

"Sounds like a plan. Would you like me to enter Woodland Park PD into the GPS?"

"Might as well." She worried her lower lip for a moment. "Pete knows the police chief at WPPD. He said he'd call and give him a heads-up about our arrival."

"You guys are amazing."

"We just want to help."

"What you're doing goes beyond that, and I can't adequately tell you how grateful I am."

Liza smiled and shot her a quick glance. "We're happy to do it, sweetie." Her eyes back on the road, she said, "Pete and Noah are manning the barbeque tonight, grilling tri-tip and all the fixings."

"Tri-tip?"

Liza nodded. "It's a sirloin cut, from the bottom. Tender and delicious."

"Sounds good. You're a lucky woman to have a man who knows how to cook."

Liza laughed. "Not just Pete. All my kids knew how to cook before they moved out of the house, even Noah, though he hardly ever cooks. I was never quite sure if that's because he's resistant or he really doesn't have a knack for it."

"He peels a good carrot."

Liza shot her a look of surprise, then began to laugh.

They chatted for the remainder of the trip about their respective children, which made the time pass quickly. At the Y in the road, they veered off Highway 24 to take 67 north, then turned left on Tamarac Parkway, where the police station was located. Simon's car was already there, though he wasn't in his vehicle.

"You ready?" Liza asked.

"As ready as I'll ever be. I'm expecting some resistance about showing the photos around."

"I don't know about that. No one likes to see a child stolen from his parent."

Hannah unbuckled her seatbelt. "I wonder if the law considers it stealing if the parents aren't divorced."

"In this case, with Jason faking his and Jay's deaths, I'm pretty sure there's a kidnapping charge in there somewhere."

"I have a hard time getting my head around how much Jason must have hated me to take such a radical and cruel step like this."

"I'm no psychologist, but I'm guessing he's been led down this path by Sabine."

"From all outward appearances, she does seem to have a lot of sway over him."

"That's what happens with a guy thinks with his penis instead of his brain."

"It seems like...."

"What?"

"Well, don't all men think with their penis?"

"No!"

Hannah wasn't so sure about that. Jason had used sex as both a punishment and a reward. Though most times he'd used it as a reward, she was fairly certain she hadn't benefitted from it, and when he'd withheld it as a punishment for some perceived misdeed, she hadn't missed it at all. Despite her skepticism, she didn't bother to offer Liza an explanation of her intimate marital relations.

Liza unhooked her seatbelt and turned sideways in her seat. "Someday, Hannah, you're going to find the right man and he's going to treat you like a queen. Yes, you'll argue and you'll disagree, but when push comes to shove, he'll worship you and that will go both ways. Marriage is a two-way street, and God knows, it isn't easy every day, but with the right person by your side, you can accomplish anything."

"Would you say that's love?"

"Definitely."

"I thought I was in love with Jason. In retrospect, I don't even know what he saw in me, or why he wanted to marry me."

"Don't sell yourself short, sweetie. You're a beautiful woman and you've got a brain most women would kill for...plus, you're talented." She grinned. "Specializing in art and dogs, no less."

"Oh, yeah," Hannah agreed, somewhat wryly. "In my next career, I'm definitely going to take up dog training."

Liza laughed. "Let's go in, shall we?"

Hannah was surprised to find Noah and Pete sitting in the conference room with Simon and the Woodland Park PD police chief, who identified himself as Willem Fitzgerald.

With introductions made, Chief Fitzgerald offered Liza and Hannah coffee. They both accepted and the chief waved at someone through the window using the peace sign.

While they waited, Hannah asked Pete, "Where's Bowie?"

"Marty's got him at the sheriff's office."

Hannah slid a look at Noah. "And that was okay with the sheriff?"

"That dog of yours doesn't cause a lick of trouble, Hannah. Everybody wants him."

"I'm glad he's so popular," Hannah said dryly.

"Marty's going to take him over to the diner at lunchtime." Pete chuckled. "I'm pretty sure it's more to show him off than it is to let him play with the other dogs."

"What kind of pooch is it?" Chief Fitzgerald asked.

"He's a golden retriever, almost six months old."

Moments later, two more cups of coffee were delivered and all canine-related conversation ceased.

"Noah has just been filling us in on the latest development," the chief said.

Hannah's head swung to Noah, who turned to meet her gaze. "What development?"

"Twombly got tired of spending time in his cell," Noah said. "He attempted an escape last night."

"Attempted, but didn't succeed?" she asked, hoping for clarification that she'd interpreted his comment correctly.

"I wish."

Hannah's bubble of hope popped with a big bang.

"He had a little help from the outside, unfortunately. They had him out in a New York minute."

Hannah stared at him for a few moments. "I'm trying to envision how that could have gone down."

"They broke the window in the cell and linked a chain through the bars, then made a run with their vehicle. We've got a big repair bill facing us, because they damned near took out the entire wall."

"Sounds like a breakout from an old Western movie," Liza said.

"That's probably how they got the idea," Noah noted laconically. "Barbie blocked the alley and called me and Derek, since he lives closest to the station."

"Was it Jason and Sabine?" Hannah asked.

"We're not sure. They managed to get the chain off the hitch, but Barbie couldn't be at both ends of the alley at once, so she was unable to make a positive ID. They were gone before Derek arrived, and he didn't pass them on the street, nor did I pass anyone I didn't know on my way in." Noah shook his head. "Twombly's the size of a mountain. I can't believe he made it out through the rubble."

"Tell me Barbie got the license plate number," Hannah said, as if she were a cop herself.

Noah nodded. "Plate number, vehicle make and model, and a photo of the car. The problem is, the license plate was stolen off a car parked in the Safeway parking lot in Woodland." He blew out a frustrated breath. "The plates on the car Twombly was using the night he prowled your house were also stolen. He's stupid in so many ways, and so shrewd in others."

"But with a picture of the vehicle, that will help trace it, right?"

Simon spoke up. "I've got CBI folks working on narrowing

it down through DMV records, but we won't be any further ahead if the vehicle they used is also stolen."

Hannah's euphoria fizzled. "That would suck."

"Keep a positive thought," Liza said. "It ain't over until the fat lady sings."

"On that note, we may have a lead to follow," Chief Fitzgerald said. "These gall-darned criminals all think they're so smart, but then they go and do something stupid like connect with the local Newcomer's Club."

"It's always something like that tripping up these dimwits," Pete said. "Did you get an address?"

"Oh, yeah. Of course, it doesn't exist, but I'll get my people out talking to the club members. Maybe they'll come up with something."

Hannah dug the envelope containing the photos out of her purse. "Maybe you can photocopy these, so they'll have something to show when they go out."

"That'll be a big help," the chief said, raising his arm. He crooked a finger at the woman who'd brought in the coffee. "Teddy, get some copies made of these pictures, will ya? Make sure everyone has a copy to show when they go out on the missing kid."

"Sure thing, Fitz." She opened the envelope to see what was inside. "They'll all fit on one page. That'll make things easier."

Hannah sagged back in her chair. All these ups and downs and maybes were making her crazy.

"I understand you want to take those pictures around to show to people in the shops and such," the chief said.

"Yes. We did that yesterday in Estes Park and got some good information," Hannah said. "At least, Liza did, while Simon and I talked to the law enforcement people up there."

"Oh, yeah?" Fitzgerald asked.

Hannah left it to Liza to repeat the information, which didn't make it any easier.

"I don't like to see a child mistreated like that," he said when Liza had finished. "You have the full cooperation of WPPD, Hannah."

"Thank you." She glanced at Noah, who was studying her

intently. She would've given anything to know what he was thinking.

Just that quickly, he opened his mouth, as if he were in charge. "Hannah and I will hit the North Pole, then come back up and catch the Safeway, Starbucks, and City Market."

Simon said, "I'll take care of the fast food restaurants and the post office."

"Mom and I will hit hair salons and clothing stores, including WalMart," Pete said.

"My boys will cover the grade schools," Chief Fitzgerald said, "and the community center."

"How many schools are there?" Hannah asked.

"Three. I'm thinking local police will have better luck there than any of you will."

"Agreed," Simon said, "but if you need me there to scare anyone into talking, give me holler."

The lighthearted tone of his voice told Hannah he was kidding, sort of. The message his eyes sent, however, was something else entirely.

"Thanks, Simon," the chief said wryly. "I'll keep that in mind."

"Anyone actually spots them, call me immediately," Noah said. He looked at Hannah. "Ready to go?"

She was, and she wasn't, but what choice did she have, either way?

Chapter 27

They were ten minutes into the drive to the North Pole when Noah finally spoke. "You doing okay?"

"I'm fine, considering."

"You don't look fine. You looked damned miserable."

"I can't stop thinking about how Sabine is treating Jay. He's just a little kid, for God's sake."

"You told me a while back that she was mean to Jay, in general. As they say, leopards don't change their spots."

"Is that supposed to make me feel better?" she shot back, irritated beyond belief.

"No."

His monosyllabic response doused her anger, but not her misery. "Would I be arrested for assault if I happen to punch her right in the middle of her ugly face next time I meet up with her?"

"Not if no one sees it. It would be your word against hers, but I'd recommend you rely on a self-defense excuse, if you do."

Hannah's head swiveled in his direction.

With an amused smile on his face, he went on. "I should warn you, though, that punching someone in the face is not what it looks like in the movies. The skull is hard and your knuckles have little protection. You're likely to break some bones in your hand."

"It would be worth it." After a moment of silence, Hannah admitted, "I'd rather shoot her, but I don't want to spend years in prison for killing her, when I could be with my son."

"Good thinking."

Mulling over all the other possible means of torturing Sabine for striking Jay, Hannah was surprised when Noah said, "We're here."

"Gosh, it is close to Woodland Park."

"Yep." He pulled into a parking spot near the entrance.

"There's no one here. I never even thought to check and see if they were open today. I just assumed since it's December, they would be."

"I called yesterday and gave them a heads-up that we'd be dropping by."

"I'm glad one of us was prepared. Thank you for doing that."

He gave her one of those unfathomable looks he was so good at. "It's my job to be prepared."

"I know, but I can still thank you, can't I?" She smiled at him and he sucked in a breath. "What?"

"You should really do that more often, Hannah."

"Smile?"

He nodded. "You're pretty without it, but with it...my, God, you're beautiful."

Heat infused her cheeks. "Thank you," she said in a flustered whisper. No one, not anyone ever, had said she was beautiful. She didn't quite know what to make of it.

He hopped out of the truck and went around to open her door.

"Thank you," she said again. Once her feet were on the ground, she said, "This place is way bigger than I thought it would be."

"Back in the old days, it was a small operation. Today, it has rides and gift shops and shows and animals."

"Reindeer?"

"You bet."

"If we get Jay back before Christmas, I'm bringing him here." She stole a glance at him. "Would you come with us?"

"I'd like that."

Hannah sighed. "I suppose I shouldn't be counting my chickens before they're hatched."

"It's okay to have hope. Life would be pretty lousy without it."

She couldn't argue with that.

He closed the door and locked the truck. "Ready?"

"Yes." *Please, God, let us find something useful here.*

Noah knocked on the main door and a woman of about fifty opened it.

"You must be Sheriff Ward," she said, her voice hospitable. "Not sure we can help you, but we're willing to give it a go. Come on in." She stepped back to allow them entrance, then locked the door behind them. "Let's go into the office. Santa and some of the elves are there waiting."

Hannah didn't know what to make of the conversation so far. Was the woman so immersed in the Christmasy North Pole that she couldn't distinguish that from reality?

Once they were in a room with a large round table in the center, the woman said, "I'm Billie Carmichael, and Santa here is my husband, Johnny. The elves are Daisy, Christine, Toby, Sissy, Erick, George, Megan, and Ray. On short notice, I couldn't get everyone in, but if need be, maybe you can come back on Friday, when everyone's here."

"I appreciate your cooperation," Noah said, his eyes wandering over the group. "I'm Noah Ward, sheriff of Pike County. This is Hannah Mason. Her son is missing and we got a lead that the people who took him were bringing him to the North Pole to see Santa. We're hoping that's true and that you have information that may lead us to where they live."

With everyone's eyes on Hannah, she withdrew the envelope with the pictures and handed them to Billie.

Billie said, "I'm probably not going to be of much help because I spend most of my time behind the scenes. Santa and the elves, on the other hand, mingle with the visitors all day long." She handed the photos over to the first elf, Daisy, seated to her right.

"Everyone take a look, and once you've all had a chance to see the photos, we'll pass them around again and you can tell us what, if anything, you remember about them," Noah said.

Hannah knew right away Daisy wasn't going to be of much help. Her face scrunched up into a frown and then a look of disappointment. The girl passed the photos to Christine, who passed them to Toby, who gave them to Sissy, who studied them intently and handed them to Erick, who nodded his head before giving them to George. After that, Megan got them, and she practically bounced out of her chair before handing them off to Ray, and finally they were in Santa's hands.

Johnny, aka Santa, lingered over them the longest. If Hannah was correct, his eyes watered as he studied the photo of Jay. When he lifted his head to hand his wife the pictures to start the round-the-table again, she was certain of it. Santa had an encounter to relate, and it wasn't one that was joyful.

Daisy said, "I remember seeing them in the gift store, but I didn't help them, Sissy did."

Hannah cast a quick glance at Sissy, who nodded.

Christine studied the photos again. "This big guy, he gave me some guff over having to pay for the Tubs of Fun ride. He thought he should be able to ride for free if he was taking this little boy on with him."

"How did that end up?" Noah asked.

"The little boy's mom...uh, I mean the woman with them, said too bad for the kid, he wasn't going to get to go on any rides, if that was the case." She shrugged. "I'm paraphrasing, but that's the general gist of it."

Toby spoke next. "I was working the animals. The kid wanted to feed the reindeer and the woman told him it would bite his hand off, then all the grownups starting laughing, like that was the most hysterical thing they'd ever heard. I tried to tell the kid that the reindeer didn't bite, but by then, I could tell he was scared to death, so I dropped it." He shook his head in disgust. "I don't know what's wrong with some people."

Sissy said, "When they were in the Candy Kitchen, the little boy asked if he could have a candy cane and the woman smacked him upside his head, as if he'd asked her if he could go out and kill someone. It was really an over-reaction. I mean, honestly, kids ask for candy canes all the time and I've never seen anything like her response. She hit him so hard, he actually fell down, poor little guy." She dug into her purse. "When she paid for the fudge the grownups wanted, she handed over a VISA card. I jotted down her name and the number while she was yucking it up with the two men. I was so pissed, I seriously considered calling and reporting her to the police."

"I should have asked," Noah said. "What day was this?"

"Monday."

"Last Monday?" Hannah asked, for clarification. "Or the Monday before last?"

"Two days ago Monday."

Two days. So close, and yet so far. And poor Jay, not the day after they'd been in Estes Park, like he'd been promised.

Erick was next. "I oversee the pony carts. This little guy wanted to ride in the worst way, but like what happened at the Candy Kitchen, the woman smacked him. He fell and hurt his head."

George spoke up then. "They brought him over to Mother Hubbard's Cupboard, where we have a first aid station, but they only came because Erick insisted on it. They down-played the kid's injury, and fortunately, I was able to clean and bandage it. He didn't need stitches, but he was already starting to get a bruise on his forehead and his cheek."

Megan stared somberly at the photos when they came back to her. "I'm sensing a pattern here. My cousin, Candace, works at the dinosaur center in Woodland, and she was telling me about some people who came in with a little boy and the mom hit him when he asked if he could have a stuffed dino-saur."

"Was that before or after they were here?"

"Before, but I didn't know about all this going on here at the Pole." A tear rolled down her cheek. "We deal with kids every day here. I've never seen a parent or guardian strike a child here, ever. It can't be a coincidence, can it?"

"Not likely," Noah said, his tone grim. He glanced at Han-nah.

Hannah couldn't meet his gaze or anyone else's, for that matter. All she wanted to do was find Sabine and choke the ever-loving shit out of her. While she dwelled on how good that might feel, the next employee spoke up.

Ray said, "I'm sorry, but I don't recognize them. I was off on Monday to take my mom to Denver for some medical stuff, so I wasn't here."

That left Santa, who had his head in his hands, studying the picture of Jay. "Your son wanted to tell me what he wanted for Christmas," he said, "but the woman thought it was ridiculous and told him no. She got into a shouting match with the man I assumed was her husband, and then the bigger guy entered into the fray and the three of them walked away." He shook his head, as if dazed. "It was like they forgot about the boy completely. The little tyke inched up to me and kept looking over his shoulder, as if he knew he'd be in trouble if they noticed. I pulled him up on my knee and I asked his name. He said, 'I'm Jay and I don't want much for Christmas, Santa. I just want my Mom back.'"

It took every ounce of strength Hannah had to keep her composure. She put a stranglehold on the strap of the purse in her lap and blinked furiously to hold back her tears.

"I said to him, 'Isn't that your Mom with you?' and he said, 'No, that's Sabine. She hates me.' I asked if the man was his Dad and he said yes. After that, he said, 'Dad took me on a boat and then we pretended that we drowned and I never saw Mom again.'" His voice broke. "He asked me one last question before his dad came and snatched him away."

Hannah barely managed to get out, "What was it?"

"He wanted to know if I thought his Mom still loved him." Santa pushed away from the table and went around to Hannah. He put a comforting hand on her shoulder and said, "I told him you absolutely did."

Hannah stared up at him with tears streaming down her cheeks. "Thank you, Santa."

"I'm so sorry I didn't report the conversation to the police." He looked away for a moment, his expression grim. "Honestly, I thought he might be fabricating the story. I'll never make that mistake again."

"Please," Hannah said, "don't blame yourself for any of this. The adults who have Jay are the ones responsible for this situation."

"Still," Santa said, "you have my sincere apology." Shaking his head, he shuffled back to his chair on the other side of the table.

Hannah recognized that this Santa had a conscience and she was fairly certain it would take him a while to come to grips with the full ramifications of the situation. Nothing she could say or do was going to ease his guilt.

Noah gave her forearm a squeeze. "Jay still remembers you, Hannah. Don't lose sight of that."

"The sheriff is right," Santa said. "That boy not only remembers you, he longs for you. I knew instinctively that he had a special bond with his mom. That part, at least, I believed was true." He looked at Noah. "Is what he said true? That they pretended to drown?"

Noah nodded. "The father went to great lengths to steal his son and run away with the woman you saw him with. The man with them is a former detective who hounded Hannah for two years and tried to make everyone believe she'd killed the boy and his father."

"That's despicable!" Billie said, to a chorus of similar expressions of outrage.

"I know this is unorthodox, but we really need you to keep this to yourselves for the time being. I'm not exaggerating when I say Jay's life depends on it." He stood and Hannah followed suit. "If you, or any of the others who aren't here today, remember anything else you think may be pertinent, please, contact me." Noah pulled out his business-card holder and counted out enough cards to leave for each person.

"Are you going to talk to my cousin?" Megan asked.

Noah nodded. "We're going back to Woodland next. Would you mind calling to make sure she's there?"

"Sure."

George spoke up. "I took pictures of the little boy while the adults were in the waiting room. Would you like to have them?"

"Yes," Noah said. "I definitely would, and thank you for thinking to do it."

George shrugged. "It's SOP here in the park, but when Erick told me the mom had hit the kid and knocked him down, I snapped extra shots. I also got the parents' information. Uh, I guess I don't mean parents, since the woman isn't his mom. I have no idea if what they gave me is accurate or not, but I told them I had to have it for our records."

Several minutes later, pictures and information in-hand, Noah and Hannah were on their way back to Woodland Park.

Hannah spent the entire drive staring out the side window without seeing a darned thing.

Traffic was so heavy, Noah couldn't make a left turn into the Rocky Mountain Dinosaur Resource Center. After two impatient minutes, he drove to the next stoplight, turned left, and found a place to turn around about half a block down. From there, he ventured back onto the highway and continued on to the dinosaur center.

"That looks like a T. Rex," he said of the large dino outside the building.

"It's a Daspletosaurus," Hannah said without much emotion. "It predates Tyrannosaurus Rex and was smaller."

"You're kidding me. How do you know that?"

"Dinosaur book," she reminded him.

Noah didn't question her. She was the expert on dinosaurs, not him. "You up to doing this?"

"Yes," she said, but not with conviction.

He decided not to press the issue. He understood there was no way she'd wait in the truck and get the story second-hand from him. "I have a punching bag in my garage you're welcome to attack once we get back to Fossil."

That got a small smile out of her. "Thanks. I may take you up on that." She opened her door and jumped out before he could go around and help her out.

Before they entered the building, Noah said, "I know you're probably going to have questions. Try to hold them until we get the entire story, all right?"

"I'll try, but I'm not making any promises."

Noah's phone rang. He pulled it from his pocket and said, "Sheriff Ward." He listened intently, his eyes on Hannah the entire time. "Okay. We're at the dinosaur center. We should be back there in less than an hour." He disconnected.

"Something urgent?"

"Nothing that can't wait until we meet up with the others." He'd be damned if he was going to tell her that one of Fitzgerald's officers had located Jay's school, but that the kid had been absent since the previous Friday, with no explanation regarding why. The officer had also discovered the address listed in Jay's school records didn't exist. It did, however, agree with the address that had been given to the North Pole.

Hannah narrowed her eyes on him and he knew instinctively that she suspected he was holding back. A long sigh later and she reached for the entrance-door handle before he could.

Noah covered her hand with his. "I was taught that ladies go first."

She glanced at him over her shoulder. "I've been taking care of myself for a long time."

"I get that, but I still open doors for ladies."

She tugged her hand from beneath his. "You're going to take some getting used to."

Noah breathed a mental sigh of relief. The way she phrased her response told him that she planned on being in his life, at least for a while.

If he had anything to say about it, it would be a helluva lot longer than that.

Inside the dinosaur center, he asked to speak with Candace.

"That's me," said a voice from his left.

He and Hannah turned in unison.

"Sheriff Ward?" Candace asked.

Noah nodded and introduced Hannah.

"Follow me," Candace said. "We have a small conference room where we can have some privacy."

"We appreciate you seeing us, Candace," Noah said, and waited until both women were seated before he took a chair.

"I probably should have called the cops while they were here, but...." She shrugged. "I guess I didn't want to get embroiled in family matters."

"I'm sure you've never dealt with child abuse before," Noah said.

Candace began to twist her hands together. "I've heard about it, of course, but never witnessed it before."

"Start from the beginning."

The young woman closed her eyes for a moment and when she opened them, her anguish was apparent. "I was working the gift shop that day. It wasn't particularly busy, because it was a weekday. There were probably only a dozen others throughout the center, and if I recall correctly, one family with twin toddlers in the gift shop. When the little boy came in, he was with three adults. He immediately asked his dad if he could look at the stuffed dinos. Before his dad could respond, the woman, who I thought was his mom, told him to shut up. She said if he was good, when they got to the stuffed animals, he could look at them. The big guy with them kind of snarled at the boy and the boy backed away, like he was afraid of him." She shook her head. "I didn't blame him. That guy scared me, too."

Noah asked Hannah for her photos. "Before we go any further, would you take a look at the pictures we have and see if you can identify them as the same people?"

"Sure." Candace looked over each photo carefully, then handed them back. "That's them, although the little boy looks older than in the picture."

Noah dug out one of the photos George had taken at the first-aid station.

Candace nodded. "That's him, for sure." She made a sound of distress. "Poor little guy. Megan told me his mom knocked him down when he asked to ride the pony carts. She's a real piece of work, huh?"

"She's not his mom," Hannah said, "I am." She knew Noah hadn't given the young woman a full explanation over the phone. "My son was kidnapped, Candace. That's why we're here. We're trying to find him."

Candace let out a horrified gasp. "OMG! I *knew* I should have called the cops on her!"

"Go on with your story," Noah said, shooting a quick glance at Hannah. Her face had gone completely white.

Candace swiped at her tears. "They spent a lot of time in the gift shop." She looked down at a piece of paper she'd taken from her pocket and read, "The woman bought several T-shirts, a large titanium quartz piece, a sunset quartz, and eight Perisphinctes ammonites, which are now-extinct cephalopod fossils found in Madagascar from the Jurassic period. She also purchased two Bohemian jackets, four meteorite pieces, a carved Moroccan chess set, and an amethyst globe."

"Did all that amount to a sizeable purchase?" Noah asked.

"She dropped over two thousand bucks without batting an eye, but when the little boy asked for a T. Rex stuffed animal that sold for less than ten dollars, she back-handed him so hard, he went flying." Her gaze went to Hannah. "I'm so sorry." Several more tears slipped down her cheeks.

"You couldn't have known Jay was kidnapped," Hannah said, fighting back despair. "I hold no ill will toward you."

The young woman gnawed on her bottom lip, apparently unconvinced.

Hannah said, "What happened then?"

"It was awful. Are you sure you want to hear?"

"Yes."

"The three adults…they laughed when he fell and hit his head. I rushed around to help him, but the big guy told me to back off and mind my own business. He scared me so bad, I finished the transaction and bagged it, hoping they'd leave immediately. My supervisor came in then, because the little boy was crying and obviously in pain." She hung her head, and her voice shook. "The boy's dad told him to get up and act like a man. The adults took the purchases and walked out the door. The little boy was obviously dazed as he followed them out, but they never once turned to see if he was okay or to ask if he was all right. His dad did yell once and told him if he didn't stop crying, he'd give him something to really cry about."

Hannah made a strangled sound in her throat and Noah could only imagine what was going through her mind. For damned sure, he knew what was going through his.

Chapter 28

Bile rose in the back of Hannah's throat. "I need to use the restroom."

"It's through the gift shop," Candace said, her expression one of concern. "Would you like me to show you?"

"Thanks, but no. I just need a minute." Hannah left her coat and purse and rushed out of the room. She hoped no one else would be in the restroom, and fortunately, while she tossed her cookies, no one came in.

Dear God, how could they treat Jay so badly? Did they not have a compassionate bone between the three of them?

Once she'd finished, Hannah wiped her mouth, then went to the sink and rinsed repeatedly before splashing cold water on her face. As she was using paper towels to dry, an older woman came in with a little girl who Hannah guessed was probably her granddaughter.

The woman appraised Hannah and asked, "Are you all right, dear?"

"I will be, thanks." And then, because she didn't want to seem too abrupt, she invented a lie. "I think the altitude got to me."

The woman nodded. "That can happen up here. We're at almost nine thousand feet, you know."

"So I heard." Hannah crumpled the paper towels and said,

"I appreciate your concern."

"Not a problem. If they have a soft drink machine here, you should have yourself a Seven-UP. I don't know why, but those non-caffeinated bubbles seem to help."

"I'll check and see." Hannah's eyes dropped to the little girl. "Is this your granddaughter?"

"Yes, her name is Ashley. She'll be in kindergarten next fall."

"Hi, Ashley. Do you like dinosaurs?"

"Yeah, I really do. Grandma and I come here twice a month to look at all of them."

"Lucky you and lucky grandma," Hannah said, working up a smile. "My little boy loves dinos, too."

"Is he here?"

"No, not today. He's in school." Hannah had no idea if that was true or not, but she fervently hoped it was.

"Maybe I'll meet him here sometime."

"Maybe you will. You two have a nice time."

"Thank you," Ashley said and skipped into a stall.

"You take care, dear," the grandmother said.

"I'll try," Hannah said. It was as much as she could muster.

Back with Noah and Candace, she slipped into her chair, hoping she didn't look as bedraggled as she felt.

"You okay?" Noah asked.

"I'm fine," Hannah lied.

"Can I get you anything?" Candace asked.

"Do you have any Seven-Up?" Hannah said, liking the grandmother's suggestion, since she had no toothbrush at her immediate disposal.

"Will a Sprite do?"

Hannah nodded.

"Be right back."

Noah said, "Are you sure you want to sit through the rest of this?"

"Positive."

His skepticism plain, he said, "Okay, but don't feel like you have to. If you want to get up and leave at any time, just do it."

"I had a momentary lapse," she said, "imagining what Jay

must have gone through, to be hit like that, then left to recover on his own. The three of them are animals."

"I wouldn't disagree," Noah said, his tone rough with anger.

"Here you go," Candace said, handing over a green can to Hannah. "I'm sorry, Sheriff, I should have asked if you wanted anything."

"I'm good," he said. "Getting back to the incident. You seem to have good recall on the purchases."

"That's because after they left, I sat down and documented everything, including the purchases and how they treated the little boy." She opened up a file folder and withdrew several pieces of paper. "Something was off about the whole thing, you know? I didn't know if they'd come back later and say the boy fell tripping over something in the gift shop, or blame his fall on me, or what, so I wanted to get it all down before I forgot."

Noah took the pages and read, then handed them over to Hannah.

When she finished, Hannah said, "You even got their credit card information, Candace. That's brilliant. And their license plate and the make and model of their vehicle."

Noah said, "You ever want to get into law enforcement, come see me. We're not a big agency, but we could use someone like you, who shows attention to detail."

"Thanks for the offer, Sheriff, but if I had to deal with stuff like this every day, I don't think I could handle it."

He nodded, then asked, "Was your instinct right? Did they come back?"

"No, I got a call the next day from the woman. She said I rang up one of her purchases wrong and she wanted a refund."

"Had you?"

"No, sir. She seemed surprised that I had an itemized list, and got all huffy. When I asked how the little boy was, she hung up on me."

"Not surprising."

"Do you think he's okay?"

"I don't know," Noah said. "We're hoping to find him

sooner rather than later, so we know for sure."

"This has taught me a valuable lesson," Candace said. "If it ever happens again, I'm calling the police."

"Good idea, and if these particular people should happen to show up here again, I'd like you to call me immediately. I can't get here as quickly as Woodland Park PD, but I'll notify them and they'll be on these assholes immediately." He seemed to rethink his language and added, "Please, excuse my French."

"I was calling them much worse in my head," Candace said, "so no need to apologize to me."

"Me, either," Hannah said. "I'm right there with Candace."

"Can you think of anything else?" Noah asked with a slight smirk of acknowledgment.

"Just one thing. That night, when I was tidying up the gift shop, I found a small folded piece of paper over near where the little boy had fallen. I picked it up, unfolded it, and read it." She reached across to Hannah. "I'm pretty sure this belongs to you."

Baffled, Hannah accepted the paper, which was about five inches square. Jay had drawn a picture of a Stegosaurus and beneath it, he'd printed, *Mom loves me and she loves dinos, too.* She almost couldn't breathe. He did remember her. The thing with Santa hadn't been a fluke.

She handed the little note over to Noah, who read it and handed it back.

Candace got up from her chair and went around the table. "You look like you could use a hug."

"If only you knew," Hannah said, rising to accept the embrace. "Thank you, Candace."

"I should've done more."

"You've been a big help, believe me. We're close. I can feel it."

"I'll keep an eye out."

"I have photocopied pictures of the four of them," Noah said. "Maybe you can post them in your employees-only area, so they know who to be on the lookout for."

"Good idea, since I only work eight hours a day, five days a week, I might miss them. Can I have an extra one of your business cards, too, and I'll tape it to the photocopies."

Noah pulled out two cards. On one, he wrote on the back. "This one's for you, in case you're out and about and happen to see something we should know. This is my home number."

"I don't actually live in Woodland," she said. "I live in Manitou Springs, but you know, that reminds me. I have a friend who works at the Christmas shop in Manitou. I'll contact her and see if she's witnessed anything like this."

"I appreciate it," Noah said, "especially since we know that the woman apparently has a thing for Christmas décor." He looked at Hannah, "Ready to go?"

"Yes."

Candace gave Hannah's hand a squeeze. "When you get him back, bring him in and I'll comp your entry fee and I'd love to gift him a stuffed T. Rex."

Hannah smiled at the girl. "That's very kind of you."

"It's the least I can do."

Back in the sheriff's truck, the two of them sat in silence for a few moments, contemplating all they'd learned. Finally, Hannah asked, "Who called?"

"The patrol officer who was checking at schools."

"What did he say?"

"He found Jay's school, but Jay hasn't been there since last Friday, and there's been no phone call regarding the absence."

Hannah's hopes sank so fast it was like the anchor of a freighter had been attached to them. "They're on the run."

"Not necessarily. They were at the North Pole on Monday, remember?"

Even though his reassurance eased her worry somewhat, she still felt tethered to that damned anchor.

"We were going to hit the Safeway and the Starbucks. Are you up to it?"

"Do you really have to ask?"

"No, but it was the polite thing to do, wasn't it?"

"You're a nice man, Noah."

He snorted. "No one's ever accused me of that before."

"I'm glad I'm the first, then, because you definitely are."

He stared at her without speaking, meeting her eye-to-eye

until his gaze dropped down to her lips.

Hannah knew what he was thinking and if the situation had been different, she would've crawled across the console and into his lap and let him have his way with her mouth.

But things weren't different. She was still legally married, albeit to a cruel, cheating bastard of a husband, but a marriage vow was a marriage vow. "We should go."

He lifted his eyes, blinked, and said, "Yeah."

At the Safeway, they went to customer service. There, the store manager agreed to show each checker the photos. When he found one who recognized Sabine, he called a relief checker to that checkstand so that Noah and Hannah could talk to her.

"The only reason I remember this woman is because she usually comes in with the little boy and she's awful to him."

"How do you mean?" Noah asked.

"She makes him go ahead of her through the checkout and then runs the cart into him. If he asks for something from the gum or candy display, she smacks him. She also says things to him that I find totally" —she shrugged and bit her lip, apparently searching for the right word— "totally degrading."

"Can you give us an example?" Noah asked.

"She tells him he's already ugly and if he eats candy, he'll be even uglier, or she tells him his teeth are gross and if he chews gum, no one will be able to stand talking to him because his teeth will be all black and rotted." She shrugged again. "Stuff like that." Her gaze went to Hannah. "He's your son?"

Hannah nodded. "My husband took him and ran off to be with this woman."

"That sucks. No one who treats a kid like she does should be within a mile of any child."

"Can you remember the last time they came in?" Noah asked.

"Hmm...I think it must have been on Monday. The little guy had a bandage on his forehead and his cheek was bruised. He said he'd fallen down at the North Pole."

"Did either of the men in the pictures come in with them?"

"No." She cocked her head. "Did any of the other checkers

say if they recognized them?"

"No."

"That's not surprising, I guess. She seems to always come through my line, even if she has to wait behind two or three other carts. It just now strikes me that maybe she didn't want any of the others seeing how she treated that poor little boy."

"Can you think of anything else?" Noah asked.

"Well, there was one thing. Last week when there were in, the woman snapped at him to do something and he said something like, 'You're not my mom. I don't have to do what you tell me.' That earned him a really mean, dirty look and another smack." She sighed. "I have to tell you, I almost picked up the phone and called the cops that day, but I don't really know about stuff like that, so I wasn't sure they'd even respond."

"They will," Noah assured her. "One last question. What does she buy for groceries?"

"Several types of cheeses and crackers. T-bones and ribeye steaks, russet potatoes, and Kraft macaroni and cheese. On Monday, I remember that the boy asked if she could get him something different to eat for a change and she said if he was unhappy with mac-and-cheese for lunch and dinner, he was welcome not to eat at all." She sighed again. "Like I said, she's one mean human being."

For the first time in her life, Hannah experienced the need for vengeance and it felt damned good. She began to plan exactly how she could make Sabine pay for treating Jay like he was no better than the dirt beneath her spike heels.

"There's one more thing," the clerk said. "My sis works over at the liquor store and we've kind of exchanged notes on this woman."

"Yes?" Noah prodded.

"Wine. She buys lots of wine."

As they walked back out to Noah's truck, he said, "I'm going to enjoy putting the cuffs on this bitch."

"I know Jason wasn't much of a father, but I can't comprehend him letting her hurt Jay like she does."

"He's thinking with the wrong head."

Hannah blinked at him. "Are you saying that the sex is so

good between them, he's unwilling to intervene for fear she'll cut him off."

"That's my guess."

Hannah had never considered it from that angle. For her, sex with Jason had been perfunctory from the get-go. She'd assumed before her marriage to him that once they'd tied the knot, the sparks would start flying and the rainbows would appear, but it simply hadn't happened that way.

A wave of guilt swept over her. If she'd been a better lover, if the sparks *had* flown and the rainbows *had* appeared, would Jason still have hooked up with Sabine and hatched the plot to fake his and Jay's drowning deaths? Was this, *all* of this, her fault?

The thought nearly doubled her. She grabbed onto Noah's arm to keep from falling to the ground.

"What is it?" he asked, grabbing her upper arms to steady her. "Are you okay?"

"It's all my fault."

"What are you talking about? What's all your fault?"

"Jason...the staged boating accident...him taking Jay." She avoided his gaze, embarrassed and ashamed that she hadn't been a better wife, a better lover, to her husband.

"I hope you're not thinking what I think you're thinking."

She remained stubbornly silent.

He grasped her chin gently with his big fingers and turned her head so she was forced to look at him. "Hannah, *nothing* you did caused Jason to do what *he* did."

"You can't know that," she whispered. "I wasn't good in bed. I drove him to it."

"Look, I wasn't there, but I can tell you, if anything went wrong in the marriage bed, it wasn't because of you."

"Oh, please! He went looking elsewhere because I'm a dud." As soon as the words were out, she longed to recall them. She hardly knew Noah, and here she was sharing thoughts with him she wouldn't share with anyone else, not even her sister.

"Are you forgetting that he and Sabine and Twombly were a threesome back in high school? He didn't go looking for either of them. This disgusting trio has always maintained a relationship with each other. You had the misfortune to get in the middle of that, and by association, Jay did, too."

Humiliated despite his attempt to make her feel better, Hannah nonetheless considered his words. And then she remembered their one and only kiss and she realized it took the right person to make sparks and rainbows. A brief wave of relief washed through her. Jason hadn't been that right person for her. Noah was.

The shame of it was that she couldn't do a damned thing about it because by law, she was still married to a conniving sociopath, who just happened to be hooked up with a worse sociopath than he was, and don't forget Twombly, who got his jollies by trying to have her arrested for the murders of two people who weren't dead.

"What's going on in that head of yours now?" Noah asked.

"I'm thinking. Everything's all jumbled up in my mind and I have a lot to sort out."

He reached for her hand. "This is all going to work out, you can trust me on that."

"It's not you that I don't trust," she said, and meant it in spite of her earlier doubts to the contrary.

Noah had no reassurances to cheer her up. He started the truck and they headed next to Starbucks.

Chapter 29

The Starbucks was deserted inside, save for one couple playing cribbage at a table near the window. Instead of coffee, they were drinking iced beverages, which Hannah thought odd, considering the wintry weather, but to each his own. The drive-thru, by contrast, had a steady flow of customers.

Noah approached the counter and asked to speak to a supervisor. The barista identified himself as the store manager and the conversation Noah had initiated several times already that day commenced yet again.

The manager studied the photos and called over one of the other baristas. "Aren't these the people who come in and order the expensive venti bevs?"

The young woman nodded. "And they will never let the little boy have anything but water." She made eye contact with Hannah, then said to the sheriff, "One time when he begged for a hot chocolate, his woman shook him so hard, I thought his little neck was going to snap."

"Do they come in regularly?"

"Two or three times a week," she said, glancing at the manager, who nodded in agreement.

"When was the last time they were in?"

"Hmm, Monday, I think."

"With the little boy?"

"Yes, and now that I think about it, they're usually here on

Monday, Wednesday, and Friday."

Noah pulled out his card and laid it on top of the photocopied photos. "If they come in again, please, call me immediately. Whatever you do, just act natural. Try not to pay them any special attention."

"Will you have time to get here, since you're in Fossil?" the manager asked.

"I'll notify Woodland Park PD. They'll get here first and detain them."

"We've never been involved in an incident concerning child abduction before," the manager said. His gaze went to Hannah. "Are you the mom?"

"Yes." There was nothing more for her to add. She was certain the misery she felt was written all over her face.

"We'll do everything we can," the manager assured her.

"Thank you."

Noah added his thanks and asked if she wanted a coffee.

Hannah needed a good caffeine jolt, so she said yes.

The manager refused to take any money for their drinks. They thanked him again and headed back to the truck.

Next stop, Woodland Park PD.

Hannah and Noah sat in the empty conference room in silence.

Finally, Noah said, "Let me know if you want to talk."

"I will."

Fifteen minutes later, Pete and Liza wandered in and shortly after that, the chief and two of his officers.

"Have any luck?" Pete asked Noah.

"Maybe more than we wanted," his son replied.

"Uh-oh," Liza said, her worried eyes on Hannah.

"If you all don't mind, I'll just listen," Hannah said. "I'm kind of on overload right now." She made eye contact with each one of them, then added, "Please, don't hold back. No matter how bad you think it is, it can't possibly be worse than what I've already heard today."

"Let's get started, then," Chief Fitzgerald said. "What have you got?" he asked his counterpart from Pike County.

It took Noah twenty minutes to go over everything they'd learned.

All the while, Hannah stared in silence at the holiday-adorned Starbucks cup clenched in her hands. She steeled herself against the emotions threatening to overwhelm her and focused instead on the facts they'd gathered. Were they helpful? Could there be something in there that would help them find Jay? Was her little boy okay?

Pete went next. "We visited every hair salon in town. Sabine likes the high-dollar cuts. Jason and Twombly visit the barber shop, and Jay is hit-or-miss at the Fantastic Sam's, which is a no-appointment place. The woman there...." His voice dwindled, as if he were reluctant to continue.

Hannah's head came up. "Don't sugarcoat it, Pete. Just say it."

Pete glanced at Liza, as if entreating her to continue.

His wife obliged. "Apparently, Sabine has a habit of ridiculing Jay when he gets his hair cut."

Hannah made a forward motion with her hand.

"She calls him names and sometimes slaps his face when he responds, even though he's not being nasty." Liza sucked in her lips, then said, "I'm so sorry, Hannah."

"Me, too."

"We hit the clothing stores, but had no luck," Pete said. "At the WalMart, one clerk recognized them, but couldn't remember anything specific about them except that they weren't nice to the little boy."

Chief Fitzgerald shoved his fingers through his nicely combed hair. "I'm sensing a pattern here that's making me sick to my stomach." He asked Officer Dave Hamby to go next.

"I went to all the elementary schools," Hamby said, "and as luck would have it, the last one I visited is where the boy is enrolled. He hasn't been in school since last Friday, and although the school has called his home, no one answers. They assumed there was some out-of-town emergency or something and they'd just forgotten to call in."

"What name is he using?" Hannah asked, curious at just how far Jason had gone with his new-life charade.

"Jay Merle, Junior."

"Merle."

"Does that ring a bell?" Noah asked.

"Jason's father's first name is Merle."

Noah turned to Hamby. "Did you get copies of his registration and school records?"

"Finally. The principal didn't want to, but I informed him it was either me or the FBI and that seemed to decide him in my favor." He shrugged. "I had no idea if the FBI will be involved, but I figured a little white lie was justified, and in any case, Simon's CBI and he's involved."

The chief nodded his agreement.

Hamby went on. "As to the people in the Newcomer's Club I talked to, most said they remember them, but that they hadn't been active in events for quite a while."

"Good work, Dave," the chief said. "Steve, you go next."

Officer Steve Kilgore said, "That's about what I heard from the Newcomer's I talked to, although the current president did say she'd seen Jason and Sabine at a restaurant up in Divide about a week ago. Twombly and the boy were with them." He blew out a breath. "Given that these people are rough on this little boy, I hit up the pediatricians' offices, the hospital, and the urgent care. The doctors' offices were not forthcoming, but both the urgent care and the hospital ER were helpful. Jay has been seen three times at urgent care in the last two years and twice in the ER."

Hannah gripped her empty paper cup so hard, it buckled. "They've been here that long? What kinds of injuries?"

"Stitches a couple of times, a broken arm once, fever another time, and poisoning once."

Beside her, Noah stiffened. "Poisoning? Like food poison?"

"No, they pumped his stomach and drew blood trying to figure out what it was, because the dad and the woman they assumed was Jay's mom said they had no idea what he'd gotten into." Kilgore's expression grew stony. "It came back that he'd OD'd on Tylenol. They admitted to giving it to him after the fever incident, but steadfastly maintained that they thought they were dispensing a child's dose."

"Did any of this get reported to us?" Chief Fitzgerald asked.

"No. This poor kid is completely lost in the cracks."

Hannah attempted to dull her brain to what she was hearing, but her mind was having none of it.

"What did you get, Simon?" Noah asked his brother.

"I hit the fast food places first, to beat the lunch crowds. Apparently, their place of choice is the McDonald's. Jay is usually only allowed a Happy Meal. No special treats, like ice cream cones or pies or cookies, even though the grownups indulge. Sometimes all he gets is a dollar hamburger. At the post office, the clerk recognized the photos of Sabine and Twombly, but couldn't remember if they both had postal boxes. One of the other clerks said she noticed that Sabine left Jay in the car while she came in to get her mail or buy stamps. She said one day, Jay came in and said he had to go to the bathroom. Sabine yelled at him and dragged him out crying. She said it looked like he wet his pants, which she thought was the reason Sabine hit him when they got to the car."

Hannah continued to stare at her now-crumpled cup. She imagined it to be Sabine's neck and crushed it flat. While it offered no relief to her emotional state, it did allow a thought to break through. "Is there no way to track them from the stolen license plates?"

The chief grunted. "That set of plates was one of a dozen stolen off vehicles in Belmar that day. As for the vehicle they're driving, there are hundreds of stolen-vehicle reports from around the country. They could have taken it from anywhere, or they could have bought it and dumped the plates when they got to Colorado. We just don't know."

"The plates on the vehicle Twombly was driving were registered to a vehicle whose owner lives in Castle Rock," Noah said.

The chief nodded. "Coincidentally, the couple was in Woodland the day the plates were stolen. They were passing through to view the fall foliage. They didn't notice the plates were missing until they got home."

"The three of them cover all the bases," Hannah said.

"Probably because Twombly guides them," Simon said. "What a pitiful excuse for a cop."

She sighed. "Where does all this leave us?"

"We're going to follow the leads we got today," Simon said. "We'll review every word on the paperwork from the schools, the hospital, and the urgent care."

Hannah held out no hope those leads would amount to anything. "It seems hopeless."

"We never know when a lead will pan out," Noah said.

Chief Fitzgerald said, "Dave and Steve will do a follow-up with a couple of kids who were friendly with Jay at school. They'll speak to them with their parents present. That may give us something."

"Will I be able to get copies of all the paperwork gathered today? I'd like to review everything. Maybe I'll spot something you all might miss, since I'm...." She faltered. It seemed both redundant and senseless to remind them that she was Jay's mother and Jason's wife.

"I don't have a problem with that," Chief Fitzgerald said. "Do you?" he asked Noah and Simon.

"It's irregular, but then so is this case," Simon said.

"I'm good with it," Noah said. "Hannah is, after all, Jay's mother."

"How about we all meet again tomorrow morning and start fresh?" the chief suggested.

Hannah was so wiped out, it sounded like a perfect plan to her. She could sleep on the way back to Fossil and stay up as late as she needed to, to read everything. She added her nod of agreement.

The chief and his officers left the room.

Liza said to Hannah, "Pete's going to ride back with me. Do you mind hitching a ride back with Noah?"

"Only if he promises not to talk."

Liza grinned.

Noah frowned.

Pete and Simon laughed. "You've either been insulted or warned, son," Pete said.

"Probably both," Noah said. "What's with the passenger switcheroo?"

"We're heading up to Simon's," his dad said. "I've been promising to help him install a new faucet. We're so close, now's the time to do it."

"You can come up, too, if you want," Liza said. "We can all go out to dinner together."

"I'd really rather get home," Hannah said, "but if Noah wants to stay, I can certainly rent a car to go back to Fossil."

"I need to get home and see to Fiona," Noah said.

"Gosh, I completely spaced Bowie. Will Marty still be there by the time we get back?"

"If she isn't, she'll take Bowie home. Her kids will love that."

"I'm sure Bowie will, too." She looked at Liza. "I'd better get my bag out of your trunk."

"I'll get it," Noah said.

Liza dug out her key and handed it over to him.

"I need to use the restroom before we go," Hannah said. "I'll meet you outside."

Five minutes later, with her face freshly splashed with cold water, and her thanks extended to the WPPD staff, she joined the Wards in front of the building. She carried a red-rope folder in her hand, stuffed full of photocopies.

"Try to get some sleep tonight," Liza said, hugging her.

"I'll try, but I don't know if my mind will shut down. This has been quite a day."

"Tomorrow, while the guys are working the case, you and I can wander around. You never know who we might spot."

"God loves an optimist," Hannah said with a smile.

"He also loves moms who love their kids."

"Thank you all for what you're doing."

"It's our pleasure, Hannah," Pete said.

"That's right," Simon concurred. "We all want to see Jay back where he belongs."

"Amen," said Liza. "And by the way, the tri-tip dinner is postponed, obviously, but I'll let you know when it's re-scheduled."

So tired she could barely hold her head up, Hannah nodded.

With hugs all around, they said their goodbyes. Noah in his

usual gentlemanly way, opened the truck door for her and helped her up.

Five minutes later, with her head cradled between the head-rest and the door, Hannah was sound asleep.

Noah glanced over at Hannah at regular intervals. Darkness had set in, but she looked serene in the glow of the dashboard lights. He honestly didn't know how she'd coped with all she'd learned over the course of the day. Jay wasn't even his kid and he wanted to beat the crap out of the three adults who had him.

He'd never handled a missing child case before, but he had handled missing adult cases, and those had involved hysterical, screaming people in most cases. Not once had he ever encountered anyone with Hannah's fortitude. Yeah, she'd cried once, and if he was right, she'd also escaped to the bathroom at the dinosaur museum to puke again, but she'd composed herself and come right back out to keep on truckin'.

Since Twombly was now an escapee, and Jason and Sabine were the likely jail-breakers, he was worried about Hannah being alone in her house, with only Bowie for protection.

Noah wondered how Hannah would take it if he suggested she sleep at his house until they were caught.

Dumb ass. You know how she'll take it.

Maybe he could broach it from a different angle. He could stay at her place. While he mulled over that possibility, he glanced at her again, taken again with her beauty. Jason must have done quite a number on her if she thought she was just another Plain Jane. From his perspective, there was nothing plain about her. Not a blessed thing.

Hannah moaned and with it came a frown.

He considered waking her, but thought better of it. If she let out a scream, that would be different, but a moan? Hell, she might only be dreaming about being chased by wolves, or at worse, the terrible trio comprised of Jason and Sabine and Twombly. Or, she could be reliving all the battering poor little Jay had taken at the hands of the madwoman, Sabine.

Noah gripped the steering wheel with so much force, his

knuckles ached. He'd never had to kill anyone on the job, at least not his job as sheriff, but he knew he could do it if he had to, to protect someone. Being a SEAL had taught him that and it was a lesson he'd never forget.

Sabine had most likely killed her husband Henri. She'd no doubt been involved in Bert Hague's murder, as well, and God only knew how many others she'd killed along the way.

Of one thing he was certain. If Sabine was the killing mastermind of the threesome, if she wanted Hannah dead, she'd relish doing the job herself. The woman, from all accounts, simply took too much pleasure in hurting a little kid who didn't have the ability to fight back. What Sabine didn't realize was that Hannah not only had the ability to retaliate, she'd probably relish the chance to kill Sabine first.

He'd like to help Hannah avoid that outcome. Knowing how to kill and living with it for the rest of your life were two different things. Psychopaths like Sabine knew how to do it. Normal women like Hannah did not.

The silence in the vehicle didn't bother him. By the time he reached Hannah's place, she was still sleeping. Again, he debated waking her and decided not to. With the motor still running for the heat, he climbed out of the truck and pulled out the house key she'd given him. He opened the front door, turned on a light, disarmed the alarm, then walked down to her bedroom and turned on the bedside lamp.

She slept in a king-size bed, and he wondered if that was left over from her marriage with Jason. He pulled back the covers and on the way back down the hall, checked the thermostat. Even with his coat on, the house seemed chilly. Sure enough, she'd set the temperature to hold at sixty-two. He took off the hold and the readout jumped to sixty-eight. He left it at that and went back out to the truck, opening the passenger door.

Hannah was so deeply asleep, she barely made a sound as he lifted her from the vehicle and carried her inside. In her bedroom, he laid her on the bed, then pulled off her snow boots and debated removing her coat. He decided it wouldn't hurt to leave her sleeping in it and pulled up the covers. On his way out of the bedroom, he turned off the light.

Back in his truck, he drove to Marty's, where he picked up Bowie against her kids' protests. "I'm sure Hannah will let you play with him again," Noah assured them. Next stop, his place to get Fiona and an overnight bag. The dogs greeted each other as if they'd been apart for years instead of hours.

Thirty minutes after he left Hannah's, he used the key to open her front door again. He set Hannah's wheeled bag next to the front door, along with his overnight bag, then turned off the alarm and reset it for STAY before he followed the dogs to the family room, where he got a fire going.

After that, he filled Bowie's food bowl, emptied a baggie of dog food into the dish he'd brought along for Fiona, and put fresh water in the water dish. The canines, oblivious to his efforts, were already curled up in front of the roaring fire, sound asleep.

He carried Hannah's bag down the hall and left it just inside her door. From there, he examined the other bedrooms, looking for a place to sleep. Neither spare bed had been made up, but on one were four neatly folded blankets. He turned off the light and went back to the family room to study the sofa. With a couple of pillows under his head, and if he slept with his knees bent, he could probably fit.

That settled, he went to the refrigerator. His stomach rumbled as he pulled the door open. The contents were sparse, but at least he wouldn't starve. He pulled out the container of soup, the baggie of corn muffins, and a cherry yogurt.

Less than fifteen minutes later, he ate his dinner on the sofa in front of the fire, trying to watch the news. As the sheriff of Pike County, he felt bound to keep up on current events, but these days, current events didn't seem to vary. He switched the channel until he found an old John Wayne movie. Who didn't like the Duke?

Once he'd cleaned up his dishes and loaded them in the dishwasher, he went back to the spare bedroom and grabbed two blankets and two pillows, which had cases on them. Both dogs raised their sleepy heads and watched as he readied his makeshift bed. "Need to go outside?" he asked. Both put their heads back down, which was answer enough for him.

He added a log to the fire, set the timer on the TV to ninety minutes, and turned off the lights. He didn't normally sleep in his clothes, but these were extenuating circumstances.

Twombly had broken out of jail. Being on the loose, he was mostly likely going to make another try for Hannah. Maybe that was tonight, or maybe not, but sometime. Noah had to be ready when that try came. He considered leaving his boots on, but how was a guy supposed to sleep like that? Besides, it wouldn't take long to get into them again. The only other thing he removed was his gun, which he left within easy reach on the leather ottoman that served as a coffee table.

He had the best intentions of watching the rest of the movie, but within minutes of getting comfortable on the sofa, he fell sound asleep.

Chapter 30

Hannah awoke in total darkness. A glance at her bedside clock radio confirmed it was 6:34, but was it evening or morning? Last she knew, she'd been on her way back to Fossil in Noah's truck, with the man himself driving.

As far as she could tell, she was now safely ensconced in her own bed, and by the feel of it, still fully dressed, including her coat.

She flipped back the covers and threw her legs over the side of the bed before reaching for the light switch on the bedside lamp. Immediately blinded, she closed her eyes. After a few moments, she opened them again and stood, removing her coat.

Fully dressed. That told her that Noah had carried her inside, but she'd been so deep into sleep, she'd been completely oblivious. She hadn't even felt him remove her boots. The last time she'd succumbed to sleep that deep had been the days immediately following Jay and Jason's deaths…only they weren't dead, were they?

The two days spent in Estes Park and Woodland Park would have been proof enough, if she hadn't already seen the pictures her brother-in-law had taken.

Hannah decided she needed a nice, hot shower to dissolve the cobwebs in her head, then after that, something to eat.

Once out of the shower, she used the blow dryer on her hair and climbed into a pair of flannel pajamas and her Sherpa-lined slippers. Moments later, she was surprised to find Bowie sprawled in the doorway to her bedroom. Beside him was Fiona.

"Is there a pooch party going on?" she asked as Bowie leaped to his paws and rushed her. She knelt down to give him some rubs. Fiona sidled up and licked her hand. "You want some love, too, huh?"

Fiona smiled in response.

"Where's your owner?"

For an answer, the dog turned in a circle twice, then wandered back down the hall. Bowie was quick to follow.

Hannah shut off the bedroom light and by the glow of the nightlight plugged into the hallway outlet, made her way to the family room. The scent of a recent fire lingered in the air and she wondered how long Noah had stayed after he dropped her off. Or maybe, he'd built a fire for the dogs, then taken off. She didn't mind dog-sitting Fiona, but she was rather surprised at finding her there.

"Ready to go out?" she asked the canine siblings. "Without me, of course." To her surprise, neither dog seemed to have any interest in anything except curling up in front of the fireplace.

"I don't blame you," she said. "I'll get a fire going." Bemused to find the coals still smoldering, she was further disconcerted when a voice behind her said, "Good morning."

Hannah stumbled backward and landed hard on her butt.

"I didn't mean to startle you," Noah said. "Are you okay?"

"I think so. What are you doing here?" Before she could push herself up off the floor, Noah scooped her into his arms and set her on the sofa. "Lights," she said, trying to figure out what was going on.

In the next instant, the lamp on the table at the end of the sofa lit up. "I spent the night."

"You did?"

"I did. Twombly escaped, remember? If he decided he to come after you again, I wanted to be his welcoming committee."

"Where did you sleep?" she asked, wondering if he'd climbed into bed beside her and she'd slept through that, too.

"On the sofa."

"That couldn't have been very comfortable."

"I managed."

"You could have made up one of the extra beds."

"I didn't want to cause a ruckus and wake you. The blankets and pillows were within easy grasp, so I made another choice."

Hannah chewed over his reason for staying and his reason for choosing the sofa. Truth be told, she hadn't considered that the former detective would try again to hurt or kill her. How stupid was that? Of course, he would. She was a problem for him and his companions, and problems in his world had to be dealt with in a certain way. "Do you really think he'll come back tonight?"

"It's way past tonight," Noah said, his tone slightly amused. "It's nearly daylight. You've been asleep since the moment we hit the road."

"I haven't."

"You have. I hope you weren't too uncomfortable sleeping in your clothes and your coat."

"I guess I wasn't," she said a bit wryly, "since I didn't wake up once." She calculated how long she'd been asleep. "My God, I slept over twelve hours."

"Sleep can be restorative."

"Sleep and a shower. I actually feel pretty good right now, considering everything I heard over the last two days."

"That would have been enough to make the Pope commit murder," he said. "You, on the other hand, took a different route."

She was silent for a moment, ruminating over his first analogy. "Yesterday, I thought about killing Sabine," she admitted. "I'm still not certain that I won't."

"The courts frown on vengeance killings, and if you don't mind another friendly reminder, it would be unfortunate if you were in prison instead of out, being a mom to Jay."

His tone was so wry, it took her a moment to decipher his underlying meaning—leave it to the law to take care of Sabine.

"I take your point, but there's no law against fantasizing various methods of torture for her, right?"

He smirked. "Not that I know of, but I can think of a lot of other, more satisfying things to fantasize about."

Hannah agreed, but didn't say so. No sense encouraging his wayward, provocative thoughts.

Noah moved toward the fireplace. "I'll get a fire going, then take the dogs out."

"I offered them the opportunity, but they declined," she said.

"So I heard. They'd rather stay in where it's all warm and snuggly, but I don't want to clean up any doggie messes."

A man like Noah using a word like *snuggly* made her giggle.

"What?" he asked, frowning at her over his shoulder.

"Snuggly?"

He shrugged and turned back to the fire. "I must have picked that up from my mom."

"Must have," she said, but she doubted it. There was a soft side to Sheriff Noah Ward that had yet to be explored.

"I'll fix us some breakfast when I come back in."

"Why don't I fix it, then it'll be ready when you come back in?"

"You should relax."

"I don't want to relax. I need to think and I can do that just as well in the kitchen."

"From the looks of your fridge, you have a challenge ahead of you."

"I'll figure out something." Maybe. She had a vague recollection of needing to hit the grocery store, and soon.

He finished laying the fire and struck the lighter to it. "It's your house. You can do what you want."

Her eye landed on the overnight bag in the corner. "If you'd like to take a shower, I can let the dogs out. They won't take off for parts unknown."

"I would like to shower, but I'll do it after they do their thing." He gazed down at her. "Will that throw off your breakfast plans?"

"Nope." He stared down at her a moment longer and she wondered what he was thinking. She knew what *she* was thinking, and it wasn't something a married woman should be thinking about a man she wasn't married to. "Would you mind going out through the mudroom? It's easier to dry off dogs in there, now that it's so wet outside."

"Not a problem." He glanced at Bowie and Fiona. Both had their eyes open, but neither had moved from their resting positions. "Let's go, Bowie, Fiona. Up!"

With obvious reluctance, and another verbal prodding from Noah, they both finally stood and trailed after him to the mudroom.

Hannah rose from the sofa and went to the kitchen to start breakfast. Behind what remained of Liza's soup was a small container of fresh pineapple chunks. To go with that, she peeled several Cuties and the last banana, emptying the fruit bowl. She also had Krusteaz pancake mix, to which she added water and a cup of the last-of-season frozen blueberries Liza had brought along with the soup. With the batter ready to go, she started the coffee and put the frozen breakfast sausages on to cook. Last to do before setting the table was to heat the maple syrup bottle in a pan of water on the stove.

Noah came back in with the dogs and gave them a thorough drying. Afterward, the canines collapsed in front of the fireplace as if he'd exhausted them. "Fakers," he muttered with a grin. He grabbed his overnight bag and headed to the main bathroom.

"Wait!" Hannah said, rushing after him. "I don't have a shower curtain up yet. You'll have to use my shower."

Standing at the doorway of the main bath, he turned to look at her, his eyes blazing.

She didn't have to go far to imagine where his thoughts had taken him. Based on her own thoughts, which had a little something to do with both of them in the larger shower enclosure together, well, enough said. Her faced flushed with color. "I think you know the way. I'll get the pancakes started." She whirled around and hurried back to the kitchen.

He called after her, "I'm going to shave, too."

She couldn't manage more than, "Okay." God, what she

wouldn't give to stand in the bathroom doorway watching him instead of cooking breakfast. Of course, it wouldn't be safe, because who knew how long her self-control would last?

She set the table with one place setting on each side. It was bad enough what he did to her across the table. She didn't dare tempt fate by sitting next to him.

Less than fifteen minutes later, Noah returned. His hair was still damp and his cheeks were free of dark stubble. She hadn't realized until that moment that she liked him with a shadow of beard. It gave him the air of a warrior, which fit the image she had of his SEAL persona.

"Smells good," he said. "I'm starving." He glanced down at the table. "I swear, when I looked for something to eat last night, I never would have come up with anything this lavish."

Hannah studied her breakfast offerings. She'd fixed something similar many times for Jason, but he'd been so health conscious, usually only she and Jay had eaten, while Jason had one of his green smoothies and maybe a couple of protein bars. "It's nothing special."

"I beg to differ. It looks like you put a lot of effort into this breakfast. Thank you."

"It was a pleasure to cook for you."

He made a move toward her, but Hannah turned abruptly toward the counter. "Choose whichever side you like at the table." She poured coffee into two mugs and swung back. Noah hadn't moved and she realized that he was waiting for her to sit first. It constantly impressed her that he took his gentlemanly ways to such lengths. "I'll sit on this side."

He nodded and stepped forward to pull out her chair.

Hannah set both cups on the table and slid into her seat. "Thank you."

He laid a hand on her shoulder and gave her a squeeze. "Thank you for fixing breakfast."

"You're welcome."

He settled himself across from her. "Blueberry pancakes in December. What a treat."

From there on, they enjoyed a relaxed, conversational breakfast and lingered over a second cup of coffee. Hannah imagined letting herself get used to doing it every day and was surprised by her overwhelming feeling of contentment. It was so foreign to her, she almost didn't recognize it for what it was.

"What are your plans for today?" he asked.

"I've got a deadline looming on the insect book, so I'm going to work on that."

He nodded. "Just so you know, I'll be sleeping on your couch until they're brought in."

No need to ask for an explanation of who *they* was. "I'll make up one of the spare beds. No need for you to sleep cramped on the sofa. In fact, if you'd be more comfortable sleeping in my bed, since it's a king, I can take the spare bedroom."

Again his eyes blazed. "You don't have to give up your bed for me."

"I know I don't *have* to, but you're a lot bigger than I am. I just thought it would be more comfortable for you."

"I'll be fine in the queen-size bed."

"I'll change my sheets, in case you change your mind."

The corner of his mouth lifted and she thought he might protest, but instead he said, "You don't seem upset that I'm taking up residence in your home."

"It's not the ideal situation, but I'm smart enough to know that if Twombly makes it inside, it's goodbye Hannah. On the other hand, I do have a gun, and I could shoot him, but what if he overpowers me or something?" She didn't let her thoughts linger on what that something might be. Given Twombly's propensity toward violence, it would be anything but enjoyable.

"I thought I was going to have to argue the point with you."

"Actually, I considered throwing a fit about it for all of about fifteen seconds."

He grinned.

"Don't get cocky," she advised him. "I'm saving my energy for bigger battles to come."

"I'm sure you are. By the way, Mom and Dad will be spending the day here."

"They don't have to do that! It's broad daylight outside." That wasn't technically correct, because the sky was cluttered with gunmetal-gray clouds and snow was in the forecast, but couldn't she at least have the day to herself?

"Jason, Sabine, and Twombly are on the run, Hannah. We don't know whether or not they know that we know about their crime spree, or how horrible they are to Jay, but we do know that they're after you. Until they're captured, someone will be with you twenty-four/seven." He sipped from his mug, as casual as if his orders never got challenged. "Are we clear on that?"

"Crystal." Then, just to taunt him, she added, "Sheriff."

Liza and Pete rang the doorbell at 7:40. Noah left at 7:45. Hannah cleaned the kitchen while Liza and Pete enjoyed the leftover pancake breakfast.

"Are you sure you don't want me to heat up anything?" Hannah asked.

"The syrup is still warm, so we're good," Liza said. "You're a darned good cook, Hannah."

"Thanks. I used to enjoy it, but it's no fun when there's only me to cook for now."

"It's been so long since I cooked only for myself, I can hardly remember it, but I know what you mean."

"You should get some blueberry plants," Pete said. "We have blueberry pancakes and muffins and cobblers all winter long." He gave his wife a sweet smile, which she returned.

"I think I will," Hannah said. "I may even plant a vegetable garden."

Liza said, "Hannah, I hope you don't mind, but I brought along my baking supplies so I can get started on my Christmas goodies."

"I don't mind at all. If there's anything in my cupboards you need, help yourself." She glanced at Pete. "What are you up to today?"

"I brought along all the paperwork on your case to review, plus, I'm Liza's kitchen helper, and I'll probably take the dogs out, so I have plenty to keep me occupied." He patted his stomach. "Man, that was delicious, Hannah. Thank you."

Liza picked up both their plates and brought them to the sink.

Pete's talk of reviewing paperwork reminded Hannah of all the copies Chief Fitzgerald had made for her. Sometime today, she had to make time to start reading what was in the red rope folder.

She dried her hands and gave Noah's mom a quick tour of where everything was in the kitchen and a brief instructional on how to use her new gas stovetop over the electric oven. "If you want coffee, the ground beans are in a jar in the freezer and the filters are in the drawer below the cupboard where I keep the mugs. Make as many pots as you like, or if you prefer tea or hot chocolate, you'll find both in the pantry. I usually take a break from drawing every hour or so to refill my coffee or grab a cup of tea, but feel free to interrupt me any time."

"What time do you like lunch?" Liza asked.

"I usually grab something around one."

"I brought along everything to make chicken noodle soup, with fresh rolls. How does that sound?"

Sometimes she got lonely eating alone and lunch with the Wards sounded nice. Maybe this being babysat thing would work out okay after all. "It sounds yummy, but I think there may still be enough of the chicken tortilla soup and cornbread muffins left to feed us all."

Liza opened the fridge to examine the container. "Tortilla soup it is, then. Should I reheat the muffins in the oven?"

Hannah nodded. "I put them in foil for about ten minutes."

Liza gave her a thumbs up as Hannah poured herself another cup of coffee and left the kitchen.

She settled in at her drawing table and began working on the katydid, which she'd started after the Elvis bug had been completed. Once that was finished, she planned to move on to either the Hercules beetle or the dragonfly. Her list of insects for the book were in no particular order, allowing her to work on whatever suited her fancy on any particular day.

At nine, she took a coffee break. By ten-thirty, she began to put the final colors on the katydid. When she broke for lunch at one, the outline of the dragonfly was complete. She headed for the kitchen.

"I hope we haven't disturbed you," Noah's mom said.

"Not at all. When I'm drawing, I get so immersed, I don't hear anything, including the easy-listening background music I have on. How's the cookie-baking going? It smells heavenly in here."

"See for yourself," Liza said.

In the kitchen, Hannah was flabbergasted by the containers full of cookies. "Let's skip soup and have dessert first."

"Pete's already in that mode," Liza said, grinning.

Pete laughed. "You know it's my payment for helping, love."

Liza shot him a cheeky grin. "I hope you aren't so stuffed with sweets that you don't want soup."

"No chance of that."

After lunch, Hannah walked down the hall munching a snickerdoodle. She popped the last bite into her mouth and stopped off in the bathroom to wash her hands before she went back to drawing. At three-thirty, she came out for another cup of coffee and grabbed a piece of fudge. "I could get used to this," she told Liza.

"I give most of this away to friends. I'll be sure to add you to my gift list."

Hannah grinned. "Please, do. So far, I've loved everything I tried." She looked around. "Where's Pete?"

"He took the dogs out for a walk." Her gaze went to the kitchen window. "He said he needed to think and fresh air helps him do that."

"Because of my case?"

"Yes, but don't let that worry you. He's been like this ever since I first met him. His system seems to work for him."

"Does that mean he's on the verge of a breakthrough?"

"I have no idea. Sometimes it does, and sometimes it just means that he found something to work with that will lead him to a breakthrough."

Hannah tried not to let her disappointment show.

"Noah is bringing pizza for dinner."

"I love pizza."

"We all do." She went around to check the timer. "He mentioned that he's going to be spending his nights here until Jason and the others are caught."

"Um, yeah." Hannah's face suffused with heat. "He slept on the couch last night."

"So I heard. He mentioned he'll have one of the spare bedrooms tonight. I noticed when I used the bathroom earlier that neither of the beds is made up. Can I do that for you while I'm between cookie batches?"

"It's nice of you to offer, but—"

"Please, let me help, Hannah. I'm basically playing in your kitchen and you're working hard on your drawings. It's the least I can do."

Hannah felt like she was taking advantage of a situation, but it would give her an extra twenty minutes or so to make some progress on the dragonfly. "Thank you. The sheets are in the linen closet at the end of the hallway."

"You're a very organized person."

"Jason used to say that was my most annoying attribute."

"Jason is a shit." When Hannah didn't respond, she added, "I'm sorry. I shouldn't have said that."

"Don't apologize! The only reason I hesitated is because before, when I thought he'd taken Jay out on the sailboat and they'd both drowned, I was furious with him, but I never hated him. I realize now that I don't even know a word strong enough to describe how despicable he is."

"I might be able to think of a few."

"Feel free to share anytime."

"I will. You know, I like being organized myself, but Pete operates under a different principle he calls organized confusion."

Relieved not to continue talking about Jason, Hannah grinned. "It seems to work for him."

Liza laughed. "That it does, even though it drives me crazy." She picked up a potholder. "Noah said he'll be here around seven with the pizza."

"My mouth is watering all ready."

"I'm glad you came to Fossil, Hannah. With Pete and Noah and Simon on this thing with your husband and your son, I know you're going to see results...and I'm not just saying that because I'm the wife and mother."

Hannah was starting to think so, too. "The thought never crossed my mind, but I wonder...."

"What, sweetie?"

"Do you know a good divorce lawyer? I feel so helpless right now doing nothing, but maybe if I start divorce proceedings...I mean, there's no way I want to remain married to Jason after what he's done."

"I should hope not!"

Hannah couldn't go on. She'd taken her vows seriously, but surely, neither God nor the law meant she had to live with *for better or for worse, until death do us part*, when her husband had not only stolen her son away from her, but faked his and Jay's deaths.

And stolen from his firm.

And killed people.

And hurt Jay.

If there was a marriage-vow how-to manual somewhere, wives of immoral, lying scumbag husbands surely had the right to claim an exemption from that particular promise.

Chapter 31

Noah arrived right on time, carrying two large pizzas.

Hannah slid them into the pre-heated oven to keep them warm. "What does everyone want to drink?" she asked.

"Beer," Noah and Pete said at the same time.

"I'll have one, too," Liza said.

"Four beers it is," Hannah said, and went to the fridge to grab four bottles. She wondered where the six-packs had come from, then remembered Pete had made a run to the store mid-afternoon.

"We don't need glasses," Liza said. "We're somewhat heathen that way."

Hannah popped the lids and brought the four bottles to the table, where she'd set four places. She went back to the refrigerator. "Does anyone like sliced tomatoes on their pizza?"

Liza raised her hand.

She reached inside and grabbed two tomatoes and the carton of grated romano. "How about hot sauce?"

"That would be me and Noah," Pete said, speaking for his son, who had gone off to wash up in the bathroom.

Hannah handed Liza the cheese and hot sauce for the table and set about washing and slicing the tomatoes. "How shall we serve?"

"Put the boxes on the island and we'll serve ourselves?"

Hannah nodded. "Good idea."

Dinner went on for a leisurely hour. The four of them demolished more than half of each pizza, leaving plenty for lunch leftovers the next day. Afterward, they sampled Liza's baked goods with fresh coffee and once the kitchen was cleaned up, around eight, Liza and Pete took off.

Drying the last cookie sheet, Noah said, "I hope it wasn't too overwhelming having the folks here all day."

"Not at all. I really like them and as long as they felt comfortable, everything's copacetic."

"They were primarily worried about getting in your hair."

"Didn't happen, and I was more productive today than I have been in a long time." Hannah rinsed out the dish cloth and folded it over the sink divider. "I think it's because I really like having someone else in the house. It gets lonely being alone."

If Noah found that oxymoronic, he kept it to himself.

"Any progress today?"

"None, but we're still putting out feelers. Something's going to break."

Hannah turned and leaned against the counter, watching carefully for his reaction. "I'm going back to Woodland Park next week."

"Are you."

Not exactly a question, but more of a statement. Hannah nodded, understanding from his short, but telling tone that he knew she wasn't going for the fun of it and he wasn't happy about her decision. "I'll wander around. Maybe I'll get lucky and spot them."

"You've heard about the needle and the haystack, right?"

"Yes, but I'm constantly reminded that it's a small world."

He frowned.

Hannah pressed her point. "Your sister encountered them at her Christmas shop in Estes Park. Who would've thought that was possible?"

"Point taken, but when they see you, they'll take off running and then we might never find them." He hesitated, then added, "And that's assuming they don't kill you on the spot."

Even though his blunt assessment sent a chill down her

spine, she took a breath and forged on. "I plan to be in disguise."

He blinked, then gave his head a slight shake. "That's rich."

"As you mentioned, I don't want to spook them."

"Forget it. You're not going."

"You really have no say over how I spend my time."

"I can put you in protective custody, remember?"

She blew out an impatient sigh. "Stop threatening me with that, will you? Look, Noah, if they're still in Woodland Park, it only makes sense to look for them. They may have no idea that we know where they are."

He worked his jaw so furiously, she couldn't help but stare. "It's too dangerous."

"By disguising my appearance, they'll never know it's me."

"Exactly how do you propose to make this big transformation?"

"I have some ideas...a wig, glasses, wild makeup."

"The best laid plans of mice and men go awry, Hannah."

"I'll be careful."

"Said a lot of ignorant people before you."

"I'm not ignorant!" she shot back.

"In this instance, you are. These people have killed, or did you forget that?"

"No, Sheriff, I did not." Boiling with anger that he'd called her ignorant and that he had so little faith in her ability to remain inconspicuous, she stomped her foot like a petulant child.

The battle of the wills ensued.

Hannah was about ready to cave in when Noah beat her to it.

"Look, I don't want to see you hurt, or killed, okay?"

"Neither do I!"

"Wait until the weekend, when I'm off duty. I'll go with you."

"That's nice of you to offer, but give me some credit for being sensible, will you?"

He stared her down for another fifteen seconds without

speaking.

Hannah scowled back. "This is a discussion for which I foresee no satisfactory or affable conclusion."

"Only if you insist on doing it your way."

She didn't have the energy to continue the argument. "Do you want to play Scrabble?"

Obviously thrown by the non sequitur response, he made a disgruntled sound in the back of his throat and growled, "Yes."

Resigned to having resolved nothing concerning her plan, she offered him a smug warning. "Be prepared to have someone beat *you* down for a change."

"Not likely."

"We'll see."

The evening's second battle of wills commenced.

Two hours later, the score in wins was Sheriff Noah Ward, one, illustrator Hannah Mason, two. She decided if this fourth game ended in a tie, she was going to bed, albeit alone. With Noah in the spare bedroom. Across the hall. Out of sight, but not out of mind.

Being a good girl was not as easy as it sounded.

She studied the small wooden tiles in front of her for several minutes.

"We should've used a timer," he groused.

She rearranged her tiles one more time and said, "Ah-ha!" before she played *ziplocks* horizontally by adding an *s* to a vertical word, *exhale*, connecting them for a triple-word score at both the corner and middle spots of the bottom row, for a total of three hundred and twenty-three points, *plus* fifty additional points for using all her tiles.

For a stunned moment, Noah stared at the board. "You computed wrong. You should only get a straight triple-word count on both the triple words."

"Wrong," Hannah said. "The first triple word comes from the corner block. That's in play by the time I get to the second triple word in the middle of the board." She handed him the sheet where she'd done her math computations. "With the one double letter, the word is valued at twenty-six points. Tripled, it's sixty-eight. Tripled on the second triple word score, that's two hundred and four on *ziplocks*. Add the third triple for *exhales*, which is seventeen points, and you get another fifty-one points." As if talking to a simpleton, she went on, "Sixty-eight, plus two hundred and four, plus fifty-one, *plus fifty* equals three hundred and seventy-three."

Noah's look of consternation as he continued to stare at the board made her smile. She held back the triumphant chuckle that begged to follow.

"I concede," he said, "both on your math and the game." He looked up.

Hannah expected anger, like Jason would have expressed, or disgust, which Jason also would have exhibited, but instead, she got a grin of amusement.

"You said you'd wallop me and I guess you weren't kidding. Congratulations."

"Thank you." All of a sudden, she felt petty and small. She'd wanted to teach him a lesson for bossing her around, but now that she'd managed it, she found no satisfaction in her victory. "I'm sorry."

"For what?"

"For trying to get back at you."

"Because I was worried about you going to Woodland alone?"

That threw her. "Were you? Worried, that is?"

"Of course. These are dangerous people we're dealing with, Hannah."

He had her there.

"What if I take a companion with me?"

"Like who, Bowie?"

"I meant a human, not a canine."

"I suppose that would be my mother."

"Actually, I was thinking about hiring Sonny. He's sweet, but he's got the look of someone who can take care of himself."

Noah blew out a breath of impatience. "You can't go putting a kid in harm's way. It's bad enough you want to put yourself there." He frowned, then said, "If I rearrange my schedule, I suppose I could go with you. Technically, I'd be on the job."

"That would work out really well," she said, her tone facetious, "since Twombly would recognize both of us in a nano second."

"At least you realize he'd recognize you."

"But he won't. I'm going in disguise, remember? He'd only recognize you, but that would cause him to recognize me by association." She gathered up the tiles and placed them in their little storage bag.

"If you think that solution is going to sway my opinion of your stupid plan, forget it. It won't."

"Then suggest something better!" she cried, suddenly angry.

Noah flexed his jaw and she knew she had him.

"That's what I thought. I'll be careful, and I even promise to check in, if that'll make you feel any better."

"It doesn't make me feel better, but I would appreciate knowing that you're still alive."

That cold, foreboding chill shimmered up her back again. Did he always have to be so maddeningly blunt?

Hannah laid in her big bed wondering if Noah had fallen asleep yet. For some reason, she had a burning desire to apologize to him again, though for the life of her, she didn't know what for or what it would solve.

An hour later, she slid out of bed and into the hallway. Noah's bedroom door was wide open. Was he asleep, or listening to her creep around in the dark?

She wandered into the kitchen to make a cup of tea. Sometimes, when she couldn't sleep, having a hot beverage helped her nod off. Instead of heating the teapot, she used the hot-water dispenser, then took her mug over by the fireplace where Bowie and Fiona appeared content to watch her without moving from their comfy positions in front of the hearth. She sank down beside them.

"You two have it so easy," she whispered.

Bowie's tail began to wag, not in a frenzy, but more with

contentment.

"All you have to worry about is where your next meal is coming from."

Now Fiona's tail began to wag the same way.

"What if I did take both of you with me? Wouldn't that be protection enough?"

Bowie made a little whining sound in his doggie throat.

"I know, stupid question, right? Maybe I should teach you both how to bite. You could pretend to be police K-nines."

"That would work really well," Noah said from the doorway. Shadowed in darkness, she couldn't make out his facial features, but his muscular form was clearly obvious.

Startled by his quiet appearance, Hannah jerked, slopping tea over the edge of her mug.

"Afterward, I could go visit you in the hospital and the dogs in the vet clinic," Noah went on, his tone half-wry, half-angry.

"It was just a thought," she said in her own defense.

In four long strides, he stood towering over her.

Hannah sucked in a breath she hoped he didn't notice. Wearing only boxer shorts, he was quite a sight to behold. Her thoughts leaped immediately to the big bed she shared with no one. How much of it would his big body take up...and what would he be doing to and with her while he was taking up all that space?

It didn't dawn on her right away that she wasn't exactly covered from head-to-toe herself. She might not have remembered at all that she was in her PJs if Noah's gaze hadn't dropped to look at what the scoop neck of her long-sleeved sleep tee revealed. She resisted the urge to readjust her clothing, because really, there was no readjustment to be made. Slightly embarrassed, she looked away.

"It's no wonder you can't sleep," he said, his voice a little hoarse as he sank down beside her, "if all you're doing is thinking of ways to insert yourself into this investigation."

"That's not all I'm thinking about."

"Oh, yeah?" he said with a challenge in his tone. "What else then?"

Before she could decide whether or not to be honest with

him, her mouth made the call without consulting her. "I was thinking about you. In my bed."

"At least we're on the same page about something."

Her gaze jerked around and met his. Desire burned so hot in his eyes, it almost scorched her. "You know we can't."

He sighed. "I know." The corner of his mouth quirked up. "Don't take this the wrong way, but, thank God for fantasies."

Her eyes went wide at the admission and she felt her face flood with heat. Her mouth didn't care. "If we're being completely honest here, I'd have to agree."

"Was I good?" he asked, his tone both wry and amused.

"You were." She took a small sip from her mug. "How was I?"

"You were so hot, the two of us were burning up the sheets."

A sexual yearning she'd never experienced before exploded throughout Hannah's body. She was so overcome with desire for Noah, she nearly threw herself at him, begging to experience whatever relief he could give her to quell the tingling excitement and hunger coursing through her and landing like a searing meteorite right at her core. "Is it cheating to talk about sex fantasies?"

"Probably."

"I'm going to hell when I die, then."

"Not likely, but if you are, so am I." He reached over and stroked her cheek with his thumb. "At least we'd be together."

"Your mother gave me the name of a divorce attorney."

"She did?"

Hannah nodded. "I asked for it. As soon as we find Jason, I want to serve him with the paperwork. I have an appointment with the attorney tomorrow."

Noah stared deeply into her eyes. "Was that difficult for you, to take that step?"

"What do you think?"

"I don't know. That's why I'm asking."

"Jason died for me two years ago. If I had any love left for him, it disintegrated the moment I saw Craig's pictures." She put her cup down on the hearth and cupped his hand with hers. "I want you so badly."

"I want you, too, but you're the one who set the rules…and I agree with them, so we're at an impasse."

Hannah uttered a soft sigh. "I know, and I'm sticking to them, too, but…."

"But what?"

"I keep thinking, would it be so bad if all we did was kiss?"

"Kissing leads to other things."

"Not always."

"Trust me, it would with us."

She dropped her gaze, considering her next words before she spoke. "I feel things for you I never felt with Jason." When he didn't respond, she lifted her gaze, expecting him to have some uninterpretable look on his face, but he didn't. His expression was one of tenderness and longing.

"I feel things for you, too. Things I've never felt for another woman, but" —his internal struggle manifested in a grimace that might have been pain— "it's better to wait, so there's no regrets or guilt later."

"I know you're right, but I don't know if I'm strong enough to resist the feelings I have for you."

"You are. You may be the strongest woman I've ever known."

She made a strangled sound in her throat. Screw being strong.

"Hannah."

"What?"

"I feel it, too, but we're close to finding them. Let's not mess it up now because we're too horny for each other to think straight."

She couldn't hold back a small laugh. "Horny? Isn't that for teenagers?"

"You make me feel like a teenager again."

"I've never felt like this with anyone, ever."

"Jesus, Hannah, you married Jason. Surely you felt something for him."

"Not the right something. The feelings I had for him don't hold a candle to what I feel for you." She bit her lip. "I know

this is going to sound crazy, Noah, especially since we've only known each other for less than two weeks."

She hesitated again, and he said, "What?"

"I think I'm in love with you."

"That's a relief. I'd hate to be the only one in this relationship who got zinged with Cupid's arrow."

She swallowed, hard. "You're not just saying that, are
you?"

"Sweetheart, I think you know by now that I always say
what I mean."

"I do." Her eyes lowered to study his finely chiseled lips.
"I really like the way you kiss."

"One of these days, I'll do it again and again and again."
He took her face in his hands. "I'll kiss you all over. I won't
miss an inch of your beautiful body."

"Promise?"

He laughed. "That's one promise I'm happy to make."

"I wonder if it's possible for me to kiss you all over while
you're kissing me all over."

"We'll sure as hell give it a try."

"I'm going to like getting naked with you."

"God, I hope so, because I know I'm going to like getting
naked with *you*."

"We should stop talking about sex. It's making me hotter
than I was before."

His dark eyes flared.

"There's something you should know about me."

"What's that?"

"Jason always said…well, he told me that…." God, why
was it so hard to say?

"Forget what Jason told you, Hannah. He's a loser…and a
liar."

"After Jay was born, he wasn't much interested in making
love anymore." She sighed. "Knowing what I know now, I
think maybe he only married me to have a child, and once he
got that, he was done with me." She tried again to say what
she couldn't moments before. "Jason told me I was lacking in
skill and the ability to satisfy."

"Remember who he is and what he's done, love, and that

should tell you everything you need to know about what came out of his mouth."

Hannah nodded slowly, hoping Noah was right, but worried still about the niggling doubts she harbored about herself and her ability to please a man.

Chapter 32

Over coffee the next morning, while they waited for Liza and Pete to arrive, Noah said, "I figured out an alternative plan and contacted Chief Fitzgerald about it. He's agreed to assign a patrol officer to accompany you around Woodland Park. A female officer during the day and a male officer in the evening."

"You did?"

"Called him at six a.m. and he gave me an affirmative."

Having a law enforcement partner over the next couple of days wasn't the worst idea he could have come up with. "Wow. Thank you."

"You're not mad?"

"Why would I be?" She got up to stir the oatmeal, then went back to her seat at the bar. "I was only angry because you told me I couldn't go."

"I did not."

She gave him a look. "Would you like your words quoted back to you verbatim?"

He lifted a shoulder but showed no remorse. "I guess I did, at that."

She should have known there wouldn't be a sheepish expression to go along with his mea culpa, but for some reason, it didn't bother her. His response was so Noah, and he'd only lectured her because he cared. She decided to move on and not dwell on it. "Is there a rhyme and reason to the gender assignments?"

"Yeah, Fitz figured at night, you might need more muscle with you."

That made sense, although Hannah didn't go out much in the evenings, and said as much. "I suppose I might, though, while I'm in Woodland Park looking for them."

The doorbell sounded. "That'll be the folks," Noah said. "I'll let them in." When he got to the doorway leading out of the kitchen, he turned for a moment. "Beginning tonight, Deputy Barbie Fleming will be spending the night here instead of me." He mumbled one last comment before he spun back around and headed for the door.

Had she heard right? Had he really said, *No sense flirting with temptation*?

It wasn't that she disagreed with him, but she'd already grown used to having him around and she liked it. She liked it a lot. It warmed her knowing he did, too.

Moments later, Noah followed his parents into the kitchen.

"It's a mite nippy out this morning," Pete said, helping Liza with her coat. "Dipped down to twenty degrees overnight."

"Twenty?" Hannah squeaked.

"That's practically a heatwave," Liza said. "Wait'll we get down to hovering above zero."

"Zero? Are you serious?"

"As a Rocky Mountain Bighorn climbing the canyon walls of the Arkansas River," Noah's mother shot back. "Did you do any research on Fossil before you moved here?"

"Not exactly," Hannah admitted. "I closed my eyes and let my finger circle a map. This is where it landed."

"Scientific," Pete said with mock seriousness.

"Well she is a scientific illustrator," Noah said, his tone was a bit wry.

"Before I made my final decision, I did to a bit of research about Fossil and found out it was a hotbed of dinosaur bones. That cinched it for me."

Liza nodded in understanding. "It must have been an amazing sight back then...the Rocky Mountains and the giant dinosaurs."

"Amazing," Hannah agreed.

A few minutes later, they all sat down to steaming bowls of oatmeal and twenty minutes after that, Noah left for the sheriff's office.

Hannah broke the news to Pete and Liza that they wouldn't have to babysit her for a few days.

"Are you sure this is a good idea?" Liza asked.

"No, but it's the only one I have right now," Hannah admitted.

"I could go with you, I suppose."

"You've done enough already, but thanks for offering."

"She'll be okay, love," Pete said. "If Fitz promised officers to accompany her, he'll keep his word, and Woodland isn't much bigger than Fossil. Anything happens and help will be there almost before Hannah can blink."

"Maybe Simon can help her look," Liza said, her expression worried.

"He's going down every day to search, so I'm sure he'll be amenable," Pete said. He rubbed his hands together. "Now, what's on the agenda for today?"

"I have an appointment with the divorce lawyer at nine," Hannah said.

"Guess we're going to town, then," Pete said.

"Guess we are," his wife agreed.

"You don't both have to—"

"Yes, we do," Pete said. "I don't want Liza left out here alone, any more than I want you on your own. I worried the whole time about both of you when I ran to the market yesterday."

Hannah capitulated immediately. What he said made perfect sense. Twombly could easily overpower Liza and take her down just for the thrill of it. "How are you at changing sheets?"

"I can manage," Pete said, "but Liza's better at it."

"We can do it together," his wife said. "Which bed?"

"The one Noah was using," Hannah said, hoping she sounded nonchalant. She didn't miss the look his parents exchanged. "Deputy Barbie is on night duty tonight. If you guys will take care of that, I'll get the kitchen cleaned up."

The elder Wards exchanged another glance, but didn't comment further on their son's change of plans.

"I brought more baking along," Liza said, "but I'm happy to do some housecleaning or" —she shrugged— "whatever."

And so the day began. Pete and Liza changed the sheets and Liza put the ones they'd taken off the bed into the wash. Pete took the dogs out for a quick walk up the hill and at eight forty-five, they piled into the Ward's SUV and headed into town.

While Hannah met with the attorney, Pete and Liza headed over to the diner for coffee. She imagined they would ask Noah to join them and quiz their son on why he'd handed over guard duty to Barbie.

Two hours later, Hannah found them waiting for her in the lawyer's reception area.

"How'd it go?" Liza asked as they walked back to the SUV.

"As well as can be expected, I suppose. The poor guy didn't know what he was getting into when I made the appointment, and he kind of got that deer-in-the-headlights look when I gave him the details, but by the time I left, he was practically rubbing his hands together in anticipation. I gather most of the divorces he handles are" —she searched for the proper word— "mundane, by comparison."

Pete and Liza chuckled. He said, "Hannah, I'm pretty sure you made Horatio Hume's day."

"He's awfully young to have a name like Horatio."

"In his family, first-born males are all saddled with it and they're all attorneys."

"Wow. What's his track record? Success or no?"

Liza said, "I've never heard an ill word about him, personally or as an attorney. Don't sell him short because of his age. Horatio has a fine mind and he's going to get this divorce for you lickety-split."

"He wants me to consider filing for annulment instead of divorce."

"An annulment?" Liza said with surprise.

Hannah nodded. "One of the choices on the Invalidity of

Marriage petition reads" —she reached into her purse and withdrew a folded piece of paper— "'One party entered into the marriage in reliance upon a fraudulent act or representation of the other party, which fraudulent act or representation goes to the essence of the marriage.'"

Pete leaned against the hood of the SUV. "I'm no lawyer, but I'd say if Jason has been hooked up with Sabine and Twombly since high school, and then he did what he did with the sailboat, that was pretty damned fraudulent, all right."

"I suppose it would solve some of the issues that might crop up with a divorce," Liza said. "Did Horatio give you any" —she shrugged— "I guess, guidelines?"

"He said it would work best if Jason is arrested and agreed to the annulment, or the divorce, without fighting it."

"That would be ideal," Pete said, his tone wry.

"You definitely have a lot to think about," Liza agreed.

"I need to call my sister and let her know what's going on," Hannah said. "I'm sure she'll want to chime in on the annulment thing, too."

Once they returned home, Hannah poured herself a cup of coffee and took it to her workroom. She left the door open so she could hear the Christmas music Liza had going while she baked. It brought back fond memories of Hannah's own mother baking and decorating for Christmas. Of course, unlike Liza, her mother never had to leave a loaded pistol on the counter in case someone tried to break in with murderous intent.

Hannah glanced at her own Glock, which she'd left on her drawing table the night before. Having Noah in the house with her had made her feel so secure, she'd completely forgotten to take it to her bedroom when she turned in.

A pang of loneliness swept through her at the thought of no more Noah whiling away the evening hours with her in front of the fire.

This was one of those instances when having an unwavering moral compass sucked.

Resigned to not seeing Noah again for a few days, she picked up her phone and called Emily.

"It's about time you checked in," her sister said by way of

greeting.

"Sorry, it's been crazy here." Hannah filled her in on the days spent in Estes Park and Woodland Park.

"Holy crap!" Emily said when she'd finished. "Your life has turned into a Mary Higgins Clark novel."

Emily, an avid thriller reader, was also somewhat of a drama queen. "Sometimes it feels more like a Dean Koontz book," Hannah said.

Her sister snorted. "I'd like to get my hands on Sabine and do her throat some real damage."

"You and me both, and I can't get my head around Jason letting her hurt Jay like she does."

"Any leads yet on where they are?"

"Noah thinks we're getting close. I'm going back up to Woodland tomorrow to do some searching."

"Is that wise? I mean, you're a woman alone. Who knows what might happen."

"Chief Fitzgerald is giving me a daytime and an evening officer for assistance or whatever."

"Well, that's something, at least."

"I'm going to wear a disguise, just in case, and I'll have my Glock."

"I still can't believe you've turned into a gun-totin' mama."

"I never saw myself carrying a gun, either, but I do feel safer with it." She sipped her coffee. "I saw a divorce attorney today."

"You did? My gosh, I never even thought about that. You definitely need one, don't you?"

"I certainly have no intention of remaining married to Jason, that's for sure."

"Is divorce easy in Colorado? One of my neighbors is going through one here, and it's a nightmare."

"It's much simpler here and actually, the attorney asked me to consider filing for an annulment instead of divorce."

"Annulment? How would that work?"

"I think Jason married me just to get a kid."

"If he's been involved with Sabine and that dickhead cop since high school, and Sabine hates kids, you're probably right, but how does that figure in?"

"Trickery, fraudulent intentions, lying, plus everything he's done since the day he faked the drownings."

"Hunh."

"The way Horatio explained it, it would be a lot easier."

"Horatio?"

"That's my attorney's name."

"Why am I not surprised. Go on with what you were saying."

"There are no assets to divide, no child support payments, no alimony, no nothing. All I have to do is get Jason to agree, and, *voila*, almost-instant dissolution of the marriage."

"I don't see a downside to it, then, except...."

"Except what?"

"Jay would be considered illegitimate."

"Is that worse than being associated with a father who fakes his death and murders people and commits adultery and lets his whore beat up his kid?"

"When you put it that way, no. Are you going to go for it?"

"Maybe. What have I got to lose?"

The following morning, assured by Hannah that she'd be leaving the house in a matter of minutes, Deputy Barbie Fleming got into her patrol vehicle and drove away.

Thankful she finally had some time to herself, Hannah went directly to her workroom, where she pulled open a file drawer and flipped through the folders until she found the one that said DMV. She extracted the copy she'd made of her temporary driver's license and slapped in on the scanner glass, closing the lid before she hit the SCAN button. Whether foresight or intuition, she'd known for some reason back in September that having that copy could come in handy down the road.

While the document scanned, she opened up her laptop and clicked on the icon for the drawing program she used. Technically, she might be breaking the law, but Hannah didn't care. It wasn't the original document and she was only altering it in case she met up with Jason, in which case, he or one of his cronies was certain to go through her purse.

Once the scan was complete, she saved the document as a JPG and imported it into the drawing program. From there, she altered the key pieces necessary to go with her Woodland Park disguise—her name and address, her date of birth, the expiration date on the license, and the photo. The latter would be overlaid with a selfie she'd taken with her phone.

Hannah worked quickly and efficiently, grateful that she had the skills to do what had to be done to the temporary license. She printed out a sample, made some adjustments, then printed it again, satisfied on the second try that the original grayscale rendering, along with a little crinkling of the paper, should allow it to pass muster. However, if Twombly got hold of it, it might be a different matter, one she chose not to dwell on.

Satisfied with the end result, she returned the photocopy of her temporary license to the file folder and withdrew an envelope from her desk. She dug into her purse for her wallet and extracted everything with her name on it, including her driver's license. She folded the fake temp license and put it into the slot where she normally kept the real one.

She grabbed her coat and called to the dogs, then headed for her truck. "Just a short ride this morning, guys," she told them after they sniffed their way from the mudroom door to the back passenger door of the double-cab Tacoma. She spread the old thermal blanket over the back seat, then said, "Up."

Fiona went first, but Bowie still needed a little help. Both immediately curled up on the seat and snuggled together.

"Good dogs," Hannah said and shut the door. She went around to the front passenger side. From the glove box, she pulled out the proof of insurance and car registration and added them to the envelope. With a little rearranging, everything fit snugly inside so that she could seal it before she shoved it down between the console and the driver's seat.

She went back inside and checked to make sure everything was off that should be off and set a timer on a lamp in the living room. She grabbed her purse and her small rolling suitcase and locked the door behind her. With the dogs in the back, she stored her luggage in the passenger knee space in the front.

First stop, drop Bowie and Fiona off at the Ward house. She'd been surprised that Noah hadn't stopped by to collect his dog on his way home the previous evening, but decided maybe he thought Bowie needed the company. As if.

She half expected him to be waiting to give her more instructions at his parents' house before she took off, but he was nowhere to be seen. He was taking his self-avowal to stay away from her seriously.

"Call us when you get there," Liza said, fretting over her. "Where are you staying?"

"At the hotel on twenty-four, at the west end of town. Simon recommended it because it has interior room entrances, accessible only with a key card."

"Good thinking," Pete said. "What time are you meeting him?"

"At nine, at the Starbucks."

Liza glanced at the clock. "That should give you plenty of time to get there, especially since you may have delays because of road conditions."

"Just take your time and drive slow," Pete advised.

"I'll be careful," Hannah promised.

Bowie circled her ankles, begging for attention.

Hannah squatted down and gave him a hug and some pets. "You be a good boy, okay?"

The puppy yipped at her, although today it had sounded more like a bark. The little guy was growing up.

Fiona got into the action by nuzzling Hannah's hand.

Hannah laughed. "Don't worry, I haven't forgotten you."

Fiona smiled at her, making Hannah glad all over again that she'd chosen a golden retriever, and that Bowie had a sister.

She stood and gave Liza a hug, then Pete. "Thanks for puppy-sitting." Five minutes later, she felt bad about leaving because Liza's concern was so obvious.

Second on her list before she could leave town, stop at the ATM to get some cash, since she'd stowed all her credit cards.

An hour later, and way ahead of schedule, Hannah drove

through Woodland Park to the hotel and checked in. She took her things to her room, then went back to her truck disguised as her undercover self. No one in the reception area looked twice at her.

She didn't usually carry anything in her jeans pockets, so the small Leatherman's tool felt a little bulky, but at least the slight bulge wasn't noticeable. Her Glock was in the safe in the hotel room, since she'd be accompanied by gun-carrying law enforcement. She started up the Tacoma and headed toward the south end of town to the Starbucks.

For some reason, she was starving. She ordered a venti latté and a breakfast sandwich and settled in at a corner table by the window, where she pulled out her phone to call Liza. "I'm here."

"How was the drive?"

"Scenic and uneventful, just as I thought it would be."

"Good. Have you called Noah yet?"

"I…no. I was wondering if you'd mind giving him a jingle, just to let him know I arrived safely."

"Not a problem, but are you sure you don't want to talk to him?"

Through the window, Hannah noticed Simon pulling in. "Actually, Simon just arrived, so if you wouldn't mind?"

"As I said, not a problem. Take care, Hannah."

"I will. 'Bye."

Simon came inside, looking all around for her.

Good, the disguise worked. "Simon, over here."

He swung around in surprise. "Good morning. I see you have a new look."

"I do, and good morning to you, too."

"How was your drive?"

She reiterated what she'd told his mother.

"Good. Let me grab a coffee and something to eat and I'll be right with you." When he returned to the table, Simon said, "I have to get something off my chest."

"Okay."

"I just want you to know that I admire your determination to stick by your guns."

Somewhat taken aback, she asked, "Are you talking about

my unwavering resolve to find my son…or your brother?"

With a shadow of a smile and a slight shake of his head, he said, "Noah says you're the most intelligent woman he's ever met. I have to say, I agree. I'm almost sorry I didn't meet you first."

She stared at him without speaking.

"I apologize if I made you uncomfortable."

"I'm more curious than uncomfortable. What are you trying to say, exactly?"

"Not much, just that I appreciate you keeping things on the up-and-up until your husband is found and the marriage is terminated. I know it must be hard on Noah, too, but in the end, you'll both be better off for having waited."

She decided to keep her response light, though she wasn't sure how she felt about Noah discussing their non-relationship with his brother. "I didn't know you practiced psychiatry in your other life."

That made him chuckle.

"You and Noah must be close."

"We are. I hope you're not upset because he discussed the situation with me."

"Mildly," she admitted, surprised by his candor, "but I suppose I'll get over it."

He grinned. "I look forward to having you for a sister-in-law. Shall we get on with planning our day?"

Since his admission had left her speechless, she could only nod in response.

For the next half hour, they laid out a schedule. At ten, Officer Karin Delaney arrived, out of uniform and dressed for the weather.

"Saw you at the station the other day," she said to Hannah, "but didn't get to meet you." Her gaze slid over to Simon. "Good to see you again, Simon."

"You, too, Karin." He gave her a slow, easy smile and Hannah wondered if the two of them had a thing going on, or a romantic history, or maybe they were exploring future possibilities. "Grab a coffee and let's talk shop."

Within minutes, she returned with a plain coffee and by ten-thirty, Simon was gone and Hannah and Karin were off on the first leg of their reconnaissance. At five-thirty, they returned to Starbucks and Hannah collected her truck. Karin followed her to the hotel, where Officer Bobby Stewart met them in the lobby. He, too, was out of uniform and dressed for winter weather. The three of them looked like tourists enjoying a few days in the mountains.

"Simon's going to join us," Bobby said. "What do you feel like eating for dinner?"

"Anything's fine with me," Hannah said.

"Me, too," Karin said.

"You guys are a big help," Bobby said, making a face. "Guess we'll leave it up to Simon."

"Leave what up to me?" Simon asked.

Hannah noted that, like his brother, he had the ability to creep up on silent feet.

"Where we're having dinner," Bobby said.

"Somewhere that we can have a private conversation," Simon said.

"How about take out," Karin suggested. "We can go to my place."

"That's a great idea," Simon said. "What about grabbing some burgers from MoJoe's?"

Hannah didn't have much appetite after a disappointing day of searching for Jason and Sabine. Add to that, wearing the wig had given her a horrible headache. "That sounds good to me. I'd really like to take this wig off for a while."

"Why don't you stop at MoJoe's," Karin suggested to Simon, "and Bobby can hit the market for beer." She pulled out her wallet. "Hannah and I will meet you at my place."

Hannah also pulled out her wallet. "Let me at least get dinner." When they started to protest, she added, "It's the least I can do for all the effort you guys are putting in on this."

"I'll get the beer and soda," Bobby insisted.

"But after this," Karin said, "we go dutch. Agreed?"

Everyone nodded.

"Do you remember where I live?" Karin asked Simon.

"Unless you moved, I do."

So, Hannah decided, a past romance.

"Still in the same place," Karin said. "See you guys in a

bit."

Thirty minutes later, they sat around Karin's kitchen table enjoying their burgers and fries, sipping beer.

"What's on the agenda for this evening?" Simon asked.

"We're meeting with Jay's teacher," Bobby said. "I've known her since kindergarten, so I contacted her and set it up outside the school. I thought she might be more forthcoming away from that environment. The principal is going to be there, as well, along with the art and music teachers and the PE instructor."

"Does that mean I can go as real me, instead of disguised me?" Hannah asked.

"I don't know if that's a good idea," Simon said. "We have no idea if any of these people from the school are friendly with Jason and Sabine. They could snap a picture of you with their phone and send it to them. Just like that, any chance we have of finding them here in Woodland would be out the window."

"Simon's right," Bobby said. "Even though I know Sharon Cummings, Jay's teacher, we're not like besties or anything." He polished off his burger and went on. "I plan to introduce you as a WPPD intern. You'll be able to ask questions, but don't identify yourself as Jay's mom."

Hannah wasn't thrilled about the plan, but on the other hand, after a moment's consideration, she realized it made sense. "Okay." Simon gave her a look that reminded her of one of Noah's expressions. "What?" she demanded.

He shrugged. "I heard you're not the type of woman who capitulates easily."

Had Noah really discussed her with Simon? "Your brother doesn't know everything about me," she retorted.

Simon laughed. "Did I say it was Noah who ratted you out?"

Hannah's face heated with embarrassment.

Simon laughed again. "You're right, it was, but to his cred-it, he said it more with admiration than with pique."

Hannah knew she should have let the subject drop, especially since the two Woodland Park patrol officers were listening with rapt attention. If Noah hadn't shown plenty of pique when she'd disagreed with his mandates, she might have. "Are you sure it was your brother who told you? He certainly wasn't happy with me when I told him I planned to come back here."

Simon grinned. "You're right about that, but he took care of making sure you didn't walk into anything alone, didn't he?"

Hannah did a mental double-take. Noah had given her a hard time about returning to Woodland Park. He'd been angry about it, in fact. But then, he'd gone and asked Chief Fitzgerald to give her some assistance. In retrospect, he'd won the argument, even if she hadn't realized it at the time. She could either be angry about the manipulation or embrace it and get on with locating Jason and Sabine and Twombly... and her son.

It was a no-brainer. Hannah may have had her faults, but making stupid decisions didn't rank at the top of the list.

She tugged the wig back on, grateful she'd had a short reprieve from wearing it.

Chapter 33

Sharon Cummings lived in a log-style house just north of town. The interior had a open floor plan, which worked well for the odd assortment of chairs set in a circle in what she called her great room.

Hannah and the others tossed their coats onto the pile already started on the sofa and took the last four chairs. Introductions were made: Denise Lloyd, art teacher, Sharon Kim, music teacher, Denny Flynn, PE teacher, Mark Rice, principal, and a surprise addition, Helen McKay, school nurse.

Since he'd set up the gig, Bobby introduced Hannah, Karin, and Simon, and explained the situation a little further than he'd outlined it for Sharon. "Our hope is that you'll be able to help us locate Jay."

The six people from Jay's school exchanged glances, but no one spoke. Finally, Sharon said, "I guess I'll go first, since I'm Jay's teacher." She folded her hands in her lap before she went on. "He's a really smart little boy. Even though he's in first grade, he can read at a third-grade level. He excels at math, as well, and has an avid curiosity about anything related to science. He also likes history and can name any dinosaur imaginable. In general, I'd say he loves school, though it is troublesome that he misses so many days."

"Due to illness?" Bobby asked.

"That's what we've been led to believe."

"Do you give homework?" Karin asked.

Sharon nodded.

"Does he keep up with it?"

"Yes, but...."

"Why the hesitation?" Simon asked.

"Well, typically, kids get help from their parents. It's una-voidable, you know, because everything they're learning is new to them, but several times I've asked Jay if he gets assis-tance at home and he always says no. To be honest, that flab-bergasts me, especially since some projects really do require adult help."

"Is that typical?" Hannah asked. "To give assignments that require parental assistance?"

"In the early grades, yes. Otherwise, how would they know how to start a project or see it to completion? I mean, I give instructions in the classroom, but certain assumptions are made that a parent assists at home."

"Did you pursue his response?" Hannah asked, hoping she didn't sound judgmental or accusatory.

"Actually, I did. Jay said his dad told him school was his responsibility and no one else's." She shook her head, as if in disbelief. "He also said his dad told him he had to 'sink or swim, that's the way of the world,' and that's a direct quote." Her eyes watered. "Sorry, I get emotional just thinking about what a callous lesson that is for a first-grader."

Simon asked, "Was Jay friendly with any of the other kids?"

"Mostly, he kept to himself, but during group activities, he interacted primarily with Lucy Rourke, Calvin Dietz, Antho-ny Hawkins, and Timothy Gherke."

"Do you know if he ever had play dates with any of them?"

"I'm not sure, but there's more to Jay than him being smart. He's polite, but never smiles. He's considerate, and by that I mean, he never cuts in front of anyone or talks over them, and he's always the last one out the door for recess and lunch, and at the end of the school day. He also never volun-teers any information unless asked, and even then, he's...reti-cent." She bit her lip. "I know this may sound weird, but he seems sad, and sometimes, I feel like he's afraid."

Hannah gripped the seat of her Samsonite folding chair to keep from jumping up and screaming. Of course her little boy was afraid! Look at what had happened to him. How could Jason live with himself, subjecting his child to such a life?

"Since he's been kidnapped, I'm sure that's true," Simon said. His tone held no condemnation, which Hannah felt would bode well for the other interviews.

From there, they went around the circle. The music teacher, Sharon Kim, said, "Jay always seems to enjoy music. He sings along with the other kids, is able to memorize the words and the tunes without any problems. He also listens and follows instructions, if we add any auxiliary movements, like dance steps or clapping." She shifted in her chair and frowned. "There is one thing, though. Without fail, every time we have music, he always asks afterward if there's any chance we can sing 'Hush, Little Baby.'"

Hannah sucked in a breath, which drew several looks. She tried to cover it with a cough, followed by, "Excuse me."

"Did you ask him why that song?" Karin asked.

"Yes. He said his mother always sang it to him and he missed it." She drew in a breath. "I asked why she didn't sing it to him now and he said she couldn't because she was dead."

Hannah almost came unglued. *Jason, you bastard!*

"There's something else I just thought of."

"What's that?" Bobby asked.

"Jay always makes this little clicking sound when we're listening to upbeat music. It's like he's snapping his little fingers, but instead it's a sound he makes with the back of his tongue. He said his mom taught him how to do it."

Hannah's hold on the chair seat tightened until she thought her fingers would break. She and Jay had worked on that clicking for weeks, until he'd finally mastered it. They called it the cricket click. The sound had driven Jason nuts, so they never did it in his presence, but bless her son's heart, he apparently had not forgotten it.

The art teacher spoke next. "Jay has quite an imagination, but no matter how many times I've encouraged him to use more vibrant colors in his art, he continues to stick to the dark shades…browns, grays, black, deep blues and purples. I asked him why once and he said it was because he doesn't have color in his life anymore." She swiped at her eyes. "That's the saddest thing I've ever heard a child say."

Silence followed her words for at least a minute, then the PE instructor spoke up. "Kids are supposed to bring comfy, loose clothes to change into for PE. No matter how warm the day, Jay always wears sweatpants and a long-sleeve T-shirt. I often wondered why, when all the other kids have on shorts and short-sleeve tees. The poor kid is sweating buckets by the time we're done with class."

"I think I may know why he dresses like that," the school nurse, Helen McKay, said. "Jay had a splinter in his hand week before last. Sharon sent him to me to extract it and when I pushed up his sleeve, which hung halfway down his palm, I noticed that he had bruising on his arm. I asked him what happened, and he said he fell. I knew he was lying, of course, since the marks on his little arm were obviously made by adult fingers."

"Why didn't you report it?" the principal, Mark Rice, asked.

"I meant to," Helen said, "but right after he went back to class, we had that incident with the fifth graders who started fighting and one of them had a knife…if you recall, we had to call the police and the EMTs because the teacher and both boys were injured." She shrugged. "I can't believe I forgot about Jay's arm until tonight." She frowned. "That's just not acceptable." She glanced at the principal. "I should tender my resignation."

"You'll do no such thing," Principal Rice said. "That was a day from hell. I'm not surprised you forgot."

"Can you think of anything the boy might have said that might help us find out where he lives?" Simon asked the nurse.

The school nurse frowned, thinking. "No, but I just remembered something else. Jay asked me not to tell his dad that he'd been in to see me. I asked why and he said he'd be in trouble for not taking care of the splinter himself. Poor little guy tried to have stiff upper lift, but he started to cry, so I assured him, since it wasn't a life-threatening injury, I wouldn't do more than make a note of it in my daily log book."

"Anything else?" Bobby asked.

Her face scrunched up, like she was wracking her brain for more information. "No, I'm sorry."

"I have something," the PE instructor said. "At least I think I do, although it's not about where he lives now."

"Go ahead," Simon said.

"Jay told me once that he and his mom used to go to the beach and race each other on the sand. I asked him where that was, since we don't have sandy beaches here in Colorado, and he said he couldn't tell me. He said he wasn't supposed to talk about his mom or where he used to live. When I asked why not, he said it was because Sabine would punish him, if he did. I said, 'Who's Sabine?' and he said, 'The bad lady who came with us.'"

More determined than ever to find her son, Hannah chanced another question, this one to Jay's teacher. "Would it be possible for us to talk to the kids Jay was friendly with? They might have some information to share that he wouldn't have told any of you."

Sharon glanced at the principal. "Can we do that without getting parental approval?"

The principal stood and began to pace around the outside of the circle. "I'm not sure, but I know all the parents, so it wouldn't be a problem to phone each one of them and ask how they feel about it."

His gaze locked with Hannah's and for a moment, she thought she read something in his eyes. Did he suspect she was not who she claimed to be?

He moved over to Sharon. "I can call them right now."

Sharon jumped up. "Let's do it. I'll get my contact list."

Within minutes, Principal Rice placed the first call to Lucy Rourke's home. He briefly explained the situation, asked his question, then said, "Thanks, I appreciate it." He repeated his conversation three more times, with only slight variations. Back in his chair again, he said, "Tomorrow, the four kids Sharon mentioned will remain inside for first recess. That'll be at nine forty-five. We'll do this in the classroom, so they're not intimidated." He looked at Bobby. "All four together okay by you?"

Bobby glanced at Karin, then Simon, and finally at Hannah, before he turned back to the principal. "That'll work. Will all four of us be able to be there?"

"Yes."

Hannah could hardly breathe. Anticipation mingled with hope and swelled through her like a surging tide. Could they actually be on the verge of learning where Jay lived?

Karin picked Hannah up at eight-thirty the next morning. They met Simon and Bobby at Starbucks, choosing a table in the corner for privacy.

"I made a list of questions we should consider asking," Simon said, pulling a small notebook from the front pocket of his suit coat.

"May I?" Hannah asked, reaching for the notebook.

Without hesitation, he handed it over.

Hannah read through the questions. When she'd finished, she handed the notebook back.

"Will you read them aloud?" Karin asked.

Simon nodded and began to go through the questions, one-by-one.

"I'd remove the ones that concern his health and any injuries. Recess isn't that long. We won't have time to ask them," Bobby said.

Karin said, "On that note, I'd omit the question about how long Jay's been in Woodland. Time isn't a concept little kids really understand, is it?"

"You have a point," Simon said, and scratched through the three questions under discussion.

"I have a suggestion," Hannah said. "Scratch all these questions and keep it simple with these." She held up a finger, "Do you know where Jay lives?" Another finger went up. "Have you ever played at Jay's house?" Another finger. "Does someone pick Jay up from school or does he walk home?"

"Three questions?" Simon said. "That may not net any-thing."

"I'm betting it will. You've got, what, twelve questions on your list? You'll boggle their minds. Keeping the questions simple will allow their brains to come up with related infor-mation that could be useful."

"What makes you so certain?" Bobby asked.

"I used to be a mom," Hannah said. "Kids don't process questions like we do. Trust me on this."

After several moments of silent consideration, Simon said. "Okay, one question for each of us to ask, except Hannah."

She was okay with that, to a point. "I'd like to reserve the right to ask supplemental questions."

Simon nodded. "Agreed."

"Are you really so sure they'll be forthcoming in their re-sponses?" Karin asked.

Hannah answered simply, "Yes."

At nine-thirty, the four of them checked in with the princi-pal. "Sharon and I decided only she and I will monitor the…information gathering," he said, "and the only reason I'll be there is because I'm the one who made contact with the parents and I'm the one who has to take any blowback. Better to be informed than not."

Simon nodded. "That sounds feasible, and by the way, we appreciate your cooperation."

"I'm more than happy to help," Principal Rice said. "One more thing." He turned to Hannah. "Are you Jay's mom?"

Without hesitation, Hannah said, "Yes."

He glanced at Simon. "Is it a good idea to have her here?"

"Actually, she's the reason we *are* here, so I guess I'll have to say the answer to that is yes."

The principal gave a quick nod. "Okay, then, let's head over to Sharon's classroom."

As they made their way down the hall, the recess bell sounded. Children poured into the hallway and headed south. Barely a glance was spared for the adults they passed.

"Where are they going?" Karin asked.

"To the gym. When it's really cold like this, we keep them inside and offer organized games and play to keep them from sitting around, doing nothing."

"Good idea," Hannah said. "An engaged child is a productive child."

The principal glanced at her. "Not many parents realize that. These days, most of them want to keep their kids occupied with video games."

They reached the doorway to the first-grade classroom, saving Hannah from having to respond to Mark Rice's comment.

All the chairs were small, but Sharon had set them in a semi-circle facing the children, who were still seated at their desks. She had explained ahead of time that it would help the discussion if the adults were more at eye level with the first graders. The six of them sat down, even though their behinds didn't fit the chair seats.

"I was just telling the children that they have a special task ahead of them," Sharon explained. "Kids, we need your help in finding Jay. These folks are going to ask you a few questions about him, and hopefully, it will help locate him." She smiled at them and said, "Please, introduce yourselves."

One-by-one, they did so, then Hannah and the law enforcement officers did the same.

Before they could ask the first question, Lucy Rourke, a cute little redhead with dimples and vibrant blue eyes, raised her hand. "Jay hasn't been in school since the day we had the assembly last week."

Next to her, Calvin Dietz said, "That's right."

"He was excited, because he loves dinosaurs, and the presentation was about the new dinosaur bones they discovered in Cañon City and Fossil," Anthony Hawkins added.

Timothy Gherke nodded enthusiastically. "He *really* loves dinosaurs."

Karin smiled. "That's what we understand. Do any of you know where Jay lives?"

"Not in town," Anthony said.

"No, he lives further out than us," Calvin concurred.

"Past the golf course," Timmy added.

"Waaayy past," Lucy said.

"As far out as the lake?" Karin asked.

The four children looked at each other.

Anthony said, "I don't think so, or if he does, he never mentioned it."

The other three heads bobbed in agreement.

Bobby asked, "Have you ever played at Jay's house?"

"He invited me once," Calvin said, "but his mom got mad when she picked him up and told him he couldn't have friends over."

"She's not really his mom," Lucy said. "Remember he told us, she's his dad's girlfriend?"

"That's right," Anthony said. "He invited me once, too, but she started yelling at him when he asked her permission. I told him it was okay, that he could come to my house instead, but she really started yelling then and said he wasn't allowed to go to stranger's houses." His little face puckered up into a frown. "I'm not a stranger! I mean, Jay knows me, so I don't know why she said that."

Hannah glanced at Simon, who was to pose the third question, which had basically been cancelled out by the responses to the first two. She preempted him with a time-related inquiry. "Did Jay just start school with you this year?" Despite Karin's earlier assumption, she thought the kids knew about time.

"Oh, no," Lucy said. "He came right after we started kindergarten. It took a long time for him to talk to us." She looked to the others for confirmation.

"He was scared," Calvin said.

"Not of us, though," Timmy said for clarification. His voice dropped to a whisper. "He told us his mom had just died and his dad said they had to move away from their house. He had to leave all his toys and clothes there, too, but he really missed his mom."

Also in a whisper, Lucy added, "He doesn't like the lady who's his dad's girlfriend. She yells all the time and she's mean."

Anthony said, "She hits him, too."

"I just thought of something," Lucy said.

"What's that?" Hannah asked.

"Jay likes it best when we have art. He always draws the red rocks on his road, and there's always a lady in the picture."

"He does?"

Lucy nodded, her expression solemn. "He told us once that he thought it was" —her brow puckered while she searched for the word she was looking for— "harmony, that's it! He thought it was harmony that he lived on the road where he lives."

Hannah mulled that over for a moment. Jay had always loved learning new and bigger words. "Did he say harmony or harmonious?"

Lucy stared at her wide-eyed. "Harmonious! That was it. I never heard that word before Jay said it. I had to ask him what it means."

"Do you know now?" Sharon asked.

"Sure. It means it goes together."

Simplicity from the mouths of babes. "Why did he think it was harmonious?" Hannah asked.

"Because the name of the road has paint in it."

Hannah didn't know what to make of that, but apparently the others did, judging by their expressions.

"Thank you for your time and for answering our questions," Simon said. He reached into his inside suit pocket and pulled out an envelope. From that, he extracted four gift cards. "Hope you all like McDonald's." He handed each of them a card.

Four thank yous came in response.

"I hope you find Jay," Lucy said. "We really like him and we've been worried about him."

"With the information you've given us, I'm sure we will," Bobby said, standing. "And if you wouldn't mind, please, don't discuss anything we talked about today with anyone besides Miss Cummings and Principal Rice and your parents, okay?"

They nodded again.

Anthony asked, "Will you come and tell us when you find him?"

"It's almost Christmas, you know," Calvin said, "and he was worried that Santa was going to miss him again this year."

"He was," Timmy agreed.

"He cried last year because Santa couldn't find him," Lucy lamented. "That just not right, is it?"

Hannah didn't think her heart could break any further, but in that moment, an ache the size of the Grand Canyon coursed through her right where her heart beat.

Chapter 34

Once again outside the building, the three law enforcement officials and Hannah came to a halt in the parking lot.

"Okay, tell me what you all know that I don't," Hannah said.

"The only road around here with 'paint' in the name is Painted Rocks Road," Bobby said.

"It's past the golf course, but not as far as the lake," Karin added.

"It leads into Pike National Forest," Simon said, "and has a number or residential dwellings both north and south of the road. There are two ways in and two ways out, if you don't count the maze of one-lane roads every which way."

"Let's go back to the station," Karin suggested. "We can set up in the conference room and figure out how we proceed from here."

"Good idea," Bobby said. He looked at Hannah. "We're close."

"I hope so," Hannah said fervently. "If we don't get my son away from them, he may be scarred for life."

Karin considered her with a frown. "Why don't you go back to the hotel and rest for a while? I can't imagine you've been sleeping well, judging from the dark circles under your eyes. I'll come get you later."

Hannah opened her mouth to protest, but Noah's brother spoke first. "Good idea. We'll take a late lunch and catch you up on our plans."

With a great deal of reluctance, Hannah agreed. While it was true she was exhausted, it was also pretty obvious they didn't want her involved in whatever plans they would be discussing. "All right, but you have to promise to keep me in the loop."

Simon gave her what she was coming to think of as the Ward Look. "I think by now you can trust us to do that."

She didn't back down. Simon knew the history between her and Twombly, and with that history came a lack of trust in law enforcement. She stared at him without flinching, but he didn't back down, either, which left them at a standstill.

Law enforcement, three, Hannah, zero.

Ten minutes later, Hannah unlocked her room at the hotel. She entered and used the bathroom and then came out and stared at the bed. Her body felt like it had been charged with electricity. She could lie down, but she'd never be able to sleep.

Painted Rocks Road bounced around inside her brain like some pesky vulture circling over fresh road kill.

She opened her laptop, clicked on the web browser, and plugged in *map woodland park* and *painted rocks road*.

By the scale at the bottom corner of the map, the road was just under nine miles away, to the north.

Hannah considered the downside of what might happen if Jason discovered her snooping around. How would she explain a wallet, but no credit cards or driver's license? She pulled the wallet out of her purse, extracted the paper money and coins, and the fake temp CDL, and shoved the wallet under the passenger seat. The fifty-plus dollars and her fake temporary driver's license went into the inside zipper pocket of her leather bag.

Satisfied that she'd taken all the precautions she could justified what she was about to do, at least in her mind. She hadn't promised to stay put and she hadn't promised not to go investigating on her own. What were Simon and the WPPD officers going to do, arrest her for being a naughty girl?

Hannah pulled out onto the main roadway and veered south on Highway 24. At the Wal-Mart, she purchased a pair of binoculars, then ventured back onto 24 until she reached the juncture of Highway 67. She set the mileage counter at eight miles, and when she reached that, she slowed, looking for a street sign marking her destination. She found it less than two minutes later.

It was pretty at the turnoff, with the snow and conifers and an abundance of giant red rocks. The road had been plowed almost all the way down to the gravel. The packed snow that remained looked icy to a non-Colorado native.

Hannah made her way carefully, hoping to avoid potholes that might cause her to hit an icy patch and lose control of her truck. She was thankful she'd listened to Noah and purchased a few bags of sand to weight the back end. About half a mile in, she noticed a large log structure with a number of out-buildings. The sign at the turn-in identified it as Camp Elim.

Hannah continued up the road, stopping only when she spotted what looked to be a dwelling in the woods. Each time, she pulled out the binoculars and scrutinized the surround-ings, looking for any sign of her son or the others. It wasn't until she'd gone another mile that she realized there were no more houses. She approached a pull-out and used it to turn around and head back down the road.

Just ahead, a Lexus sedan backed out of a driveway feed-ing in from the north. Hannah braked to a stop and raised the binoculars. She got a brief glance of one of the backseat pas-sengers.

It didn't take a rocket scientist to identify the child with his face pressed against the window.

Hannah began to shake all over. She prayed no one else in the vehicle had noticed her. "Keep your cool," she muttered. "Keep your damned cool."

She tossed the binoculars onto the passenger seat and low-ered her sunglasses. From behind the dark lenses, her eyes wandered the landscape, looking for a marker, so she could bring Simon and the police back to the exact driveway. Finding none, she studied the dwelling as she passed, making note of its architectural features. Somehow, she managed to maintain her speed and keep her head on straight.

At the end of Painted Rocks Road, she made the right turn heading back to town. She pressed her foot harder against the accelerator, intent on following the Lexus. She had to get closer, but not too close.

Tailing the vehicle wasn't difficult on the highway, but once they reached town, it was a challenge to keep them in sight. Still, Hannah managed it without breaking a law or hitting anyone.

When the sedan pulled into the dinosaur center, she couldn't believe it. They really had the balls to take Jay back there after the way they'd treated him the last time they'd visited?

Hannah squeezed the steering wheel with all her might, again imagining it was Sabine's neck.

Jason took the parking space nearest the door. Sabine and Twombly climbed out of the vehicle and a moment later, Jay followed. They entered the building, never looking back to make sure he was following. Jason backed out and waited at the driveway exit to enter traffic.

At the other end of the parking lot, Hannah considered following Jason, but the chance to be close to her son was so powerful, she gave up the idea, although she did wonder where her bastard-of-a-husband was going.

She parked three spaces down from the entrance. Within moments, she had her sunglasses off and her non-prescription eye glasses back on. She checked her appearance in the rear view mirror to make sure the remaining parts of her disguise were still in place. She also thanked her lucky stars that she was incognito, otherwise, Candace would have recognized her, and who knew what kind of shit storm that would have produced, with Sabine and Twombly in the building.

Inside, Hannah paid the admittance fee, then slowly worked her way into the dinosaur area, where she located Jay, admiring the T. Rex. As with every child, it was his favorite.

Hannah looked around for Sabine and Twombly, but saw no sign of them. She ventured closer to Jay. "This tyrannosaurus is a beauty, isn't it?" she asked him.

He started, then looked up at her, blinking as if he were discombobulated.

"It's one of the largest Tyrannosaurus Rexes ever found," he said, his expression solemn.

"Is that right?"

He nodded, but didn't take his eyes off her.

"What else can you tell me about him?"

"He has big teeth."

Hannah spared a glance upward at the skeletal creature's mouth. "He sure does."

"The biggest ones are the size of a large banana."

"That's big, all right."

"They're rounded on the tip, but there's serrations on the sides. That's so when he bit into his food, he could get a good grasp on it, then he'd shake his head and the serrations would kind of saw at the meat of the animal he was going to eat, and it would cut it up for him."

"Impressive. You must really like dinosaurs, to know all that."

"I do." He continued to stare at her. "I like your voice."

"Thank you." Hannah worked to keep her emotions at bay. More than anything, she wanted to grab her child and hug him and kiss him and let him know she was alive and wanted him back with her, where he belonged.

"Do I know you?"

"Maybe."

"Jay!" came a screech that Hannah recognized as belonging to Sabine.

The boy scuttled away from her before Sabine came into view.

"Why do you always waste time looking at the T. Rex?" Sabine demanded.

"I like him," Jay said.

Sabine scoured the area with narrowed eyes. Hannah pretended to read the material posted on the tyrannosaurus.

"You're not talking to anyone, are you?" Sabine hissed.

"No. You told me not to, so I'm not."

Sabine glared at him, then at Hannah. "You bothering my

kid?"

When she didn't answer, Sabine approached and poked her in the arm.

Hannah decided to play deaf, literally. Knowing the bare minimums of sign language, she turned and extended both hands in front of her to make the sign for *what*.

"What are you, deaf or something? I asked if you're bothering my kid?" Sabine snarled again.

This time, Hannah pointed to her ears and made a motion with her right hand to signify *no*. She sealed it with a shrug.

Sabine laughed. "You are deaf! Poor, stupid bitch." She looked back at Jay. "Ricky and I are going next door to grab something to eat. Stay in this room, do you hear me? No gift shop and no wandering into the bird room today. Understand?"

Jay clasped his hands behind him and nodded.

"I mean it."

"I know you do," he said.

"Don't get smart with me, you little shit."

His little body stiffened.

Hannah dropped her purse to divert Sabine's attention.

"Stupid mute," Sabine sneered, then spun around and left the dinosaur room.

When she'd gone, Jay said, "That was smart of you, faking that you can't hear. I wish I could do that. Maybe then, she and my dad and Rick would forget I'm around and leave me alone."

God, how she ached for her son. "That woman isn't your mom."

"No, my mom is dead."

Hannah debated the wisdom of giving him the truth straight out and decided to bide her time. "Are they having lunch close by?"

"There's a place next door that has beer and stuff."

"When will you have lunch?"

He shrugged his small shoulders. "I'll eat something when we get back home, I guess."

"Did you have breakfast?"

"I ate a banana. Sabine needs to go to the grocery store, but she only likes to shop for stuff for herself and she never cooks."

The admission spoke volumes. "Are you hungry?"

Again the shrug and his direct gaze skittered away. As if to confirm what his mouth refused to say, his tummy rumbled.

"I have a protein bar in my purse."

His head whipped around and his gaze dropped to her purse.

Hannah dug into the bag and grabbed both the bars she'd brought along in case she got hungry. "Keep one for later," she said as she handed them over to him.

"Thank you." He shoved one bar into his coat pocket, then ripped open the other one and began to devour it.

Hannah was sickened by the path her thoughts took. Not only did they discipline Jay physically and aggressively, but apparently, he wasn't given regular meals, either. He ate like he hadn't had any food for a week.

Once he finished the bar, he took the wrapper to the trash container then came back to her side. He tilted his head at her. "You remind me of my mom, especially your voice. It's all soft and warm, like my mom used to talk to me."

"What else do you remember about your mom?"

His head whipped around and he seemed to examine every nook and cranny, looking for someone who might overhear and report him to Sabine. "I'm not supposed to talk about her."

"Who told you that?"

"Dad and Sabine."

"But you have memories of her, so you still think about her, right?"

"I have lots of memories of her. I'd give anything if she wasn't dead." His voice caught and he said, "My mom never treated me bad and she gave me the best hugs."

That nearly leveled her. "How are you at keeping secrets?"

"Pretty good. I didn't used to be, but I've had to learn how. Why?"

Hannah hunkered down beside him and lowered her voice to a whisper. The lyrics she sang weren't original to the song, but they were true to her heart. "Hush, little baby, don't you cry, mama's going to sing you a lullaby." She put her hand gently to his cheek. "Mom's coming for you, sweetheart. Hang tough until I get there, okay?"

"Mom?" he asked in a low, warbly voice. His expression registered both confusion and hope.

"It's me, buddy. It's me, and I'm coming back for you."

"Dad said you were dead." His big green eyes filled with tears. "Take me now," he pleaded.

"I wish I could, but Dad and Sabine and Rick, they're mean. They might hurt you or other people who are here if I try now. Do you understand?"

He nodded slowly. "They *are* mean. Sabine hurts me all the time."

"I know, baby, and she's going to pay for that." She used her neck scarf to dry his eyes and wipe his cheeks. "The most important thing right now is, don't mention to them who I am or they'll take off running again, and next time, I might not be able to find you."

His eyes widened in fear. "I won't tell, I promise!" Another tear dribbled down his cheek. "You're not a ghost, are you? Your hair's all different now."

"Sweetie, I'm as real as real can be." She tried to think of an analogy he'd understand, then remembered how much he'd loved Batman." I'm in disguise, sort of like Bruce Wayne is when he wears his Batman costume. I promise I'll come get you as soon as I can."

"We need a secret code," he whispered.

"The cricket click," she said without a moment's hesitation.

He nodded and made the clicking noise twice with his tongue.

"You haven't forgotten." Hannah responded in kind and he grinned.

"No, but I only do it when they can't hear. Otherwise, Sabine or Dad will hit me. They hate it."

Before she could say anything more, a man's voice she recognized as Jason's shouted, "Jay! Where are you?"

She gave her son a quick hug, then turned away, hoping Jason hadn't witnessed the embrace.

"What are you doing?" Jason demanded of Hannah.

So much for hoping.

"She's a deaf lady," Jay said. "She dropped her purse and I helped her pick up the stuff that fell out. She gave me a hug for helping her."

Hannah's heart filled with pride at Jay's ability to improvise. She kept her eyes glued to the tail of the T. Rex, playing along, pretending she couldn't hear a thing. She did, however, feel Jason's eyes boring into her. Did he recognize her profile, even though she had on a red wig and wore eyeglasses? Was there something else about her he found familiar?

Glaring down at their son, Jason said, "C'mon, Sabine and Rick are waiting for us." He swung around and strode away with an impatient huff, leaving Jay to trail in his wake as they made their way to the exit. Once, Jay turned around and gave her that precious little half-wave that always tugged at her heartstrings.

Hannah didn't dare follow immediately, but counted to thirty, as if half a minute would give her the distance she needed. Finally, after what seemed like an eternity, she made her way outside and climbed into her truck. A quick survey of the lot confirmed the Lexus was long gone. Jason hadn't wasted any time driving away. Bastard.

Shivering, she started the engine and cranked up the heat. She really needed to get back to Woodland Park PD, but first, she wanted to get the wig off her head. She had another killer headache and from here on, she doubted the disguise would be necessary, but before she headed back to the hotel, she had a call to make.

She pulled out her phone and dialed Noah.

"How's it going?" he asked.

"As if you didn't know."

He grunted. "Simon doesn't tell me everything, and besides, I like my information straight from the horse's mouth."

"Gee, thanks for comparing me to a horse."

"You are a pretty little filly."

For a moment, his intimate tone threw her.

"Too much?"

"No, it's just that I never think of myself as pretty."

"Then you've been looking in the wrong mirror."

Inexplicably, his words warmed her, and not just in places where a body might normally feel the cold. "Thank you."

"For what?"

"For making me feel good."

"Let's not go down the path of what I could do to make you feel good," he said, his tone wry and wary at the same time.

Hannah allowed herself a moment to imagine what his words insinuated, then slammed that door shut and got down to business. "I assume Simon told you we were talking to some of Jay's classmates at the school this morning."

"He did."

"After we left the school, I ventured out by myself while the others went into their secret law enforcement confab over how to proceed."

He swore softly under his breath. "Please, tell me you didn't."

She ignored both his dismay and his disgust. "I can't, because I did."

"Jesus-H, Hannah! What the hell were you thinking?"

"I was thinking I might finally get lucky."

After several moments of silence, he said, his voice tight, "And did you?"

"Yes and when I spotted them, I followed them to the dino center."

"And you went in after them."

"Of course."

The string of curses he let loose was quite inventive.

Fortunately, they were speaking by phone. From her perspective, verbal explosions via the airwaves were far better than those encountered in person. With any luck, Noah would cool off by the time he next came face-to-face with her. With some reluctance, Hannah admitted, "You might as well know, I talked to Jay."

His snort of disgust spoke volumes.

"Sabine and Twombly left him in the dino room with a warning not to go anywhere else, and they went off to a tavern next door to have something to eat and drink."

"So you felt compelled to have a conversation with the boy, did you?"

"Of course, I did." She decided not to give him a blow-by-blow account of what they said. "Sabine and Twombly were in that bar stuffing their faces and all Jay had for breakfast was a banana and he didn't expect them to bring him any lunch."

"Did he recognize you?"

"Yes, but he won't tell them it was me."

Another huge sigh of disgust rumbled against her ear, or maybe it was impatience. "Hannah, it's been two years since you've seen your son. They've been terrorizing him. He's likely so scared shitless of them, he'll tell them immediately."

"He won't," she shot back, for the first time, experiencing some uncertainty about her impromptu sleuthing. Damn Noah for raising doubts that hadn't been there before!

"How can you be so sure?"

"He said Sabine hurts him all the time. He wants to get away from them, and he's smart, Noah. He'll be careful."

"Okay, what aren't you telling me?"

Busted. "I told him I'd come get him. We devised a code for when the time comes to run."

"A code."

"Yes, it's a clicking sound made at the back of the tongue. Not everyone can do it and it took me a while to teach Jay how, but he still knows it. We call it the cricket click."

"As codes go, that's a long way from cryptography."

"And a lot simpler." She assumed the ensuing silence meant he agreed.

Eventually, he spoke again. "Where are you now?"

"In my truck, in the dino center parking lot. I'm headed back to my hotel next, then to Woodland Park PD." She glanced around the parking lot, then into the rear view mirror and noticed a car that looked exactly like the one Jason had been driving earlier pull into the parking lot. Before she could decide what to do, the vehicle eased into a marked space directly next to hers. "Ah, shit, gotta go. They think I'm deaf."

"Hannah, wait!"

As unobtrusively as possible, she disconnected and turned

the phone off before she slid it down between the seat and the console.

A moment later, someone pounded on her driver's-side window.

Thank God she'd noticed Jason pulling in and had time to psych herself up for whatever confrontation lay ahead. With her foot on the brake, she shifted the gear into reverse and brought her head around slowly, as if checking to see if anyone was behind her before she backed out.

She feigned a surprised recoil when she faced Twombly through the glass.

At the same time, she worked the gear shift into DRIVE.

Chapter 35

With every ounce of control she had, Hannah schooled her features into what she hoped was a questioning expression.

"Roll down the window," Twombly screamed.

Hannah raised her eyebrows.

"Roll down the fucking window," he shouted again, and to prove he was serious, raised his arm. The gun in his hand was aimed at her head.

Hannah didn't have to fake her fear. Having a weapon leveled on her put an entirely new perspective on things. In particular, it made her wonder why the former cop was even doing what he was doing. Had she given herself away?

She let go of the steering wheel and covered her face, all while easing her foot over to the gas pedal, depressing it. The truck shot backward. The side-view mirror caught Twombly, spinning him around and away from the vehicle. She hit the brake and threw the gearshift into PARK.

A moment later, Twombly regained his senses and lunged toward the truck, maneuvering his gun so the butt of it was raised. Did he intend to use it to shatter the window glass?

Without looking down, she scrabbled for the door lock, thinking she could surprise him by opening it and shoving it hard against him. Instead, she accidentally pressed the window control. The glass began to lower.

Snarling and growling profanities, he reached inside with his free hand and opened the door, then dragged her out, still holding on to the pistol.

Hannah prayed she could keep up her deaf charade. With little effort, she made mewling sounds of distress in her throat.

"Shut up!" he bellowed at her, spraying her with spittle.

Hannah sent up a brief, silent prayer. *Please, God, don't let Jay give me away. Please, please, please.*

In the next instant, Twombly shoved the gun into his coat pocket, raised his right fist, and took aim at her face.

And then, everything went black.

Hannah came to, tied to a chair in a darkened room.

She opened her eyes to slits, then all the way and blinked, trying to bring things into focus. Even that small effort was too much. Her face hurt like a bastard. Her eyelids went back down and stayed there.

Was she at the house Jason and the others lived in? Somewhere else? Some *place* else? For all she knew, she was dead and experiencing a new life in hell.

Before she could begin to think clearly, the door flew open and crashed against the wall. Despite her best intentions, Hannah jumped and her eyes flew open. The overhead light came on, blinding her. She quickly lowered her eyelids. Her head hurt so badly, the brightness was like having acid in her eyes.

Sabine let loose with a cackle.

Hannah prayed her captor was so engrossed in her maniacal glee that she hadn't noticed either the jerk of her body or the twitch of her eyelids. She continued to pretend that she was still out cold.

"She awake yet?" Jason hollered from another room.

Sabine screeched again. "No! Ricky really popped her a good one."

Hannah's head lolled forward as Sabine circled her. Her shoes rasped against the wood floorboards, echoing so loudly, it sounded like a herd of horses had entered the room.

"You think she's going to be a problem?" Sabine asked, her tone hopeful, like she'd love to take care of the *problem* in an excruciatingly painful way.

"She is now, thanks to you." Jason must have entered the room, because his voice had grown closer.

"Something's off about her."

"I'm starting to think something's off about *you*."

"Watch yourself, Jason."

Hannah heard the warning, which sounded more like a threat, even if Jason didn't. He seemed to toss caution to the wind as he jumped further into the fire of Sabine's wrath. "You're out of control, Sabine."

The next thing Hannah heard was a hand connecting with a face. Hard.

"I am *not* out of control, Jason. You're a pussy, that's all. Ricky's got all the balls at this party."

"Hit me again and you'll find out if I have balls or not." Jason didn't sound like he was passionately in love with Sabine at that moment. "I'm going out for a goddamned beer. Or two."

"Maybe I'll come—"

"Alone."

"Sometimes, you're just no fun, Jason."

"I'm sure Ricky will find some way to entertain you as soon as he finishes up whatever the hell he's doing."

Which made Hannah wonder where Twombly had gone.

"She'd better be conscious by the time I get back."

"If she isn't, I'll wake the bitch up for you."

"Via waterboarding or electric shock treatment, no doubt."

"You're so cute when you're pissed. Have fun getting sloshed."

Jason's reply was to storm off with angry footsteps. Seconds later, he slammed the front door as hard as he possibly could on his way out.

Only minutes after that, the front door opened again. Heavy footsteps sounded through the house, getting closer and closer. Twombly was back.

"He's gone," Sabine said.

"So I noticed. I thought the fucker was never going split."

A pause, then, "I see she hasn't come around yet."

"You got her good, Ricky."

"I wish I knew why she looks so familiar."

"Maybe I can keep you occupied while you think about it some more."

The snakes slithered over to each other. The sound of their hands and bodies rubbing together was enough to make Hannah want to puke.

"Jason's starting to be a problem," Twombly panted, giving away his arousal. "For one thing, he's around all the time, so I always gotta share you, and he's getting pissy about his fucking kid. We gotta do something about both of them."

Sabine moaned, which told Hannah that whatever manhandling Twombly had engaged in was happening in a way that turned her on. "You're such a *man*, Ricky."

"Only for you, baby. I get hard just thinking about you."

"I should've killed Jason when I did Henri."

Hannah could hear clothes coming off. Really, were they going to have sex right there? What if Jay walked in?

"Nah, we needed his money, baby. You've timed everything just right."

Judging by the slobbery sounds, the two of them had moved on to kissing.

The thought of having sex with Twombly sickened Hannah. He was a pig. That he was ready to have sex with Sabine proved he rutted in slop, plus, there was nothing sexy about him.

"Fuck me, Ricky. Fuck me doggie style right now."

"I will, baby. Bend over. God, I love your tits."

Sabine giggled.

Twombly's zipper rasped as he lowered it and after that, it was a steady pounding of his groin flesh against Sabine's butt.

Where was Jay? Was he out of sight, and out of hearing range? God, these people were animals! Did they have no sense of decorum or privacy?

And then Sabine screamed. "Oh, Ricky…what a stud you are, baby…that's it…give it to me good and hard…." And then she must have reached her climax, because she screamed and screamed, all the while praising his "big, hard, beautiful cock." Moments later, Twombly grunted and moaned and groaned over his own release.

From there, their encounter degenerated into a masturbation session for Sabine, with her lover coaxing her on with language so depraved, bile actually crawled up Hannah's throat. If only ears could close like eyes did!

After another twenty minutes of Sabine pleasuring herself, Twombly said, "I'm getting hard again baby. Let's take it to the bedroom. I gotta eat me some pussy."

"What about that little shit?"

"It ain't nothin' he hasn't heard before, but if it'll make you feel better, I'll bring him in here."

"You're the only thing that can make me feel better, Ricky-Dicky," Sabine said, her voice husky with her version of desire. "You and your nice big dick."

Wet noises ensued, followed by more screaming.

"Bed, baby."

"Carry me riding you, big boy."

Twombly grunted.

Hannah thought longingly of the Glock she'd left in the safe at the hotel. She should have worn it in the under-arm holster she'd bought in Fossil. She could blow them both away and be done with them forever.

"You think this bitch will wake up any time soon?"

"Nah, I smacked her a good one."

"Be sure you put the fear of God into the kid. Tell him he better not even look at her."

"I will. Besides, he's glued to that stupid tablet Jason bought him. Ain't a TV good enough for a spoiled brat like him?"

"Jason's too easy on him."

Twombly laughed. "The kid's so scared of me now, he practically pees his pants every time he sees me."

Sabine's responding laugh was so evil, it renewed Hannah's desire to kill her on the spot.

"Jason should take lessons from you."

"Jason should do a lot of things, sugar."

"You got that right...."

"Brat!" Twombly bellowed. "In here, now!"

After a lot of shuffling bare feet and grunts and moans along the way, Twombly and Sabine apparently arrived at their bedroom destination and were doing more of what they'd been doing.

Several minutes later, the door to the room where Hannah was held captive closed softly.

At least now Sabine and Twombly's disgusting encounter was muted. Talk about evil mating with evil.

Hannah opened her eyes, then lifted her head. With the door closed, the light out, and room-darkening drapes at the window, her surrounds were left in near darkness again.

Her head turned slowly toward the only other light in the room.

Jay sat in a corner, staring at his tablet. The illumination from the device gave his face an eerie, almost ghostly appearance that made her shiver.

Her sweet little boy had been exposed to too much. His attention may have been on the tablet, but his expression told her that he'd gone blank inside.

Hannah guessed it was his way of coping with what was going on around him.

Not even seven years old yet, Jay had experienced the worst of humanity first hand. That was a helluva way to spend your childhood.

Hannah cricket-clicked, twice.

A moment later, Jay responded.

Relief washed through her. "Come closer, Jay. Bring the tablet for light."

Her son popped up and hustled over. "Get me out of here, Mom."

"I will, honey, I will, but we have to be really quiet, okay?"

"I can be so quiet you'll think I'm not even here," he said with such seriousness, it pricked her heart.

"Thank goodness you are. I've got a knife in my back jeans pocket. Take it out and open it carefully. I don't want you to cut yourself."

He set the tablet on the floor and dug into her back pocket. "This is cool," he said.

"It's called a Leatherman Squirt. You can have it once you get my bindings cut. It has both a knife and scissors. You choose which you want to use."

He studied the Leatherman. "I can't decide."

"Let's try the scissors, first. This cording doesn't look too tough and once you get it cut, it should be easy to unwrap."

Jay moved the tablet around so it shined toward her right hand, which was bound to the back spindle. The tiny scissors kept getting away from him.

"Take your time."

"We don't have time. Sometimes they go in the bedroom and make those noises for a long time and sometimes, they come back after a few minutes." He muttered a few choice words he'd no doubt learned from the three adults with whom he lived. "Sometimes, when Dad's here, he goes in with them. I shut myself in the laundry room so I don't have to hear them."

"I'm sorry, Jay."

"It's not your fault," he said, intent on controlling the scissors. "This isn't working too good."

"Try the knife instead, but be careful opening it, okay?"

"I will." He took a moment to work out the blade and tried cutting the cord again.

Hannah felt the binding give way immediately.

Jay moved over to the other arm and cut through those cords, as well.

Hannah jiggled and wiggled her hands, trying to get her circulation going again while Jay moved on to concentrate on the cords around her ankles. Soon, she felt those constraints give way, too. "Good job, Jay!" With both hands loose, she leaned over and finished the job on her ankle bindings.

Jay stood and closed the Leatherman. He handed it back to her, but she said, "It's yours now, remember?"

"Thanks, but are you sure?"

"I haven't been able to give you a gift for two years, love, so I'm completely sure. Just remember, it's not a toy, so treat it with respect."

He cocked his head at her. "I'm not sure what that means."

"It's a function tool, not a toy, so you have to remember that it can cause damage or hurt someone."

He nodded. "I get it now."

Though she longed to take him in her arms, the time for hugs had to wait. Getting away was their priority at the moment. "Go quiet as a mouse now. Get your coat and snow boots, and also bring your hat and gloves. Come right back."

"Are we going to escape?" he asked, his eyes wide with both apprehension and awe.

"Yep. We're going to go right out that window."

"Wouldn't it be easier to walk out the front door?"

"It will be," she said, and left it at that. "Is there more than one vehicle here?"

"Yeah. Dad always takes the fancy car, but there's an SUV no one ever drives in the garage, and a truck."

Hannah's heart took a hopeful leap. Was it possible it was her truck parked in the garage? "How about the keys?"

"All the keys are on the nails by the door."

"Is there a reason the SUV doesn't get driven?"

He looked down at the floor.

"Jay?"

His head came up. "I think it's because Ricky stole it from someone."

When he didn't go on, Hannah said, "That's okay, honey. I think I know who it belongs to."

Jay snuck a glance toward the bedroom door. "They're bad people."

"I know."

"They're trying to make me bad, too."

"You'll never be bad, Jay. Now, go and get your stuff, and if you see any keys, grab them, okay?"

He nodded and tiptoed toward the door.

By the light of the tablet, Hannah moved over to open the drapes. She activated the window lock mechanism and pushed it open, grateful that the frame moved without squeaking or lurching. As soon as she had it all the way open, she removed the screen and set it outside.

After that, she took the tablet to the closet and had a look inside the small space. Jay returned, carrying everything in his arms. He dropped his load on the bed, then went back to close the door.

"What'chu looking for?" he asked her.

"I was hoping to find some snow boots."

"This is Sabine's room. She doesn't actually sleep here, but she does buy a lot of stuff and she has to have somewhere to keep it all. She has plenty of boots."

"So I see," Hannah said, examining the selection. She picked up a pair and checked the size. One size too big, which was better than one size too small. She set them outside the closet and shucked her own snow boots. "Where's the best hiding place inside the house?"

He frowned. "There's only one they don't know about."

"Where is it?"

"It's a space I get to through my closet."

"Good. Grab your stuff and let's go."

Without questioning her, he did as she instructed and led her to his tiny bedroom. It was so small, it barely had room for his twin bed. He opened the closet door, which revealed his meager belongings, including one pair of well-worn shoes.

"Get your gear on and then get yourself inside the hidey hole."

His eyes widened. "I just remembered...we had a hidey hole at our house, didn't we, Mom?"

"We sure did. Remember how we practiced being really quiet when we went into it?"

He nodded.

"I need you to be even quieter here. Can you do that?"

"Sure." He frowned. "Why'd you open that window?"

"I'm going to try and make them think we ran away from the house that way, and while they go out looking for us, we'll use the SUV to get away."

His frown deepened. "Will that actually work?"

"If it doesn't, I have a back-up plan."

"I hope so, because I don't think the keys I grabbed are for the SUV."

She smiled at him, hoping to ease his worry, even though

her own had just escalated. "Trust me, okay? One way or an-other, I'm getting you out of here."

He threw his arms around her middle. "I love you, Mom. I'm so glad you found me."

"Me, too, honey. Me, too." She gave him a quick kiss on the cheek, then said, "Now get inside the hidey hole. When I come back, I'll probably make a little noise, so don't open the door unless you hear the cricket click, got it?"

Solemn, he nodded.

"Are you scared to go into the closet alone?"

"No, I've been put there plenty of times."

Renewed anger swept through Hannah. "By who?"

"Sabine. She gets mad at me a lot, so she punishes me by putting me in the closet." He shrugged. "I always make sure and act like I hate being in there, but really, I like it because I get away from all of them for a while."

"If she put you in the closet, are you sure none of them knows about the secret hiding place?"

"Yeah. I only found it myself on accident."

"On accident?"

"Yeah, Sabine told me I had to stay in the closet for two hours one day. I really had to pee, but she told me to hold it. I got mad and after she left, I kicked the bottom of the book-case on the end wall. The next thing I knew, the bookcase opened up. I'd been wishing I could just disappear, and I did." He giggled. "I went right through to the secret place, even though my toes hurt like crazy."

Hannah winced. "You're lucky you didn't break one. Does the hidey-hole lead outside?"

Jay nodded. "I heard Dad say once that this was a burn house."

"What he probably said was berm," she said, and spelled it for him. "That means it's built into a dirt hill on one side."

"That's right. There's three stairs leading down and then pretty soon, there's a door that leads outside. There's lots of stuff stored along the way, like someone was preparing for an emergency or a war or something."

"Is the outside door locked?"

"It must be." He hung his head. "I was going to run away,

but I couldn't get it open."

"You're a brave boy."

"I don't know about that. I get scared sometimes."

"If this is one of those times, it's okay, because I'm scared, too." She couldn't resist giving him a quick hug. "We'll be scared together, and the fact that we *are* together means we're going to get out of here."

He settled his knit cap on his head and pulled on his gloves.

Hannah pressed her foot against the bottom of the bookcase. The entire unit slid backward without making a sound. Curious as she was to investigate the hidey-hole, now was not the time.

Jay scooted inside with his tablet.

"How much battery life is left?" she asked.

"It's almost full," he said, "but I'll try to save the light, in case we need it later."

"Good thinking, but if you do get scared, don't be afraid to wake it up."

She waited until he was inside the small area, then peered in for a quick peek. If they had to, both of them would fit inside comfortably until Jason and Sabine and Twombly vacated the property, which they were sure to do once they realized that she and Jay were really gone. "Tell the spiders to take a hike before I get back."

He smiled at her silliness. "I will."

"I love you, Jay."

"I love you, too, Mom."

Hannah pulled the bookcase back into place, reluctant to leave her son, but determined to implement her ruse to make Sabine and Twombly believe she and Jay had fled the house and taken off into the woods.

Back in Sabine's room, she carried the chair over to the window, then retrieved both pairs of boots. She pulled on Sabine's and climbed over the window sill carrying hers in her free hand.

Twilight was fast approaching, which meant the moon would soon be rising in the east. Eventually, it would light everything, leaving the snow coated with a silver shimmer, which would aid her plan, especially if the sex encounter between Sabine and Twombly carried on for a while.

She took off running toward the trees, where the canopy of pine boughs had kept the forest floor clear of snow. On the return trip to the window, she walked backward in her own boots, which was no simple feat, and took more than twice as long.

Climbing back into the house wasn't as easy, or as quiet, as she thought it would be, but she managed it. Inside, she dried Sabine's boots with a cotton shirt hanging on the rod and returned them to the exact spot they'd occupied before. She sat down on the floor and dried her own boots, as well, then wiped up the wet shoe prints between the window and the closet. She shoved the blouse under the bed to hide it, then ripped off the cursed wig, and kicked it toward the bed, too.

She gazed outside one last time. For all intents and purposes, it looked as if two people had escaped through the window and run into the woods. Thankful she'd even had the idea, Hannah mentally patted herself on the back and made her way back to Jay's tiny bedroom.

The closet size was correspondingly small, which meant she didn't have much room for hiding herself. The good news was, the door opened out and the corner nearest the hinges would remain in the dark, should someone come in and turn on the lights. That corner would be her hiding spot.

Hannah barely got herself situated when she heard the front door burst open. The paper-thin walls not only allowed the sound to carry, but seemed to magnify it. Jason was back.

If footsteps could have expressed emotion, his were either angry or eager as they pounded through the living room and on to the room where Sabine and Twombly had gone off to have sex.

Another door crashed open, this time slamming against a wall.

"I figured you two would be at it like rabbits!" Jason said, laughing. He didn't sound amused, but he did sound a little plastered. Something was definitely rotten in Denmark.

Raucous laughter spilled down hallway from the bedroom.

No matter what his mood when Jason entered the house,

eagerness now prevailed.

Sabine, apparently experiencing another orgasm, screamed for Jason to fuck her.

Hannah would have given anything in that moment for a pair of noise-cancelling earphones.

Twombly's voice rumbled like a tornado every time he pounded into Sabine. Finally, he reached his climax and eventually, he ground out, "Your turn," which Hannah assumed meant her rat-bastard husband had taken over.

Jason began to utter unimaginable noises that sounded like a wild animal rutting in agony.

Sabine screamed vulgar instructions suitable for triple-X-rated pornography.

Hannah had never heard such a cacophony before. It halfway terrorized her, and would have sent her completely over the edge, if not for her worry that Jay was hearing exactly what she heard.

Then came the sound of gunfire. Not multiple shots, but a single round.

And after that, Twombly shouted, "Jesus, Sabine, are you fucking nuts?" A moment later, he broke into laughter. "You gotta stop trying to use Jason for target practice."

Chapter 36

"You bitch! Are you trying to kill me?" Jason demanded, his voice incredulous.

Sabine screamed, "Shut up!"

Uncertain if someone had actually been shot, Hannah let loose a trapped breath. To a person, the three of them were certifiable.

She waited for what would come next. Within minutes, they carried on. Sex, sex, and more sex. And after that, more sex.

At the rate the trio was going, they'd be in the bedroom all night. She and Jay could have been long gone by now. Hannah began to consider other means of escape, aside from the vehicles in the garage.

After an hour, the moaning and groaning and screaming subsided. One after another, the sex machines shuffled down the hall. The door opened to the room next door, where she'd been held captive. Twombly bellowed, "The bitch is gone!"

Two additional pairs of footsteps quickened, slapping frantically against the hardwood floors.

"Holy fuck, it's cold in here!" Sabine screeched.

"She's gone out the window," Twombly said, his voice angrier than Hannah had ever heard it, even when he'd been interrogating her. "I think she took your fucking brat with her,

Jason!"

Jason yelled, "Get dressed! If we don't find them, we can kiss this cheery little life we have goodbye."

"Wait!" Twombly bellowed. "Look at this. The bitch was wearing a wig. Goddammit, I knew she looked familiar. It was your fucking wife, Jason."

Hannah experienced a brief regret, but too late now to remedy her hasty action.

"Oh, great!" Sabine screamed. "I told you we should've gotten rid of her before we left San Diego."

Moments later, tempers soaring, fury building, blame flying, the three of them scrambled for clothing and footwear. Jason ran to the kitchen shouting, "Where's the fucking flashlight?"

"Jay had it last," Sabine screamed back.

"I took it away from him and put it back in the drawer," Twombly roared. "I should'a bashed his skull with it, instead. If it's gone, the little fuck took it again."

If the situation hadn't been so serious, their angry give-and-take might have been funny. A who's-on-first moment, or Moe and Larry screwing with poor Curly's mind. Hilarious.

Finally, the three of them relocated to the garage, apparently certain they'd find a backup flashlight there. After fifteen minutes, they made their way outside.

Hannah made a cricket click twice and Jay opened the door. "Do you have the keys?"

"In my pocket."

"Let's go. We don't have much time."

Jay left the hidey-hole stooped over. "I thought I heard something on the outside of the house, while they were in the kitchen."

"A critter maybe?"

"We have bears around here." He shivered visibly. "Sabine said she was going to feed me to one if I ever talked back to her again."

Hannah ground her teeth together. Another reason to wish Sabine a slow tortuous death that ended with her spending an eternity in Hell. "No bears are going to get you today, Jay, or ever, for that matter. I promise you that."

He blinked his big brown eyes at her. "Are you sure?"

Grateful he hadn't inherited his father's blue eyes, she said, "Positive."

He gave her a slight nod and reached for her hand.

"One quick detour before we go." She hurried to the bedroom, hoping the window was still open. "You wait here," she said at the doorway and hustled over to see how far out the trio had made it. About half-way to the treeline, three lights bobbed and swept the growing twilight.

She hustled back toward the door, then spun around and grabbed the white Sherpa blanket draped over the end of the bed. Her wig went flying. She had another moment's regret about taking it off, but too late now to worry about it.

As they passed through the kitchen, Hannah noticed the garish pink Christmas wreath hanging on the wall behind the table. It was every bit as ugly as Jules had said. Hannah had half a notion to take it down and stomp the heck out of it, but she resisted the urge.

Disappointment knifed through her as soon as they entered the garage. The truck wasn't hers. They'd have to resort to the SUV. She settled Jay safely inside on the back seat. "I need to borrow the knife for a minute."

He dug it out of his pocket and handed it over. Hannah raised the garage door, hoping the sound wouldn't carry around to the back of the house to the trees. She also said a silent prayer that Jason still maintained his bad habit of not locking his car. After a quick tug on the door handle, she whispered, "Thank you!" She pulled open the door and popped the hood. With no idea of what she was cutting, she severed several cables and wires. That should stop pursuit long enough to put some distance between them.

Even as she lowered the hood, two vehicles approached on the roadway. Hannah ducked down, out of sight. Once they'd passed, she ran back to the garage and fired up the SUV. Afraid of attracting attention, she backed out without turning on the headlights.

Jason's vehicle blocked the end of the driveway, forcing her to rely on the rear-view camera to make her way. Unfortunately, without backup lights, it was impossible to see where she was going and the SUV made a startling drop into the roadside drainage ditch. Furious with her own stupidity, Hannah slammed the palms of her hands against the steering wheel. "I screwed up, buddy. It looks like we're on foot from here."

Jay unfastened his safety belt and hopped out of the SUV. "Can we get away without a car?"

"You didn't happen to grab the keys to the truck, did you?"

"No, they weren't hanging on the key rack." He cast a worried glance toward the house. "That's Ricky's. He never hangs his keys up on the rack."

"It's okay, let's go."

"Take the SUV key," Jay said. "Since they stole it, they don't have a spare."

Hannah reached in and extracted the key fob from the ignition. "Good thinking. Thanks for the reminder." She grabbed his hand and said, "We're lucky the full moon is coming up, but by the same token, it'll make it easier for them to spot us if they give up looking in the woods. Let's try and get a good head start."

Almost running to match her stride as they started down the road, Jay said, "I think I know where your truck is."

Hannah didn't dare stop. Time was of the essence. "You do? Where?" she asked, gasping from exertion. Why hadn't she acclimated faster to the altitude?

"Down at the religion camp."

"Religion camp? You mean Camp Elim?"

"Yeah. I'm pretty sure Ricky threw the keys in the snow. I might be able to find them."

Keys. Hannah's hopes sank. Finding anything in the snow would be near impossible, and her fob only had one key on it, so they must have stolen someone else's truck.

Jay shone his flashlight around as they neared the gate to the camp. "This is about where he threw them."

"There's a red leather heart attached to the key fob," she said. "That might help find it."

Jay hustled over to the south side of the road and ran his light over the snow mound left by the plow. "Got 'em!" he shouted.

She didn't have the heart to shush him, but she hoped the sound of his jubilation hadn't carried up the hill. She also didn't have the heart to burst his bubble. Maybe they'd get lucky and the keys would fit whosever truck was hidden at Camp Elim.

With the keys still clutched in his gloved hand, he ran toward the gate at full steam. "It's behind the big house."

By the time they reached the entrance to the property, both of them were breathing hard. Hurrying was difficult enough in the snow, but overworked lungs breathing frigid air was no picnic, either. Every expelled warm breath billowed forth as a giant white puff when it met the arctic air. The only saving grace was that their escape route had led downhill. If they'd had to run in the other direction, Hannah had no doubt they'd never have made it, or at least she wouldn't have. Jay's lungs seemed to handle the altitude slightly better.

"I hear a car coming," her son whispered, his voice frantic.

"Me, too. Let's wait until it passes, then we'll make a run for the building."

"What if it doesn't pass? What if they see us?"

"They won't." Hannah had a brainstorm. "Climb over the fence, quick, and lie in the snow."

Jay didn't question her. He scaled the fence and went down on his back. Hannah threw the blanket over and followed him. Fast as she could, she shook open the blanket and laid down next to him, covering both of them just seconds before the car came abreast of the gate.

The vehicle continued up the hill without slowing. Hannah waited until the sound of the engine faded, then jumped up. She shook the blanket and the two of them took off for the back of the main building.

Thank goodness for the moon. It was a big deal today—a super frost moon, the weatherman had called it on the news the night before. Since when did moons come in super-frost varieties, anyway? Who cared, if it helped save their lives.

Even with the trees blocking some of the moon's brilliance, she knew her son was right. It was her truck. "Bless your heart, Jay!"

"Why?" he asked, a little breathless.

"You were right. It is my truck."

He grinned at her. "Told you so."

She unlocked the Tacoma and made sure Jay was buckled in and under the blanket in the backseat before she settled in behind the steering wheel. "I'm not going to wait for the truck to warm up."

"Good idea," her son said, his teeth chattering, "but what about the gate?"

"I'll figure it out as soon as we reach it." If nothing else, she could ram it with the truck and worry about sending a check for the repairs later.

As it turned out, the gate was latched, but not locked. Hannah took time to close it again after they passed through. No sense giving Jason and the others the idea that they may have used the Tacoma to make their getaway.

About halfway back to town, the sky began to spit a snowflake here and there. By the time they reached the hotel, the size and volume of the flakes had increased.

"Are we going to hide out here?" Jay asked, his tone worried.

"No, this is where I was staying. I want to get my stuff and then we'll head for home."

"They won't find us, will they?"

"They'd have no reason to look for us here," she assured him, "and we'll be in and out in five minutes."

"I gotta pee."

"Me, too. We'll have time to use the bathroom."

They entered the lobby and crossed to the automatic doors. Hannah opened the envelope she'd shoved down between the driver's seat and the console and pulled out the keycard.

"What's that?" Jay asked.

"It's opens the automatic door. Only the people who are staying here are allowed to have one."

"Can I do it?"

"Sure."

Almost giddy with excitement, he went to the card lock and inserted the plastic key with the arrow pointing down. "Wow!" he said when the doors slid open. "That's cool."

"You can open the room door, too. It's number one-ten."

He ran ahead, examining room numbers, and inserted the card as he had on the first lock. "Hurry, Mom!"

Hannah quickened her step. Once inside the room, she said, "You use the bathroom while I gather up my stuff."

He nodded and scooted off to use the facilities, closing the door behind him and locking it.

Hearing that lock click disturbed Hannah. Her child had become a kid who cherished his privacy above all else. Jason and the others had done that to him.

By the time Jay came out of the bathroom, tugging his coat and gloves back on, she had everything back in her suitcase. She slipped her laptop into its carry-case and zipped the bag shut. With one final look around, she said, "That's everything. I need to use the bathroom, too, then we'll go."

Several minutes later, they stood at the front desk. Hannah paid the bill and handed over the key, assuring the clerk that she wasn't worried about paying for the night, even though she was leaving early.

Back in the truck, Jay said, "I'm hungry, Mom. Can we get something to eat?"

"Sure, what do you want?"

He hesitated.

She eased up to the stop sign and glanced at him in the rear view mirror. "Jay?"

"Do you think we could get a bacon cheeseburger at McDonald's?"

She smiled. "Is that your favorite?"

"I don't know. I've never had one before. Sabine and Dad would never let me order anything but a plain hamburger."

That now-familiar anger at her husband and his lover snaked through her. "You know, I've never had one, either. Let's both have one."

He grinned. "Thanks, Mom!"

She made a right turn onto the highway. "Here's what we're going to do. I don't want to take a chance that they'll come looking for us and see my truck in the McDonald's parking lot. We'll go through drive-thru, then drive on down to Walgreen's and park at the back of the lot, which isn't visible from the highway. We'll eat in the truck, then I need to run inside and pick up a few things. Sound okay?"

"Sure, but what kind of things?"

"A couple of pillows and another blanket or two and maybe some snacks and water."

"How come?"

"Just in case."

"Just in case we have to sleep in the truck?"

Hannah gave up the subterfuge. "Have you ever heard that expression, hope for the best, but expect the worst?"

"No, but it makes sense. We hope Dad and the others don't find us, but if we have to hide out, we might get cold or hungry, so we have to be prepared."

Her heart burst with love and pride for her child. "That's right."

At the order window, Hannah asked exactly what was on the bacon cheeseburger. "What do you think?" she asked Jay.

"I'd like mine with no onions, no ketchup, and no mustard. Can they add mayo?"

Hannah asked the voice in the order kiosk, who said, "Yes."

"Make it two of those." She turned to look at Jay again. "Shall we share a large fry?"

He nodded.

"How about a drink?"

"A strawberry milkshake."

"And dessert?"

"Chocolate chip cookies."

She finished the order and drove forward to pay. At the second window, the person handed out their drinks and then a sack containing their dinner. "Extra napkins, please," Hannah said, "plus some salt and ketchup packs."

Minutes later, they were in the Walgreen's lot. Hannah invited Jay to climb into the front seat to join her.

"You sure you can eat all that?" she asked, eyeing her own bacon double burger.

He grinned. "No, but I'm sure as heck gonna try. Thanks for ordering all this for me, Mom."

"It's my pleasure, buddy."

Fifteen minutes later, both burgers had been devoured and all the fries. Half Jay's milkshake was also gone. He decided to save the cookies for later. Hannah bagged up their trash and stowed the cookies in the console. Together, they went into the Walgreens and shopped.

Back in the truck, she said, "Ready?"

"Ready."

"Let's do this."

Less than half an hour later, they were on their way up the mountain, headed for home.

Chapter 37

The red PCSO truck belonging to the Sheriff stopped fifty feet short of the entrance to the house where Jason Clarke and his friends had been living. Noah pulled out his binoculars and scanned the area. Directly behind the truck, Chief Fitzgerald exited his vehicle and approached the driver's side.

Noah lowered the binoculars and the window. He said to his brother, sitting next to him, "There's an SUV, tail-end down, at the end of the driveway. Looks like someone backed it into the ditch."

"That wasn't there when Fitz and I came by earlier," Simon said.

"No, it wasn't," Chief Fitzgerald said. "There's been activity in the woods behind the house, too. I've called in my crime scene team. They should be here shortly."

"What kind of activity?" Noah asked, dreading the answer.

"A body. My people say from the looks of things, there were two down initially, but one was able to get up and walk away."

Noah's own body felt as if it were being fed through a combine. If he hadn't been a ten-year combat veteran or a county sheriff, his thoughts might never have tracked to Hannah and Jay being the victims, but he was and he did and there wasn't a damned thing he could do about it.

The radio on Fitz's shoulder crackled. "Chief, come in."

"Go for Fitzgerald."

"What's your location, boss?"

"We're just east of the driveway," the police chief said. "Have you checked the inside of the house yet?"

"Yeah, it was clear."

"I know you've got a bad feeling about this," Simon said to Noah, "but don't let your mind go there."

"Too late," Noah shot back.

"Chief!" someone called out. "We got a body in the ditch, too."

"Jesus, is this a fucking slaughter?" Fitz muttered.

"Why couldn't Hannah just do what she said she was going to do?" Noah asked. He shut off the ignition and pocketed the key before he opened his door.

Even though Simon didn't have an answer, he had a question. "Shouldn't we have a plan?"

"At this point, our only option is to wing it."

Outside the truck, Noah and Simon both withdrew their weapons and mini-Maglites and joined the chief just past the disabled SUV.

"This one's alive," Fitz said. Beside him, a patrol officer summoned an ambulance. Fitz knelt down to cover the man in the ditch with a blanket another officer handed him. "Can you tell me what happened?" he asked.

"My wife is a nurse at Penrose. I was headed down to meet her for a late dinner. I came around the curve and there was a woman standing smack in the middle of the road, stark naked. I stopped to see if I could help her and she aimed a baseball bat at my head. I ducked, but not fast enough. I guess I passed out and when I came to, she and my Jeep were both gone."

The chief pressed for a description of the assailant. The man described Sabine Borreau to a T.

"I hope to God you can find my Renegade. I just put the plates on today and I haven't even made my first payment yet."

"Jeep Renegade?" Noah asked for clarification.

The man nodded.

"Plate number and color?" Fitz asked. His patrol officer

wrote as fast as the man talked.

Noah and Simon exchanged a glance. "Let's have a look inside," Noah said.

His brother answered with a curt nod.

The chief instructed his officer to remain with the victim and followed behind them.

They entered through the garage and conducted a room-by-room search of the interior, landing last in the bedroom with the open window.

"Judging by the cut cords and the chair, I'd say they kidnapped Hannah and she was tied up right here," Simon said, glancing at the floor. "That's the wig she was wearing."

"So they knew who she was," Noah said.

Fitz moved over to the window. "She took her son and escaped through here." He examined the treeline beyond. "We'd better find them before they freeze to death."

Noah came up beside him and stared out into the night, unconvinced, then shined his light over the snow. "I think Hannah pulled a fast one on them."

"How so?" Simon asked, standing between them.

"The footprints in the snow indicate two pairs of boots of an near-equal size. There's no way Jay wears a boot the size of his mother's."

"By God, I think you're right," Simon said.

"How would she manage that?" Fitz asked.

"I have a theory." Noah whirled away from the window and went to the closet. He examined the boots and lifted one pair. "These are damp. What if Hannah made both sets of tracks?"

"I wouldn't put it past her," Simon said.

Noah moved on to the bedroom at the end of the hall. Fitz and his brother followed. By all accounts, a threesome had gone on in the room, and fairly recently, judging from the condition of the bed, the discarded male and female undergarments, and the used condoms on the floor. "The three of them were having sex and somehow Hannah got loose and went out the window, setting up the escape that never happened."

"You think she and the boy are still in the house and we

missed them?" Fitz asked.

"I'd prefer that to thinking it's one of them out there in the trees."

Fitz activated his shoulder mic. Without following protocol, he barked, "Bobby, who the hell you got out there?"

"It's the husband," Bobby said, "and judging from the size of the imprint in the snow, the other one was the detective."

"No sign of anyone else?"

"No one, but we're still looking."

It felt as if a two-ton weight had been lifted from Noah's shoulders. He asked the chief, "Are you positive she hadn't checked out of the hotel?"

"As sure as I can be, based on the fact that all her stuff, including her laptop, was still in the room when Karin had a look-see."

Frustrated, Noah ripped off his ball cap and jammed his fingers through his hair. "Would you mind sending someone over to check again?"

The chief scratched his chin. "Not a problem."

"Noah, you need to chill, man," Simon said.

"How can I?" his brother snarled. "Everything's so goddamned surreal right now, I can't tell what's real and what's Memorex."

The chief activated his shoulder mic again. "Delaney, come in."

"Go for, Delaney."

"Karin, get back over to that hotel again and make sure Hannah hasn't come and gone."

"We're on the same wavelength, Chief. I was worried she might have done that, too. She came in with the boy and checked out about an hour ago."

Noah's brain almost exploded. An hour! She could be anywhere by now, including off the road somewhere because she had zilch for experience driving in snowy weather or on icy roads. "How did she get there?"

"Let me ask." He relayed the question.

In a moment, Karin said, "The clerk is pretty sure she left in a truck."

Half a wave of relief washed through Noah, but where the

hell had she gone and why hadn't she called him? He yanked his phone out of his pocket. As with the previous fifteen times he'd dialed her, the call went straight to voice mail. "Wonder woman," he muttered, his tone laced with disgust.

"We know her truck wasn't here," Simon said.

"Do we?"

"C'mon, Noah, think about it. The garage had two vehicles in it, the SUV is now in the ditch, and the Lexus is disabled, which is why Sabine got naked to stop that poor sucker driving his brand new Jeep Renegade."

"The SUV in the ditch is bothering me," Fitz said.

"Me, too," Noah agreed. "Let's take another look."

"Chief!" Bobby shouted through his mic from the treeline. "We got something rummaging around up here in the trees."

Noah and Simon looked at each other and said, "Twombly," at the same time.

Since Fitz had another four officers already on site to send up to assist Bobby, Noah and Simon made their way back to the driveway to examine the interior of the SUV.

"Nothing here to indicate who was driving," Simon said.

Noah nodded in agreement and turned to study the sedan. He opened the door and popped the latch to release the hood, then shone his flashlight over the engine. "Look at this."

Simon peered inside and whistled. "The lady knows how to cover her bases."

"She's probably feeling pretty good about her getaway plan right about now, but it's damned cold out here. If she should skid off the road, she and Jay could freeze to death."

Before Simon could respond, the sound of gunfire resounded in the cold night air.

Officer Dave Hamby, who'd stayed behind at the Chief's direction, made a move to run up toward the treeline, but his shoulder mic crackled. "Everybody stay put," the chief ordered. "We had to take down a bear. Goddammit! Somebody get me an ETA on when the Deputy ME will be here."

Noah said, "Screw this. Sabine and Twombly are both long gone, and most likely after Hannah. Both of them have killed before and they'll do it again without blinking an eye."

"You think Hannah's headed back to her place?" his brother asked.

"Where else would she go?"

"Good question. She doesn't know anyone else here except the folks and Jules." An instant later, Simon dialed their sister. "Have you seen Hannah?" he asked when she said hello. "Okay. ... No, she's missing. ... Look, I don't have any other information. I'll call you tomorrow, all right? ... About how you'd think. He's here with me, in Woodland. We're headed back to Fossil now. ... Yeah, you, too."

"Call the folks and ask them," Noah said, striding toward his truck.

Simon hustled after him, his phone to his ear. "Hey, Dad, have you guys seen or heard from Hannah tonight? ... No, we're in Woodland, and heading back to Fossil now. Can I bunk at your place tonight? I'll fill you in on the details when I get there. ... Thanks. See you in a couple of hours." He disconnected before he got any more questions.

"It's not going to take a couple of hours to get there," Noah informed him.

"Yeah? You do know we're heading into a major winter storm, right? I'd like to at least get there alive."

"Fuck you."

"Fuck you back. You won't do her any good if you kill us both."

And because Noah knew he was right, he said, "Sorry for being a shithead."

"It's okay," Simon said. "Just remember, you owe me one if I'm ever in a similar situation."

Noah fist-bumped him and they were on their way.

Hannah decreased her speed, hoping to improve her visibility.

Why'd there have to be a whiteout tonight of all nights, and how was that even possible when the moon had been so beautiful in the night sky only a few hours earlier?

She glanced in the rear view mirror. Jay was belted in and sound asleep, with one of the pillows tucked behind his head and the Sherpa blanket doubled over him. Where before, his countenance had been worried, it now reflected one of serenity.

If she'd been alone, she might not have worried so much about arriving safe and sound at their destination.

Why did life keep throwing curve balls at her?

Over an hour later, Hannah breathed a sigh of relief when she made out the WELCOME TO FOSSIL sign on the side of the road, about fifteen miles in from the county line. Now, all she had to do was make it through town and up the gentle incline of Creight and they'd be home.

Main Street was deserted. Fossil had bowed to the storm and buttoned up for the night.

She glanced at the dashboard clock, surprised to find it was already after ten. Time flew when you weren't having fun.

She thought about detouring to Pete and Liza's to pick up Bowie, but that would have to wait until daylight, when she could actually see where she was going. The house would be cold, because she'd left the furnace on sixty-two. Still, compared to outside, it might feel like the Banana Belt.

About half a mile from home, the storm worsened. Hannah reduced the pressure of her foot on the gas pedal, praying she wouldn't drive off the road. Rationally, she knew if she kept the steering wheel straight, she'd be okay. From here on, Creight had no curves. It could have been a brother to a yardstick.

The windshield wipers worked furiously to clear the half-dollar size flakes from the glass. Was it like this every winter in Colorado?

As she neared her driveway, Hannah slowed to a crawl.

Were those tire tracks going up to her garage door?

She peered at the house as she inched closer. Something was wrong, but what?

It took her a moment to realize that the lamp she'd plugged into the timer wasn't on. Had the bulb burned out or....

If her world hadn't taken on the proportions of Nurse Ratched's psychiatric ward over the last two weeks, she might not have worried about Jason and Sabine and Twombly lurking in her darkened living room, awaiting her arrival.

But her brother had said it best recently. *Everything is*

fucked up right now. Her mind had no choice but to go immediately to the worst-case scenario.

Did she have no options at all?

Maybe.

One.

She resisted the urge to slam her foot against the gas pedal and instead applied a little more pressure, achieving crawl mode again.

She didn't take time to dig around for her phone. Noah would take her in, no matter what. He didn't need a heads-up that she was on her way.

Just to be on the safe side of that assumption, Hannah took Liza's advice and called upon her guardian angel to help assure she found a safe sanctuary for herself and Jay.

The drive that normally took five minutes from her house, took twenty in the blizzard conditions. Hannah couldn't risk hurrying with Jay in the truck.

Once she passed under the BELLA VISTA RANCH sign, she began to relax a little. Unlike Creight, Noah's driveway was slightly serpentine and more noticeably uphill. She used the four-rail white PVC fence as a guide. Noah had told he'd installed it the summer before, to avoid wood-fence repairs that didn't stand up to Colorado weather.

Like her house, his was dark. She put the truck in PARK and unbuckled her seatbelt so she could rummage between the seat and the console for her phone. When she turned it on, she didn't expect the battery icon to immediately start flashing that it was dead. She opened up the console and dug for her car charger. Not there.

With a sigh of disgust, she cast a glance at her sleeping son, then opened the truck door and slid out into the nightmare storm.

The wind had come up and the force of it nearly flattened her. Great. What next, a hurricane? Or thunder-snow? Or maybe a volcanic eruption?

It took her awhile to orient herself to the location of the front door. After several minutes, she realized Noah wasn't home and no amount of knocking and ringing the doorbell was going to miraculously open the door.

Hannah trudged back to the truck, grateful for the heat inside the cab. Jay slept on soundly, and she was so tired, she'd have given anything to join him in dreamland.

What a horrible freaking day.

She considered her options. The wind came from the north, so parking her truck on the south side of the house would provide some protection from the elements and maybe a little extra warmth inside the Tacoma.

Hannah squinted at the rambling ranch house. She'd only been here twice, and only once when it was daylight. What would she hit or ruin if she drove around to the south side?

After she thought about it, she remembered that the barn lay to the south, so there must be a driveway of sorts leading to it.

She grabbed the small flashlight she kept in the console and climbed out of the truck again. It was so cold, her teeth began to chatter. Still, she kept on until she found what she was looking for. In the truck again, she shoved the gearshift into REVERSE and moved back about twenty feet before she drove forward. Minutes later, she eased the Tacoma up next to the south side of the house.

The downside of her bright idea was that when Noah came home, he might not notice them until daylight broke. By then, they could be frozen like Popsicles.

That grim realization birthed another brainstorm involving the barn. Did Noah lock it?

Disgruntled but determined, Hannah climbed out of the truck yet again and made her way over to the large red structure. Expecting resistance because of the size of the double-door sliders, she grabbed the left handle and gave it a hard tug. It moved with such ease, she flew backward and landed on her backside in the snow.

Mumbling a choice expletive, she managed to right herself and open the other door. A quick look into the looming darkness confirmed her vehicle would fit inside. She ran back to the truck, if loping awkwardly through the quickly growing depth of snow could be called running.

Thankful it was more of a dry snow, she brushed herself off before climbing up into the cab again. Jay slept on. Within minutes, she was inside the barn, with the doors closed. The truck sputtered and died.

With dismay, Hannah's gaze fell to the gas gauge. The indicator arrow hovered just below the E. Why hadn't she checked the gas gauge before leaving Woodland Park? A shudder wracked her at the realization of how close they'd come to being stranded on the road. With no gas to run the truck to keep them warm, they might have frozen, even with the extra blankets she'd bought.

Someone upstairs had definitely been looking out for them. *Thank you, guardian angel.* Despite her poor planning and every wrong decision she'd made that day, they at least had a roof over their heads for the night.

She shut off the ignition, pulled out the key and shoved it into her pocket, then made sure the doors were locked before she climbed over the console to join Jay in the back seat. After unwrapping the two extra blankets, she unbuckled him and pulled him away from the window. She situated herself in the opposite corner, with his pillow behind her, leaving him covered with the doubled Sherpa. She pulled the two lighter-weight blankets up to cover them both.

Within minutes, she was sound asleep, snuggled up with her son as she had been so many times in the past before his father had stolen him away from her.

Chapter 38

A tapping on the side window startled Hannah out of sleep. She lurched upward, struggling to remember where she was and why.

Fossil. Noah's barn. With Jay.

Her eyes wide with fear, she swung her head around.

"Open the damned door," Noah growled.

So, it was going to be like that. Hannah dug into her pocket for the key fob.

Once he heard the click, Noah jerked open the door she'd been leaning against.

Her pillow tumbled out and she would have followed if he hadn't ignored it and grabbed her around the middle. She managed to resettle Jay before Noah dragged her out of the truck.

"What the hell do you think you're doing? Where have you been? People are crazy worried about you."

She was so glad to see him, Hannah ignored his anger. Somehow, she squirmed around to face him and throw her arms around his neck.

"God, I thought Sabine had you," he said, his voice rough with emotion. "Don't ever pull anything like that again, do you hear me?"

"I didn't ask them to kidnap me."

"You might as well have, playing Nancy Drew like they'd never notice you."

Before Hannah could respond, Jay leaped from the truck and started beating on Noah's legs. "You let my mom go, do you hear me? Let her go!"

Hannah released her hold on Noah and squatted down to take Jay in her arms. "He's not hurting me, honey. This is Sheriff Ward. He's been looking really hard for you, so you could come home to me."

Stiff as a porcupine right before it shot off its needles, Jay assumed a pugilistic stance, ready to go another round with Noah's legs. "He yelled at you."

"Because he was worried about me."

Her son narrowed his eyes on Noah. "Are you sure?"

"Very sure."

"That doesn't make sense. Why would he yell at you, if he was worried about you?"

"It's a grownup thing," Hannah said, for lack of a better explanation. "I know that sounds crazy, but it's true."

Jay's posture relaxed somewhat, but he kept an eye trained on Noah. "Where are we?"

"In Sheriff Ward's barn."

"It's cold out here."

"It sure is," Noah said. "Let's get inside before we freeze off something important."

Hannah released her son and moved toward the truck. She grabbed the Sherpa blanket and wrapped it around Jay.

"Leave everything else. I'll get it in the morning," Noah said.

"There are things I need tonight."

He gave her one of his looks, then reached for the remaining blankets and picked up the pillow. "What else is there?"

"My travel bag is in the front knee space and my gun is...." She trailed off, hoping she hadn't frightened Jay by mentioning the weapon.

Her son stared up at her. "You have a gun?"

"Yes."

"Have you ever shot anyone with it?"

"No."

"Will you teach me how to shoot it, in case Sabine or Dad or Ricky try to take me away again?"

It was such a grown-up question coming from his little body, she almost said yes, but instead said, "Someday."

"Anything else?" Noah asked.

"My cookies," Jay said.

"I'll get them," Hannah said. She grabbed the Walgreen's bag and tossed the cookies on top of what remained of her purchases. For whatever reason, Twombly had left her purse in the truck. She tucked her gun and phone inside, along with her wallet and the envelope containing all her credit cards and driver's license, and secured the strap over her shoulder.

Outside, the blizzard had picked up speed and intensity. The three of them made a mad dash for the house. Jay slipped and fell once, scrambling unsuccessfully to right himself before he reached the back door.

Noah dropped the blankets and pillow and reached down to grab her son around the middle. "I'll come back for this stuff," he said when Hannah made a move to retrieve the pile. At the back door, he set Jay on his feet and stomped the snow off his boots. With his free hand, he dug into his pocket for his house key and opened the door. He set Hannah's bag inside the door and flipped on the lights. "You two get inside. I want to close the barn doors and I'll grab the blankets on my way back."

Grateful Noah had come home, Hannah urged Jay to go in ahead of her.

"Are you sure he's okay, Mom?"

"Absolutely positive. His family has also been helping me try to find you."

His expression both serious and curious, he glanced around the kitchen, examining everything. "This is nice."

"Yes, it is."

Jay readjusted the Sherpa blanket.

"Are you still cold?"

He nodded.

"Would you like a hot chocolate?"

"With marshmallows?" he asked, perking up.

"If Noah has some." She filled the teapot she found on the

stovetop and turned on the burner.

A minute later, Noah returned. "Looking for something?" he asked Hannah as she rummaged through a cupboard.

"Hot chocolate packets."

Noah crossed the kitchen and opened the top cupboard beside the refrigerator. He removed three packets from the box.

"Do you have marshmallows?" Jay asked.

Noah nodded. "Mini or large?"

"Mini," Hannah and Jay said at the same time.

From a drawer down below, Noah extracted a bag that hadn't yet been opened. The tea kettle began to whistle at the same time. "I'll get the fire going." He looked at Jay. "Want to help?"

Jay glanced at his mother, who gave him a nod. "Sure."

"I'll bring the hot chocolates in," Hannah said.

In the spacious living room, Noah pointed toward a switch near the fireplace and asked Jay to flip it on. Flames shot up around the faux logs immediately.

"Wow, instant fire!" Jay said. He looked at Noah with a grin. "I thought you were going to teach me how to put in the logs and stuff and give me some matches to light it."

Noah grinned back. "I'll do that at your Mom's house. She doesn't have a gas-log fireplace."

Jay stood in front of the fire, seemingly mesmerized by the flames. When he turned around, he started when he discovered two dogs staring at him.

"Don't be afraid, Jay," Noah said. "They won't hurt you. They're both golden retrievers, which is one of the gentlest and smartest dog breeds around. " He dropped down on his knees, holding each dog back by the collar, and made introductions. "This is Fiona and she belongs to me. The puppy is Bowie, and he belongs to your mom. He and Fiona are brother and sister from different litters."

"What's a litter?" Jay asked.

"It's what they call the group of puppies that the mom dog gives birth to."

He nodded, his expression thoughtful, but still a little reserved.

Hannah arrived carrying three steaming mugs on a small

tray.

"When did you get a dog, Mom?" Jay asked.

"When I moved here."

"I always wanted a dog."

"I know."

"Dad always said no."

"He doesn't like dogs."

Jay inched forward. "Is it okay to pet them?"

Tails wagging, the dogs strained against Noah's hold. "You bet. They love petting, and belly rubs, and scratches between their ears." He released both collars and the dogs rushed Jay.

The Sherpa blanket fell away as the boy stooped to disburse equal amounts of attention on the canines, who wiggled in ecstasy. Within moments, Jay plopped down on his behind. The dogs followed his lead by going down on all fours. They licked, squirmed, and finally rolled over for the belly rubs, which made her son giggle.

Relief began to melt the worry encasing Hannah's heart. Jay still had the ability to laugh and enjoy a simple pleasure, like petting a dog. In that moment, she understood that Bowie and Fiona were going to be instrumental in helping her son recover from the ordeal he'd undergone for the past two years.

"Fiona and Bowie like dog biscuits, too," Noah said. He squatted down and handed two treats over to Jay. "The trick is to make them mind you before you give them one." He shared a brief, amused glance with Hannah. "Bowie is pretty good about it, but Fiona is still learning."

Jay looked puzzled. "But isn't Fiona older?"

Noah nodded. "She is."

"What do I have to say to make them mind?"

"Try saying *sit*."

Jay's brow furrowed. "That's it?"

Noah smiled. "Pretty simple, huh?"

The boy nodded. "Sit."

"You have to be a little more forceful," Hannah said. "Like this. Bowie, sit."

Bowie looked from the dog biscuit to Hannah, then back at the doggie treat again. He rolled over to his belly, forgetting about a rub, and promptly went into sit mode.

"Wow," Jay said, impressed, handing the treat over to the pup. "Fiona, sit," he said, mimicking Hannah's tone.

Like her brother before her, Fiona assumed the sit position.

Jay rewarded her with a biscuit, which she demolished in about three crunches.

Noah gave his dog a scratch between her ears. "Good girl, Fiona." He glanced at Hannah. "I can't believe she's never, ever sat when I told her to, but you managed to teach it to her, in what? Ten seconds?"

"Bowie sets a good example," Hannah said, amused.

Noah pushed to his feet. "I don't know. Mom says you're a dog whisperer, and I think maybe she's right. I wonder how you'd do with horses."

Hannah laughed. "Horses? I never even been close to a horse."

"You will be," Noah said.

"I doubt that," she shot back.

"You did notice there were horses in the barn, right?"

"What?" she said at the same time Jay cried out the exact same thing. "God, I must have more tired than I realized, because I swear, I did *not* see them."

"To be fair, the stalls are at the other end," Noah conceded.

"I'd like to ride a horse," Jay said, then added, "That is, if you're not mad at me about hitting you."

Noah went back down so he was eye-to-eye with Jay. "Buddy, if I thought someone was going to hurt my mom, I would have been beating him up, too. You did the right thing, considering you had no idea who I was. I'm not mad at you at all."

Jay shot his mother a quick look, then met Noah's gaze again. "Thank you."

"For what?"

"For not being mad. It seems like I'm always in trouble because all I do is make people mad."

Noah put a hand on his shoulder and squeezed lightly. "Son, those days are over, okay? Your mom loves you and nothing you do or say will change that. Between the two of us, we're not going to let anyone hurt you again."

Jay's expression remained uncertain. "How will you stop Dad from taking me away again?"

"I'm making you a promise right now that you'll never see your dad again, and I always keep my promises."

"What about Sabine and Ricky?"

"I'm working on that."

Hannah wanted Noah to explain himself about Jason, but that would have to wait until she got Jay tucked in for what was left of the night. "Do you have a spare bed for us to sleep in?"

"I have two spare beds, so you can each have one," Noah said, straightening. His breath caught and his expression turned grim.

Hannah wondered what she'd done now.

Noah said to Jay, "The bedrooms are right next to each other." He pointed toward the hallway. "You can pick the one you want."

Snuggled up with the dogs again, he said simply, "Okay." He looked at Hannah. "Would you hand me my hot chocolate, please?"

"Sure. Why don't you scoot back against the fireplace hearth, so you'll have a place to set your cup?"

Jay did as she suggested. Both dogs inched along with him.

"Will you be all right in a bedroom by yourself?" Hannah asked. Two years without her son had left her reluctant to leave him alone, which seemed to equate to unprotected.

"I'm alone most of the time, anyway, and you'll be in the next room, right?"

She nodded, though she hadn't actually seen the layout.

Thirty minutes later, Jay's mug was empty and his head bobbed in a failed effort to stay awake.

"Let's get you ready for bed, honey."

Once her son had brushed his teeth and changed into the pajamas she'd bought at Walgreens, he asked, "Can the dogs sleep with me?"

"In your room, but not on the bed," Hannah said.

Jay flashed her a sweet smile. "Thanks, Mom."

"Do you need to use the bathroom?"

"I did after I brushed my teeth. I like that toothpaste, by the way. It tastes a lot better than that stuff Sabine made me use."

Noah located a nightlight from his electrical stash in the garage and plugged it into the socket nearest Jay's bed. He also hauled Fiona and Bowie's beds into the room.

"Will you leave the door open?" Jay asked.

"Sure," Hannah said, "and if you need me, just call out or come get me, okay?"

He nodded, though his eyes were on the dogs. "I will." He climbed into bed and kept close to the side so he wouldn't lose sight of Bowie and Fiona.

Hannah pulled up the covers and leaned down to kiss him. "I love you so much, Jay. I'm so glad I found you."

"Me, too, Mom. I think I'm gonna sleep good tonight."

She smiled at him and ruffled his hair. So much time to make up for. "Goodnight, love."

"Goodnight, Jay," Noah said from the doorway.

"Goodnight," Jay mumbled, already half asleep.

Hannah stood and crossed the room. She shut off the overhead light and left the door open all the way, but didn't move away until she was sure Jay was sound asleep.

Noah took her hand and led her to the kitchen. The tea kettle whistled softly over a low flame. He turned off the burner, then took her in his arms and hugged her. Not with the intensity of a lover, but with the kindness and caring of a good friend. "I almost lost my mind when we got up to that house on Painted Rocks Road. I was scared shitless we'd find you and Jay dead inside or up in the woods."

Leave it to Noah not to mince words. "I think that's the way we would have ended up if they hadn't take time for a sex marathon." She shuddered, thinking about how close she and Jay had come to dying. "I didn't know you'd gone up there."

"After the way you cut off our phone conversation?" He made a sound of disgust in his throat. "I headed up there immediately." He put a finger under her chin and eased her head up gently. "What happened to your face? You have a black eye."

"Twombly hit me. I guess that's his way of asking for co-operation when he's kidnapping you."

His expression grim again, he led her over to a barstool and lifted her at the waist to settle her on one. Noah took both her hands again and listened intently while she went over everything that had happened, from the moment she'd disconnected her call to him, to the moment she'd pulled into his barn.

"There's something you need to know," he said when she'd finished. "Sabine was serious when she discharged the firearm earlier."

"I thought so, too, but they all kind of laughed about it."

"Once they were outside, she was apparently intent on making sure both Jason and Twombly never came back from the forest."

Hannah stared at him, not quite comprehending.

"Do you understand what I'm saying?"

"No...I...unless...are you saying Jason and Twombly are dead?"

"Yes, or at least Jason is. She shot him in the back of the head."

Dead. Execution style. Hannah had no feelings about it one way or another. Her grieving had been done long ago, and now, knowing all the horrible things Jason had been involved in.... She put up a mental barricade to stop the direction of her thoughts. She had Jay back, that's all that mattered.

"What about Twombly?"

"There were signs of another body in the snow and more blood. Most likely, she thought she'd killed him, but she didn't hang around to make sure."

"I'm confused. What they were doing in the bedroom...the way they talked to each other...why would she want them dead?"

"When we find her, I intend to ask her."

"Jason really *is* dead now. That's almost...."

"Almost what?"

"I was going to say incomprehensible or surreal, but he's been dead to me for two years already...." She trailed off with only a helpless shrug, unable to finish her thought. "Is it horrible that I'm glad he's dead?"

"No."

"It feels like I should repent or something for feeling that way."

"Why? He was a piece of shit who hung out with two others just like him. Since I was a kid, I can remember my mom saying that people always get what they deserve in the end. Jason wanted Sabine and he got her. He should have realized somewhere along the way that she was a self-serving bitch who would get tired of him and Twombly, like she had her husband."

"I can't get past the way all three of them carried on, and then to end up like that."

"I'm sorry you and Jay were exposed to their degenerate behavior."

"I'm an adult, so I can probably deal with it, but Jay, living there and constantly in the midst of their depravity...and all the meanness they hurled at him."

Noah's jaw flexed. "I hope when this goes to trial, the jury is sympathetic toward Jay."

"Why wouldn't they be?"

"In today's world, jury verdicts are unpredictable."

Shocked, Hannah said, "You mean that killing Jason and Henri, and trying to kill Twombly, not to mention kidnapping and child endangerment, aren't enough to find someone guilty?"

"It's complicated. For one thing, juries today watch too much TV, so they think they know more than the cops and the prosecution. Defense attorneys play on those misconceptions and emotions. I can envision them saying, 'Poor Sabine, used as a sex toy by two men, forced into a life of depravation, blah, blah, blah.'" His expression hardened. "Since he's dead, Jason will be an easy scapegoat, and Twombly will be, if they don't find him."

"What if they do find him?"

"He'll sing like the proverbial canary. I'm betting he's not happy that Sabine tried to kill him, too."

"Has she admitted to anything?"

Noah hesitated. "Sabine hasn't been arrested."

"Why not?"

"She was long gone when we got there." He told her about the nude act in the roadway and the stolen vehicle.

"My God, she must be one of the most brazen people on the planet." Another thought struck Hannah. "I kept driving past my house because it was dark. Do you think she's there?"

That gave him obvious pause. "I actually stopped there before I came home. I used my key to go in and check if you were there, because it looked like recent tire ruts in the snow. Everything looked okay."

"I don't suppose you checked all the closets."

"No, but...." He swore softly under his breath. "Shit, I didn't even open the garage door to see if there was a vehicle inside." He narrowed his eyes on her. "Why did it concern you that the house was dark?"

"I left one of the living room lamps on a timer. Unless the bulb burned out, it should have been on until midnight. It wasn't."

Noah glanced at his wristwatch. "It's one-thirty now. It's possible the timer was off slightly and the light had already gone out, but if she *is* there, she'll still be there in the morning, waiting for you to come home."

"Is that supposed to make me feel better?"

"No, it's supposed to make me feel better, because I don't want to go out in this weather to check. Instead, I want to stay here and hold you and—"

Hannah intuited the direction of his thoughts and cut him off. "I can't sleep with you when Jay's in the house."

"That's not what I was going to say." He lifted a hand to cradle her face. "But now that you bring it up...."

"Don't go there, Noah. I can't take it right now."

He hesitated before he spoke. "Your honesty is one of the many things I like about you, Hannah."

She thought about asking him to expound on the other things he liked, but said instead, "You don't make it easy to resist you."

His dark eyes began to twinkle. "Good to know. I'd hate to be sitting on this fence alone."

"Is that a cowboy-ism?"

"Hell if I know. It just popped into my head."

Amused, she smiled.

"You know I'll do whatever it takes to keep you and Jay safe."

Hannah nodded and leaned into his hand, closing her eyes. He already made her feel safe, whether he realized it or not. "Thank you."

"Hannah?"

She opened her eyes.

His thumb stroked her cheek. "I'm going to kiss you. Don't try and stop me."

Jason was dead, she was no longer married. As long as kissing didn't lead straight to a more intimate encounter, and no moral or spiritual laws were being broken, she was okay with locking lips. She leaned toward him, ready and eager.

The kiss was even better than she remembered. Soft at first, it grew ravenous. Noah tugged her into his lap so that she straddled him. His desire for her was so obvious, she almost threw caution to the wind. Would it really be so horrible to follow him down the hall to his bedroom?

She was saved from her own mental wavering when her son screamed, "Mom, help me!"

Chapter 39

Jay was hysterical by the time Hannah reached him.

Caught in the throes of a nightmare, her little boy was absolutely certain Sabine had broken into the house and was ready to feed him to a bear. Nothing Hannah said could convince him otherwise as he thrashed wildly beneath the covers.

Noah approached the bed and lifted her son from the tangle. "Listen to me, Jay," he said in a gentle voice, holding him securely in his arms. "Sabine isn't here and there's no bear. Do you hear me, son? No Sabine, no bear."

Jay bucked and whimpered. "Don't let her get me. Don't let the bear eat me!"

"Wake up, Jay. Open your eyes and look around. It's safe, buddy. It's just you and me and your mom. No Sabine, no bear."

Jay stopped flailing and listened as Noah repeated himself in a calm, soothing tone. Finally, his eyelashes fluttered and he nodded, as if he understood. A little at a time, he opened his eyes, all the while, clinging to Noah's shoulders with a death grip. His eyes still wide and dilated from the dream, he scanned the room. "We're not at the house with Dad and Sabine," he said on a whisper.

"No, you're not at the house where you were living, you're at my house. Sabine isn't here and she doesn't know where you are. We don't have any boy-eating bears around here, either."

Jay's head swung in every direction again, his breathing still slightly ragged. "You and mom aren't going to leave me, are you?"

"No, we're staying right here." Noah settled on the edge of the bed, holding Jay in his lap. "Tell me about the bear."

Hannah stayed where she was, listening, marveling that a man with no children had such a way with Jay. She wondered if Noah'd had his own experiences with scary nightmares, then realized, after ten years serving in the military, he probably had a boatload of demons to deal with. Jay had known him for less than two hours, but her son accepted Noah's kindness and inquiry by snuggling closer to him.

Jay related the dream and Noah told him about the bear the police had killed in Woodland Park. Jay gaped up at him. "There really *was* a bear! Are you sure it's dead?"

"Deader than the proverbial doornail," Noah said.

"What does that mean?"

Noah explained the idiom.

"Wow, a real bear. How big was it? What did it look like?"

While Noah answered all Jay's questions, Hannah went off to her bedroom to change into her pajamas. When she returned, Noah was telling Jay about the horses in the barn.

"What are their names?" Jay asked.

"Lucy and Desi, and the horse Sonny boards here is called Mr. Spock."

"Who's Sonny and why does he call his horse mister?"

Noah grinned. "Sonny is a high school kid who takes on a lot of odd jobs because he wants to go to college and become a vet. He calls his horse Mr. Spock after the character in *Star Trek*."

"What are odd jobs? What's a vet? And what's *Star Trek*?"

Noah glanced at Hannah. To his credit, he didn't appear to be overwhelmed by all Jay's questions. "Odd jobs are things like mowing lawns, and shoveling sidewalks, and grocery shopping for people who are sick. A vet is a veterinarian and that's a person who administers medical care to animals. *Star Trek* is a TV series from the Sixties, and it's also a string of movies made for the theatre. I take it you've never seen any of them?"

Jay shook his head. "The only TV shows I ever got to watch were whatever Dad or Sabine or Ricky wanted to see. I wasn't allowed to watch TV if they weren't."

"Tomorrow, we'll try to find *Star Trek* on the TV guide," Noah promised. "I'm sure we'll come up with something."

"Will Sonny be here?"

Noah nodded. "He comes every day to look after his horse, and usually, he takes Mr. Spock out for a ride every other day."

"Can I ride one of the horses, too?"

"If it's okay with your mom."

Jay craned his neck to look at Hannah. "Can I, Mom?"

"We'll see. You might not be big enough yet."

"I'm big enough!" Jay shot back. "Honest."

"I'm not talking about age," Hannah said, although, in part, she was. "I'm talking about your size, in comparison to how big the horses are."

"Dad says I'm big for my age." He frowned. "Is that bad?"

"Not at all," Hannah said, "but this is a discussion we'll hold for tomorrow, okay? It's time now for us to get some sleep."

Jay cast a worried look at the disheveled bed. "I don't want to sleep alone tonight."

"I'll stay with you, honey."

He brightened. "You will? Thanks, Mom." As an afterthought, he added, "It's not like I'm a baby or scared or anything. Well, maybe I am a little scared, but I'm not a baby like Sabine says."

"You're definitely not a baby," Noah assured him. He gave Jay a quick hug, then lifted him off his knee. He bid both of them goodnight, then waited in the doorway until they were situated in the bed before he turned out the light.

Snuggled once again under the covers, with his mother beside him, Jay fell asleep immediately.

Hannah was not far behind, but at four-thirty, she woke with a start, wondering where she was. When it came back to her, she snuggled further under the covers, but from that moment on, sleep was elusive. After half an hour, she climbed out of bed and made her way to the kitchen, where she put on a pot of coffee. Noah found her at the antique oak table, drinking a cup, a short while later.

"You're an early riser," she said.

"Not usually this early. I thought I'd head to the grocery store and pick up some supplies. Since you're up, you can make a list for me."

"I wouldn't know where to begin."

"Pretend I have nothing and go from there."

"Do you really not have anything?"

He lifted a shoulder. "Marshmallows and hot chocolate."

She smirked at him. "Seriously?"

His responding grin was unrepentant. "There's Corn Pops in the cupboard, but I'm out of milk. Beyond that, there's not much." He went to a drawer and pulled out a small pad and a pen and handed them to her. "In case I've never mentioned it, you look cute in pajamas with penguins on them."

He raked her from head to toe with a heated gaze that left her flushed and a little breathless. She shot back with, "In case I've never mentioned it, you look studly in your uniform."

Noah barked out a laugh. "Studly? Is that even a word?"

"If it isn't, it should be."

He bent down and stole a quick kiss. "Who am I to argue with complimentary logic like that?"

List in-hand, Noah wandered up and down the grocery aisles with his mother.

"Why do you need me here if Hannah gave you a list?" Liza asked.

"I'm sure it's not as comprehensive as I asked her to make it."

Liza scanned the items Hannah had written down. "I think you're right. For one thing, there's no ice cream. Everyone loves ice cream, even when it's snowing like the dickens outside."

He couldn't argue that.

"And Hannah loves to bake, but there aren't any baking supplies. Did you stock up recently?"

"No, I told her to pretend that I had zip for supplies, which is the truth."

"I see." She *tsk-tsked*. "I thought I raised you better than that."

Noah laughed. "And I thought you knew me better than that."

And so it went. The cart got fuller and fuller until Noah decided he had to nip his mother's enthusiasm in the bud, or he'd be pushing two carts through checkout. "There's something else you can help with."

"What's that?"

"Would you be willing to go over to the mercantile and pick up some clothes and other stuff for Jay? Hannah gave me her credit card and another list of what he needs, with sizes."

"Of course! Hand it over."

Relieved, since shopping was not his forte, Noah dug into his shirt pocket and pulled out another piece of paper wrapped around a credit card. "She also wants some stuff from her house and she was none too thrilled with the idea of me rifling through her unmentionables."

Liza grinned. "I wonder why. Oh, look. Here's comes Simon and Dad."

Thank God for small favors, Noah thought, grateful for the interruption of his thoughts and how they related to Hannah's unmentionables.

"Dad's giving me a lift back to Woodland to pick up my car," Simon said, "then I'll head back here. Sabine Borreau no doubt has Fossil in mind as a destination hotspot, which means Twombly is probably not far behind."

"Pretty sure you're right," Noah agreed. "Do you really need to go get your car now, though? You're welcome to use my 4Runner."

"I told him he could use Mom's car, too" Pete said, "since I'm her transportation when the weather gets like this, but he's not hearing it."

"He's stubborn, like his father," Liza teased.

Noah studied his brother, trying to communicate without speaking.

Simon apparently got the message and capitulated about the vehicle.

"C'mon, transportation man," Liza said to Pete. "We have errands to run."

"Wait!" Noah said, digging Hannah's key out of his pocket. He handed it over and asked his dad, "Are you carrying?"

"Of course. Why do you ask?"

"If you see anything suspicious or out of place at Hannah's, get the hell out of there and call me immediately, okay?"

"Mind explaining yourself?" Pete asked.

"Hannah came on up to my place last night because she'd left a lamp on a timer on in the living room, but her house was dark. I did a check to see if she was there before I headed home, and everything looked all right, but it's better to be cautious than sorry."

His parents exchanged concerned glances, said their goodbyes, and left the store.

Noah turned to his brother. "What's so all-fired urgent that you want to get back to Woodland?" When Simon didn't respond, he said, "I suppose it involves Karin."

"Maybe."

Noah reached for two boxes of Corn Pops and tossed them in the cart. "I thought you'd moved past that relationship."

"I thought so, too, but seeing her again...." He shrugged. "You got a problem with that?"

"No, she seems like a nice enough woman, and it's your life, but I might encourage you to remember why you broke it off with her."

His brother grunted. "Is that a leopards-don't-change-their-spots reminder?"

"You said it, not me."

"I get your drift and I'll think about it. I take it you think Sabine's headed this direction."

"If she'd not already here."

"What about Hannah."

"What about her?"

"Is she going to stay at your place until Sabine is caught?"

"If that's what it takes."

"Not very practical and maybe not very smart, either."

"Says you."

"C'mon, Noah, you know how fast things can go sideways."

"Hannah has her own bedroom and it's not mine."

"I figured, with the kid there, but I'm talking about the danger involved, and how you, all by your lonesome, is going to protect them. Your place sits on a hilltop. How do you propose to protect her and the boy?"

Noah had it figured out for the immediate future, which really only covered the next twenty-four hours, but his brother was right. Long-term, his solution wasn't viable when Sabine was still on the loose and most likely being pursued by a vengeful Twombly.

Besides, Hannah and Jay were going to want to venture outside sometime.

"Looks like Sonny's been here," Liza said.

"The kid's a worker bee, that's for sure," Pete said.

"Kind of like our boys, huh?"

He smiled at her. "Kinda. Unless you need my help, I'll wait here. The piece about community policing is scheduled to broadcast right after the news. I told Noah I'd listen and give him a critique."

Liza laughed. "I bet you did." She opened the door. "I'll be back in a flash."

"Wait!"

She looked over at Pete, who was holding his gun toward her. "Seriously? Why not just walk up to the door with me?"

With a grunt, he glanced at the dashboard clock and said, "I still have five minutes, so I guess I will."

Liza climbed out of the truck and made her way up the cleared walkway with her husband trailing behind her. On the porch, she dug into her pocket, feeling for the key. The front door opened, startling both of them. She had no trouble recognizing the woman who greeted her.

Beside her, Pete's hand inched toward his gun.

"Can I help you?" Sabine Borreau asked.

Liza thought fast. "We're looking for a lost dog. We wondered if you'd seen it?"

"What kind of dog?"

Liza improvised. "A chocolate lab. Full grown."

"Nope, haven't seen him." Sabine's gaze traveled past her and examined Pete from head to boot. With a expression of dismissal, she started to close the door.

"We haven't met yet," Liza said. She plucked a name from thin air. "I'm Spring Byington, and this is my husband, Roy. We live down the road, about a half-mile."

"I'm Hannah Mason," Sabine said. "Gotta go. I have breakfast cooking." And with that, she closed the door in Liza's face.

Liza didn't press the issue by knocking. Both she and Pete hurried back to their vehicle.

"I'd say Hannah was smart to keep on driving last night," Pete said, once they were both situated inside the truck again.

"No kidding. Get us out of here."

Pete turned the key in the ignition and backed down the drive. Once on Creight, he glanced at Liza's hands, which were visibly trembling. "My God, you're shaking like a leaf."

"You probably would be, too, if you hadn't spent your entire career dealing with bad guys. I can't believe she had the gall to introduce herself to us as Hannah."

"Better call Noah and give him a heads-up."

Liza pulled out her phone, working hard to still her quaking fingers. In lieu of a greeting when her son answered, she asked, "Where are you?"

"On my way home," Noah said.

"Is Simon still with you?"

"Yes."

"Good. Come straight there," Liza said. "Don't stop at Hannah's under any circumstances."

"Mom, what the heck is wrong with you?"

"Sabine is there, pretending to be Hannah." She disconnected, but still caught Noah dropping the f-bomb.

Five minutes after Pete and Liza arrived at the gate, Noah and Simon pulled in next to them.

Pete and Liza got out of their vehicle and went to the driver's side window of the red Ford F-150. "Better to talk out here," Pete said. "Hannah could take the conversation, but we don't want to scare Jay."

"What happened?" Noah asked.

"We went up the door," his mother said, "but before I could get my key out, it opened, and there stood Sabine. I recognized her from Hannah's photo. I had to think quick to make up an excuse for why we were there."

"What did you say?"

"I told her we were looking for our lost dog, then I introduced us."

"Mom, you didn't!" Simon said.

"I didn't give our real names," Liza said, giving him the names she'd chosen. "Spring was an actress from the fifties who hailed from Colorado Springs, and Roy really was her husband."

"You're one smart cookie," Pete said, giving her a squeeze.

"I have to be smart to keep up with all of you." She glanced back at Noah. "It's too cold to stand out here discussing this."

"We stopped and bought a PlayStation at the mercantile and a couple of games," Simon said. "I'll get it set up and you and Jay can play it together."

"I don't know anything about video games," Liza said.

"These are kid games, Mom. You'll catch on."

"If you say so."

"Let's head up to the house," Pete said. "We can take things as they come, and besides, Mom's right. It's colder'n a witch's tit out here."

Chapter 40

Thinking about his nightmare, Hannah decided she couldn't put off telling Jay about his dad.

They sat on the floor constructing a dinosaur from Legos. It was a three-in-one package and they'd started with the T. Rex.

"Something's happened to your dad and Twombly." Now that she'd begun, she didn't quite know how to carry on.

"Twombly?" he asked.

"The guy you call Ricky."

Jay made a face. "Oh, him." He connected two pieces. "What happened?"

"They were both…shot."

He turned wide eyes on her. "Not by you."

"No, not by me."

He held the nearly finished T. Rex in one hand and the first piece of the tail section in the other. "Sabine did it."

"Why do you say that?"

"She's the one who was shooting in the house last night, and she's done it before."

"She has?"

"Yeah, a couple of times. It always happens when they're in the bedroom." He cocked his head. "She did do it, right?"

Hannah nodded, swallowing over the lump in her throat.

Jay had endured so much. "The police are pretty sure it was her."

He attached the tail piece and grabbed another Lego. "She's not a nice person."

"No, she isn't." Hannah bit her lip, then said, "Jay, your dad was seriously injured."

His hands dropped to his lap. "Is he dead?"

"Yes."

"What about Ricky?"

"He's still alive."

"What about Sabine?"

"No one knows where she is at the moment."

"I'm sorry she's not dead."

Hannah was no child psychologist, but she knew she should tread carefully. "How do feel about your dad's death? Do you have any questions?"

He tilted his head, thinking. "Did it hurt when he got shot?"

"Probably."

His chest rose and fell with a huge sigh. "Mom, maybe it's not very nice for me to say this, but I'm glad Dad's dead and I'm sorry Ricky isn't and I wish Sabine was, too. They were all mean to me and they hurt me. Dad was supposed to take care of me and he didn't."

"I'm so sorry, baby."

"It's not your fault. Dad's the one who took me away from you and told me you were dead. That's not something a nice person does, is it?"

"No."

"Could you do me a favor?"

"Sure, what?"

"Don't ever call me baby again. That's what Ricky and Dad call Sabine, and she always tells me not to act like a baby. I don't want to be reminded of them ever again."

Hannah worked hard not to cry, but it was difficult, because her heart ached so for her son. Seven-year-olds shouldn't have to make such requests. "I promise, I won't ever call you that again."

"Is Sabine going to kill us, too?"

"I won't lie, Jay, she might try."

"Who's going to stop her, Noah?"

Hannah nodded. "And me, and all the people who work for Noah, and his brother, Simon, who's also a police officer, and every other police officer in this state. Sabine killed your dad and she tried to kill Ricky. She's going to be arrested, and then she'll go to trial, and after that, she'll spend the rest of her life in prison."

"Are you sure? What if she escapes or something?"

"I'm positive, and she won't escape. Once she goes to prison, she'll stay there forever."

"But there's a chance she'll try and kill us before she's caught."

Hannah silently cursed herself for being so honest with her son. "Yes."

"Maybe you can use your gun to shoot her."

She kept her mouth shut for a full fifteen seconds, then said, "If that's what it comes to, I guess I will."

"Will that make you sad?"

"Probably. I don't like the thought of killing anyone."

"Not even someone who's really bad, who's trying to hurt us?"

"Not even. She's still a human being."

His head jerked in a quick nod and he went back to finishing the dinosaur. "But not a nice human being."

"Definitely not." She watched him work, then asked. "So, no questions about your dad?"

"Nope."

On that note, Hannah decided to change the subject. "I can see we're going to need to buy more Legos."

"They're cool. Didn't I have some before Dad took me away?"

"You did and they're in a box in my garage."

"You kept them?"

She nodded. "I have everything that belonged to you. You're too big now for most of the toys, and all of the clothes, but there are still some things you can play with."

"Dad wouldn't buy me any toys because Sabine said I didn't need them. She always said I could occupy my time other ways."

"Sabine didn't like kids, Jay. It wasn't just you specifically."

"Every time she hit me, it sure felt like it was me specifically."

Hannah's anger bubbled to the surface again, but she managed to keep her tone temperate. "I'm so sorry she hurt you, honey."

"She scared me with her words, too."

"There's probably nothing she said to you that was true."

"Maybe not, but she did threaten me a lot." Jay shrugged. "I heard Dad tell her once she was full of shit and I think that's true, because shit is stinky and nasty, and she was stinky and nasty, too."

A little shocked by her son's cavalier delivery of such language, she said, "Do you know that shit is not a word little boys should be using?"

"It isn't?"

"No. It's a grown-up word and people usually say it when they're angry, or being mean."

"Hunh. They all said a lot of words when they were angry. Should I tell them to you so I'll know if they're bad words, too."

Hannah nodded, though she didn't want to hear profanities coming from her son's mouth. With each progressive word, she curled her hands tighter and tighter into fists until her nails dug painfully into her skin. "None of those are little-boy words."

He lifted his shoulder again. "I won't say any of them, then, okay?"

Hannah reached over and hugged him. "I'd appreciate it, and you don't want to get yourself in trouble for saying them at school, either."

"My teacher did talk to me once about saying 'crap.'"

"I'm sure she did."

"I like school. When can I go back?"

"We have to get you registered at Fossil Elementary, but I'm going to wait until after Christmas break. That means you'll get an extra long vacation."

"Will I ever get to see my friends at my old school again?"

"Of course."

"What about my teacher?"

"Her, too."

He nodded with a smile. "Speaking of Christmas, can we get a tree?"

"Sweetie, we are definitely getting a tree."

He grinned. "Good. Sabine didn't like decorating Christmas trees, so we never got one. Did you see that ugly pink wreath in the kitchen when we were leaving?"

Hannah nodded.

"She bought it at a Christmas store when we went to Estes Park. It was the best store ever, and they had so many cool things there, and she picked that stupid wreath. Dad and Ricky made fun of it all the way home. Sabine got really mad at them and called them all kinds of bad names." He looked up at her. "Do you think that's why she killed Dad and tried to kill Ricky?"

"With Sabine, I guess anything is possible, but I imagine it was a lot of things that drove her to it."

He studied his T. Rex. "Do you think maybe we can go see Santa, too? I talked to him at the North Pole, but Sabine told me not to, so I really didn't get to tell him everything I wanted for Christmas."

Hannah smiled. "Absolutely! You know, I met him and he remembered you. I think he'll be pleased to see you again."

"Cool!" Jay grinned. "I love you, Mom."

"I love you, too, buddy."

"Do I have to take the T. Rex apart?"

"Not if you don't want to."

He placed the dinosaur on the coffee table and collected all the wrappings, which he took to the kitchen wastebasket. When he came back, he placed the instructions in the box with the spare pieces for the other two dinos and closed the lid. "Where shall I put this?"

"How about in the bedroom?"

"Can I keep the T. Rex in here?"

"I don't think Noah will mind."

"Cool!" He jumped up and ran down the hall with the box.

Hannah wondered if his easy acceptance of his father's death was all the reaction he'd have. She decided to ask Liza's opinion when she saw her next.

"Can I watch TV?"

"Sure."

"Do you think *Star Trek* is on?"

She grabbed the remote to turn on the widescreen on the wall and went directly to the SEARCH function. "The *Star Trek* movie is on tomorrow. I'll set it to record, okay?"

He nodded.

She then did a search for the Nickelodeon channel. "Do you like SpongeBob?"

"I don't know."

Hannah selected the cartoon program and Jay plopped down cross-legged, engrossed immediately.

Knowing Noah should be returning shortly, she went to the living room window. If she craned her neck, she could see the gate, but even from here, she knew something was up. Otherwise, why would Noah and his parents be having a confab under the BELLA VISTA RANCH sign?

She glanced at Jay, who was engrossed in "SpongeBob SquarePants." Should she walk down to the gate and see what was going on?

Even as she had the thought, Pete and Liza climbed back into Pete's truck and within seconds, both vehicles were on their way up the drive. Hannah was surprised when Simon climbed out of Noah's truck. All four Wards came up the walk with a sack. Noah and Simon went back a second time and returned with two sacks each and Pete pulled two more large sacks out of his truck.

Once everyone was inside, Hannah hit PAUSE on the TV remote.

Jay looked around, but didn't complain.

"Honey, I want you to meet some of Noah's family. These are his parents, Mr. and Mrs. Ward, and this is his brother, Simon."

Jay stood and clasped his hands behind his back. Solemn, he studied each of them, then said, "Hi."

"If it's okay with your mom, you can call me Liza and this

is Pete," Noah's mother said.

Hannah nodded her permission.

"We're so glad to meet you," Liza said.

"Thank you," Jay said, still looking serious.

"I'll be in the way in the kitchen while Liza and your mom get breakfast going," Pete said, smiling at Jay. "Let's you and I finish watching this episode of SpongeBob, and after that, Simon is going to hook up a PlayStation to the TV."

Jay nodded and Noah's dad joined him on the floor, also sitting cross-legged. "What's a PlayStation?" her son asked.

Pete looked up at Simon, who offered an explanation.

Liza grabbed Hannah's hand. "C'mon. I'll put the groceries away and help figure out what we can fix for breakfast. I'm sure everyone is hungry."

"Jay snacked on Corn Pops," Hannah said. She snuck a glance at Noah, who was looking about as serious as she'd ever seen him.

Whatever the four of them had been discussing at the gate, it was significant.

Noah said to Hannah, "We have a lead on Sabine's location."

Hannah stared at him, uneasy and overcome with a sudden sense of foreboding.

Noah reiterated his mother's story.

Hannah shook her head, baffled. "I was hoping she'd run as far away from here as possible, while she had the chance." When no one responded, she continued. "Apparently, she wants me dead so badly, she's willing to take a chance on being caught."

"Her movements do reek of desperation," Noah agreed.

"She knows it was me they had tied up."

"Because of the discarded wig," Noah said.

Hannah nodded. "I should have made sure I kicked it completely under the bed, or better yet, I never should have taken it off. Twombly had already commented a couple of times that I looked familiar, plus, they knew I left with Jay."

Noah worked his jaw, apparently trying to decide whether

or not to berate her.

"You're lucky they didn't recognize you right off," Simon said from the doorway. "They would have killed you immediately."

"They couldn't risk leaving any witnesses behind," Noah said.

Hannah frowned. "Did I make things worse?"

"No, but you didn't make them better, either."

Slightly stung by Noah's dressing-down, she managed to remain mute for about two seconds before she relayed the information Jay had given her about previous incidents of gunfire in the house.

"That poor kid," Simon said.

Hannah put away the last of the perishables. "I don't understand why Sabine killed Jason. Faking his and Jay's deaths, taking Jay away, cleaning out our bank accounts... everything Jason did, he did for her." A flurry of thoughts whirled around her brain, and right there in the eye of her mind's hurricane was the answer. "Money," she said. "It was always about the money, wasn't it?"

"They say money is the root of all evil," Noah said. "Given the facts as I know them, I'd say you hit the nail on the head." He tilted his head, listening. "Someone's coming up the drive. Everybody stay put. I'll go out and see who it is."

Chilled by the depth of Jason's cunning and deceit and what a horrible death he'd wrought for himself in the end, Hannah said to no one in particular, "I'm cold. I'm going to go grab a sweater."

In the bedroom, she rummaged through her suitcase. Curiosity got the best of her before she located the sweater. She moved over to the window and looked out. Shock froze her in place.

A light tap on the doorjamb preceded Liza's entry into the room. "You okay, sweetie?"

Hannah backed away with a jerky shake of her head.

Liza's eyes followed the direction of her gaze. "Who is it?"

"Jason's parents. My God, is this nightmare never going to end?"

Liza went to stand beside her. A moment later, she moved

to the window, slid her fingers through the blinds midway up, and unlocked it. She worked the window open, then turned and crooked a finger at Hannah and whispered, "Come closer. We'll eavesdrop."

"They'll see us," Hannah whispered back.

Liza shook her head. "They're not looking this way."

Hannah took three steps forward and tilted the blinds up a bit more, in case they turned around.

Outside, his tone friendly, but sheriff-like, Noah asked, "What can I do for you folks?"

"Are you Sheriff Ward?" Merle Clarke responded in his trademark stuffy manner.

"Yes, I am, and you are?"

"Merle and Susan Clarke. Our son and grandson were murdered two years ago and the woman who killed them is living in your town. We thought you should know, so you can do something about it."

If ever the events of life tumbled into place with perfect ironic synchronicity, this was it, Noah thought.

He couldn't help but wonder who'd tipped off the Clarkes that Hannah had taken up residence in Fossil, or if it even mattered. Regardless, his money was on Twombly, the diehard who persisted in pursuing a woman for a crime he knew damned good and well she hadn't committed. The former detective's devotion to his friends would have been impressive, if not for the vile repercussions of their unified actions.

Noah schooled his features like the good lawman he strived to be. "I'm in the middle of a kidnapping investigation," he said. "Are you staying in town?"

The Clarkes stared at him as if he'd spoken in some language they couldn't comprehend.

Noah tried again. "Are you available to meet with me at the sheriff's office later this afternoon, say around three?"

Susan Clarke, her feathers obviously ruffled, said, "Well, I never!"

Merle Clarke, apparently more verbose than his wife, said,

"This is important!"

"So is a missing child," Noah informed them. "If three isn't good for you, it's possible I can make time to see you tomorrow or the next day."

Blustering a little more, Merle bit out with anger, "We'll be there at three."

"I assume you know the location."

"We do." He threw back his head and looked down his arrogant nose at Noah, even though Noah was several inches taller. "They wouldn't tell us how to find you. We had to stop at the Podunk gas station on Main Street to get the information."

Noah made a mental note to talk to Stan Sheldon about his employees at the Fuel Stop giving out personal information on law enforcement officials.

"Don't you even want to know who this murdering bitch is we're here about?" Susan demanded, taking a step forward. The sole of her high-heeled shoe slid on the packed snow, but a quick move by her husband, who grabbed her elbow, prevented a fall.

"Yes, ma'am, I do."

"Her name is Hannah Clarke. Have you met her yet?"

"No, ma'am, I don't know anyone by that name."

"She's no doubt hiding out."

"Can you recommend a good hotel in town?" Merle asked, giving his wife a stern glance.

"No hotels, sir, but there are a couple of motels on the east end of town."

"Motels?" Susan repeated, making a face. "Seriously?"

"Never mind," Merle said to his spouse. "We'll head back to Colorado Springs. We're not staying the night in some rat-infested motel."

"What are we going to do between now and three o'clock?" his wife responded in a whiny tone.

"Darry's Diner is about a block from the sheriff's office," Noah offered. "She serves great home-cooked meals."

"I can only imagine," Susan said with a sneer.

"I'm sorry, but I really need to take off. Can you find your way back to town?"

Merle stiffened. "Are you impugning my ability to drive?"

"No, sir, but it's cold out here and your wife is already starting to shiver." Noah turned away and walked over to his truck.

The Clarkes returned to their vehicle and within moments, they were on their way back down Creight toward town. Noah followed as far as the end of his drive, then turned in the opposite direction, went up a mile and turned around in the Johnson's driveway, and headed back home.

His family and Hannah were probably wondering where he'd gone off to.

He could only imagine how far south the encounter with the Clarkes would have gone if Hannah had been aware of them taking this inopportune moment to reenter the fray.

Chapter 41

Hannah was furious. Who did the Clarkes think they were, following her to Fossil, spreading their vicious lies about her? Were they on a coast-to-coast vendetta?

What would they say when they learned their only child, the perfect bad seed, really *was* dead now? Jason was the worst, most callous son ever, letting his parents believe he'd died a horrible death with his child in the Pacific Ocean. In Hannah's mind, that, coupled with everything else he'd done, made him a monster.

And who'd told them she was here in Fossil? Not Jason, obviously, or Sabine. That left only one person, the one-man wrecking ball known as Twombly.

"You're not going after them," Simon said, holding tight to her upper arms.

"You can't tell me what to do!" Hannah shot back.

"What's wrong, Mom?" Jay asked. Pete stood behind her son, his hands on the boy's shoulders, like he was Jay's protector. Or maybe he was holding Jay back from going after Simon.

"Nothing, honey. Go back and watch TV."

Jay glared at Simon. "You'd better let go of my mom."

Pete tried to get Jay to turn around. "C'mon, son, let's let the grownups get this straightened out. Liza, how about making us that breakfast?"

Liza cast a worried look at Hannah, then smiled for Jay's benefit. "What's your favorite thing for breakfast, Jay?"

"Banana pancakes, but I haven't had any since Dad took me away. Sabine always said it was too much trouble to make them for a kid."

"I love banana pancakes," Liza said, reaching for Jay's hand, "and it just so happens we have everything it takes to make them." Between her and Pete, they managed to divert Jay's attention and steer him toward the kitchen.

"Let me go," Hannah said to Simon through gritted teeth. "What is it with you Ward men? Do you always have to control things in caveman fashion?"

"Hey," Noah said at the open doorway. "I heard that." He glanced at his brother. "What's going on?"

"Hannah is intent on reaming her in-laws a new one."

Noah shut the door behind him. "I was hoping you wouldn't see who was here."

"I not only saw," Hannah said, jerking free of Simon's hands, "I heard! I've had enough of their bullshit. It's time for a confrontation. Where are they?"

"They're gone."

She gaped at him. "Just like that? What did you do when you followed them down the drive, run them out of town?"

"No, I told them I'm on a kidnapping case, which happens to be true, and that I'd meet them at the SO at three. I didn't want them to know I was shining them on, so I took a short drive up Creight and came back." He leveled one of his looks on Hannah. "I thought you might like to observe the interview."

For a stunned moment, she couldn't find her tongue, but she did lose some of her steam. "Of course, I would."

"You're joking, right?" Simon asked.

"My county. Things run my way."

"It's your funeral," his brother said. "I'm hungry. You guys coming?"

"In a minute," Noah said, pulling off his coat.

"In a minute, my ass," Hannah said, feeling feisty again. She realized she was still cold, because she'd gotten sidetracked and never found the sweater and the window was still open. She spun around and tore down the hall to her bedroom.

Noah's footsteps, loud and determined, followed behind her.

Hannah closed the bedroom window first, then continued searching through her suitcase. She found the sweater at the bottom. She pulled it on over her head, then swung around, still looking for someone to vent her anger and frustration on. Noah made the perfect target.

"So, I get to observe the interview, but I don't get to face my accusers. That's really fair of you, Noah. Thanks a lot." If her tone had been any more acerbic, and had he actually had a heart, he might have withered, but did he? No! He stood tall and broad-shouldered, like he'd had plenty of practice dodging verbal bullets. She planted her hands on her hips. "Don't you have anything to say?"

"If you're through ranting."

"I am not ranting!"

He crossed his arms over his wide chest, practically obscuring his name and the stupid star emblem that had been sewn over the left pocket.

"I assume you have a strategy in mind."

Noah's gaze dropped briefly to study her heaving chest. When he looked up, he said, "As a matter of fact, I do."

"Care to share?"

"Hannah, why do you always have to do things the hard way?"

Her eyes bugged out. "*Hard* way? Are you *kidding* me?"

"Think about it. What recourse do I have to get the Clarkes out of your life forever?"

It took her twelve seconds to get his drift. "A death notification."

"Exactly."

"And why is it I can't be there in person while you do that?"

"What kind of satisfaction will their renewed grief give you?"

Now that he mentioned it, none.

"If you're looking for an apology from them, that will take time."

She barked out an incredulous laugh. "You have no idea what you're talking about, Noah. I've known them for almost ten years. They've hated my guts from the moment Jason met me. Regardless of what they've said to me or how they've treated me, the words *I'm sorry* are not going to suddenly crop up in their vocabulary."

"You might be surprised."

"I'd be more surprised if little green men suddenly popped out of a space ship in your front yard, but I promise you, neither is going to happen."

He drew in a resigned breath. "Let's go get some breakfast."

"Go ahead. I'll be along in a minute."

As soon as he left the room, she looked around for something to kick that wouldn't result in a broken toe. Finding nothing, she sank down to the floor and let the tears come.

No one, but no one, was ever going to understand what she'd endured for the past two years.

Sonny arrived while they were eating. He helped himself to four banana pancakes and sat down at the table next to Jay.

The two of them struck up a conversation about horses, which prompted Noah to give voice to his earlier conversation with Hannah's son. "Jay, how would you like to go on a horse ride with Sonny today?"

"Wow! Could I?"

"If it's okay with your mom." He looked at the teen. "Could Jay ride your horse and you can ride Desi?"

Sonny's eyes lit with excitement. "That's cool with me."

Noah turned to his father. "Would you go out with them on Lucy?"

"I think I should go," Liza cut in, and added wryly, "since I'm not all that good at discussing law enforcement stuff, but I do know my way around horses."

"I don't know, honey," Pete said. "I think you're pretty good at bluffing fugitives."

Liza gave his arm a playful biff.

"Mom, how fast can you make up a lost-dog flyer?" Noah asked.

"Who lost their dog?" Jay asked.

"One of the neighbors," Simon improvised.

Jay's gaze wandered to the two goldens seated near him, raptly watching his every move. "I hope you find it."

Back to the original question, Liza said, "I can do it in about five minutes." She took a bite of her pancakes, then said, "Hunh. I guess I'm a key player, after all."

Noah glanced toward the doorway, wondering what was keeping Hannah. Thankfully, her truck was out of gas, but he wouldn't put it past her to march down to her house on foot for a face-to-face confrontation with Sabine. That was when he realized he'd never gotten around to telling her Sabine had taken up residence in her house. "Be right back."

From the bedroom doorway, he didn't see her right away, but he heard her, sniffling. He entered the room and found her on the floor on the other side of the bed. "What's going on?" he asked, settling down beside her.

"I have Jay back," she said, her voice clogged with tears. "Everything should be all right again, but it's not. Sabine and Twombly are still out there, probably looking to kill me and Jay, and the Clarkes are still hell-bent on destroying me. When is it going to end?"

"Soon," Noah said, gathering her into his arms. "I promise."

"Don't make promises you can't keep."

"When I make a promise, I keep it," he said. "You can count on it." He cupped the back of her head with his hand and rubbed his thumb over the silky softness of her hair.

"The most absurd thing just popped into my head," Hannah said, laying her open palm over his heart.

Noah had never imagined that he'd be content to hold a crying woman in his arms. "What's that?"

"I'm in love with you, dammit."

Noah sighed. "Good, because I fell in love with you the moment you looked at me with those big, beautiful eyes of yours."

"As I recall, I was in fear for my life at the time."

He grunted. "Fearful or not, you showed more guts than anyone I've ever scared before."

Hannah giggled.

"I want to kiss you."

"I'm all snot-nosed."

"I'll get you some tissues."

"I've got one." She dug into her jeans pocket and found two. She used both of them. "Okay, I'm good."

A look of amusement softened his features. "I could take that a number of ways."

She tossed the tissues on the bed. "Shut up and kiss me."

By the time Noah returned to the kitchen with Hannah, only Simon still sat at the table.

"Where is everyone?" Hannah asked. Part of her brain was thinking about the phone call she needed to make to her sister, but the larger part was still on that kiss Noah had given her. The man could really knock her socks off.

"Dad, Jay, and Sonny are out in the barn, saddling up the horses, and Mom is working on the missing-dog flyer."

Hannah came to a standstill, connecting *Jay* and *horses* and *missing dog* and trying to make coherent sense of it. "Who's going riding and whose dog is missing?"

Simon leaned back in his chair. "Sonny, Mom, and Jay, on riding—that is, if it's okay with you—and no one's dog is actually missing."

Hannah looked at Noah. "You said your horses are too big for Jay to ride."

He nodded. "But Sonny will ride Desi and Jay will ride Mr. Spock, who's a good hand shorter."

Hannah didn't understand that comment, but she let it go for now. "Your mom and Sonny are experienced horsemen?"

The brothers laughed. "Mom's been riding horses since she was three, and she's happy to tell the story of her first ride to anyone who'll listen."

Before Hannah could reply, the woman in question entered the kitchen and handed Noah a sheet of paper. "How's this?"

Noah read the flyer and nodded. "Perfect."

Liza grabbed her coat. "I'm going out to supervise the boys." She opened the door, but said to Hannah before she left, "I hope you like banana pancakes."

"I do. Thanks."

Noah looked at Hannah. "Sit."

She regarded him with incredulity. "Really, Sheriff? You talk to me like I'm a dog now?"

He grinned. "You know Fiona doesn't mind when I give her instructions, so no, I'm not talking to you like you're a dog." And since he apparently couldn't leave well enough alone, added, "You're more like a recalcitrant child."

Hannah had never flipped anyone off before, so no one was more surprised than she when her hand came up with only the middle digit extended. More than a little miffed as she took the only chair in front of an empty plate, she ignored the brothers' howls of laughter.

"You like milk with your pancakes?" Simon managed to get out.

"Yes, please."

He scooted his chair back and returned moments later with a full glass.

"This is what's going to happen," Noah said. He picked up his fork to finish his own breakfast. His expression went from amused to grim as he began to outline his plan.

When he'd finished, Hannah stared at him with an expression that reflected equal parts of consternation and disbelief. "You make it sound so simple."

Simon, leaning against the counter with his arms crossed over his chest in a pose that mirrored the one his brother had taken earlier, said, "Sounds plausible to me."

"I think you're both crazy," Hannah said, "but...the more I think about it, the more I think it will work."

"It's definitely better than calling in the FBI and having a mini Branch Davidian event on our hands," Noah said.

Simon said, "Don't let Dad hear you make comparisons like that."

Noah made a sound of agreement, or at least Hannah thought that's what it was.

She couldn't quell the vision of her new home going up in flames, or of what could happen to Noah. After all was said and done, she wanted him alive, not injured, or worse, dead. The thought of it sent a vicious chill down her spine.

The back door flew open and Jay rushed in. "I'm going on a horseback ride, Mom! Mr. Spock is the coolest. He ate an apple right outta my hand." He threw himself at her.

Hannah opened her arms and hugged him. "You are one lucky boy."

"So, it's okay if I go?" he asked, his eyes lit with excitement.

"Yes, but you have to mind what Liza and Sonny tell you."

"I will."

"Promise?"

"Promise!"

"C'mon," Hannah said, extending her hand to him. "Let's go look at your new clothes and get you bundled up nice and warm so you don't freeze out there." She looked down at his feet. "How do those new snow boots feel?"

"Great, and my feet are completely dry. Thank you!"

"Hannah," Noah said, his voice quiet, "Finish your breakfast. You'll have time to get Jay into warmer clothes after that."

"Yeah, Mom," Jay said, sliding into the vacant chair beside her.

Pete, Liza, and Sonny wandered in, kicking the snow off their boots. Hannah popped up out of her chair. "I'll clean up the snow Jay tracked in."

"You sit and finish your breakfast," Pete said, putting his hand up. "I'll do it."

"I'll get it, oldtimer," Sonny said, grinning.

"I'll oldtimer you, you young whippersnapper," Pete responded, laughing.

"Hi, Hannah."

"Hi, Sonny. Thanks for letting Jay ride Mr. Spock."

"Hey, it's not a problem, especially since I get to ride Desi."

Noah directed the teenager to the laundry room for the mop and whatever else he needed to clean up the floor.

"We got a plan?" Pete asked Noah.

Noah nodded. "You in?"

His father grinned. "Of course."

Hannah appreciated that they kept their exchange short and cryptic for Jay's benefit.

The last thing she wanted her son to know was that his Sabine-the-Tormenter was holed up so close by.

Chapter 42

At two forty-five, Hannah, Pete, and Noah's deputy, Kenny, moved from the conference room at PCSO to the observation room.

It was a long fifteen minutes until three o'clock, but it had to be that way. Noah didn't want the Clarkes to know that Hannah was listening to the interview he and Simon would conduct.

Noah, Simon, and two other PCSO deputies on day shift remained in the conference room. When the Clarkes arrived, Marty would escort them to the interrogation room.

Chief Fitzgerald, Bobby Stewart, and Karin Delaney were on their way from Woodland Park. Two Colorado State Patrol officers and an additional CBI investigator were also on the way. As soon as the Clarkes left town, the plan was to converge on Hannah's house to arrest Sabine Borreau and, with any luck, Rick Twombly.

Noah had already confirmed that Sabine was still in the house.

On the way into town, Simon had knocked on Hannah's front door, purporting to be a detective at PCSO. Under the guise of making a wellness check on the new resident, he'd also handed over the lost-dog flyer to cement his neighborly inquiry.

So far, everything was going according to plan.

At 2:58, the Clarkes entered the sheriff's office. Marty escorted them to the interview room and asked if they wanted something to drink. Both asked for coffee. Marty beelined for the kitchen area and poured two cups of coffee, which Simon carried in to the couple. Noah asked if they were comfortable, then got the tape going and identified the four in the room by name.

At the same time, Chief Fitzgerald entered the obs room.

"Are you ready to listen to our story now?" Merle Clarke demanded.

"Please," Noah said, "continue."

Jason's father related the story as it had been fed to him by Twombly. "She went out with the two of them, as surely as the sun rises each day. We believe she had a boyfriend waiting for her out there, who helped kill them, then provided her transportation back to shore."

"How did you arrive at the conclusion this woman went out on the boat?" Noah asked.

"There were three empty soda cans in the cooler, and three lifejackets floating nearby." His hands shook as he picked up his paper cup and sipped his coffee. "Who else would have been there drinking that third soda or wearing the other adult lifejacket?"

"That's right," Susan Clarke concurred. "I've never liked Hannah. I've always felt there was something off about her, and now, to my great regret, I know what it was. She's a cold-blooded killer."

"Who provided you the facts concerning this incident?" Noah asked.

The couple exchanged a glance, then Merle said, "Detective Twombly, from San Diego PD."

"He was a friend of your son's."

Merle started. "How do you know that?"

Ignoring the question, Noah said, "Did you ever bother to speak to anyone else at Harbor Patrol or San Diego PD about the incident?"

"No," Susan said. "Why should we? Rick had the facts."

"Did you ever question that your son and grandson died

that day?"

"Of course not!" they said at the same time. Merle went on, "Why would you even suggest something so outrageous?"

"The bodies were never recovered."

"We were told that recovery is not that common, and we've lived near the ocean long enough to know that there've been many instances where bodies were never found."

Simon, who'd been sitting with his hands clasped on the table in front of him, staring at the couple, said, "Did you know that because of the distance the sailboat was found from shore, and the current in that particular area, everyone who's drowned in that vicinity has surfaced within a ten-mile stretch of the beach?"

The couple exchanged another, surprised glance. "That...that can't be right," Susan said. "Rick said—"

"What are you trying to pull here?" Merle cut in, his voice raised in anger. "We've come here to tell you that you have a ruthless murderer in your town and you're posing asinine what-ifs to us."

"Here's a real what-if for you," Noah said. "What if your son took your grandson out on the sailboat that day intending to *fake* their deaths? What if he took his girlfriend with him and she helped him pull it off? What if no one died that day? What if Jason took Jay and went to live in another state with Sabine Borreau?"

For several shocked moments, the Clarkes gaped at the sheriff in horror.

Susan finally managed to speak. "I can't believe you're even suggesting something so...so...."

"Ridiculous!" Merle sputtered. He pushed back from the table, toppling his chair. "I want to see your superior! *Now!*"

"I am my superior," Noah said, unruffled. "Sit down, Mr. Clarke, and let me tell you what really happened that day." When Merle didn't move, Noah said, "You can either sit of your own accord, or I'll help you back into the chair and I'll handcuff you to the ring to prevent you from moving until I'm ready to let you walk out of this room."

Susan grabbed her husband's sleeve and tugged until he sat.

"Have either of you spoken to Jason since the sailboat incident?"

"What?" they squawked in unison.

Apparently satisfied they hadn't heard from their son, Noah instructed them not to interrupt him while he filled in the details of what had actually taken place.

By then, Hannah was pretty certain the Clarkes had already been shocked into silence, if not apoplexy.

When Noah got to the part where Jason, Jay, and Sabine had been spotted at DIA, he took a breather. "Any questions so far?"

"I don't believe you!" Susan said. "Jason would never, *ever*, do anything like that."

Noah opened the file folder on the table and withdrew the photocopies Hannah had provided him. He swiveled them with his fingertips so the Clarkes could see the proof for themselves.

Susan Clarke put a hand to her mouth and began to sob. Tears ran in streams down her pale cheeks.

Merle said, "That looks like Jason...and Jay." He glanced at his wife. "And Sabine. We...we...that is, once when Jason came up, she joined us for dinner. Jason said" —Merle's voice caught— "he said they were attending a conference together, and she didn't know anyone there, so...."

"She was a friend of his and Twombly's from high school," Simon said. "For God's sake, man, stop sugar-coating the truth!"

Merle's shoulders visibly sagged.

"He lied to us," Susan said, her voice little more than a whisper. "Oh, God. Where is he? Our son is alive, Merle." Her head swung to face Noah. "Where is he? Please! I need to see my son."

Noah's expression became grim, yet somewhat reluctant, and no wonder. It wouldn't be easy to tell these people for the second time that their son really was dead.

Regardless of how this had played out, Hannah knew he had some sympathy for two parents who had been cruelly duped by their only child.

Noah said, "I'm sorry to be the bearer of bad news, but

your son was murdered two nights ago."

"My God, Hannah got him, after all!" Merle boomed, slamming his palm hard against the table. "Will you arrest her now and make it stick?"

"It wasn't Hannah who killed him," Simon said.

"Oh, please! Who else would want him dead after what he did?"

"Every indication is that Sabine Borreau killed him and also tried to kill Rick Twombly at the same time," Noah said.

"Impossible. They were—"

"Mr. Clarke, this is a murder investigation. If you fail to cooperate with us, or lie to us one more time, I'm going to charge you with hindering an investigation."

Merle blustered for a moment, then spat out, "The three of them were friends. Is that what you want me to confirm? They've known each other since high school, all right? Satisfied now?"

"I think it's time for me to get in there," Chief Fitzgerald said, and left the obs room. Moments later, he knocked on the interrogation room door, opened it, and walked in.

For the recorder, Noah said, "Chief Willem Fitzgerald, Woodland Park PD, entering at three-thirty-six p.m."

Fitz said, "We've been trying to reach you folks. Since your son was killed in Woodland Park, the investigation falls within our purview."

"We've been trying to tell the sheriff that we know who killed Jason," Merle said. "He's not listening."

"We're one-hundred-percent certain the woman who shot your son is Sabine Borreau," Fitz said. "The reason we've been trying to locate you is that we need a next-of-kin identification to verify that the victim is Jason Hiram Clarke."

"What's to verify? You have pictures," Merle said, swiping his hand across the table. Sheets of paper went flying everywhere.

"Your son died as a result of a gunshot wound to the back of his head. There's not much left of his face to identify. He does, however, have some markings on his body that you are probably familiar with."

Susan began to sob uncontrollably.

"What kinds of markings?" Merle demanded.

"A birth mark and a couple of scars."

"Can't you take photographs and let us look at them?"

"No, I'm sorry. ID has to be made in person."

"I don't want to see my son with his face blown off!"

"You won't," Fitz assured him. "Every effort is made to keep his injuries covered. I have a patrol officer here who can drive you to Woodland and back, if you don't feel up to making the drive yourself."

Merle ignored the offer and asked of Noah, "You said she also tried to kill Rick. Where is he now? I want to talk to him."

"He's not yet in custody, and when we find him, it may be a long while before you can speak to him."

"What the hell would he be charged with, if he's a victim?"

"Among other things, kidnapping, impeding an investigation, attempted murder, obstruction of justice, assault." Noah shrugged. "I could go on."

Susan grabbed her husband's shoulder. "I want to get out of here. I want to see my son."

Clearly discombobulated by everything he'd heard, Merle glanced at Fitz. "How long is the drive to this place, Woodland Park?"

"We could have you back here in about three hours," Fitz said.

"Let them drive us," Susan said. "We'll come back and spend the night at a motel, then get out of this hellhole first thing in the morning."

Hannah liked her mother-in-law's plan. A lot. She also found it telling that neither Susan nor Merle had inquired about Jay, but she wouldn't put it past them to show up down the road and try to get custody of him.

The thought threw her into a frenzy of possibilities about how to deal with such an attempt. "I need to get some fresh air," she said to Pete and Kenny, anxious to leave the building while the Clarkes were still in the interrogation room. "I'm going to walk over to the diner to get a coffee. Come get me when you're ready for Phase Two."

Noah checked for traffic, then crossed Main Street and headed for the diner. He pushed open the door and scanned the few tables that were occupied.

"Hey, Noah," Darry said. "Can I get you something?"

"I'm looking for Hannah. She said she was coming over here."

"She ordered a cup of coffee, but took it in a to-go cup."

"Thanks," Noah said, and ducked back out. He looked up and down the street, then over across the way. No Hannah.

The door opened behind him. "I heard you say you were looking for Hannah," Charlie Crispin said.

Noah turned to face the owner of Crispin Heating and Sheetmetal.

"Me and Bethie met up for a slice'a pie and cupp'a coffee." He turned and pointed toward his wife, sitting next to the window.

Beth Crispin waved at Noah, who nodded back.

"I didn't think anything of it at the time, but since you can't find Hannah, I guess maybe I know why."

Charlie was a genius with heating and air conditioning systems, but sometimes, his roundabout way of reaching a point bordered on aggravating. Impatient and trying not to show it, Noah asked, "Did you see her?"

"I did. We even said hello. When she left the diner, Hannah stepped off the curb and this Jeep Renegade comes tearing down Main, like it's the Interstate or something. The driver skids to a halt and jumps out. Of course, I couldn't tell what she was yelling, but the next thing you know, she grabs Hannah's arm and drags her around to the passenger side." He scratched his cheek. "Now I can't be certain about his, but thinking back on it, the woman may have hit Hannah once she was in the Jeep."

The reported scenario and the possible outcome left Noah's blood running cold. "What color was the Renegade?"

"Red, with black trim. Even though it was dirty from the snowy roads, it looked brand new."

"And the driver? What did she look like?"

Charlie described Sabine exactly. Even when she was hitting guys in the head with a baseball bat, or kidnapping women, someone who looked like Sabine Borreau left an impression. "You didn't happen to get the plate number, did you?"

"Tweren't a number," Charlie said. "It was a personalized plate, 'Jeeped Up.'" He then spelled it out as JEEPDUP. "Peculiar choice, if you ask me."

But one that was memorable and matched the one on the vehicle of the poor sucker who'd had his new Renegade stolen by Sabine in Woodland. "Thanks, Charlie." Noah clasped the man's shoulder in gratitude, then bolted back across the street and into the station. "Sabine's taken Hannah."

After some debate on where they might have gone, Pete said, "Hannah has a smartphone. We should be able to pinpoint her approximate location."

"If we had the proper equipment," Noah said, his tone and expression equally forbidding.

"Or," his dad suggested, "we could just call someone I know at the FBI and let them do it for us. This is a kidnapping, after all."

Fifteen minutes later, they learned that Hannah was somewhere in the vicinity of her own house.

Sabine might be a knockout, but she had absolutely no imagination, and apparently not as many smarts as Noah had given her credit for.

The moment Hannah regained consciousness, her body informed her that it hurt, from head to toe. She opened her eyes, surprised to find little stars dancing in her vision.

With her brain groggy and her nerve centers on excruciating pain alert, it took her a minute to remember what had happened.

Sabine. Pointing a gun at her. Issuing threats. Promising to find Jay and kill him.

Hannah hadn't been inclined to disobey an order to get in the Jeep with a gun pointed at her gut, which was why Sabine smacking her in the head with the butt of the gun, in retrospect, seemed like overkill. Of course, Jason's lover did have a dramatic streak about a mile wide, and a vindictive streak that was even wider. She'd whacked Hannah because she felt like it and for no other reason.

She opened her eyes a little wider. Sabine stood at the bar, her back to Hannah.

Hannah couldn't believe Sabine had actually brought her back to her own house, like no one would look for them there. And how had Jason's lover managed to get her into the house? Had she dragged her? That certainly would explain the massive aches and pains she felt throughout her body.

Her eyes scanned the room. Her favorite lamp lay on the floor nearby, although the cord was missing. A pair of scissors lay next to it. Hannah concluded that, lacking a rope, Sabine had used the electrical cord to secure her arms to the spindles in the chair back.

Hannah wiggled against the restraints. Obviously, Sabine had not been the one who'd tied her to the chair in Woodland, because the lamp cord was so loose, she was practically free already.

Sabine had several wine bottles lined up on the countertop. She poured herself a healthy serving from one that she'd already opened. By the time she turned to face Hannah, the goblet was half empty. "I see you're awake, you lousy bitch."

Hannah likened her tone to that of the Wicked Witch's voice in *Wizard of Oz*, when she promised Dorothy, *I'll get you, my pretty, and your little dog, too!*

Still, Sabine showed no indication that she was ready for an immediate kill. Hannah decided to take the opportunity to ask some questions. She prefaced them by goading. "I hope you're enjoying my wine. My brother-in-law left it for celebrating a special occasion."

"I'd say putting a bullet in your head is going to be a pretty fucking special occasion," Sabine said, pouring a second glass.

"Where's Twombly?"

"Dead."

"Wrong. He got up and walked away after you shot him."

"Liar!" Sabine drank from her glass like she was dying of

thirst, then choked on the last sip. Red wine dribbled down her chin on onto her white sweater. "How would you know anything about it? You weren't there."

"Wasn't I?"

She whirled around and grabbed the wine bottle, refilling her glass before she spun back to face Hannah. "You bitch!" she snarled. "Ricky was right! We had you in our grasp and didn't even know it."

"That's right. You missed your golden opportunity."

"I still have a golden opportunity, Hannah, and it's going to feel damned good when I kill you."

Hannah took her goading a little further. "You better hurry up. Twombly's going to be after you." She paused for effect. "He may already be here."

"He's dead."

She forced out a short laugh of derision, silently cursing the pain in her head. "You're wrong. You only managed to kill Jason."

A look of uncertainty wrinkled Sabine's normally perfect features. "Jason was right. You'd say anything to get your way."

"Let's cut to the chase, Sabine. Jason was a liar, and you know it."

Dismissing Hannah's words with a shrug, Sabine drank from her glass.

"If you aren't scared of Twombly, you're dumber than I thought."

"If I hadn't made sure he was dead, I might be, so you're wasting your time trying to convince me otherwise."

"It's your funeral." If Twombly showed up before Sabine killed her, he'd go after the woman who'd tried to kill him first, so maybe she'd still have a chance to get away.

Sabine laughed. "After I put a bullet in Jason's head, I turned around just as pretty as you please and grabbed Ricky's balls for one last squeeze. He never knew what hit him." She sneered at Hannah. "You always were too inquisitive for your own good."

Hannah's gut clenched. What was that supposed to mean? She'd seen Sabine drunk before. To say she had no inhibitions or limitations once the alcohol hit her blood stream would have been a massive understatement. "Apparently, not inquisitive enough, because I never suspected you and Jason were an item."

That sent Sabine into gales of laughter. "Oh, we were more than an item, Hannah."

"From the orgy you had at the house, I thought you and Jason and Twombly had a good thing going."

"We did, but you know men, they only think about themselves and I was getting tired of the same old thing. Besides, why should I share Jason's money with Ricky?" Her tone went from blasé to almost giddy. "This time tomorrow, I'm going to be on a hot, sandy beach somewhere, having sex with a bronzed god or two. And after that, I'll choose another beach and hook up with two new bronzed gods." She polished off her wine and refilled the glass for the fourth time, which emptied the bottle. "Life is going to be good for me from here on out. Sex and money and more sex. What more does a girl need?"

"Did you kill Henri, or did Jason and Twombly help you?"

"My God, you are a fount of knowledge, aren't you?"

"I don't understand why you don't simply leave the men you hook up with. Why do you have to kill them?"

"You're joking, right? If I leave them alive, I have to leave all that beautiful money behind. I'm not stupid, you know. I never even told Jason or Ricky how much I really got from Henri, or what I really sold the house for." She snorted. "When men think with their dicks instead of their heads, they can't see two feet in front of them."

"Not all men are as stupid and gullible as Jason and Twombly."

"Ohmygod, you are so wrong! What a naïve bitch you are."

"You might as well know, I'm pretty pissed about the way you treated my son."

Sabine studied her with narrowed eyes as she gulped half her goblet. More red liquid dripped down from the corner of her mouth. "You might as well know, I didn't want your brat along for the ride. I told Jason that, but he insisted." She frowned. "He said it was because I wouldn't give him a kid.

Hell no, I wouldn't! No way was I getting swollen up like the goddamned Goodyear blimp. I fucking hate kids and he's known that since forever. What did he think those two abortions were about, anyway?"

"Were they Jason's babies?"

Sabine shrugged. "I have no idea, and frankly, I don't give a rat's ass. I don't do kids. Ever. Period. End of fucking story."

"Did you and Jason and Twombly kill other people before Jason married me?"

"Maybe." She snickered in a getting-drunk sort of way. "See, I told you, you're too inquisitive for your own good, but since you're asking, I wanted to kill you in San Diego. I liked it there, you know? Sunny, and warm, and I loved that mansion you lived in. God, fucking in your bed with that view of the bay…what a rush, but Jason said it would be too obvious."

Hannah, working on her bonds as unobtrusively as possible, didn't dwell on how close she'd come to being dead already. She wanted information she could pass on to Noah, in case Twombly got to Sabine before she could be questioned. "Who else did you kill?"

Sabine drained her glass. She struggled with the corkscrew on the next bottle, but a few minutes later, she had it open and refilled her goblet. When she turned back to Hannah, her eyes were glassy and her speech was starting to slur. "What was the question?"

"Who else have you killed?"

She lifted a finger on her free hand. "Oh, yeah. One of our classmates in high school, Tommy Craig. We made it look like he'd killed himself. God, what a rush. Have you ever watched anyone die? It was so amazing, it was almost as good as having an orgasm." Her free hand slipped down the front of her jeans to her crotch.

"Why did you kill him?"

"Two reasons, really. We wanted to see what it was like" —she giggled, then moaned— "and just because we could."

Appalled by Sabine's lackadaisical attitude about murder and masturbation, she asked, "Who else?"

Sabine finished what she was doing and pulled her hand out. "What?"

"Who else did you kill?"

"One of the partners where Jason used to work. He figured out Jason was cooking the books, so we had no choice. He liked to drink, though, so it was easy enough to run him off the road after we liquored him up. He didn't die right away, but we hung around until he did." She giggled. "We had sex while we waited. I could tell, even though he was dying, he wished he was the one fucking me."

Hannah couldn't help wondering if Sabine had been born psycho, or if the two men she'd been friends with had initiated her into a debased, narcissistic lifestyle. Or maybe it was the exact opposite, and Sabine had tainted them. "Don't you want to know who else?"

Revolted by the woman's mind-set toward killing, Hannah almost said no. "I'm waiting to hear with bated breath."

"Janine Fredrickson." She licked her lips, as if in anticipation of eating something really yummy. "I met her in one of my college classes and when Jason and Ricky saw her, they hounded me to ask her if she liked group sex. I was pissed initially, because I should be plenty for two horny guys, right? But the more I thought about it, the more possibilities I conjured up between her and me, so finally, I did ask her. God, I swear, she was a closet nympho. She liked being with the three of us so much, she was like our lapdog. Then one day, she brought a guy with her and that's when we knew we had to kill her." She giggled again. "We did him, too. Made it look like a murder–suicide." She frowned. "I've always missed that slut. She was amazingly good at so many things, you know?"

Hannah didn't, but that was beside the point. The pounding in her head didn't allow for concentrating on anything more than freeing herself from the restraints that held her to the chair.

Sabine drank more wine, her expression almost dreamy. Her walk down her sex-filled memory lane must be quite a blast.

A screeching sounded from the direction of the patio door.

Hannah jerked her head that way, immediately sorry she'd moved so fast when everything started to spin.

The world finally righted itself. Was she seeing things? Was it really Bowie trying to get in?

Sabine was slower to respond to the noise. "A dog. Hunh. Somebody came around looking for a lost dog yesterday and the cops brought a flyer by today." She squinted at the patio door. "Not this dog, though. It's just a puppy...and the wrong color."

Before Hannah could advise Sabine not to let Bowie in, Sabine stepped over to the patio door, unlocked it, and slid it open.

Bowie rushed over to Hannah, sniffing and whining.

Sabine wobbled on her feet. "He's cute. Maybe I'll take him with me."

"Over my dead body," Hannah said.

Sabine snorted again and held up her glass, as if in salute. "That's true." She turned toward the door. "Brrr." Even though she grabbed the handle to slide the door closed, it stuck. Uttering a disgruntled sound in her throat, she set down her glass and put two hands on the door handle.

Hannah took the moment of diversion to wriggle her arms one last time. The cord restraining her dropped with a whisper of sound to the floor. Silently, she entreated her guardian angel, *Guardian angel, please, help me do what I have to do to get out of this mess.* She hoped Liza's advice worked, because she had just one plan, and not only was it a stupid one, it was risky as hell. "Bowie, sit."

Though obviously unwilling to do so, the puppy did as he was told.

Sabine, still struggling with the patio door that had never given Hannah one ounce of trouble, finally gave up when she got it within six inches of closing. She retrieved her wine glass from the counter. "God, this is good wine." She swallowed what was left and went to work opening another bottle, completely ignoring the second one she hadn't yet finished.

Given the circumstances, Hannah wondered briefly why her captor was slowly but surely getting stinking-ass drunk, but she had no time to ponder that further. She also didn't engage in self-debate over whether or not she could kill a woman who had been her friend in another life. Nor did she consider that she might not make it out of her current situation unscathed.

She knew what she had to do. With both Jay and Noah at the forefront of her mind, she had to move and she had to move quickly.

It never occurred to her that Noah might be outside planning a rescue.

Or that Bowie might have doggie thoughts of his own.

Chapter 43

Hannah pushed up out of the chair. Of course, being part of the antique table-and-chairs set she'd bought years ago, the chair squeaked and announced her movement.

Slow to react due to the amount of wine she'd imbibed, Sabine whirled around and lost her balance, but managed to recover by grabbing the edge of the island countertop. She swung back and began to scrabble for something behind the row of wine bottles.

It took Hannah a moment to realize Sabine was reaching for a handgun.

Sabine swiped at the bottles, sending them flying off the island and onto the floor. Had the floor been something other than oak, the bottles might have broken, leaving a sea of broken glass for her and Bowie to navigate, but they didn't.

Bowie yelped and came up on all fours, seeking cover.

Hannah lunged and shoved Sabine sideways, but Sabine already had the weapon in her hand.

Bowie surged into the fray and sank his teeth into Sabine's ankle. She screamed and lowered the weapon, pointing at his wriggly body.

Hannah grabbed the only wine bottle left on the countertop, which happened to be the one tipped over and dribbling white wine like a faucet. Holding it by the neck, she took a wild swing and connected with the side of Sabine's head. "This is for Jay and Juliette...and me."

Sabine screamed. Simultaneously, the sound of gunfire filled the room.

Bowie yelped.

Sabine fell to the floor.

Whether she was dazed or dead, Hannah didn't bother to wait around to find out. "Bowie, come!" she screamed.

The pup didn't respond.

"Bowie, come!"

With a whimper, he peeked out from behind the end of the island. He was too heavy to lift, so Hannah headed for the open patio door, which as far as she could tell at that moment, was the surest and fastest way out of the house.

Finally understanding her intent, Bowie nearly tripped her as he whizzed past her and out onto the patio, where a light snow had begun to fall.

If she hadn't been curious about how close Noah's house was to hers, and looked at a satellite map online, she wouldn't have even considered heading up the hill and over to his property to get away from Sabine. But she had, so she did. For one thing, there was no way Sabine could follow her in a vehicle, like she might if Hannah had taken to the road to make her escape. Besides, she walked up that hill at least once a day and she could do it now without stopping to catch her breath. Of course, her daily jaunts involved walking not running, and Hannah found herself breathless halfway up.

Outside, Bowie tore up the incline. Hannah had nowhere near his speed, but she made it in a respectable time, considering the depth of the snow and her inability to draw a regular breath.

Down below, Sabine screamed from the patio, "I'm going to kill you, bitch!" The threat chased after them, surprising Hannah all over again by how sound carried outside when it was snowing, as if it were muffled.

From a quarter-mile up the road, Noah studied Hannah's house through binoculars. "There's a truck in the driveway, but no sign of the Jeep." He lowered the binocs. "Hannah said there was a blue Dodge Ram double-cab in the garage when she left the Woodland Park house, but it wasn't there when we arrived on-scene. I'm guessing Twombly has joined the party."

"That's going to make things a little trickier," Simon said, reaching for the binoculars so he could take a look.

Noah activated his shoulder mic. "Any sign of CBI or CSP?"

Kenny came back. "Not yet. Maybe we should have asked the Woodland people to hang around."

Maybe they should've, Noah thought, but too late now.

Simon said, "CBI, at least, should have been here by now."

"Snowy roads and weather. Who knows what's holding everyone up." Noah glanced at the sky. The snow, at least, had abated. "This would be a helluva lot easier with them than without them, though, goddammit."

"What do you want to do?"

"We'll give them five more minutes. If they don't show, we stick to the plan and hope to hell it doesn't go south on us." He activated his mic again and issued his five-minute deadline. "If they're still not here, proceed in your vehicles to the property line, as defined by the fence. Proceed from there on foot."

From Noah's perspective, the minutes dragged by as if they were hours. All he could think about was Hannah and what Sabine and Twombly had done, or were doing, to her in that house. He glanced at his watch. Five seconds, four, three, two, one. His radio crackled.

"No sign of them, Noah," Kenny said. "We're headed your way."

Noah started up the F-150 and went at a crawl down to the fence line on the east side of Hannah's property. With no re-inforcements in sight, and two maniacs who loved to kill in-side, this was going to be tricky, but he had confidence in his people and his brother. He opened the door and said, "Let's go."

His mother hadn't given back Hannah's key, so he slid out the hidden tray on the bottom of the mailbox and took that one. He issued one final instruction. "Think smart and stay safe, people."

He waited for an verbal acknowledgement from each one of them before they moved up the driveway, weapons drawn. Kenny and Barbie broke off and headed toward the rear of the house. Toad went left to cover the mudroom door. Flip remained at the garage door and Noah and Simon took the front entrance.

Noah slid the key in the door lock and turned it. With only the slightest of clicks, the door was unlocked. He depressed the lever and opened it. "Sheriff's office," he announced in a commanding voice. "We have the house surrounded. If you have a weapon, place it on the ground and raise your hands above your head."

No one responded, nor was there any indication anyone was even in the house.

Utter silence reigned until Kenny shouted from the rear of the house. "Sheriff! Patio door is wide open and there's footprints going up the hillside."

Noah took a moment to say, "Stay put. We'll clear the house."

Several minutes later, certain no one was hiding in a closet or under a bed, Noah and Simon met again in the kitchen. To Kenny, he said, "What've you got?"

"Three sets of footprints and one set of paw prints, all going up the hill."

Three sets of footprints. One set of paw prints. What the hell? "Two women, a man, and a dog?"

"Looks like."

Noah took a moment to examine the kitchen. Three unopened wine bottles on the floor, two empty ones, also on the floor, one full wine glass on the counter, and white wine everywhere. One chair in the middle of the room. Behind it, an electrical cord. In the family room, a lamp on the floor with the cord missing. Beside it, a pair of utility scissors.

Simon squatted down to examine an empty bottle. "Got some blood on this one."

Either Sabine had hit Hannah, or Hannah had gotten loose and attacked Sabine. Noah's phone rang. His non-law enforcement persona considered ignoring it, but the sheriff in him overruled.

"Noah, Sonny just came in from combing the horses and said Bowie took off a while ago, running toward home. Is he down there?"

Everything happened for a reason, right? His dad calling to say Bowie had escaped explained the paw prints out back. "Looks like he was. It also looks like Hannah got away and Sabine is after her, and Twombly is after both of them. We don't have any idea how long ago any of them left the house, but since Hannah's at the head of the chase, I'm guessing she's heading toward my place."

"You headed back?"

"Soon as I get my people situated. CBI and CSP still haven't shown up."

"You've got to be kidding me. Want me to put out some calls?"

"That would be helpful."

His father hung up without saying anything more than, "Will do."

"Kenny, get everyone to the patio."

While they waited for the deputies, Noah went to the garage and disabled the Jeep. Simon did the same to the Dodge Ram in the driveway.

From there, he stepped out back via the patio door to study the footprints. Straight up the hill. He ran to the top to confirm everyone had headed east. Damn, he could've have used the binoculars right about now to confirm they were on a straight trajectory for his place.

Back on the patio, he examined everyone's footwear. "Who has snow shoes in their rigs?"

Every hand went up.

"Go get them. The drifts are going to be deep up there and you're going to travel faster wearing them."

"It's going to be deep enough to impede Hannah and the two following her," Simon noted.

"Maybe not for Twombly. He's a lot taller and stronger than Hannah or Sabine." Noah turned to the others. He didn't want to leave a deputy alone in the house, but every indication was that the action was headed toward his place. Besides, he needed the four remaining deputies to chase after Hannah and the others from this end. "Derek, you stay here. Call Shari in to start processing inside the house."

The deputy didn't look happy about being left out of the action. "What do you want me to do with CBI and CSP if they ever show up?" he asked.

"CBI should stay with you and send CSP up to my place."

"Is it really necessary for me to stay here, boss?"

"There's a remote possibility either Sabine or Twombly will circle back. I need someone here to stop them if that happens. You're it."

That seemed to soothe Deputy Parker's ruffled feathers.

"I hope to God Dad takes Mom and Jay into the safe room," Simon said as they ran back to the F-150.

"He will."

"After he gets them situated, I bet he thinks you're going to let him come out with us."

It was a family curse. The genetics of the Ward men didn't lean toward taking a back seat while others did the work.

Noah pressed his foot down harder against the gas pedal, which sent the rear of the truck fish-tailing.

Hannah stopped, doubled-over, trying to catch her breath. Where was a damned tree when you needed one to hide behind?

She straightened and glanced back the way she'd come. Sabine was still hot on her trail. She wasn't making good time like Hannah, probably because she was sloshed, but she was still too close for comfort. Even as Hannah had the thought, a bullet whizzed past her head.

Too close for comfort was right.

Then it dawned on Hannah that Sabine was still moving, and her arm wasn't raised, aiming a gun at her. She searched the landscape beyond Sabine. There, bringing up the rear of this odd parade, was a large hulking man who could only be Twombly. She wasn't the least bit surprised, but she did wonder if the bullet shooting past her head had been meant for her or Sabine. No doubt, they were both his targets.

She twisted around, praying for the fortitude to continue.

God, it was hard to run in the snow. Bowie managed it okay, but then he had four legs and he was a lot lighter, though he did sink in. Every boot step Hannah planted in the deep snow seemed to take forever to release so she could take the next step. Her only consolation was that Sabine had to be experiencing the same problem. The other thing going in her favor was that she had her coat on and Sabine had run out without one. Of course, Sabine had drunk enough wine to stoke an internal fire, so she might not feel the cold at all.

Ten or so steps later, Hannah got stuck, mid-thigh. The harder she struggled, the worse she wedged herself in. She could only conclude that she'd stepped into a major depression in the landscape. The snow would either swallow her up completely, or she'd die from hypothermia and her bones would be found in whatever year the snow melted.

The thought of never seeing her son again after she'd just found him nearly undid her. So cruel were the ironies of life.

Bowie came back and puppy-barked at her.

"I'm stuck," she said. "I can't move." She had to be close to Noah's by now, didn't she? Her head hurt so bad, she could barely form a coherent thought, but she had to. It was think or die! "Go get Noah," she finally said to the pup.

Bowie tilted his head at her and smiled.

Helpless and hopeless at the same time. Could it get any worse? Hannah pulled herself together and tried once more. "Go get Noah, Bowie. Find Noah!"

Bowie circled twice, then turned and loped off through the snow.

Hannah held out no hope that he'd come back with Noah, but at least he'd survive, and his survival meant Jay would have both a playmate and an protector.

She had no such illusions that she'd manage to do the same when Sabine eventually caught up with her, which at this point, seemed inevitable.

Noah pulled into his driveway just as a small helicopter

flew in overhead. The bird landed in the pasture to the north of his house.

Pete opened the front door and ran down the steps. "Called J.T., just in case!"

If Noah'd had time, he would have hugged his dad for his foresight. "Good thinking, Dad!"

Sonny barreled down the steps behind Pete. "How can I help?"

Noah didn't like to involve civilians in a dangerous situation, but in this instance, he was up Shit Creek with no goddamned paddle. He put a hand on Sonny's shoulder. "I'll give you an assignment, but so help me God, if you fail, you'll never work anywhere in Pike County again, got it?"

Sonny nodded, his expression both solemn and worried.

"Get up into the barn loft. There's a pair of binoculars hanging on a hook next to the loft doors. Keep a sharp eye out, but don't go making yourself a target, do you understand? If you see someone coming besides Hannah, make yourself invisible."

Again, Sonny nodded.

"I could do that," Pete said.

Noah and Simon both leveled a look on their dad that made his shoulders slump. Noah said, "We need you in the house, protecting Mom and Jay. Sonny can shoot, but he's not a marksman like you are, and he's not experienced at keeping people alive. Get the walkies out. You keep one and give one to Sonny." He glanced back at the teenager. "Anyone besides Hannah shows up, you let Dad know."

Sonny's head bobbed. "I will. You can count on me, Noah."

Pete also nodded. "I'll make sure Mom and Jay are okay until this is over."

Noah glanced back at Sonny. "It's going to be cold up there."

"I got my coat and stuff inside. Don't worry about me." And with that, he bolted back up the stairs and into the house.

Pete was slower to follow. At the door, he turned and said, "Any news?"

"No, but I'll try to keep you informed. You know cell service sucks up here when the weather's bad, though."

"What about the outside agencies?"

"Still no-shows. You hear anything?"

"Only that they're on the way. If you can believe it, there was a small avalanche on the highway, but it's cleared now. They should be here in half and hour or so."

"Too bad we can't wait that long," Noah said.

"We'll manage," Simon assured him.

"I hope so." He looked back at his father. "You'll be able to check the video feed if someone comes knocking." He thought about adding, *Make sure it's not Sabine or Twombly*, but decided not to. His father wouldn't appreciate being treated like an idiot. He glanced at his brother. "Ready?"

"Yep."

"Good luck and stay safe," Pete said before he closed the door.

Noah grabbed the binoculars and his rifle from the rack mounted next to the console in the truck, then went to the box, where he pulled out two pairs of snowshoes. He handed those to Simon, and together, they ran across the yard and jumped the fence into the pasture.

J.T. Holcomb, a rancher who had modernized his cattle drives by utilizing a helicopter, waited in his bird with the engine running. He had a reputation for always being willing to help law enforcement.

They were up in the air in minutes. Noah gave directions, hoping his thinking and Hannah's jibed. He put the binoculars to his eyes, trying to locate her and the dog. He saw Bowie before he found Hannah. From what he could tell, she'd gotten stuck in the snow. About a hundred and fifty yards behind her, Sabine closed the distance between them with determination. Fifty yards or so behind her, Twombly plowed his way closer.

"Put us down as close as you can to the first woman," Noah said to Holcomb. He turned to Simon. "You take care of Hannah and I'll grab Sabine."

"Wrong, bro. It looks like Hannah's gone and got herself stuck in the snow. Two of us can get her out quicker than one." Noah opened his mouth, but Simon cut him off. "We'll have time."

"There's a little folding shovel behind the back seat," Holcomb shouted over the noisy rotor blades. "Might come in handy."

Noah reached behind the seat and released the catch holding the shovel in place.

Holcomb said, "I'll take the bird back up so I don't make things worse. Signal me when you're ready for me to come back down."

Noah nodded and sat in the open doorway to attach his snowshoes. Simon followed. Snow whirled around them as if a cyclone had come in and whipped it into a frenzy. Lifting off was a good idea, but it made sight impossible for a few minutes.

Once the flurry had settled, the two brothers headed toward Hannah.

Bowie came out of nowhere and jumped up on Noah, barking.

Noah took a moment to pat his head and said, "So, you're the rescue dog, huh?"

Bowie barked twice, then took off loping through the snow back toward Hannah, who seemed completely unaware that a helicopter had just landed and taken off.

Noah reached her soon after and it was a moment before he realized that she wasn't moving. "Hannah?"

No response.

Bowie whined.

Noah dropped down on one knee and gently lifted her. The right side of her face was black-and-blue and she had a huge egg forming at the temple. Blood had dribbled down her face from whatever head injury she'd sustained. He ripped off his glove and felt for her pulse. Thready, weak. She needed medical attention and she needed it quickly. He had no idea how long she'd been stuck in the snow, or how long she'd even been out in the cold.

"Hold her head up and I'll dig," Simon said, unfolding the shovel.

Noah pulled his glove back on and ripped off his snowshoes. With one hand, he supported Hannah's upper body and with the other, he began to dig at the snow around her.

Moments later, the report of several rounds of gunfire split the air. Without thinking about it, he automatically moved behind her, using his body to shield hers.

Simon took his place and began to dig around the front of her. "Thank God we wore the Kevlar, huh?"

Noah grunted in response.

"Was it Sabine firing or Twombly?"

"Hard to say."

No other shot was forthcoming.

Five minutes later, they had her free. Noah got his snow-shoes back on and signaled Holcomb to land again. Between the brothers, they managed to carry Hannah to the helo, where they buckled her into a seat and pulled a blanket up over her.

"She needs medical attention," Noah shouted.

Holcomb nodded. "I'll take her directly to Penrose Hospital in the Springs." He shouted one last question, "What about the dog?"

Noah called to Bowie, who stood back away from the chopper. The dog refused to move. He snowshoed over to him and picked up the pup. Moments later, Bowie was situated in the empty front seat, shivering.

"He'll be fine," Holcomb assured him.

Noah wanted to go along with them in the worst way, but he had two killers to bring in. He slapped the back of Bowie's seat, backed out of the helo, and closed the door.

Ducking, he and Simon moved away.

"You ready?" Noah asked his brother.

"As I'll ever be. Let's go get these assholes."

Noah worked hard to tamp down his anger. Right now, he was a lawman, not a man in love with a woman on her way to the hospital. Hannah was safe now, or at least, that's what he had to focus on to keep sane. The problem remained that others could be in danger. Namely, his deputies, and possibly, his parents and Jay.

He and Simon took their pursuit a step at a time.

At first, Noah couldn't figure out why both Sabine and Twombly continued to move forward, but then it dawned on him. Sabine was running now from the man she'd tried to kill.

Another shot rang out, and then another, and another.

Noah and Simon crouched low, then flattened against the snow, trying to make smaller targets of themselves. Noah lifted the binoculars. "Sabine is down."

"He'll keep coming. He'll want to make sure she's dead."

No sooner were Simon's words spoken, than gunfire erupted again. Still looking through the binocs, Noah said, "He's shooting at my deputies." He reached inside his coat and pulled out his mic. "Derek, grab your snowshoes and your rifle and proceed up the hill."

"One step ahead of you, Noah. I'm ready to go and halfway up the hill. Let me know when."

"Will do."

The Ward brothers rose in unison and increased their efforts to make headway toward Twombly. The moment they came into view of the Pike County deputies, the return fire ceased. Noah knew they wouldn't risk hitting him or Simon.

They reached Sabine, who lay on her back in the snow.

Dressed only in street clothes and her feet bare, she stared up at them with a glazed expression. "I was certain I killed him. I guess the bitch wasn't lying, after all."

Simon reached down and grabbed the pistol that was only inches from her fingertips. He removed the magazine and checked the chamber for a live round before shoving the gun into the pocket of his coat.

"Am I going to die?" she asked, her voice raspy.

"I don't know," Noah said, tempted to add, *and I don't care*. Somehow, he managed to refrain from uttering the words. He studied her, watching with apathy as her white shirt grew redder from the weeping, gaping exit wound in her chest.

A bullet tore through the sleeve of his down coat. He went down automatically, though he knew he wasn't hit.

"Go kill the fucker," Sabine said, her face contorted with what looked like both pain and excitement.

The snow between him and Simon spewed into the air.

"It's him or us," Simon said.

"I don't want to risk hitting any of my deputies."

"I hear you, but what are our options?"

"Derek is a marksman." He pulled out the mic again. "Derek, you in place for a shot?"

"Almost. Hold on." He came back a minute later. "Got him in my sights."

Fifteen seconds later, Twombly fired downhill at the four deputies he could spot.

The report of a rifle sounded from the one he couldn't see.

"That will be the kill shot," Noah said.

A moment later, the mic on his shoulder crackled. "Derek got him, Noah," Kenny said. "You're clear to proceed."

Noah glanced back at Sabine. Her dead eyes stared at the sky, no longer seeing anything. He grabbed the mic from his shoulder again. "Is he in need of medical?"

Kenny hooted. "Are you kidding?"

Noah exchanged a look with his brother. "Guess that answers that."

The investigator from Colorado Bureau of Investigation and the two Colorado State Patrol officers arrived just in time to help carry crime scene equipment up to the site where Sabine Borreau had died. Flip and Toad strung up battery-powered lights so the coroner could pronounce and the meat-wagon team could get to the body.

Once the coroner had confirmed Sabine was dead, and Shari had taken all the photos she needed and measured everything that could be measured, the meat-wagon team bundled the deceased up in a body bag and somehow managed to get her back to their vehicle for transport to the morgue in Colorado Springs.

A second meat wagon awaited Twombly's body. Again, Shari did her crime-scene thing before the meat-wagon team bagged him. They rigged up a tarp with ropes to slide him over the snow to Hannah's driveway. No one had been willing to try and carry the two-hundred-twenty-pound lump down on their shoulders.

"You doing okay?" Noah asked Derek, who stood apart from the others, observing with a blank expression on his face.

"I've never killed anyone before."

"I'm sorry you had to kill Twombly, but I'm grateful you saved one of your co-workers from a similar fate."

Derek sent him a startled look. "I hadn't thought of it quite like that."

"You were doing your job, Derek. No one can fault you for that."

"How long before I can go back to work?"

"We all know what the rule book says. You've gotta see a shrink, the DA has to review the events, yada, yada, yada."

"So, you're saying I'm going to have a mini vacation."

"Something like that."

"I guess it could be worse," Derek said, sounding a little morose.

"It sure as hell could've been." Noah clasped his shoulder. "Try not to dwell on it overmuch, okay?"

"You're speaking from experience."

"Yes, I am."

By the time everyone came and went who thought they should be involved, or who thought they needed to give everything a good look-see, it was ten p.m.

Darry's Diner had sent up a slew of sandwiches and coffees around seven, so no one was starving, but everyone was exhausted. One by one, they departed. Even Flip, who'd been covering graveyard, got a reprieve, although the 911 line had been redirected to ring on his phone if anyone needed a cop overnight.

As he watched the last SUV cruiser pull away, Noah thought it would be a helluva lot easier on his team if they had backup sometimes, like a local police department. Not for the first time, he considered making a proposal to the city council and mayor to add a small police force to the Fossil payroll.

"What now?" Simon asked, staring as the last red taillights disappeared.

"I need a change of clothes and a shower, then I'm headed to the Springs."

"I'll go with you. Will you lend me something to wear?"

Noah nodded.

"I could use a shower, too."

They climbed into Noah's truck and headed up Creight toward Bella Vista Ranch. "Have you talked to the folks?"

"Not since they called to say they were headed down to Penrose." Simon shook his head. "This is going to be hard on the kid, seeing his mom in the hospital."

"Maybe, but Jay's got guts. He's had to be tough to survive the last two years living the way he did."

"True." Simon's mouth almost made it to a grin. "I'm going to enjoy having the little guy as a nephew."

Noah nodded. "I hope he'll like having me as his new dad."

"You've already popped the question, have you?"

"No, but I plan to the minute I see her." God willing, and Hannah was all right.

Chapter 44

Noah and Simon pulled into the Penrose Hospital parking lot at 11:35 p.m.

Simon dialed his dad. "We're here. Where are you? ... Okay, see you up there." He unhooked his seatbelt and said to Noah, "Hannah's in the ICU."

They made their way into the building, onto the elevator, and up to the Intensive Care Unit. Pete met them in the lobby and led them into the family lounge. Jay was sound asleep under a blanket in one of the recliners.

Liza popped up and rushed over to hug each of her sons. "I'm so glad you're both all right."

"Tell me about Hannah," Noah said.

"She has a concussion, and they were worried about a hematoma, which is why she's in the ICU."

"She had quite a lump on the side of her head," Simon said.

"Being hit by Twombly one day, then Sabine the next, did a number on her," Pete said. "They're playing it safe."

"She has about fifteen stitches in her head and...." Liza trailed off, looking helplessly at Pete.

"What?" Noah asked.

"She took a bullet, son," Pete said.

Noah had seen guys in the military take a bullet and not bleed. It had never boded well for them. "We didn't see any blood when we put her in the chopper. Was she bleeding internally?"

"No. It was a clean shot. Miraculous, really. No organs damaged, which is a good sign."

"Did they have to remove the bullet?"

"No, it went straight through."

"What caliber?"

"Twenty-two."

Sabine's gun. Twombly had a nine millimeter.

Liza put a hand on his arm. "She looks a sight, and she's unhappy about having bullet-wound scars, but at least she's alive."

Noah had seen worse, he was certain of that, and besides, this was Hannah, the woman he loved. "I need to see her."

"C'mon," Pete said. "I'll take you back."

Although, technically, visiting hours were over, they were allowed admittance. Pete stopped at the nurses station. "This is my son. He'd like to see Hannah."

The nurse looked up from her computer and nodded.

"How's she doing?" Pete asked.

"She's resting comfortably," the nurse said. She glanced at Noah. "I hope you're the guy she's been waiting for."

"I hope so, too," he said.

The nurse smiled. "I think there's enough light in the room to see by, but if not, hit the third switch by the door."

Noah left his dad at the nurse's station and proceeded to Hannah's room. He took a deep breath to gird himself before he stepped inside. The door whispered shut behind him.

He approached the bed with a mixture of reluctance, fear, and happiness. He must have made some sound that alerted Hannah to his presence, for her beautiful eyes slowly made their way open.

"Noah."

"Hello, love." He leaned over the bed, wanting more than anything to kiss her, afraid that if he touched her, it would cause her pain. Her poor face, bruised from her temple down to her chin on the right side, and from her left eye to the cheek on the other side. Her scalp had been shaved to accommodate the stitches.

"I thought you'd never get here. Are you all right?"

"Yes, I'm fine."

"Did you get her?"

"Twombly got her and we got Twombly."

"I wondered if he'd show up."

"What happened after you left the station?"

It took her a while, but Hannah managed to get out the story.

"So, you beaned Sabine with a wine bottle. Nice going."

"She was so drunk by then, I'm not even sure she felt it, but she did go down." She closed her eyes and Noah thought she'd fallen asleep. A moment later she opened them. "I can't remember what happened after you found me."

Noah looked around for a chair, found it, and pulled it over toward the bed. He slid his hand through the rail's safety bars and grasped hers. "Is that uncomfortable?"

A slight smile lifted her lips. "No. It makes me feel better."

Noah spent the next hour going over everything that happened from the time he and Simon got off the helicopter.

"They're both really dead?"

"Really."

"Then Jay is safe, unless…."

"Unless what?"

"The Clarkes decide they want to take him."

"That's not going to happen," Noah said. "They didn't even bother to ask about him when we talked. No family court judge is going to slide past that."

"I hope not."

He surveyed the room.

"Looking for something?"

"Bowie," he said with a hint of amusement.

"Your dad said he's with the guy who flew the helicopter."

"Ah, he's in good hands then."

She closed her eyes again, and once more he thought she'd fallen asleep. "Noah?"

"What, sweetheart?"

"Will you kiss me, or am I too ugly with all the bruises and the shaved head and the stitches and two bullet holes in me?"

"You look beautiful to me, Hannah." He stood and lowered

the rail so he could reach her more easily.

When their lips touched, he did his best to keep the kiss chaste. The last thing he wanted was to cause her discomfort.

"I want a real kiss, Noah. I want a lover kiss."

"Hannah—"

Her eyes opened. "After what I've been through, you don't think I can take it?"

He studied her, amused as he so often was by her sassiness. "I think you can take anything anyone throws at you, Super Girl." He leaned down again and this time, he claimed not just her lips, but her mouth.

Sometime later, she smiled and said, "That's better, now climb up in this bed and lay down next to me."

"No way," he said. "I'm too big and the bed's too small and you're hurting all over and the nurse will kill me, if I do. For tonight, you'll have to be satisfied with holding hands."

She forced her bottom lip out in a pretend pout. "Do you always have to be so damned bossy?"

Noah laughed. "Yes."

"Can you at least ask me to marry you, so I know for sure there's going to be some sex involved in this relationship down the road?"

Noah belted out another laugh. "God, I love you."

"I love you, too." After another two seconds, she said, "I'm waiting."

"Will you marry me, Hannah Mason?"

"Yes, Noah Ward, I'll marry you." She lifted her hand, reaching for him. "Lean down so I can touch your amazing face."

He obliged, cupping her hand with his, kissing the open palm she laid against his cheek.

"How soon?"

"How soon, what?"

"Can we get married?"

"We need to get you well first."

"I'm well enough. I bet they have a preacher somewhere in the hospital who can perform the ceremony."

"I'm not taking you for my bride in a hospital."

"How about next Sunday, then?"

"Done. Do you think Jay will approve?"

"I'm sure he will."

"Mom's right, I do," said a voice from the doorway.

They both glanced toward where Jay stood, smiling.

"As long as I'm getting a new last name, I'd like a new first name, too. What do you think of Jax, Mom? All I'd have to do is change the last letter of my name to the letter before it in the alphabet."

"I love the idea! Come here…Jax."

"Grandma said she thought you'd like it."

"I do."

"Me, too," Noah said and smiled. He extended his free hand to the boy. "Jax Ward it is." He looked at Hannah. "Our son."

"Our son," she whispered with tears in her eyes. "I suppose you've already discussed me and Noah getting married with Liza," she said, her tone wry.

Jay-now-Jax wagged a finger at them. "You mean you and *Dad* getting married."

Noah felt something suspiciously like emotion overcome him. "I like the sound of that."

"Me and Grandma and Grandpa all think you guys getting married is a great idea, and Uncle Simon agreed when I asked him about it. He says Auntie Jules and Uncle Brant will like it, too."

"I'm sure they will," Noah agreed. His siblings would especially like it if it took the heat off of them to tie the knot.

"Can we get married at your new house, Mom? I know Sabine was there for a while, but I've never seen it, and we can decorate it for Christmas and think how pretty everything will be for your wedding."

"That sounds like a great idea, honey. What do you think, Noah?"

"Thumbs-up, buddy."

Jay-now-Jax's smile grew into a grin. "You sure, Mom? Dad?"

Noah nodded. "Absolutely."

Hannah smiled. "Positively. I can't think of a better way to cleanse our house of evil than to fill it with love."

Author Note

Here and Gone started out to be a Christmas love story under a completely different title. However, once I started writing, as sometimes happens, both my brain and my fingers on the keyboard took me down an entirely different path. Don't ask me how that happens, when I'm supposed to be in charge of my mind *and* my fingers, but it does.

As it turns out, this book is still a love story, but it's also a story of lost-and-found and as Noah says he learned from his mother, everyone gets theirs in the end. I'd say that happened here to those who deserved it, but the more important piece is that Jay was found and reunited with his mother, who loved him like a mother should love a child.

I really enjoyed writing this book. It was somewhat of a challenge for me, because I usually have my two main characters consummate their relationship about half-way through the story. With Hannah and Noah setting the parameters of their relationship in the beginning, and sticking to their decision right up until the end, I hope I succeeded in keeping the sexual tension between them sufficient to keep you interested in their romantic relationship.

If you're wondering about my locale, Fossil and Pike County are a creation of my imagination. The North Pole and the Dinosaur Center actually exist in Woodland Park, as does Painted Rocks Road. All the people are, of course, fictional. Except for Santa.

Thanks to my husband Frank, who is always my first reader and keeps me in line if I happen to misspeak in any technical or mechanical jargon. Thanks also to my editor, Nancy Jankow, for her support and dedication in helping me ensure that *Here and Gone* is the best book it can be.

Oh, and if you're curious about what the Elvis Presley Shield Bug looks like, here it is.

Happy reading!

Thank You!

Thank you so much for reading
HERE AND GONE!
I'd love to hear what you think about it.
You can email me at **ann@annsimas.com**, or post a
comment on my **Ann Simas, Author** page on
Facebook. I hope you'll "like" me while you're there,
and if you are so inclined, please, leave a review on
Amazon.com or Goodreads.com.

Just For Fun

If would like to submit a picture of yourself reading
this or any book by me, please, send your JPG to
ann@annsimas.com
and I'll post it on my FAN page!

Available now, **BLACK MOON RISING**,
a sexy paranormal thriller.

Turn the page for a preview.

BLACK MOON RISING

~ The Vision ~

The first vision came on Monday.

At least Sunny thought it was a vision. Her eyes were wide open and she wasn't sleeping, so she didn't think it was a dream.

A dense fog enshrouded her. She couldn't move and when she opened her mouth, she couldn't scream, let alone speak.

What she saw was crystal clear.

She was driving down College Avenue in bumper-to-bumper traffic, often at a snail's pace. Up ahead, a young woman lay sprawled on the curb, her bicycle on top of her. No one stopped to help, but that just wasn't the way Sunny did things. She put on her blinker, pulling in just shy of the bicyclist, and jumped out of her car, phone in hand.

She hurried over to the young woman, but a moment later, a large truck hit the back of her SUV, pushing it directly onto Sunny and the bicyclist. The vision disappeared, just like that, but Sunny had no doubts of the outcome. She and the girl had not survived the impact.

On Tuesday, a variation of the first vision appeared. This time, Sunny pulled her vehicle ahead of the downed bicyclist. A rubbernecker realized at the last minute that Sunny's car was stationary in the bike lane, swerved right, and landed her vehicle right on top of Sunny and the girl. As before, the vision vanished abruptly, but Sunny knew the end result was the same as the day before.

On Wednesday, the vision showed Sunny pulling into the next driveway and running back to help. That resulted in a multicar rear-end collision that netted the same fate for Sunny and the bicyclist and probably had sent someone from the traffic flow to the hospital.

In Thursday's vision, she pulled all the way into the parking lot behind the bicyclist. A car in the middle lane changed lanes without signaling, forcing a pickup in the outside lane closest to the bicyclist to swerve toward the curb to avoid impact. Sunny and the girl were directly in his path.

On Friday, the vision changed yet again. Sunny pulled up just past the downed bicyclist and eased her vehicle up onto the curb, straddling the bike lane. She put on her flashers, got out, dropped her phone. She managed to get to the girl and offer assistance until she heard the sound of a siren from the approaching ambulance. And then she took off. Alive.

Then came Saturday.

This time, there was no vision.

Only reality.

~ Chapter 1 ~

Traffic was a bitch. Sunshine Fyfe cursed a blue streak inside the confines of her older but sturdy and well-maintained Durango.

Why today, of all days, did her plane have to be late arriving? And why today, of all days, did her mother, who was babysitting for her, have a gala event scheduled in an hour that she absolutely, positively could *not* miss? And why today, of all days, did the shortcut to her parents' place, which took her tooling down Car Dealer Row, have to be bumper-to-bumper, stop-and-go traffic?

"Because, stupid," she muttered, answering her last question aloud, "it's rush hour and everyone's trying to avoid bumper-to-bumper, stop-and-go traffic just like you are!"

She slapped her palm against the steering wheel. "Shit!"

Fumbling in her purse for her phone, she took her eyes off the road for an instant. By the time she had her hand on the device and her eyes back on the road, a space the length of several vehicles had cleared in front of her. The opening gave her an unobstructed view of a bicyclist lying just ahead on the side of the road, her two-wheeled method of transportation a mangled mess on top of her.

Sunny's heart began to pound as a week's parade of visions trampled through her memory.

She momentarily debated her options. Incur her mother's wrath or leave an injured person unattended on the side of the road? The debate was short-lived. Passing by as if she had seen nothing had not been one of the scenarios presented to her in the visions, nor was it an option Sunny seriously considered.

Signaling, she pulled over into the gutter, ahead of the downed bicyclist, and eased the front wheel of her SUV up over the curb, then the back wheel. That left her half in the bike lane, but out of the traffic lane. She jammed her finger in the general vicinity of the emergency-flasher button, and despite the heavy traffic and the narrow space between the passing cars and her vehicle, managed to open her door enough to squeeze out. In the process, she dropped her phone. It bounced once then went straight out into traffic, where the next wheel ran over it with a sickening crunch.

Muttering the f-bomb, Sunny hurried along, pressed against the side of her vehicle, until finally, she reached the relative safety of the curb. Why hadn't she shoved the damned phone into her pocket? For crying out loud! She'd had fair warning what would happen if she didn't.

"Are you okay?" she asked the young woman, lifting the bike off of her, hoping not to cause her further injuries or discomfort. Blood poured from a wound somewhere on the right side of the girl's head, liberally covering that side of her face and dripping profusely onto her white T-shirt. From personal experience, Sunny knew that head wounds usually bled a lot. This one, however, looked like a gusher. She tried not to freak.

"I don't know...my head hurts." The young woman was pale and looked stunned. Tears pooled in her big brown eyes. "My bike! He hit my bike!"

Sunny ripped off the colorful scarf she had around her neck, bunching it up as she handed it over. "Here, put this against your head wound. It might help stanch the bleeding."

The woman accepted it with trembling fingers.

Upon closer inspection, Sunny decided the bicyclist looked younger than she'd originally guessed, maybe in her late teens. "I'm Sunny. What's your name, sweetie?"

"Della."

Sunny smiled at her, thinking, *Keep calm, keep calm.* Remaining calm herself would encourage the bicyclist to remain calm, too. "Do you think you're hurt anywhere else?"

"I don't know. My right leg...hurts...bad."

Sunny glanced down, dismayed to see something sticking up out of the bloody denim just above the girl's knee. *Please, God, don't let it be bone!*

"Okay, Della, I'm going to call an ambulance. You don't happen to have a phone, do you?"

"I do, but...battery's dead," Della said. "I think...going to be sick." With that, she turned her head quickly and tossed her cookies all over her shoulder and into the grassy strip.

Sunny kept a hand on the girl's opposite shoulder, offering the only thing she could—comfort. When Della had finished, she helped her scoot away from the barf, cognizant of the fact that she shouldn't be moving an accident victim. Nonetheless, she couldn't leave the girl to sit in her own puke. She whipped off the lightweight sweater she wore over her cotton tank and used it to wipe Della's mouth and shoulder.

"You'll...ruin it," Della protested.

"Don't worry about it, sweetie. Listen, I dropped my phone when I got out of my vehicle and it got run over, so I'm going to go up to the car dealership and call from there. Will you be okay while I'm gone?"

Instead of an answer, big tears rolled down Della's cheeks.

She swiped at them with the trembling fingers of her free hand and nodded.

Sunny straightened and bolted toward what she hoped was the dealership office. No sooner had she passed between two Honda sedans than a guy with a name badge approached her.

"I called an ambulance," he said in an unusually deep voice. "It's on the way."

"Oh, thank you!" Sunny glanced at his name tag—JAMES MORGAN—before reversing direction.

Once back at Della's side, she knelt down and put a hand on the girl's shoulder. The car salesman loomed over them, not offering any assistance. "Della, are you doing okay?"

"Not feeling…good. Kind of…light-headed."

"I'm not surprised. Hang in there, okay? The ambulance is on it's way." In fact, she could hear a siren and wondered how the emergency vehicle would make its way through the ridiculous traffic jam.

"Need to…lie down."

"I'm not sure you should," Sunny said. Throwing up most likely meant that Della had sustained a severe concussion. Blood, Sunny could deal with. Head trauma was a different matter. Weren't you supposed to try and keep people with head injuries awake?

"Feel like…going to…."

If possible, Della went even whiter. The hand she used to hold the scarf up to her head wound fell limply to her side and she slumped forward. Sunny grasped her by the shoulders, righting her. She looked up at the car salesman. "Help me!"

He backed away, holding his hands up in front of him. "No way! She's covered in blood."

Disgusted with his craven attitude, Sunny eased Della gently to her back, debating the wisdom of turning the girl on her side in case she vomited again. What other option did she have? If Della choked to death on her own barf, it wouldn't matter if the other injuries were exacerbated.

Before she made the shift in Della's position, she put two fingers against the girl's carotid artery. She still had a pulse. Even though the sweater had the contents of Della's stomach all over it, Sunny found a small clean section she used to pad the girl's face from the grass.

She glanced at her watch and looked up at the car salesman again. "Would you let me borrow your phone, so I can—?"

"Are you nuts? Your hands are covered in blood and puke!"

Realizing he was right, but pissed beyond belief at his ridiculous behavior, Sunny said, "Oh, for God's sake, grow a pair!"

For the moment it took him to register what she'd said, he glared daggers down at her. When the full import of her comment sank in, his expression grew ugly. He made half a lunge in her direction, his hands fisted, and snarled, "Fuck you!"

Sunny recoiled, as if his words had breathed fire on her. Once she felt composed again, she stood, wiping her hands on her blue jeans, even as she back-stepped. "Look, since the ambulance is nearly here, I really need to get going—"

Both his words and demeanor came across as threatening. "You better not leave!"

"I have to. I have to go pick up—"

"You'll turn an accident into a felony," he warned.

"What are you talking about?"

"You leave the scene and it'll be felony hit-and-run."

"I didn't hit—"

"I saw you!"

"Look, I don't know what your problem is, but I did no such thing!"

The siren grew louder. Sunny glanced down the boulevard. Vehicles in all three lanes looked like bumper cars being driven by grade-schoolers, desperately and ineffectively trying to get out of the way of the ambulance. Finally, in obvious desperation, the red-and-white emergency vehicle climbed the curb and made the last one hundred feet half on the sidewalk, half on the grassy parkway strip. It stopped just short of a light standard.

Confident Della would immediately get the medical care she needed, Sunny ran back to her Durango, opened the passenger door and extracted a business card from her purse. She hurriedly scribbled a note on the back and ran back to put it into Della's pocket.

The EMTs climbed out of their vehicle, grabbed their gear, and approached. Sunny ignored the car salesman and said to them, "Her name is Della. She just passed out, but before that, she vomited. I need to go."

And with that, Sunny Fyfe ran back to her vehicle and took advantage of the opportunity presented by the lookie-loo drivers. She pulled quickly into a nice open space in traffic, making a note of the time.

Her mom was not going to be happy about this delay.

She didn't notice the car salesman pull a small pad out of his shirt pocket and a pen from his pants pocket, making a note of his own.

• • •

BLACK MOON RISING
Available worldwide in paperback or as an ebook at
amazon.com

Also available in paperback from
annsimas.com

About the Author

Ann Simas lives in Oregon, but she is a Colorado girl at heart, having grown up in the Rocky Mountains. An avid word-lover since childhood, she began to pen her first novel in high school. The author of 22 novels, one novella, and seven short stories, she particularly enjoys writing books that are cross-genre—a mix of mystery/thriller/suspense, with a love story and paranormal or supernatural elements.

In addition to being a three-time Romance Writers of America Golden Heart Finalist, Ann is also an award-winning watercolorist and budding photographer who enjoys needlework and gardening in her spare time. She is her family's "genealogist" and has been blessed with the opportunity to conduct first-hand research in Italy for both her writing and her family tree. The genealogy research from century's-old documents, written in Italian, has been a supreme but gratifying and exciting challenge for her.

Contact the author via:
Magic Moon Press
POB 41634
Eugene, OR 97404-0386
or at **ann@annsimas.com**

Or visit:
annsimas.com *and*
Ann Simas, Author on Facebook

Ann's books are available worldwide at
amazon.com